Lost
Inheritance

Lin Stepp

Books by Lin Stepp

Novels:
The Foster Girls
Tell Me About Orchard Hollow
For Six Good Reasons
Delia's Place
Second Hand Rose
Down by the River
Makin' Miracles
Saving Laurel Springs
Welcome Back
Daddy's Girl

Christmas Novella:
A Smoky Mountain Gift
In *When the Snow Falls*

Regional Guidebooks
Co-Authored with J.L. Stepp:
The Afternoon Hiker
Discovering Tennessee State Parks

Lost Inheritance

A SMOKY MOUNTAIN NOVEL

LIN STEPP

MOUNTAIN HILL PRESS

Cover design: Katherine E. Stepp
Interior design: J. L. Stepp, Mountain Hill Press
Editor: Brittany Dowdle
Cover photo and map design: Lin M. Stepp

Library of Congress Cataloging-in-Publication Data

Stepp, Lin
Lost Inheritance: A Smoky Mountain novel / Lin Stepp
         p. cm – (The Smoky Mountain series; bk. #10)
ISBN: 978-0-9985063-3-3
First Mountain Hill Press Trade Paperback Printing: April 2018

eISBN: 978-0-9985063-4-0
First Mountain Hill Press Electronic Edition: April 2018

1. Women—Southern States—Fiction   2. Mountain life—Great Smoky Mountains Region (NC and TN)—Fiction. 3. Contemporary Romance—Inspirational—Fiction. I. Title

Library of Congress Control Number: 2018901332

Printed in the United States of America

This book is dedicated to my long-time friend Jayne Matthews (December 7, 1947 – January 13, 2015). Jayne, a full-time journalist—smart, creative, full of laughter and fun—passed away a few years ago – much too soon for all who loved her. Jayne and I met when students at The University of Tennessee and quickly became fast friends. Jayne was full of wonderful stories and it was Jayne's incredible story about a lost inheritance that inspired the idea for this book.

ACKNOWLEDGMENTS

"There is always, always something to be grateful for." – Anon

Acknowledgement and thanks go to these wonderful people who helped to make this book the best it could be …

My excellent editor Brittany Dowdle for her thorough and meticulous work in editing *Lost Inheritance*. I treasure her as a fine professional and as a friend.

My fan and friend Charlene Heirman Povia who allowed me to model the gallery cat in this book after her cat Sugar Lips. Cats make the world a better place.

My daughter Katherine Stepp for her help with cover art and design, proof editing, and for her ongoing creative assistance and encouragement with my books. How blessed I am to have such a talented graphics designer in my own family.

My husband J.L. Stepp for always being the first, enthusiastic reader of my books and for his excellent production skills. He makes writing a joy and an adventure.

Thanks also to all
my wonderful fans.
Keep reading and loving my books
and I'll keep writing them!

*"That I may publish with the voice of thanksgiving
and tell of all thy wondrous works."* (Psalm 26:7)

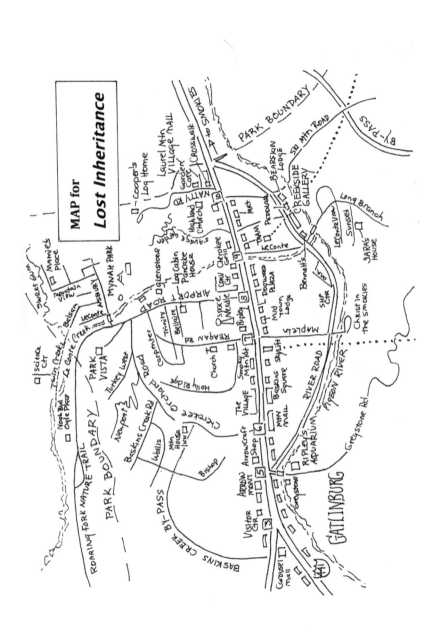

MAP for *Lost Inheritance*

CHAPTER 1

Her thoughts a mile away, Emily almost bumped into the boy shoveling drifts of white snow away from the restaurant doorway.

"Sorry," she said, slowing her pace.

The boy nodded, continuing to scrape snow across the icy sidewalk.

Emily angled around him, not saying more. It was simply too cold for conversation. Temperatures hovered below freezing today, frigid even for early February in Philadelphia. The remnants of the last snowstorm had partially melted, and the downtown streets hummed with the noise of city traffic. However, flurries in the air hinted of more snowfall to come.

Wrapping her scarf over her face against the cold, Emily walked on, her boots crunching through the untidy piles of snow packed along the edge of the sidewalk. She scanned the street ahead, trying to judge the distance remaining to Reuben Parrish's office.

Despite the cold, Emily had decided to walk the few blocks to her appointment. Time in the out-of-doors helped to soothe the hurt in her heart.

A cab skidded to a stop as she started up the steps into the brownstone office building, dislodging a man wrapped heavily, like everyone else, in winter clothing. He sprinted for the steps and then stopped as he noticed her.

"Well, well." The man snarled the words into the frosty air, his breath a white cloud in the cold. "I would say it's nice to see you again, Emily Lamont, but it would be a lie." He glanced towards the doorway. "I guess we're the only heirs, from what Reuben Parrish said. I don't see any reason why we had to come today for a formal reading of the will. There's no legal need for that in this day and age, despite the hype in the movies. Besides, we all know how the little orphan ingratiated herself into the graces of the Newmans all these years." He scowled. "Uncle Hal told me pointedly he was leaving the house and gallery to you. He called you 'the responsible one.'"

Emily bit her lip. "I'm sorry there are hard feelings between us, Leonard, especially at this time with both Mary and Hal gone."

He pushed past her. "Let's go get this travesty over with. I hope there will be at least some fairness in this whole procedure and that Hal will have left me a portion of his estate, anyway. I am his only nephew, after all; you'd think that would count for something."

In Reuben Parrish's legal office, the receptionist ushered them into a comfortable conference room where they found Reuben sorting through a pile of paperwork stacked on an antique table that nearly filled the room. Emily and Leonard each stripped off their winter wear, draped it over a mahogany coatrack, and after getting a cup of coffee from an old credenza against the wall, settled in around the table to savor the room's warmth.

"I'm glad you could both come today," Reuben began. "I want to say first how grieved I am over Hal's death. Caring for Mary these last years wore out his health, I'm afraid." He looked up with caring concern, and Emily felt tears smart at the back of her eyes. Reuben, with his familiar bulbous nose, somewhat florid face, and freckled bald head, had been a friend to the Newman family for as long as Emily could remember.

"Nice words," Leonard interrupted. "But I don't see why you called us here today. We know Hal and Mary left a clear will and all you needed to do was send copies to us. We didn't need to meet together and pretend to be fond of each other."

Emily saw Reuben wince. He and Leonard held no affectionate feelings between them. Reuben had handled several loans between

Leonard and Hal in the past, and some of the meetings about non-payment had been unpleasant.

Reuben shuffled the papers on his desk again, obviously uncomfortable with the situation. "I called you both here today because there are some irregularities with the last will Hal made. As you know, Hal drew up a new will about ten years ago, but the old will he and Mary made earlier was still kept on file, too."

"And?" Leonard passed him a look of irritation.

"And on examination, we've realized the second will was never fully executed." His eyes moved to Emily's with a grievous expression. "Of course, the new will that was drawn up is very clear in detailing Hal and Mary's desires on their deaths."

Leonard leaned forward, his attention aroused now. "The will was never executed." He repeated the words slowly, a slight smile curling the corner of his mouth. "How interesting. That means the former will stands in its stead. Emily had only lived with Uncle Hal and Aunt Mary about five years when that new will was written. I remember I turned thirty-five that year. It's when Hal and I had some of our first disagreements." He made a face, not adding any clarification.

"Yes," Reuben put in. "And I know he advised you of the changes he made to his will at that time and why."

Emily watched Leonard's face take on a nasty expression. He wasn't a bad-looking man, with blue eyes, a handsome if somewhat effeminate face, and spiky, prematurely white hair. Leonard's father, Raymond Newman, and Raymond's brother, Hal, had both sported heads of thick white hair at a young age, too. Unfortunately, Leonard lacked his father's distinguished bearing, and he certainly lacked Hal's sterling character.

"Mr. Parrish." Leonard's voice took on a sarcastic tone. "I think you and I both know that only what is written in a *legally executed* will matters in the end. I assume your beating around the bush and calling us in here means you regret that you somehow dropped the ball and didn't get some proper legal signatures on that last will. In which case, I think you should read to us the will that stands in its place." He crossed his arms, smiling. "It might be more to my advantage than the latter one."

Thirty minutes later, Emily still sat in shock at the conference table while Leonard continued giving directives to Reuben as he pulled his coat on. With the old will in place, he had become the primary beneficiary of Hal and Mary Newman's estate.

"Tough luck, little orphan." He gave Emily a malicious grin. "I'm having locks put on Hal and Mary's house today and a guard posted, so don't be getting any ideas about heading over there to retrieve anything. Tomorrow I'll be down to the gallery to start making changes there, too, since it appears I will now be the new owner and manager rather than you."

Reuben sputtered out some words about the fairness of this, but Leonard waved a hand at him in dismissal.

"Emily's had her day," he stated. "I'll keep her on at the gallery as an employee if she'd like. She does know the gallery well and it will keep continuity." He turned a warning glare towards Emily as he draped a wool scarf around his neck. "But if you make any efforts to usurp my authority, Emily Lamont, you're out. I hope I make that perfectly clear. It won't be like the last time when you and that clannish little staff ganged up on me and got Uncle Hal to oust me. I haven't forgotten that. I'll be giving every one of the employees the same cautionary warning, you can be sure. You tell them I'll be there at eight in the morning for a full staff meeting before the gallery opens, and I expect every one of them to show if they want to keep their jobs."

Reuben followed Leonard out, and Emily could hear their muted voices in the vestibule. She tried to clear her mind and process all she'd just learned about the will. Reuben mentioned she could contest, but Emily knew she'd have little chance in court against a legitimate blood heir.

"Emily, I am so sorry," Reuben said, coming back into the room. "I asked Hal so many times to come in and take care of finalizing that will, and then I let one of my associates, who moved shortly after, meet with Hal when he did drop by. I was sure he verified that all had been properly taken care of. I was out of town at the time, but there was no reason for me to doubt the will had not been properly executed." He sat down at the table, sighing. "I was simply stunned when I got out the paperwork to go through it after Hal's death. I thought it would be very straightforward." He gave Emily an anguished look. "I will testify as to what Hal wanted. You do have the right to contest."

Emily smiled. "I am Mary Newman's godchild, the daughter of her best friend from college days. I have no kinship link to Hal and Mary Newman, but they were good enough to honor their guardianship agreement when my parents were killed when I was ten. I had no other family, you know. I was so blessed that Mary and Hal took me in, raised me, and that I got to be a part of their lives all these years. They were wonderful people."

"They thought the world of you." Reuben ran a hand around his collar. "They'd have been so distressed about this. Leonard is not a responsible business person and Hal was not fond of him. Hal always said his brother, Raymond, and especially Raymond's wife, Adele, spoiled Leonard and made him fit for nothing except being pompous and pretentious. It would break Hal's heart to know the gallery will go to Leonard now, plus their home and their collection of art. I know Hal talked many times with you about what he wanted to see done with the gallery in the future. Leonard will never do those things. I can't imagine anything except disaster if he puts his oar into that business again."

"He won't simply put his oar in this time, Reuben." Emily sighed. "He owns the gallery now."

"Yes, but Hal trained you since only a girl to run the gallery. You know every aspect of it. You've managed it all these years with skill and diplomacy—especially in these last years while Hal stayed with Mary when she was so ill." He rubbed a hand across his head nervously. "I really hope you'll contest."

Emily shook her head. "No. It would be nasty, and it would hurt Hal and Mary's memory and reflect poorly on the gallery. I'd have little chance to win, too. You know that."

The attorney argued a little longer, but Emily finally put a hand across his. "I've made up my mind, Reuben. If I contest it would fill the news and discredit Hal and Mary."

"It's a very big estate; you know that."

"I do. But as Leonard said, I've had my day." She propped her chin on her hands, trying to keep back the tears as she repeated the hurtful words. "Hal and Mary educated me, taught me useful work and good life ethics, took me around the world on trips, shared their lives and hearts with me, loved and cherished me. It's more than I might have expected, considering, and probably far more than I deserved."

"I hardly agree with that." Reuben bristled. "Hal and Mary thought of you as a daughter. We both know very well what they wanted for you—and what they wanted to leave you." Reuben paused, shaking his head. "I, for one, will deeply regret this miscarriage of justice all of my days."

"Well, there is little to be done about it now, and unfortunately, regrets can't change the past." Emily straightened. "Why don't you tell me what I do inherit in the estate, Reuben? I know there was something you mentioned, but I was so stunned I didn't fully take it in."

Reuben looked down at his papers, sorting through them. "There is a trust fund, but Hal set it up to be something you could draw on later in life. You can't access that money now. The town house you live in is yours free and clear, as is your car and all your personal possessions, of course." He paused. "Anything you've been given, in gifts of money or possessions, that are not contained in either the gallery property or in Hal and Mary's home are yours to keep."

"I moved out of Hal and Mary's home only a few years ago when I turned twenty-one and graduated from college. Not long after that Mary got sick. Sometimes I wanted to move back, but Hal kept saying I should keep my own place." She rubbed at the tension in her neck. "I'm glad I did stay there now. Otherwise I'd have an even greater problem—locked out of my own home." She looked at Reuben. "What about the things I kept stored at Hal and

Mary's house—can I retrieve those?"

Reuben shook his head. "Only if there are legal papers stating they were deeded to you."

"Well, of course there wouldn't be any. Those things were all to be a part of the house property in the will." Her mind drifted over the furniture in her old bedroom at Hal and Mary's, items boxed in the attic, and special treasures packed in a hope chest for her potential wedding one day.

"Again, I'm so sorry, Emily. I don't know what else to say." Reuben hesitated. "Maybe I can talk to Leonard about some of the items you'd like to have, or if he holds an auction later, you might bid on them."

She toyed with the copy of the will before her. "No, what I yearned for most were personal keepsakes, things I knew Hal and Mary loved that would remind me of them. Fortunately, they gave me many items when I moved out on my own." She glanced up. "I have their photos in my possession. I was working on putting them into books for Hal. Can I keep those?"

Reuben nodded. "Yes."

"That's good. I doubt Leonard would treasure them."

"I'm sure that's true." He scratched his head. "You know, you did inherit that little gallery Hal and Mary bought from their friend Nelle Jacobs after her husband died. The two families had been friends for years, and after Leon Jacobs passed away, Nelle wanted to move farther south to live with their daughter in South Carolina. Hal helped her out and bought the gallery from her. When I did the paperwork for the sale, Hal put all that property jointly in your name and his. So that property is yours free and clear. You could sell it now and that would give you more money to live on." He paused. "I think Leonard will reduce your salary at the gallery. He's the spiteful type."

Emily shook her head. "I think Leonard would make every day of my life a misery if I stayed at the gallery. You know that. I couldn't possibly stay on there now."

"But they will need you at the gallery with Hal gone." Reuben tapped a pencil on the table in irritation. "Hal wouldn't want to see the gallery run down."

"Whatever happens now at that gallery will happen regardless of what Hal might have wanted. I am no longer in any position to make a difference."

"I suppose it would be difficult." Reuben glanced at his watch. "I have an appointment coming in. We can talk some more afterwards. I won't be long."

"Fine." She smiled. "Would you leave me the paperwork on the Jacobs' gallery to look through while you're gone?"

"Oh, yes, that's a good idea." He gathered up a large file to bring around to her. "There are photos here, account statements, all the documentation. I think you could get a good price for it."

After he left, Emily got up to pour herself another cup of coffee before sitting down again to open the portfolio. The quiet of the room seemed a welcome change after the stress of the morning. She leafed through the folder, glad for a little time to be alone with her own thoughts.

Reuben returned about twenty minutes later. "There, that didn't take long. Just some quick papers to sign." He settled back into his chair at the head of the table beside Emily. "Did you get a chance to look through everything? That small gallery has been quite prosperous. Hal didn't make a bad investment by buying it eight years ago."

"No, I can see that." She gave Reuben a small smile. "The gallery is in Gatlinburg, Tennessee. I went there often as a child. I actually grew up nearby in Knoxville, Tennessee, where my parents owned a small shop before they died."

"Well, what a small world."

Emily tapped the folder. "Yes, it is. Reuben, I want to move there and manage the gallery."

"What?" He looked shocked. "But that's a mountain tourist town and you're used to this life in the city, in Philadelphia. Besides, your friends are here. Your world is here. Your work is here."

"Not any longer," she replied patiently. "I need a change, and I'm only trained to run an art gallery. It's all I've ever known since I was ten and started carrying out the trash and dusting the display cases for Hal and Mary."

Reuben Parrish twisted his hands. "It's a much smaller gallery than the Hal Newman Gallery and it will have a very different clientele."

"I don't have a lot of choices." She looked down at the file. "The Creekside Gallery looks like an interesting small gallery, and there are two rental businesses on either side of the building that are part of the property. The rentals bring in steady money for when the gallery experiences down times. That's nice."

"Yes, the rentals give stability and an ongoing income. The frame shop in the gallery helps with revenue, too. You would enjoy a comfortable income from the business to live on—although it would be nothing like what you're used to."

"I came from much less, Reuben. And it will give me something to put my heart and thought to now. I really need that."

"You won't stay here?"

She frowned. "I don't want to stay here and watch what Leonard will do to the gallery, nor do I want to watch him auction off Hal and Mary's things—or hear the talk about it."

"I can see your reasoning." He heaved a sigh before pulling her folder towards him. "There's an apartment above the gallery you can use if you'd like, at least until you get settled. The floor plans are here, with photos from when Nelle and Leon Jacobs lived in it. It's not rented now, hasn't been for a year or two. It may need cleaning up and some paintwork done, but it would do for you." He pushed the photos towards Emily. "You can see that it can look nice when decorated."

She studied the photos. "That will make things easier, already having a place to live. And I'm used to living near the gallery here." Emily looked up at Reuben. "Have you notified the gallery manager in Gatlinburg that there is a new owner?"

He nodded. "I sent some formal notification about the will, but I haven't talked to the manager directly. Her name is Adelyn Garrison. She's managed the gallery for years. She used to work for the Jacobs and continued to handle things after Hal bought the gallery. I know Hal and Mary met and liked her. She seems to have done a good job there."

"Would it be all right if I call her about the apartment—to make sure it would be okay for me to move in?"

"You can, but it's your property to do with as you want now. She won't really have any say."

Emily shook her head. "Reuben, how can you say that after what you've seen happen today? Of course I want to call her, and I want her to feel valued and not threatened by a change in ownership." Her eyes moved to the folder in front of Reuben now. "Can you make copies of all the material in this folder for me before I leave and note all the contact information?"

"Sure, I'll get Gladys to do it right now." He started to stand up.

"And, Reuben, could you also help me with moving contacts and recommend someone to put my town house on the market?"

"You're selling the town house?" He looked stunned. "You fully inherited that."

"Yes, and the money from the sale will help supplement my savings. It will cost me to move and settle into a new place."

"You aren't going right away, are you?" Reuben looked pained.

"As soon as I can make arrangements." Her eyes moved to a skyline photo of downtown Philadelphia on the wall. "There's nothing left here for me anymore except a few cherished friends. It's time for a new beginning—either in Gatlinburg or somewhere else. There's no sense in putting it off."

He sighed. "I'll get some names for you while Gladys duplicates the file." He gathered up the papers as he stood. "Once again, I can't tell you how grieved I am that Hal never finalized the new will. My associate evidently failed to clarify to Hal that final signatures were needed before he left the firm. Hal was here often while Mary was dying and never mentioned it. Usually a close death, especially a spouse, makes a person eager to be certain everything is in order, to be sure all the wills and paperwork are as they should be. It would have taken only a little time to resolve what he wanted." He gave her a strained look, pulling at his tie. "Maybe Hal thought it was done, that I'd taken care of it."

"I don't blame you, Reuben, and I don't blame Hal. These last years watching Mary slowly die were horrible for him. It's no wonder he let things go. I saw it at the gallery, too. I had to pick up so many matters he ordinarily would have handled himself."

"You're a good person, Emily. Hal told me time and time again he didn't know how he'd have gotten through that difficult time if you hadn't been a support and comfort to him and Mary . . . and taken over at the gallery—you and Daniel." He stopped over that name, his eyes widening. "Daniel is going to be devastated over this, you know. When Hal tried to bring Leonard into the gallery ten years ago, it proved a disaster. You remember that. Daniel and the whole staff will be up in arms about this change. It will make it much worse that you are leaving, too."

Emily stood and walked over to get her coat. "I learned when only a little girl that we can live through bad things when we must. And Hal and Mary taught me things have a way of working out even from sorrows. I'm still young. I have a good education and a sound work background. I'm in good health, and I have a strong faith. God will take care of me, and I'll be all right."

"I hope you will keep me as your attorney so I can help you as you make this move and so many other changes." He started towards her with an arm extended to hug her and then paused. "Although, if you never wanted to see my face again, I'd certainly understand."

Emily moved under his arm to hug him. "Nothing that happened here was intentional, and I will be glad for your continuing friendship and support as I move through all the legalities of this change."

A short time later, Emily headed out of the legal office into an icy blast of arctic air and a swirl of incoming snow. The new blizzard was already piling snow heavily on the sidewalk, streets, and parked cars.

"Whew! It's gonna be another big one," one man said to another as they walked by her, both bent to the cold. "Just one sorrow after another this winter."

"Yes," Emily whispered, wrapping her scarf around her neck. "And in more ways than only the weather."

CHAPTER 2

Cooper Garrison climbed down from his stepladder, moved it, and then climbed up the steps again to angle his paintbrush into the last corner of the wall he couldn't reach before.

"I can't believe we had to take time from the Mayfield house we're building on the mountain to paint this dang apartment." Cooper swept the paintbrush in neat strokes down the wall as he complained.

Rafe Harlan, who was rolling yellow-cream paint on the opposite wall, turned to look at Cooper. "You've been bellyaching all day about this job when you know we're doing this work as a favor to your mother."

"Yeah and that's what burns me." Cooper paused after filling in the last block of wall above a section Rafe had previously covered with his roller. He turned to scowl at Rafe. "We shouldn't have to be doing this, but Mother would have paid someone if we hadn't. I didn't want her spending gallery money on painters. It's bad enough the gallery has changed hands again without anyone giving her a chance to buy it. You'd think they'd have offered her an option after all the years she's slaved here."

"Aw, Cooper, you know she loves her work at the gallery." Rafe ran a hand through his sun-bleached blond hair, which—as always—hung down his neck in a style overly long and in need of a trim. "Besides I heard you *offer* to do the work for her. She didn't twist your arm none."

"I know," he grumbled. "But I'd have felt guilty if I didn't of-fer." He scraped a hand through his own dark hair, cut shorter and neater than Rafe's.

"What's really got you so sniffed off?" Rafe leaned over to skim his roller through the paint tray.

Cooper climbed down from the ladder and propped an arm against it.

"Just the whole chain of events, I guess. My mom was the first employee the Jacobs hired when they opened the gallery twenty-two years ago. From early days, after they trained her, they traveled and left her running things, basically let her manage the gallery as time went by. Of course, they knew she really needed the work after Dad died in order to raise my brother Lance and me. Some-times I think they took advantage of her because of that."

"Yeah, it was tough you lost your dad so young. Leroy asked me the other day how old you boys were when that happened and I couldn't remember exactly."

"I was sixteen and Lance twenty-two." He frowned as a sweep of painful memories skittered through his mind. "Lance had just graduated from the community college the year before with his as-sociate's in business and started working with Dad and Delbert in the business. Then he had to take everything over; it was hard for him. Fortunately, Delbert's expertise in the building and construc-tion end helped Garrison Log Homes stay afloat, and Lance soon showed a gift for working with people on the sales and adminis-trative side. We made out all right despite it all, especially with me working part-time after school and on weekends."

Rafe moved his paint tray to start the last half of the wall. "You know, I started with Garrison Log Homes part-time before your dad died and then came on full-time after high school." He paused. "I remember Lance—a great guy and fun-lovin' by nature. Real tragic he died so young. Lance wasn't even thirty, if I recollect rightly."

Cooper frowned, looking towards the window. "He was only twenty-eight, and I'd turned twenty-two that year."

They worked in silence for a moment. Cooper knew Rafe hoped he'd talk more about Lance, but it was a subject Cooper avoided whenever possible.

"Yeah, well, you've done a great job with the business," Rafe said at last. "I know it wasn't easy for you, either."

"No, it wasn't, and it made everything harder for Mom. She had a *right* to get an offer before Nelle Jacobs sold the gallery to that Newman guy up north. They didn't even give her a shot at it. She deserved a chance to buy the gallery when Newman died last month, too. Instead it went to some woman in Newman's will who worked with him, not even blood related. The whole thing burns me up, that's all. Rightfully, Mom should have inherited the place to my way of thinking—after all she's done here. She's run the gallery these last eight years since Leon Jacobs died and Nelle sold out. And now some new owner is moving down here to take things over from her."

"Did your mom want to buy the gallery?"

Cooper didn't like the question. "Whether she did or didn't has nothing to do with the fact that she didn't even get a chance to make that decision at all. I might have bought it for her if she had. Like I said, she deserved to get this place after all her years here."

"Yeah, life sucks sometimes."

"That's a fact." Cooper studied the wall before him, nearly finished now, and then glanced at his watch. "You know, we need to get cracking to get this room completed."

"No problem." Rafe turned back to the job. "My part's done with this last wall anyway. I'll let you finish here and I'll drive up the mountain and check on the Mayfield house, see what I need to do there tomorrow for Delbert." He ran a long line of paint down the wall. "Do you still want to paint the porch and do the wallpaper in the back bedroom on your own tomorrow? I can come help again if you need it—the two of us can knock it out quicker."

Cooper climbed up the ladder again to get to the wall near the ceiling. "No. I don't want to pull you off the Mayfield house with Delbert for another day. We finished most of the paintwork today. I can do the rest tomorrow by myself and clean up on Friday."

They worked in silence for a time until Rafe commented, "Pretty color, this Buttercream Yellow. Kind of girly." He raised an eyebrow. "We use so many neutrals, like sandalwood and sage, in the log homes we build that I don't get to handle pretty paint like this very often."

Cooper snorted. "The new owner, this Miz Lamont, called Mother to talk about the apartment and when she wanted to move in. Asked if Mother could work out getting someone to clean up the place and paint it. She even sent down paint chips of the colors she wanted and had wallpaper shipped in for the bedroom and the kitchen."

"It's cute wallpaper she picked out for the kitchen with them colorful roosters on it." Rafe chuckled. "I kind of enjoyed sticking it up, and I noticed that bedroom wallpaper she sent has yellow stripes and little flower sprigs. Real sweet." He wiggled his free hand in an airy fashion.

Rafe's good humor failed to lift Cooper's surly mood. "You'd think the woman could have been content with us being good enough to clean out the place and then go through the whole apartment with a uniform coat of white paint," he groused, not ready to let a sore subject go. "But no—she had to send us paint chips and ship in special wallpaper, making the whole job take longer. She even wanted the hardwood floors refinished throughout. That took two dang days of work last week, thank you very much, Miz Lamont." He paused. "So you be sure to keep those drop cloths over the floor, Rafe, and don't drip any paint on the wood."

"Yeah, I'll do that, boss."

"We don't want our new gallery owner arriving on Saturday and not finding everything *absolutely* perfect in every way." He gave a disgusted snort.

"Ummm. Yeah, sure, boss."

Something about Rafe's reply sounded odd. Cooper turned to see Rafe raise his eyebrows at him and then glance towards the doorway. A dark-haired girl stood there with a hurt expression on her face, biting her lip. *Where had she come from?*

Cooper's eyes scanned her from head to toe. Rich brown hair, neatly parted down the middle and pulled up loosely in some sort of girly style in back. A soft heart-shaped face, blue eyes. Pretty thing. Nice figure, rounded in all the right places. She wore a bright crimson sweater, one of those long cashmere types that dropped over her hips, with black slacks tucked into low-heeled black leather boots. When his gaze reached the girl's face again, Cooper's eyes caught on hers and held.

He didn't notice girls much—always so busy with too much to do and too much to be responsible for. But he noticed her. There was something about her that drew him, made him take a second look. She seemed all polish and sophistication on the outside with an unexpected touch of sweetness hiding underneath. Interesting girl. It felt like she looked right through him with those clear blue eyes, searching him out.

Rafe cleared his throat, pulling Cooper's attention away from the girl. "Uh, miss," he said. "If you're looking for the gallery or the coffee shop, the entrances to both are around in front. Neither business has a back door for the public."

She lifted her chin. "I'm Emily Lamont," she said in a quiet but refined voice.

Cooper registered the name. "The new gallery owner?"

She nodded, offering a thin forced smile.

"Well, dang." Rafe slapped his palm against his forehead. "And you walked in and caught us both bellyaching about the work we're doing fixing up your place. Gee, ma'am, we're sorry. You don't think nothin' of it, you hear? Cooper here offered to fix up this place for you, and we neither one meant anything disrespectful by those words you heard. We were just going on, flappin' our jaws, like men do sometimes."

"I see." She tried that smile again, shifting in the doorway.

Cooper watched her. "You weren't expected until Saturday. That's the date you said. We're not finished for you to be able to move in. I hope a moving van isn't sitting outside. There's wet paint everywhere." He glanced around. "And a work mess, as you can see."

She shifted again, moving so the light skittered over her hair and winked off what looked like diamonds on her earrings and a thin bracelet glittering on her arm.

Rich Philadelphia girl, he thought. Boots alone must have cost several hundred bucks and no telling what the rest of her clothes were worth, much less the jewelry.

She twisted her bracelet, as if noticing his glance there. "The van won't arrive until Saturday. I came early. I didn't expect to stay at the apartment until the furniture comes. There's a motel down the road on the corner, the Bearskin something. I thought I'd stay there."

"The Bearskin Lodge," Rafe put in. "Nice place. You'll like it." He grinned. "Have you been downstairs to the gallery yet and met Mamie?"

"Who?" She looked confused.

"Mrs. Garrison," he clarified.

"Oh." Her eyes lit then. "Do you mean Adelyn Garrison?"

"Yeah." Rafe gave her one of his handsome-boy smiles. "But everyone just calls her Mamie."

"I see." Again she offered a tentative smile in return.

Rafe began to gather up paint supplies. "Look, Cooper, I'm going to start hauling all this gear out to the truck. You only have a little painting to finish tomorrow and that wallpaper work to do. Most of the rest of this stuff you won't need." He paused, shooting Cooper a cocky grin. "Why don't you show Miz Lamont around the place a little, give her an idea about how nice her new home will look when we're all done. Then you can take her downstairs to meet your mother, Mrs. Garrison."

Cooper saw Emily's eyes blink wide at those last words.

"Son of a weasel," Cooper muttered under his breath. He'd get even with Rafe Harlan later for putting him in the Mr. Hospitality role. He glared at him now, but Rafe only gave him a wink and a wide grin before starting out the door, loaded down with paint supplies.

"Rafe, you put that extra paint in the storage room downstairs in case we need it for touch-up later," he hollered after him. "And put those drop cloths in there, too. We're done today but I might need them tomorrow when I finish up."

"Sure thing, boss." Rafe's voice floated back.

Cooper leaned over to settle his paintbrush across the top of the nearly empty can. When he looked up, the girl still stood in the doorway, watching him.

"Actually, I would like to look around," she said at last, a touch of polished Yankee accent to her voice. "But you don't need to take me. I know the floor plan and I'll be watchful for the fresh paint."

"It won't be a bother," he said at last, knowing he was acting churlish. "But watch going through any doorways. There's still a lot of paint not quite dry throughout, especially here in the dining and living areas."

Cooper pulled a handkerchief out of his back pocket and wiped his hands. Resigned to the inevitable, he gestured around the room. "From where you're standing in the main hallway, left takes you to the bedrooms and right leads you to the living areas. You're looking into the dining room now."

He walked into the dining room and put his hand against built-in cherry cabinets covering one wall. "Leon Jacobs had this shelving put in years ago when he converted this upstairs space." Moving to the middle of the room, he pulled up the edge of a large drop cloth to reveal a dining set. "Under here is a big dining room table and chairs they left behind. Nelle didn't need it where she was moving."

The girl walked closer to run a hand over the table. "It's nice. I didn't expect to find any furniture."

"Well, this is the only furniture in the place you'll find except for some beat-up rattan pieces in the porch room. Those will need to be thrown out or cleaned and painted—whatever you want. I left them for now."

Her eyes moved back to the cabinets. "The cabinets match the dining table," she commented.

"Yeah, they were custom built. Delbert Hilton made them; he's a fine carpenter and cabinetmaker."

She nodded, looking towards the doorway.

Cooper gestured her in that direction next. "This door leads into the living room. We just finished it, so take care for the wet paint." He watched her glance into the large living room, with its soft buttercream paint nearly dry on the walls. "We refinished all the hardwood floors in the apartment, too, like you asked."

"So I heard earlier." She winced over the words. "I'm sorry that was a problem for you. Mrs. Garrison indicated she knew someone to contract for the work and said she didn't mind to arrange it."

Cooper felt like a heel at her words. He turned towards the next room, eager to avoid her eyes. "In here is the kitchen with a small eat-in area next to it, a laundry in back, and a big pantry closet."

She walked around, smiling, and running a hand over the wallpaper. "The wallpaper looks nice," she said. "I bought it, and the paper for the bedroom, over a year ago, meaning to put it up in my place in Philadelphia, but I never had the time. It seemed a shame to waste it—and I knew I'd bought extra rolls—so I shipped it down."

Hmmm, Cooper thought. That explained the paper.

She walked into the kitchen's eating area. "I own a little round table that will fit perfectly here, and I love the view out of these big windows."

"That's the West Prong of the Little Pigeon River you can see at the end of the property. On a warm day, if you open the windows wide, you'll hear it bubbling along its way."

Another quick smile touched her face—a pretty smile.

"The kitchen appliances—stove, refrigerator, dishwasher—aren't the newest but they all work good," he said. "So do the washer and dryer in the laundry room." He gestured towards the doorway to that space.

She glanced in, her face lighting up softly again.

Cooper started towards the door. "I'll walk you to see the bedrooms and the sun porch." Moving down the hall, he gestured to a bathroom off the hallway before carefully pushing open the door beside it, trying to avoid the wet paint. "This is the spare bedroom. I think you specified a brighter paint for this room, Daffodil Yellow. Is it all right?"

"Yes." She glanced around, obviously pleased. "I like yellow."

No kidding, Cooper thought, leading her on to the master bedroom, still painted a dull ivory.

Her eyes brightened. "Oh, I love all this space. There's room for all my bedroom furniture plus a little sitting area."

"The walls here still need papering."

"I'm aware of that. I heard you talking about it." Her face dropped. "I can hang the wallpaper myself," she told him, lifting her chin. "I do know how, and then you won't have to do it."

"I said I'd do it." He snapped out the words.

"I see," she replied again, looking away from him. Clever how those two words conveyed a whole lot while avoiding any confrontation and not giving away what she was thinking.

Cooper wisely made no further comment.

"You can go out to the sun porch through the French doors off the bedroom here." He walked across the bedroom to open the doors as he spoke. "Or you can access the porch through a door at the end of the hallway."

"Oh, my," she said, stepping into the sunny porch room, the floor painted a shiny white.

"We didn't strip the floor here—just cleaned it," he said. "It's always been white for as long as I can remember, and you can see the old wicker pieces I told you about look a little worse for wear."

She ran a hand across the back of one of the old chairs. "I can redo these. All they need is cleaning, some paint, and the cushions re-covered." She glanced at him. "I can paint as well as paper and I can do simple reupholstering."

Cooper wasn't sure what to say to this. She wasn't the kind of woman he was used to. She made him antsy for some reason, but he didn't know why. He pointed to the doors leading to a covered outdoor balcony. "There's more outdoor furniture on the open porch. It looks worse, of course, since it's taken the weather, but it could be cleaned up, too, I guess."

"It will give me a project." She turned to look at him, crossing her arms. "Was there any white paint left from the interior trim work?"

"A couple of cans." He picked up on her thoughts. "It's probably enough to do all these chairs and tables if you want. The paint's downstairs in the storage room behind Garrison Log Homes."

She lifted her brows. "Is that your business that rents space from the gallery?"

He nodded. "Yeah. I like being near my mom, to keep a watch."

She didn't reply to that, obviously not a chatty, talkative sort.

"I scheduled time to paint this porch room tomorrow," he told her. "If you recall, you picked out a moss-green shade for it. Ought to look nice with the white painted floors."

"Yes." She considered this, looking around. "It will pick up the green sprigs in the bedroom wallpaper, too."

"It will." He nodded. "I painted part of the bathroom, off the bedroom, in that same moss color from the floor to the chair rail. Thought it would look better than just white with the wallpaper above to match the bedroom."

She offered him that soft smile again. "Yes, and I already have bed coverings, towels, and accessories to match that wallpaper. I'll look forward to seeing how it all comes together."

"Sounds pretty." He paused. "I'll bring the paint up here later for the wicker chairs and tables and such—whenever you want it— plus some drop cloths and brushes. There's no need to buy what we already bought."

"Thank you." She walked out onto the open porch to look across the expanse of property leading down to the river.

He came to stand beside her. "You might not know it but the Creekside Gallery building was an old lodge in the early days of Gatlinburg. Rich industrialists and other city folk came down here to enjoy the beauty of the mountains, to hunt, fish, or hike. Even to take the waters in nearby resorts. The outdoor patio and walkways that you see, and the garden atmosphere, were created in those years. You'll find statuary scattered around the grounds, nice flowers and shrubs, and a covered picnic shelter down by the stream."

"A gazebo?" She turned those clear blue eyes to his, and he felt his stomach clench in an odd way.

"No, nothing fancy like that, but a nice wood structure with a good roof. There are a few Adirondack chairs there and a picnic table, too. It's a fine spot for sitting and thinking."

Her eyes met his, seeming to look inward at him again. "I like a place for sitting and thinking." Her voice softened.

They stood close now, too close—staring at each other, time seeming to stand still, like the first time when he saw her in the doorway. Cooper wasn't familiar with the odd feelings she caused in him, wasn't sure he liked them either. She seemed to suck him into some kind of force field he couldn't pull free from.

His eyes linked to hers, and he felt the oddest urge to touch her face or to put a hand in her hair. When his eyes moved down to her mouth, soft and inviting, he shook himself, turning away.

"I guess that's about it," he said, finding his voice again and starting towards the door into the apartment, not trusting himself to even look back at her right now. Whatever was the matter with him?

Cooper walked quickly down the hallway, eager to put some

space between himself and the girl. Back in the dining area, he scanned the room, looking for any final areas he needed to touch up before calling it a day.

She followed a short time later. Cooper felt her standing in the doorway again before he turned towards her.

"Thank you for your time," she said. "I can see myself downstairs to find Mrs. Garrison on my own."

"No, I'll take you down." He looked around a last time. "I'm finished here for the day. I can introduce you to my mother, and then come back to clean up."

He pulled his Garrison Homes ball cap down, shading his eyes, before starting towards the door. "Off the entry area leading up to the apartment, where you came in from the back patio, you might have noticed a door on the right. It leads directly into the office of the gallery. It's always locked, but you can use it to get to the gallery from your apartment without needing to walk all the way around to the front entrance. The Jacobs always used it."

"Were they the ones who made the lodge into a gallery?" She followed him down the stairs.

"No. It was renovated into a commercial space before—developed as a gallery with the two smaller business spaces on either side. The Jacobs changed things, of course, when they bought the property. And they renovated the upstairs into a big apartment to live in."

"It's very gracious," she commented.

"Yeah. I remember going up there sometimes as a kid. They kept a dog and I took care of it for them when they traveled."

He heard a quick intake of breath.

"Oh my goodness," she gasped. "I left my dog in the car. I'd better go check on her before I go to the gallery."

Cooper turned at her words, and she nearly ran into him starting to rush down the stairs—creating another of those strained moments. Confound it. She made him feel like an awkward teenage kid again. What was it about her?

She straightened and cleared her throat. "You go on back to your work while I check on Mercedes. She's used to being in the gallery with me in Philly, so I can take her in with me to meet your mother."

He chuckled at her words. "You might not want to do that, ma'am. Sugar Lips might not like it—not one little bit."

Her brows lifted. "Sugar who?"

Cooper laughed. "Sugar Lips is the resident gallery cat here. Showed up small, pitiful, and meowing one morning by the door, scooted inside, and then after a little milk decided she'd stay. She's been ruling the roost around here for about five years. I'm not sure she'll take to sharing her space with a dog."

Emily let herself out the downstairs door, not waiting for Cooper to open it for her. Obviously, the independent type.

"Mercedes is used to being around all types of animals and people. She'll find a way to get along with the cat." She picked up her pace as she started down the walkway towards the parking area in back. "What was the cat's name again?"

"Sugar Lips."

"Interesting name."

"The cat likes to give people sugar—a little lick on the chin or on the finger—if she likes you. Affectionate thing."

"I see." She turned to send a small smile to him over her shoulder.

At the end of the drive, Cooper saw what had to be Emily's car parked beside his brown Ford F-150 pickup—a sporty silver convertible, with the top up, and a big gray poodle looking out the window with excitement. *Son of a gun*, he thought. The girl drove a BMW Z4 sports car. His work crew would throw a fit to see this number. If he wasn't mistaken, it was one of those models imported from Germany, not even made in the USA.

"Sweet car," he said, watching her lift the hem of her sweater to pull a set of keys from her slacks pocket.

"Yes, it is." She sent the car a wistful look. "Hal and Mary bought this for me when I graduated from college."

Cooper made no comment. He remembered when he graduated from college his mother gave him one of his father's rings she'd saved. There'd been no money for extravagant gifts. He glanced down now at the platinum ring on his finger with its blue tanzanite stone—worn and battered from years of wear by an outdoorsman, but precious to Cooper.

How in the dickens, he wondered, was a city girl like this—used to diamonds and BMWs for presents and sporting a French poodle for a dog—going to get along with his mother and the people around here in Gatlinburg?

Emily clipped a leash on the dog as she let it out of the car. The dog, a large poodle probably twenty inches high, had a thick, gray curly coat, trimmed short, but thankfully not in one of those prissy cuts with part of its legs shaved and a pom-pom tail. Cooper always felt sorry for dogs trimmed out like that, unnatural like. She spoke to the dog, and it minded exactly what she said, sitting down on the sidewalk while she locked the car door again.

After a woof of welcome to her, the dog didn't bark or fidget, or try to make a dash towards the yard. It didn't act aggressive towards him either.

"Nicely trained dog, your Mercedes," Cooper said, watching the dog's ears prick at her name. "Where'd the name come from?"

"We ran a name-the-puppy contest at the gallery when I first got her. It drew a lot of interest and some publicity." A small smile touched her mouth again, crinkling the corners of her eyes, too. "Everyone at the gallery helped to vote for the best name. Mercedes seemed the favorite—and the most appropriate for a gallery dog for the Hal Newman Gallery."

"Posh kind of place, the Newman Gallery?"

"Yes, I suppose so." She pocketed her keys again. "It's an old established art gallery with a national reputation situated right on the Rittenhouse Square in downtown Philadelphia."

She pointed to the walkway leading towards the stream. "Will it be all right for me to walk Mercedes there?" She glanced back at the car. "I usually carry doggy waste bags. I have some in the car."

"A little trinkle today won't kill the shrubs."

He followed along as she started down the pathway, the dog walking beside her, as well behaved an animal as he'd ever seen.

They passed a bronze statue of a boy holding a jar of fireflies, one of Cooper's favorites since childhood. It sat tucked into a bed of candytuft that would be a glory of white blooms to see come spring.

A little farther along, Emily stopped to study a red metal bird feeder on the top of a pole.

"A feeder built high like this on a pole keeps the squirrels from accessing the seed supply." Cooper turned to point back towards the gallery. "You can see this feeder—and others around the yard—from your porch."

"I'm sure I'll enjoy watching the birds from the porch, and hope-fully, from that big picture window in the kitchen dining area."

"Yeah, there are nice views down across the garden and to the stream from all the back windows." He paused with her, waiting for the dog to irrigate a nearby shrub. "The gallery holds eve-ning events in the springtime on the broad back patio. People get dressed up to come. The Jacobs usually had the outdoor events catered. Mom has kept the tradition going in a limited way."

She glanced towards the broad patio spanning the back of the gallery. "I imagine it's beautiful here in spring when all the flowers and trees bloom. I see dogwoods and redbuds, forsythia and ja-ponica. Oh, and there's a beauty bush over there and one of those gorgeous pink Kwanzan cherry trees. I love those." She pointed down the walkway.

Cooper found himself surprised again at her, knowing the names of shrubs and trees. "You'll see it all come into bloom in the spring, if you're still here."

Her eyes lifted to his in surprise.

"It's mighty different here in Gatlinburg, Tennessee, from downtown Philadelphia and the city life you're used to, Miz Lamont. You might not stay around."

She frowned at him. "I imagine you'd like that." She walked on with the dog.

"I didn't say that." He followed, annoyed at her comeback.

She turned to gaze at him. "I think you made it very clear earlier that I wasn't exactly welcome here."

He frowned. "I might have grumbled, but don't take that to mean others feel the same, Miz Lamont."

"It's Emily."

"Emily," he repeated. "My mother has been real excited about your coming. I haven't heard her say a negative word."

Her eyes found his, and she lifted her chin. "I hope that's true, Cooper Garrison, because I intend to stay. This is my home now. I have nothing to go back to."

She walked on without further comment, and Cooper wondered at her words.

CHAPTER 3

Emily hadn't expected the glorious garden behind the Creekside Gallery. It brought a bright spot into her day to discover it. She'd seen no pictures or found any mention of it in the attorney's file she examined.

The last few weeks had proved hectic, stressful, and often unpleasant as Emily resolved all her affairs in the city, said her goodbyes, and packed to move. She didn't want to reminisce about those painful days in her mind right now. She'd had more than enough time to do that—and to cry a boatload of tears—in the night hours and on the drive to Tennessee.

Eager to put the past and its entanglements and sorrows behind her, Emily left Philly earlier than planned, right after the movers came. Her furniture traveled on one of those joint loads carrying another household's possessions before heading south to deliver hers. She could have stayed the extra days in Philadelphia with several friends who offered, but chose not to.

She drove seven hours of the trip yesterday to a small town called Wytheville, Virginia. There she'd spent the night in a Classic Revival bed-and-breakfast called the Trinkle Mansion, tucked into a cozy, romantic room filled with antiques. She'd lingered over a three-course breakfast at the inn before heading out again this morning, stopping at several points along the way and taking her time on the three-hour drive still remaining to Gatlinburg.

After arriving in the busy tourist town, and discovering absolutely no parking spaces on the River Road even on a weekday, she found her way to the private park area behind the gallery. Curious to see her new home, she decided to slip upstairs through the back entrance for a quick look before going around front to the gallery to meet Adelyn Garrison. She hadn't counted on finding workers when she let herself in the apartment or on overhearing the conversation she did.

Emily glanced over at the man walking alongside her now. He didn't want her here. He'd made that rather clear. And Leonard Newman had made it clear, as well, before she left Philadelphia that he didn't want her around either. She pushed all these unpleasant thoughts from her mind and sighed. Welcome or not, she was here to stay. This was all she had now, and she needed to make the best of it. As Reuben Parrish had reminded her, the gallery property belonged to her free and clear. It wasn't essential that she be liked—although it would be nice.

"Mercedes and I are ready to go into the gallery," she said to Mr. Garrison, while wishing at the same time she could explore more of the back property and walk down to the river.

He nodded, turning to lead the way back up the path.

"I'll get you a hangtag for your car so you can keep it in the park area without getting towed," he said. "Mamie has a few extras, I think. Parking is at a premium in Gatlinburg."

"I certainly saw that," she replied.

Opening the door into the back entry again, Cooper took out a ring of keys and used one to unlock a bright blue door. "I guess you saw the turquoise trim on the front of the building. The back door matches."

"I did notice that as I drove up and in the photos I reviewed earlier. All the tall window frames and doorframes are brightly painted, too. It's an unusual color for such a rustic wood structure."

"A splash of color can make a place memorable. People always say it's one of the things they remember most about the gallery. The Jacobs added the turquoise color to the weathered browns of the lodge building when they bought it to give the gallery personality." He hesitated. "It seems to have worked."

"Don't worry. I won't change it. It makes the place distinctive, as does the landscaping."

He nodded, relieved at her words. "You'll like the gallery inside, too." He gestured for her to go in.

The door led straight into a hallway that ran past two small offices. Through one doorway, Emily glimpsed a large empty desk by a back window, the nearby shelves almost barren, and through the next door she saw a desk piled with a clutter of papers and catalogs, the tops of the file cabinets stacked high, and the bookshelves bulging with books, mementos, and photos.

"Mom's office," Cooper said, gesturing to the second. "The one to the back will be yours. It was the Jacobs'."

The hall led into the gallery sales area where more file cabinets stood along a wall behind a long checkout counter. Cooper paused. "To the right leads into the frame shop with storage and a workshop behind it." He gestured. "To the left leads directly into the gallery."

As they advanced farther into the room, a threatening hiss and a low feline growl met them.

Cooper chuckled. "Sugar Lips has spotted your dog." He pointed to the cat, rising from a bed on top of the counter. "She spends a lot of her day curled up in that basket on the sales counter near the front window. Likes to keep an eye on things."

The cat stood on the counter now, eyeing the dog, with her fur bristling. She was a gray-and-white shorthair cat with a gray back, head, and tail, a white underbelly, and a pretty white nose, whiskers, and vest. And she did not look happy at the moment.

Mercedes sidled behind Emily, ears lifted, observing the cat.

A voice called out from inside the gallery. "Cooper, is that you?" A short woman with closely cropped yellow-white hair stepped out from behind one of the gallery walls. She wore a neat blue blouse covered in decorative tucks over trim navy slacks and had a gamine smile, sparkling gray eyes, and a neat, petite figure. She dumped the empty cardboard box she carried into the corner as she walked towards them.

"You must have slipped in the back, Cooper. I didn't think I heard the front bell." She dusted off her hands. "Who's this you have with you, dear?" Her eyes moved to Emily with warmth.

"This is Miz Lamont," he said. "She came down from Philadelphia early. This is my mother, Adelyn Garrison."

"Oh, what a delight." The woman stepped forward to wrap Emily in a warm hug. "I am so pleased to meet you." She pulled back to survey her. "And aren't you a beautiful young girl! I don't know why I expected an older woman, but I guess I did." She paused to smile at Emily. "Welcome, my dear."

Ordinarily, Emily would have offered a hand to shake in greeting, but it seemed a little late for that after the impulsive and affectionate greeting already given. "Thank you," she said instead. "I've heard only the nicest things about you, Mrs. Garrison."

"And I of you."

Another hiss from the cat drew Adelyn Garrison's attention. She noted Sugar Lips's hostile glare towards the dog and shook her finger at the cat. "Oh, dear. I regret Sugar Lips is not very welcoming to dogs. It's a failing of hers."

She fussed at the cat, and then, not moving directly into Mercedes's personal space, she dropped to a partial squat and held out a tentative hand when she saw Mercedes wagging her tail. "And who is your charming friend?"

"This is Mercedes." Emily gave the poodle a signal that she could approach Adelyn to make friends. "She's been practically raised in the gallery in Philly and she is very well trained. She won't chase Sugar Lips. She learned early as a pup that cats can be rather dangerous playthings."

Adelyn laughed. "Well, the two will have to find a way to get along." She turned to the cat. "Sugar Lips, this is our new owner, Emily Lamont, and her dog friend, Mercedes. You might as well settle your mind to being gracious to both of them or you might lose your place of royalty in this little gallery."

Emily walked over to pet the cat. Sugar Lips, not seeing Mercedes advancing towards her, settled down in her basket once more, keeping a careful watch on the poodle. She even offered Emily a rumbly purr.

"Where did you run into Cooper?" Adelyn asked, seeming to sense him growing restless.

"I parked in back and thought I'd walk up to see the apartment before I came around to the gallery. You remember you sent me a key. I found Cooper and another man working there."

"That was Rafe Harlan, one of my carpenters with Garrison Homes and a fine worker," Cooper put in before turning to his mother. "I walked Emily around the apartment and then downstairs to meet you."

"Oh, dear." Adelyn put a hand to her face in concern. "You know the place isn't ready yet, Cooper. I hope the moving van isn't coming today."

"No." Emily soothed. "My furniture is on one of those split loads, so the movers are going to another city first and then will be here, as scheduled, on Saturday morning to unload. With no furnishings remaining in my place in Philadelphia, I came ahead early. I told Cooper I thought I'd stay down the road at the Bearskin Lodge. I can enjoy looking around the city for a day or two until the movers arrive."

"Well, I'm thrilled you decided to come early, and I absolutely insist you come and stay with me until Saturday."

"Oh, no, Mrs. Garrison," Emily interrupted. "I wouldn't want to put you out, and with the motel so close, Mercedes and I will be almost right by the gallery."

Mamie leaned down to pet the dog again. "Emily, I promise you Mercedes will be much happier at my little place. And I really don't think the Bearskin allows pets." She paused. "Besides, it would hurt my feelings if you don't stay with me. It will give me a chance to get to know you and for us to visit. We'll be working closely together and that would be nice, don't you think?"

Emily thought it was hardly professional, but what could she say?

Cooper cleared his throat. "Mom, if Miz Lamont wants to stay at a motel you should let her. The River Terrace down the road allows pets for an extra fee."

Adelyn's face dropped, her eyes moving to Emily's. "Well, of course, if you'd *prefer* to stay at a hotel tonight and tomorrow, dear, I'd understand, but I live alone and have two extra bedrooms. It would be no bother."

Not wanting to see more disappointment on her face, Emily gave in. "Mrs. Garrison, if you're sure it won't be too much trouble, I'd be delighted to stay with you until Saturday. It's very kind of you to offer."

Mamie clapped her hands, her face lighting up. "Oh, that's wonderful! Monty will be in shortly to take over the gallery for the evening, and you can follow me right on home. I only live a mile or two from the Creekside."

Emily watched Cooper frown and shift restlessly. "Mom," he said, "I need to get on back to work upstairs."

"Oh, of course, dear, you run right along." She reached up to pat his face. "I'll show Emily around the gallery before Monty gets here and then take her to the house so she can relax and freshen up. I'll see you later on tonight. How fortunate you were coming to dinner tonight so I already had a pot of that wonderful fagioli soup you love simmering in the Crock-Pot, plus a big salad and a nice loaf of French bread ready to serve. You be sure to show up on time, you hear?"

He shifted restlessly in the doorway. "Mom, I don't need to come tonight since you have Emily to entertain."

"Nonsense." She waved a hand. "You need to get to know Emily, too. We want her to feel welcome and comfortable in her new home."

He pasted on a feigned smile. "Well, then, I'll see you at six," he said, turning to head towards the office hallway and back upstairs. He tipped his cap to Emily as he left.

Emily twisted her hands. "Mrs. Garrison, I can't say again how kind it is of you to invite me into your home, but truly it isn't necessary."

"Of course it isn't necessary, but it's my pleasure. There's a difference." She reached over to pat Emily's cheek. "And you must call me Mamie. No one calls me Adelyn except people who don't know me."

A bell on the front door chimed as two couples walked into the gallery.

"Mr. and Mrs. Craddock! How delightful to see you again!" Mamie moved across the room in welcome. "Are you in town at your cabin this week?"

A little conversation ensued as Mamie visited with the Craddocks and met their friends. She turned back to Emily. "Dear, why don't you slip back to the office and rest a few minutes while I show the Craddocks the new Cawood Gentry print they're eager to see. I know you're tired from the drive." She moved closer to Emily, whispering. "There's no need for you to get into sales work just yet in the gallery. I'll tell you about the Craddocks later." She pointed past the sales counter area. "That door there, with the long waterfall painting hanging on it, leads into the restroom. Use it if you need to, and if you want to snoop around in the mat and frame shop, you feel free. I won't be long with these clients."

With that, she swept away with the Craddocks and their friends towards the back of the gallery. Glad for a few minutes of reprieve, Emily found the restroom—nicely decorated—and then went back to the empty office Cooper Garrison had pointed out to her earlier.

In it sat a large oak desk with a leather chair tucked underneath it, several file cabinets, a long row of bookshelves down one wall, and two cozy side chairs with an end table between them. Both guest chairs were nicely upholstered in a plush green-on-green stripe, and Emily settled gratefully into one of them.

Mercedes padded up to put her nose in Emily's hand.

"Yes, everything is unfamiliar and we're both tired," she told the dog in comfort. "But we'll settle in and we'll be all right."

She noted, glancing around, that the walls of the office were papered in grass cloth wallpaper in a subtle, two-tone green stripe to complement the chairs. The room's colors were soothing, like the view out the double window to the back gardens.

Emily felt glad she wouldn't have to share an office or usurp someone else's office space. A quiet place like this, in which to savor a few moments of peace during busy days in a gallery, was always welcome. This room would be a pleasant oasis once she filled it with her own things.

With a sigh, Mercedes settled down at Emily's feet to curl up for a nap. Seeing the dog so comfortable, Emily leaned her head back and closed her own eyes for a moment to rest while she could.

"You're worn out," a quiet voice said a little later.

Emily, at first disoriented, opened her eyes to see Mamie leaning against the doorway. "I've finished with the Craddocks and Monty is here. I think the two of us should head for the house where you can get some rest. The gallery will be here for a grand tour tomorrow. I don't think you need any more to focus on today."

"I guess I'm more exhausted from the weeks getting ready to move and from the trip than I thought. I fell asleep."

"It's only natural." Mamie smiled. "Is your car out back?"

Emily nodded.

"So is my little Honda. Let's slip out the back door and you can follow me home. After you get settled in, I think you should take a tiny nap while I get supper together. Then you'll feel much more like yourself."

Relieved, Emily smiled. "Thank you. I think that would be nice."

A few minutes later, Emily followed Mamie's maroon sedan through the Gatlinburg traffic, down a busy side street, and gradually away from the cars and people onto a quieter back road. They turned by a rustic sign that read Mynatt Park and then traveled down two more short roads to a small barn-red cottage at the end of a shady lane. The quaint house, with its gables and steep roofline, sported bright yellow shutters and a yellow front door. Emily followed Mamie into the driveway, parking her car under a spreading maple tree.

"Oh, my," she said, getting out of her car and snapping a leash on Mercedes. "If I'd known how absolutely charming your house was I'd never have hesitated for a minute to say I'd stay with you. It's like a cottage out of a children's story."

Mamie laughed, coming to help Emily get her bags out of the car. "I'm so glad you like it. Cooper is always trying to get me to move into something more modern, but I love my little house here in the woods."

Walking towards the porch, Emily spotted a wooden bench across the road, with a stream running along merrily in front of it.

"You even have your own stream!"

"Well, it's hardly mine, dear, but it feels like it is. It's called Sweet Gum Branch and it's a small tributary out of LeConte Creek that we crossed on the bridge coming into Mynatt Park." She led the way towards the front door. "You can take Mercedes walking along the creek road later. I told you she'd like it here better than at a motel."

"Oh, yes." Emily looked around at the woodland setting in fascination.

They entered a house cozy and comfortable with family furnishings and an array of warm colors. "I hope you don't mind climbing stairs," Mamie said, leading the way. "My two extra bedrooms, that used to be the boys' rooms, are both upstairs. There's a nice bathroom between them and you'll have a little privacy from any of the noise down here."

She trooped up the stairs and led Emily into a bedroom under the eaves with a double bed in the center smothered in handmade quilts and eyelet pillows. The furniture pieces, obviously older, had been painted in soft colors, and framed English garden scenes hung on the walls.

"Who did the paintings?" Emily asked, seeing immediately they were originals.

"An older lady in the community who passed away several years ago." She made a tut-tutting sound. "Can you believe her children put these lovely paintings out in a garage sale after she died? I bought every one I could. I think they're charming."

"So do I." Emily sat on the edge of the bed to study them.

"They're sort of a mix of Impressionism and Primitive Realism."

"Yes, and Bertie Hammond was the sweetest thing you ever met and a beloved neighbor of mine for many years." Mamie paused in front of one of the paintings. "I think about Bertie every time I look at her work."

Mamie pulled a luggage rack out of the closet and set it up, dropping one of Emily's bags on it. She put the other on a trunk at the end of the bed.

"You settle in now." She leaned over to give Emily a kiss on the cheek, just as if she'd been one of her children. "I'm going downstairs to putter in the kitchen and then I plan to put my feet up and read a good book until dinner." She pointed to a small bookcase. "You may find something there you'd like to read yourself. Pile up on the bed for that small nap, and come down to find me later when you're rested. I'll take the dog out for a short walk, give her a little water to drink, and after that I imagine she'll run right back up here to be with you."

She clucked at Mercedes as she left, who padded after her as if they were already the best of friends.

Emily moved around the room, putting her things away and settling in. She found the bathroom, put her toiletries there, and came back to look through the books in the bookshelf. Picking out an old L. M. Montgomery title she'd loved as a girl, she pulled off her boots and curled up on the bed to read.

Shortly, she could hear Mamie singing in the kitchen, something lyrical and sweet. Tears filled her eyes as the sounds drifted up to her. Someone, at least, seemed happy to have her here. It felt blessedly welcome after such a hard season of disappointments.

CHAPTER 4

Cooper felt disquieted all afternoon after leaving Emily with his mother. It bothered him that his mother had taken that girl into her home, knowing so little about her, and it troubled him that he'd be subjected to an evening with her later. She made him uncomfortable, although Cooper wasn't sure why. Probably because they'd started off so awkwardly, the girl overhearing his conversation with Rafe. And as for the attraction, well, that would pass. Cooper certainly wasn't interested in starting a relationship with his mother's new boss.

After cleaning up the apartment over the gallery, Cooper found a can of primer and put a coat of paint on all the wicker pieces. It would save time for Emily tomorrow to have a base coat already on and dried. After finishing, he went down to the Garrison Homes office to check on messages. Bettie Chase sat at the front desk, filing a nail.

"Danged if I didn't tear off one of my nails changing out the cartridge in the copier." She studied it with annoyance.

"If you wouldn't put those stupid paste-on nails over your own nails you wouldn't have that problem."

"But they're fun." She made a face at him. "Besides, I wanted my nails to look pretty for my niece's wedding this weekend." Bettie glanced at the wall clock. "If it's okay for me to leave a little early, I can run by the salon to get this nail fixed before they close."

"Sure," Cooper replied absently, looking through the mail he'd pulled from his in-box.

Bettie began tidying up her desk to leave. "A middle-aged couple visiting from Ohio want to come in tomorrow to talk to you about possibly building a vacation cabin here. I set the appointment for ten in the morning, knowing you'd still be upstairs finishing the Jacobs' apartment."

He snorted. "It's *hardly* the Jacobs' apartment anymore."

Ignoring him, Bettie leaned forward, a glint of interest in her eyes. "I heard the new owner arrived this afternoon and that you got to meet her."

"Where'd you hear that?" Cooper scowled.

"Monty Russo in the gallery told me. Said she's staying at your mother's house, too, until her moving van arrives on Saturday." She made a pouty face. "But Monty didn't get to meet her yet. What's she like?"

Cooper had no desire to give Bettie Chase any more information than she'd already ferreted out. She was a terrible gossip, although an excellent administrative assistant.

"I'm sure we'll all get to know her soon enough." He evaded her question. "And ten is fine for a meeting tomorrow. Who are the couple?"

Bettie launched into a full description. It amazed him how she managed to wrangle so much information out of people at a first meeting. Bettie, in her midfifties with grown kids, had worked first for his father, then for Lance, and now for him. She'd grown a little plumper through the years, changed her hair color several times, and wore glasses on a jeweled chain around her neck for close work now, but she was still a crackerjack at running the office.

After catching him up on a few more office matters, Bettie left, and Cooper settled into his own office, propping his feet on his desk, to sort through the mail and to check and answer his e-mail. It was hard keeping up with everything in three arenas—in the small sales office here in the Burg, at the model-home office out on Highway 321 above Gatlinburg, and with his construction crew working on whatever building projects were in progress. He wished his father and brother had lived so they could have split up the work more equitably. Cooper did his best, but often believed he fell short in many ways of what his dad dreamed the business would be.

Noting the time, Cooper realized he needed to head home, clean up, and change clothes in order to get to his mom's on time. She'd be annoyed if he arrived late, especially with Emily Lamont at her place.

Not long after, he pulled his Jeep Renegade into his mother's driveway at five thirty, ahead of schedule. Cooper drove a construction-size pickup for business, but he liked to drive his little Jeep on his own time. His golden retriever leaped out of the open Jeep as soon as he turned off the motor.

"Brinkley, wait up," Cooper called to him, but to no avail. Brinkley dashed around the side of the porch towards the kitchen door. The dog knew Cooper's mother's home as well as his own and loved to come here. If Cooper even said the words *Do you want to go to Mamie's?* the dog went nuts. Brinkley stayed with Mamie, too, when Cooper traveled.

"Oh, well." Cooper knew Emily's fancy dog, Mercedes, would be here, but he couldn't deny Brinkley the chance to visit, despite that. "Dang it, they'll just have to find a way to get along." After all, this was more Brinkley's home than the Philadelphia poodle's anyway.

He pulled two sacks from the back of the Jeep—one an extra bag of dog food from his own place his mother might need for Emily's dog. The other held two bottles of wine he'd picked up from the Sugarland Cellars on the way over.

Seeing his mom's garbage container still at the curb, he walked down to roll it back to the garage with his free hand before letting himself in the back door. "Hey, Mom," he called, heading through the side porch and laundry area into the kitchen. "I see you let Brinkley in. Is he behaving himself with the new dog?"

She reached up to straighten his collar and give him a kiss. "They're getting along as sweet as pie. They've already sniffed, circled, and done the whole canine socializing act. Mercedes wisely played the charmingly submissive role, dropping her body and tail a little to let Brinkley know she didn't intend to threaten what was obviously his territory. Smart girl. I've given them both a chew bone and they're busy with those now."

Cooper leaned down to pet Brinkley and then to give Mercedes a scratch behind the ears, so Brinkley would know he approved of her.

His mother studied the dogs. "It's a good thing I thought to put out a different feed and water bowl for Mercedes—and to put Brinkley's dishes on the counter until he came. That helped."

Cooper laughed. "Yeah, I'd say it did. Brinkley's a little territorial about his stuff sometimes." He glanced around. "Where's the girl?"

"Upstairs, taking a rest. She was worn out and I suggested she take a nap. She fell asleep in the chair in her office while I talked with the Craddocks at the gallery. Poor thing."

"Smells good in here," Cooper said, sniffing the air and avoiding a response.

His mother turned to lift the lid of her Crock-Pot to stir the contents. "I hope she won't mind soup and salad for dinner. It's only simple fare."

"If she doesn't love your pasta fagioli there's something wrong with her. I think it's better than the Olive Garden's." Cooper dropped his grocery bag on the counter.

"Well, aren't you sweet to say that." His mother smiled. "It is one of my favorite recipes and gives me leftovers to heat up for several meals after." She glanced at the bag he'd placed on the counter. "What did you bring?"

"Dog food in case you were short." He pulled the sack out. "And two bottles of wine from Sugarland's. I thought they'd add to our dinner. I got the Martha Jane Rose you like and a Century White."

"That was thoughtful of you. Emily may prefer the white, like you do."

Cooper wrinkled his nose. "That Martha Jane is too sweet for me."

He watched his mother add three wine glasses to the family-size kitchen table setting. The small house had no formal dining room, but Cooper loved the heavy oak table in the kitchen his father had made many years ago and the tall ladder-back chairs. He even liked the bright placemats and homey decorations his mother always used with her meals.

"Are you sure you should have invited this Miz Lamont to stay with you, Mom? We don't really know her and I'm not sure how professional it is to entertain your boss so informally in your home."

His mother crossed her arms. "She's a young girl, and from what I understand she left everything she knows in the city to come here to run the gallery. I have a strong feeling there's a story behind all this, Cooper. I seem to remember Nelle Jacobs telling me Hal and Mary Newman took in a friend's child to raise in the past. This may be the same girl and if so, she'll have lost Hal Newman this winter and Mary not long before."

"Why didn't she stay in Philadelphia with her life there and sell the Creekside Gallery? I could have helped you buy it then."

She sent him an exasperated glance. "Cooper, I don't want to buy the gallery. It's enough responsibility for me to work there, and at this age and stage of life I don't want more stress and bother. In fact, I'd like less. I'm glad the girl is coming to take some of the weight off my shoulders. I might get to travel a little or take a vacation now and again without worrying about things so much."

He scowled. "Well, you should have at least been given a chance to buy the gallery after all the time and love you've put into it."

"Owning things doesn't make you happy, Cooper." She opened the oven door to stick in a buttered loaf of French bread. "But satisfying work does, and the love of friends and family. I have both of those."

Her comfortable ease with life and her lack of ambition often bothered Cooper. "I suppose so," he said, not wanting to argue.

Mercedes's ears pricked, and she jumped up and headed to the door, collar jingling, at the sound of Emily's footsteps coming down the stairs.

"There you are," Cooper heard Emily say to the dog before she headed into the kitchen. Emily paused in the doorway, seeing them both there. "I hope Mercedes hasn't been giving you any trouble."

Brinkley rose, eyeing Emily across the room.

"Relax, Brinkley." Cooper spoke to the dog. "This is Mamie's house guest."

Emily, in wisdom, stood quietly, waiting for Brinkley to edge across the room towards her. After a moment, she spoke to him and put down a hand for him to sniff. "I'm glad Mercedes has a new friend," she said to the dog.

Deciding she must be okay, Brinkley went back to his bone.

"Something smells wonderful in here." Emily moved farther into the big family kitchen. "Is there anything I can do to help?"

"You can pour some of that cold water in the refrigerator into those glasses on the table," Mamie said, giving Emily a task. "I'll spoon out some bowls of soup and get the bread out of the oven." She turned to Cooper. "You put that salad bowl on the table and then pour a glass of wine for each of us."

Cooper watched Emily out of the corner of his eye while he put the big bowl of mixed salad on the table. She still wore the long red sweater and black slacks he remembered from earlier, but she'd pulled on a pair of black canvas walking shoes now instead of the boots.

"I brought a rosé and a white wine," he said to Emily as she finished pouring out the waters. "Which would you prefer?"

"The pink is a little sweet," his mother put in, setting a basket of hot bread on the table, "but it's my favorite. The white is Cooper's choice. Give her a taste of both, Son, so she can decide."

Obliging, he poured her a sample of each, rinsing her glass between.

"The rose is sweet and good, but I think I'd like the white tonight. I'm fond of most all white wines—rieslings, chardonnays, even sangrias." She paused at the table with her glass.

Mamie gestured to a chair, encouraging her to sit down. "These are wines from the Sugarland Cellars right on the Parkway, not far from the gallery," she said, settling into a seat herself. "They make their wine right on the premises. You'll have to go over and take their tour of the winery one day."

She offered a short blessing, sparing Cooper an uncomfortable moment of wondering if he should welcome their guest in a meal prayer, and then his mother kept up her usual amiable chatter as they began to eat.

"Tomorrow I'll take you for a get-acquainted tour around the gallery," she told Emily between bites. "It's a lovely little gallery, and I'm sure you will love it and love our artists. Leon and Nelle Jacobs bought the gallery twenty-two years ago this summer. I started working in the fall the same year after they opened, just after Cooper turned six and started first grade."

Cooper rolled his eyes.

"I've been with the gallery ever since. As the gallery grew and needed more help, I took the role of assistant manager, and later gallery manager when Leon's health began to fail."

Emily glanced up from her dinner. "I seem to remember Daddy Hal saying Mr. Jacobs had Parkinson's and then fell and contracted pneumonia while in the hospital."

Cooper noticed the intimate term Emily used for Hal Newman.

His mother passed the bread around again. "Yes, that's right, and it was a hard time for Nelle. Leon had carried the weight of running the gallery and Nelle simply didn't want to try to keep it up after he passed away."

"Had you hoped to buy the gallery then?" Emily asked.

"Gracious, no!" his mother replied, causing Emily to lift a brow at Cooper across the table. "I'm hoping to slow down a little after you settle in and are able to pick up more responsibility." She smiled at Emily. "Hal and Mary Newman always said you ran the gallery in Philadelphia with artful diplomacy and skill. If you could run that grand city gallery, you'll have no trouble with our small-town gallery." She spread a little butter over a piece of bread. "However, we have our own unique challenges here in Gatlinburg, and during the tourist seasons we can get very busy. It will be different for you, but I think you will enjoy it."

Cooper cleared his throat. "Why didn't you stay on managing the gallery in Philadelphia?"

Emily looked away and didn't answer for a moment. "The gallery changed hands when Hal died last month," she said in a soft voice. "Hal's nephew Leonard Newman inherited Hal and Mary's estate and the gallery in Philadelphia."

His mother seemed surprised. "Wasn't that the boy Hal tried to groom to work in the gallery in the past, the one that made such a muck of things and that Hal had to dismiss? I remember Nelle and Leon talking about it after one of their trips to Philly to visit with the Newmans. Those two couples were fast friends." She scratched her head. "I seem to remember the Newmans didn't have much use for that nephew. How did he end up with the gallery?"

Emily twisted her hands in her lap before looking up with a strained expression. "He was their only nephew and their blood kin."

"So he got the big gallery and you got the little gallery here." Cooper studied her, hoping she would share more.

"Yes," she said, stirring her spoon in her soup and keeping her eyes on her plate.

Cooper's mother gave him a warning look and then reached across to pat Emily's hand. "Well, for whatever reason you're here, we're tickled to get you. And I'm sorry you lost Hal, and Mary, too, the year before. That had to be hard for you."

"Yes, I loved them." Tears threatened at the corners of her eyes. "And I will miss them."

"Cooper and I have known loss, too, dear, and we understand that pain. Don't you feel embarrassed about it." She reached behind her to the counter to get a tissue for Emily. "I lost my husband, Price, when Cooper was only sixteen and his brother Lance twenty-two, and then we lost Lance six years later."

Emily glanced up. "Oh, I'm so sorry. I didn't know."

"Well, of course you didn't, but loss is a part of life and time moves on. The pain grows dimmer, but you don't forget those you love or stop missing them or thinking about them."

Uncomfortable with this conversation, Cooper changed the subject. "Emily, I should get the last of the paintwork in your apartment done in the morning and the wallpaper up in the bedroom tomorrow afternoon. If you want to start painting that porch furniture either tomorrow afternoon or Friday morning, it would get dry before the movers come on Saturday. Then you'd be done with paint smells and drop cloths."

"Now, Cooper," his mother chided. "Emily may not want to deal with that right now when she's just arrived."

"No," she interrupted. "He's right. I'd like to work on it, so when I move in most everything will be done. After I unpack my sewing machine, I can find some material and work on re-covering the cushions in the evenings."

"They certainly need it." Mamie laughed. "And there's a nice fabric store and a Walmart in Sevierville. You'll find fabric options at both."

"Oh, good." Emily offered them one of her sweet smiles again. "I'm sure I'll need other things for the apartment, too."

More idle chitchat on a lighter note ensued. Cooper's mother made sure of it, noticing Emily's reluctance to discuss the recent past.

"I love this soup," Emily said at one point. "I hope you'll share your recipe with me."

"Absolutely, or I'll invite you over when I make it again." Mamie gestured towards the counter. "As you can see, it makes a large amount, too much only for myself."

"Is that cake for dessert?" Cooper gestured to a cake under a glass dome on the counter.

"Yes, and I hope you'll like it," she said, getting up. "It's a Hummingbird Cake from a recipe Maureen Cross gave me. She said it was one of Tanner and Delia's favorites, so I thought I'd try it."

Cooper glanced Emily's way as his mother went to cut the cake. "Maureen Cross is my mother's longtime best friend. Her son, Tanner, is the accountant for the gallery and for Garrison Log

Homes, so I'm sure you'll meet him and Maureen at some point."

"Maureen lives only a few streets away from me on Balsam Lane," his mother added, bringing a piece of cake to Emily and one to him. "She's a dear; you'll like her. And her son, Tanner, and his wife, Delia, live across the street from her. Cooper helped add on to their house when they married some years back." She paused. "When was that, Cooper?"

"About five years ago, I think."

"Hmmm, that should be about right. Their little boy, Thomas, named after Maureen's late husband, is about four now." She smiled as she sat down with her own cake. "Maureen says Delia is expecting again, Cooper."

Cooper dug into his cake, deciding not to reply to that. It might start his mother on the subject of wishing he'd marry and provide some grandchildren for her. "This cake is great, Mom," he said instead.

"Yes, it really is," Emily added. "What's in it to make it so moist?"

"Cream cheese plus mashed bananas and crushed pineapple."

"Well, it's wonderful, and I rarely get homemade cake."

Cooper felt grateful for his mother's chatter and conversation to fill in the spaces with Emily Lamont. He wasn't much for social chitchat with people he didn't know well, but his mother had never met a stranger. He supposed that was what made her wonderful at managing the gallery; she made everyone feel immediately welcome and comfortable.

Carrying his plate to the sink a short time later, he wondered how quickly he could make an excuse to leave.

"Cooper," his mother said, "I want you to go with Emily to walk Mercedes around the neighborhood while I clean up the kitchen. I took Mercedes out earlier, but I know she'll want to go out again. Brinkley will be glad for a walk, too, and you can point out some sights to Emily along the way."

"That's not necessary, Mamie." Emily rose to carry a stack of plates and silverware to the counter. "I'll help you clean up here and then take Mercedes for a short walk afterwards. I'm sure Cooper has things he needs to do."

Seeing his mother's pointed glance in his direction, he replied, "Brinkley and I would be glad of a walk. It's no problem, and Mother's had a long day. We can clean up before we walk so she can go sit down to watch that TV series she enjoys on Wednesday nights."

Mamie sighed. "It's dreadful how you get caught up in these television shows." She glanced at the clock. "But I still have ten minutes before it begins, plenty of time to load the dishwasher and put away a few leftovers. You two run on before it gets dark out. Emily will enjoy seeing the park."

Resigned to the inevitable, and with Brinkley on alert after hearing the word "walk" several times, Cooper turned to Emily. "I'll hit the bathroom and then get my jacket. You'll want a coat, too. It's about fifty-three degrees out but still cool."

With Mercedes also picking up on the excitement of an upcoming outing, Emily conceded. "Any temperature in the fifties sounds like a heat wave to a girl who's been living in Philadelphia. I'll run upstairs and get my coat, Mercedes's leash, and some doggy bags in case we need them."

A short time later as they headed down the driveway, Emily paused to look back at the house. "I love your mother's house," she said on a wistful note. "I told her it looks like a storybook illustration."

"My dad built the house when they first married. Mom raised Lance and me there and doesn't want to move. I've offered to build her a bigger place."

She sighed. "I don't blame her for wanting to stay. Bigger isn't always better. I remember I felt absolutely overwhelmed when I first went to live with Hal and Mary."

"They owned a big place?"

"A huge place with high ceilings, a sweeping staircase, fine antiques, incredible art, sculptures and glassware everywhere. They even had a Norwegian couple, Claus and Edda Sorensen, who lived in and did all the cleaning, cooking, housework, gardening—

even answering the door. I'd never seen anything like it."

Surprised at this bit of candor from her, he asked, "How old were you then?"

She laughed, a warm rich sound. "I had just turned ten."

"Would you have stayed at their house if you inherited?"

"I didn't live at Hal and Mary's home anymore. I moved into a small town house after graduating from college, but I'd have felt obligated to live in their home if I'd inherited. It had an incredible history and it meant a lot to Hal and Mary."

"Would you have continued running the gallery there, too?"

"Yes, it's what Hal and Mary wanted. I loved the gallery. I went there every day after school from the first week I moved to Philadelphia to live with them. I started doing odd jobs as a girl and gradually took on more and more responsibility."

"So why didn't they leave all this to you instead of their nephew?"

She looked at him with pained eyes. "A new will that Hal and Mary made ten years ago wasn't fully executed, so the older will stood in its stead. In that earlier will Hal's only brother, Raymond, now deceased—or his only son, Leonard—were the named heirs."

"Bummer. So how did you get the gallery here?"

"When Hal bought the property from Nelle Jacobs, he wrote me in as the co-owner for the Creekside. So on Hal's death, that property came fully to me."

Cooper ran a hand through his hair. "Listen, Emily, I didn't mean to push on you to hear this. It sounds like you've been through a rough time."

She looked up at him. "Yes, and I'd like not to be quizzed and pushed to answer any more questions about all this, if you don't mind. I know you feel your mother should have been offered a chance to buy the gallery but perhaps you'll understand now why I wanted and needed a change. The gallery in Philadelphia is in a turmoil with all that's happened, and Leonard dismissed the couple that lived in Hal and Mary's house who helped to raise me. Sadly, an inheritance meant to help them in their latter years was also lost."

Cooper felt like a heel. He tried to think of something to say. "I guess you heard Mom say she didn't really want the gallery. I suppose I just wanted it for her, wanted her to have the chance to decide if she wanted it or not."

"Yes, it's hard not to get choices. I understand that."

They walked on in silence for a space.

Cooper decided to change the subject. "The street Mom lives on, if you noticed the sign, is called Garrison Lane—for obvious reasons, since it's the only house on the short road. We turned onto Mountain View after leaving that street and ahead is the intersection with Asbury, the main road into Mynatt Park. This area was once an old assembly grounds with many private retreat homes, then later a children's camp, and now a city park with the homes in the area privately owned. If you drive a short distance past the entrance to the park and neighborhood, you come to the boundary for the Great Smoky Mountains National Park." He paused. "Have you ever been to the Smokies or to Gatlinburg before?"

He watched a small smile touch her face. "When I was a girl, I remember trips here to Gatlinburg and the Smokies to picnic or wade in the cold streams. I was raised not far from here in Knoxville, Tennessee."

"Small world," he said.

"That's what I said when I learned the gallery was in East Tennessee."

"I go to Knoxville a lot. Where did you live there?"

"In a neighborhood called Bearden. My parents ran a small shop off a side street and we lived within walking distance of it."

"Been back since then?"

"No. This is my first trip back to Tennessee."

He laughed. "I guess you saw a lot of changes as you drove into Gatlinburg."

Cooper was pleased to hear her laugh again, too. "It's hardly the same quiet tourist town I remember, and Pigeon Forge certainly looked different. It's grown into quite a tourist attraction in its own right."

He pointed ahead. "That's Mynatt Park. Pretty place situated along LeConte Creek. It has a pavilion, playground, picnic tables, tennis and basketball courts. The park is a nice perk in living here, a good place for gatherings and a fine place for kids to play."

Brinkley stopped to spritz a bush Mercedes had just watered. The poodle, as he'd noted earlier, was well behaved. Even in a new place, where Cooper knew she was eager to explore, she walked neatly beside Emily, with no need for Emily to yank on her leash. In this way, Brinkley was obedient, too. You needed a dog that knew how to heel, and how to stop and sit on command, in a busy city like Gatlinburg and especially around all the hazardous construction sites where Cooper worked. Brinkley minded Cooper's commands most of the time. But as a retriever, some things got him excited, and he'd take off and forget himself.

"Mercedes is well trained," he commented.

"Yes. Thank you."

She spoke to the dog. "You're getting compliments, Mercedes. Good girl!" She gave the dog a small treat from her pocket, and after an inquiring look towards Cooper, offered Brinkley one, too. "You're a very good dog, too, Brinkley," she said. "Good boy!"

Brinkley wagged his tail like a flag at her praise and gave Emily a big doggy smile. *Hmmph*. People who said dogs didn't smile didn't know much about dogs.

After walking the dogs along the creek, Cooper paused. "It's getting dark now," he said. "We'd better head back. Mom will worry."

"You have a good mother."

"Yeah, and you've been kind to her. Keep it up."

She laughed that warm, throaty laugh again. "You're very direct, Mr. Garrison."

"Yep. I pretty much say what I think. Some say that's a failing of mine."

"Well, I've seen you be diplomatic a few times, as well, and not blurt out what you were thinking." She pulled her jacket a little closer. "You didn't want me to stay at your mother's, but you minded your tongue about it, and you didn't want to come walking tonight with me but you did it to please your mother."

"A guy tempers himself around his mother."

"No, a *good* guy tempers himself around his mother. I think, possibly, you're not as gruff or rude as you first appeared."

He looked down at her in the gathering darkness. "Don't be deciding you know me, Miz Lamont."

"Or you me, Mr. Garrison," she said, walking a little ahead of him.

Cooper grinned to himself, following her. She had pluck. Seeing a touch of that soft, vulnerable side of her had made him forget she'd been running a big-city gallery for several years despite her young age.

"How old are you, Miz Lamont?"

"I'll be twenty-five on my birthday in April. And you?"

"I turned twenty-eight last month in January."

"Well," she replied, walking ahead to turn the corner onto Mountain View, obviously remembering the way.

Cooper fell a few strides behind while Brinkley stuck his nose in a bush, and then followed after her, watching her walk. She had a graceful, confident stride with a tiny sway to it, and her figure drew a man's eyes—that was a fact.

As if sensing his eyes on her, Emily slowed until they walked along side by side again. "After your mother shows me around the gallery tomorrow, I'd like to come up and work on the wicker furniture. Will I get in your way?"

"Depends on how you act." He grinned at her.

Her eyes brightened. "I don't see you smile like that often. It makes you much more attractive, Mr. Garrison."

"Better not sweet talk a man alone in the dark, Miz Lamont." Cooper's voice dropped, and he found his eyes moving to her face and lips as he said the words.

She cleared her throat and fidgeted with Mercedes's leash. "I was only making an observation. And perhaps we should both return to using our first names again. It's Emily."

He put a hand to her face. "And maybe it might be wiser for me to stay a little more formal."

She pulled away, crossing her arms defensively. "I don't want to get into a relationship with my gallery manager's son, Cooper. I'd like to make that very clear. It wouldn't be professional and I'm not looking for a little fun on the side, either."

It annoyed Cooper that she threw back the words to him that he'd thought earlier. "My same thoughts exactly, Emily Lamont." He stomped on ahead of her and turned into the driveway.

"Cooper," she called.

He stopped to turn and look at her.

She walked closer to him. "I haven't had much practice with men; I've always been too busy for dating and all those girly things." She studied her feet. "I don't know how to act around feelings that get stirred up. . . ." She stopped, not finishing her thoughts.

Cooper respected her effort at honesty. "I'm not much good with that sort of thing either, Emily, and I admit some emotions do kick up around us. I probably haven't handled it well either."

She sighed. "I'd like us to be friends."

"Well, that's what we'll be then," he said. "And I'll put down the drop cloths on the porch in the morning, bring up some paint and brushes for whenever you decide you want to do some work." His eyes passed over her. "You might want to wear some old clothes, if you have any."

"I admit, I didn't think to bring painting clothes. My casual clothes are all packed in the moving van." He could see that little smile touch her lips again, even in the darkness. "Perhaps you or Mamie could loan me an old shirt I can put on over my jeans and T-shirt."

"I'll rustle one up," he said, leading Brinkley around towards the kitchen door.

She followed, not acting huffy and independent over him holding the door for her. Evidently even in big-city Philadelphia, old-fashioned manners hadn't gone completely out of style.

Hearing them come in, Mamie walked through the kitchen doorway. "I hope you had a nice walk."

"Yep," he replied. "And I'm going to head out now. Big day tomorrow." He leaned over to give his mom a quick kiss on the cheek and—glancing across the room at Emily Lamont in the soft light of the kitchen—wished he could give her the same. *'Let's be friends,'* *be danged*, he thought. There was something about this girl that stirred him. He'd just have to learn to rein it in, that's all.

CHAPTER 5

The smell of coffee woke Emily the next morning. She'd slept well and felt rested and better. Stretching and yawning, she noticed Mercedes wasn't by the bedside and smiled. The dog obviously liked Mamie.

Knowing she'd be heading to the gallery, Emily dressed in a long-sleeved open-neck white shirt, tan velveteen trouser-style pants, a neat belt, and a long, open-front black cardigan that provided a tailored-suit look to a casual outfit. Instead of her boots today, she slipped into black leather Clarks mules she favored for long days on her feet.

Mercedes's woof of greeting alerted Mamie to Emily's presence as she came into the kitchen. "You look rested," she commented, "and very nice." Mamie wore brown slacks, a pink blouse, and a cardigan embroidered in flowers—a cheerful look for a winter's day.

"I didn't mean to sleep so late." Emily glanced at the clock, shocked to see it was almost ten. "Doesn't the gallery open at ten?"

"Yes, but it's Leona's day to work so we could both enjoy a sleep-in." She sent Emily a sunny smile. "Ready for some breakfast?"

"That would be a treat. What can I do to help?"

"Pick out some jam, cream cheese, or butter to your liking in the refrigerator. I made some biscuits and I'll scramble a couple of eggs for us. You're not allergic, are you?"

"No," Emily replied, rummaging in the refrigerator.

Mamie cracked eggs into a bowl. "While you're in there, get out one of those pink grapefruits and cut it in half for us to share." She pointed to the coffeemaker as Emily headed to the table with jars of blueberry and peach jam. "You can pour us both a cup of coffee, too, after you cut the grapefruit."

"I love it that you give me tasks to do." Emily sat the jams on the table and began to section the grapefruit halves. "At Hal and Mary's house Claus and Edda Sorensen acted like it was an offense to their sensibilities if I did a thing in the kitchen. I had to teach myself to cook when I moved out on my own."

Mamie distributed the cooked eggs onto two plates, put them on the table, and gestured for Emily to sit down as she did. "Nelle and Leon always used to tell me the Newmans lived high on the hog."

Emily blinked at the term and then laughed. "I guess that's a good way to put it. I told Cooper last night, when we walked, that I felt awkward at first when I went to live with them. They lived a more lavish lifestyle than I'd known."

"How old were you then?" Mamie stirred cream into her coffee.

"Ten. My parents were killed in a car wreck. I had no other close relatives and Mary Newman had been my mother's best friend and roommate in college. Hal and Mary were my godparents, too." She spread blueberry jam over a hot biscuit. "I remember as a small girl our families often vacationed together, usually at a beach house or a mountain cabin out west. And sometimes my mother, Mary, and I went on little trips together. I was always fond of Hal and Mary, which helped at that hard time when my parents were killed." She paused to eat a few bites, remembering those times. "They came down after the accident and took care of all Mother and Daddy's affairs, arranged the service, everything. I don't know what I would have done without them. They were so good to me."

Mamie ate quietly for a moment. "I don't mean to be nosy or to pick at a scab, but I gather they meant to leave you the gallery and their home but something went awry with the will." Her eyes met

Emily's. "You don't have to discuss this with me if you don't want to."

Emily sighed. "No, it's all right to ask, Mamie. Hal and Mary made a new will about ten years ago but somehow it didn't get fully executed. It was their intention to leave the gallery and their house to me. Hal's brother, Raymond, had cancer at the time of the second will and was dying, and Hal didn't think his son, Leonard, a good choice to inherit. However, with the new will never properly finalized, the old will stood in its stead. That's the law."

"That's a shame." Mamie made a face. "Nelle Jacobs told me their nephew made a muck in the gallery years ago when Hal tried to bring him in and train him."

"Yes, and there were many other ongoing problems between Hal and his brother and sister-in-law, as well as with Leonard, their only son. Relations were strained between the two families long before I came to live with Hal and Mary and then only grew worse."

"Was there nothing you could do about the will?"

Emily finished her eggs and considered this. "Hal and Mary's attorney, Reuben Parrish, said I could contest, but I felt I'd have little chance of overturning the old will—having no blood relation to the Newmans. Even Mr. Parrish admitted before I left that a legal battle would have been hard. He'd looked into the matter more thoroughly by that time, and Leonard Newman's attorney had contacted him, suggesting this course of action not be pursued. In court, it could easily have been interpreted—by those not knowing Hal and Mary Newman—that Hal changed his mind about finalizing the new will and decided the house and gallery should stay in the family." She got up to pour a little more coffee. "More than anything I didn't want to bring any scandal and discredit to Hal or Mary's name by fighting and squabbling over assets."

Mamie shook her head. "All of this had to be difficult for you."

Emily nodded and then smiled at Mamie. "Which has made it all the nicer to be so graciously welcomed by you. I truly appreciate your kindness."

Mamie waved the compliment away. "Even though you've lost a lot, Emily, I hope you'll be happy here. I've always loved working at Creekside, and I believe you'll enjoy our other two employees, Leona Berry and Monty Russo." She sipped at her coffee, breakfast finished. "Leona has a master's in art history and taught at a college near Cincinnati, Ohio, before coming to Gatlinburg after retirement. Of course, immediately she became bored. As soon as you meet Leona you'll realize why—so she came looking for a part-time job and found us. She also adjuncts a class or two in art history at Walters State Community College."

"She sounds very qualified." Emily got up to carry some of their dishes to the sink. "Tell me about Mr. Russo."

"Monty doesn't have Leona's academic background. His expertise is in business and graphic arts instead. The main reason he started working with us at Creekside was because he could cut mat. He takes care of much of our in-house matting. The rest we send out to Benwen Lee. Ben runs a mat and frame business in Gatlinburg. He does excellent work, not only for us but for several other galleries and businesses in town."

Mamie got up to help Emily clean up from breakfast. "Monty will be in later today," she said. "He favors the evening shifts and Leona is more a morning person and likes to open. I try to work with individual preferences as much as possible when I make out the schedule. We've settled into a routine we follow most of the time for the hours we work and then we fill in for each other when the schedule needs adjusting." She glanced at Emily. "Of course you can change any of that if you wish."

"I see no reason to change anything that's working well."

Mamie looked relieved. "Well, I'll finish up here while you take Mercedes outside and then we'll go down to the gallery. The dog will be fine here today while you tour the gallery and get into that painting work." She paused. "Do you have old clothes to paint in?"

"Some jeans and a knit shirt that will do. Cooper said he'd bring me an old shirt of his as a cover."

"Hmmph. And it would swallow you whole, too. I have a better shirt I can loan you." She turned to study Emily. "You're about my height. I may have some old jeans that would fit, also. No sense in spoiling good clothes with paint. I'll dig both out while you walk the dog. You can try them on and, if they'll do, you can take your paint clothes with you to the gallery and change there. I'm not scheduled to work today, so I planned to come back to the house to do a few chores this afternoon. I'll keep Mercedes company and take her for a little walk."

"Oh, that would be kind of you. Mercedes really likes you."

She gave Emily that pixie smile of hers. "Raising two boys, I've taken care of a lot of dogs over the years. I kept Lance's dog, Spike, after the accident, but when Spike died a year ago I decided to simply enjoy Cooper's dog, Brinkley, when he comes by."

Emily nodded. "It's awful to lose a pet you love. Hal and Mary owned a white poodle named Lulabelle when I went to live with them. I loved that dog so much; it nearly broke my heart when she died. It took me a long time before I felt ready to welcome another dog into my heart."

Mamie looked at Mercedes. "And then you chose another poodle."

"Yes, I learned how intelligent they are and knew I needed a dog I could train well for the gallery. They're also nice to strangers, shed little, and are practically odorless—additional pluses for a gallery dog."

"And tolerant of territorial cats!" Mamie laughed. "Another plus."

Emily laughed. "Sugar Lips may be a challenge, but I think she'll come around in time when she realizes Mercedes is no threat to her."

A half hour later, Mamie led the way into the gallery, stopping to introduce Emily to Leona at the front counter. Taller than Emily or Mamie, Leona had short-cropped, silver-threaded hair, a neat middle-aged figure, and wore round, black-rimmed glasses, perched low on her nose.

Putting down the paperwork she'd been reading, Leona dropped her glasses to hang from her neck on a black chain. "I'm pleased to meet you," she said in a deep radio-announcer voice, shaking hands with Emily formally.

"Thank you," Emily replied. "Mamie's had only good things to say about you. Your background sounds like a wonderful asset for the gallery."

They chatted for a space, and when a customer came in needing Leona's attention, Mamie started Emily's gallery tour. "The gallery has seven main areas." She gestured around. "This is the main entry with the checkout counter by the door and across from it you see a small gallery section where we keep tourist items." She walked Emily closer. "The shelves here are full of reasonably priced items from local artists—most who contract other art with us—and the bins are stuffed with matted prints visitors can easily buy and carry home from vacation."

Mamie selected a small print from a nearby bin of a black bear climbing a tree, handing it to Emily. "This is a popular seller by Mack Harrington. It's one of the prints he makes multiple copies of, versus one of his signed and numbered prints. Many tourists want a bear print to take home and put on the wall." She smiled at Emily. "Gatlinburg is a tourist town, Emily, and in order to make money we have to cater to average tourists who often know little about art, except whether or not an item appeals to them and isn't very costly. It's a different sales atmosphere than I'm sure you're used to at the Hal Newman Gallery in the city."

"I like this print." She dropped the bear print back in the front of the bin. "And besides, art is about finding a way to reach all people, not only a select few."

"Well, I'm glad you hold that philosophy because Nelle and Leon Jacobs soon discovered, in their first years here, that if they didn't keep art and collectibles for the average tourist, as well as art for connoisseurs, their business wouldn't survive. In a sense, it makes our little gallery here more diverse. We carry something for everyone."

"Even in a big city, with a prestigious gallery like the Newman, we had to offer reasonably priced prints and items. We had print bins, too, and tried to keep an array of small items, such as artists' note cards and small sculptures."

"Well, I'm feeling relieved to hear that." Mamie led Emily across to another section. "Because in most of our main gallery sections, along with the pricier paintings on the walls, glass cases sit between the wall displays full of small, affordable items by the same artists. Leon, Nelle, and I evolved this idea over time. It's benefited our artists individually as well as our overall profit line."

She pointed to the gallery wall closest to them, well lit by ceiling lights from above and painted a soft ivory to not detract from the color of the paintings. "On the wall to the left here are Christopher Tolley's wonderful watercolors of bugs, Elkmont fireflies, frogs, ladybugs, and bees. You're probably familiar with his work already, although we're blessed he lives in the Southeast not far from us."

Emily studied Tolley's gallery section, a smile forming on her mouth at the joyous, close-up scenes he depicted. "I've seen his work before and it's absolutely brilliant—so bright, crisp, and colorful."

"In the case in front of his wall are Christopher's river rocks." Mamie opened the case with a key to take one out. "He paints many of his same bugs and critters on smooth river rocks and then glazes them. Many people collect these painted rocks who can't afford to collect his prints."

Emily turned the rock in her hand. "That's a clever idea."

Mamie looked smug. "We thought so, and now we only accept artists in the gallery as regulars who will also create a related type of small item for us to sell. Christopher does his rocks, Frank Marcus—who does these incredible realistic birds—also paints wood-carved birds that his father whittles in his spare time." She pointed them out in the case. "And Mark Harrington, who you heard me mention earlier, nationally known for his black bear paintings, paints carved bears that Dempster Marcus also creates. Our fourth artist in this room section, Kim Yung, does these exquisitely detailed butterflies." She pointed towards the wall display.

"How beautiful." Emily let her eyes drift over Yung's delicate watercolor paintings. "They are really incredible. I don't think I've seen her work before."

"Her designs always draw attention and sell well." Mamie pointed into the case again. "Her small signature items are these porcelain boxes she covers in her lavish little butterflies."

Emily leaned over to study them. "Oh, my. I want one of these for myself—perhaps that lovely yellow swallowtail."

"Sold, and with an employee discount." Mamie laughed.

"Is the rest of the gallery set up like this?"

Mamie nodded. "Almost every section. We have each part themed, four artists to a section . . . this one wildlife, the next one landscapes." She led Emily around the corner into a new section, gesturing as she talked. "These are Elton Gibson's sleek, glossy landscapes—modern with limited detail." She tapped a shiny black frame. "On the opposite wall, you'll see Eloise Newton's lush acrylic close-ups of flowers—they're very popular—and Rosemarie Corde's country landscapes featuring pathways, doors, and windowsill boxes spilling over with flowers. Beside Gibson's work are Brooks Davies's busy, peopled scenes filled with tubers, hikers, and tourists milling around Gatlinburg."

Emily moved closer to one of Davies's paintings. "These are certainly attention getters, almost like looking at a *Where's Waldo* book chock-full of people and things to see."

Mamie laughed. "Funny you should mention that, because Davies always hides a small bumblebee somewhere in his work for his followers to look for."

Emily found herself searching for it. "I love art that is also fun, don't you?"

"I do and so do tourists." She directed Emily across the aisle to a third area. "This section is especially appealing to the children."

Emily looked around at the walls plastered with warmhearted, playful art. "I recognize two artists here." She pointed. "Those are Tovah Ricci's happy, colorful scenes of children and Anna Fortunoff's sweet close-ups of animals—bunnies, sheep, squirrels, cats, and dogs."

"The other artists here are a sister team, Elsey DeMarco and Marlene DeMarco Lee, who share a wall space with paintings of their fairies, nymphs, and woodland scenes. And on the back wall are Hadley Bennack's angels."

"Oh, my," Emily said, walking closer. "These angels are very realistic, unique and striking. I'm not familiar with this artist's work."

"Hadley Bennack is a very strong Christian and he feels people have seen entirely too many unbiblical, wispy women angels and cute, fat, baby cherubs." She laughed. "Wait until he stops by the gallery some day. He'll give you an earful."

"Well, his angels in these guardian angel scenes, all dressed in full battle gear, are really spectacular. He brings light into his work, too, in a very distinctive way."

"Yes, he does." Mamie propped her elbow on a case filled with whimsical ceramic fairies, painted angels, and charming, carved woodland houses that Emily knew she'd want to study more later on. "Bennack and the other artists in the sections you've just seen are our regular contracted artists with the gallery. We carry their work as long as they continue to produce it, and bring us new work regularly, and for as long as their work continues to be popular and to sell."

"And if their work stops selling or if they stop producing?"

Mamie crossed her arms. "This is a business, not a charity. We make allowances for a hard space in an artist's life when personal tragedy or problems slow their art for a season, but if things don't change shortly after, we sever the relationship. All our artists clearly understand the rules of the gallery."

Emily smiled to see this firm business side to her otherwise warmhearted manager. "A very wise policy," she said. "It's hard to sever ties to artists whose works are not selling or who stop producing, but it has to be done."

She nodded, moving on. "At the back of the building are the three final areas of our gallery. To the left is our regional Smokies artist room, containing several well-known national artists who paint Smoky Mountain scenes and a number of newer regional artists we're helping to promote. In the middle room is the Cawood Gentry gallery."

Emily walked into this area to look around in awe. "Wow. I read that Cawood selected this gallery as one of the few around the United States to represent his work. However did you manage that?"

Mamie looked puzzled. "I'm not sure. He came into the gallery one day when I was working. I didn't even know who he was—an older gentleman, white-haired and whiskered, with a gruff manner. He asked me a million questions, it seemed—some rather personal. I'm not sure I behaved as graciously as I should have that first visit, but his questions seemed intrusive." She looked away, embarrassed. "I thought, at first, he was making a play for me."

"Really?" Emily was fascinated. Cawood Gentry, known worldwide for his landscapes and portraits, had a reputation for being reclusive and difficult to even get an interview with. Any gallery would value an alliance with him, even if only to exhibit his work in a single event.

"Cawood moved to Gatlinburg later—bought a big house behind a gated drive on the mountain. Perhaps he knew he planned to move here when he visited that day, and for some reason he took a liking to our little gallery and to me. I always handle everything in relation to his work." She moved to straighten one of his paintings. "He signed an agreement to show his work here. He even helped to decide on the space he wanted to display his work in—right beside the main exhibit room where the traveling shows are housed."

Emily studied Cawood Gentry's stunning, rich work, set in the heavy, gold-embellished frames he favored exhibiting his art in. "He is such a master at manipulating light and shade."

"Yes." Mamie paused by a luxuriant landscape of a small lake tucked at the end of a green valley. "It's brought our gallery a tremendous amount of national recognition to be associated with an artist of his stature."

"I read in the gallery's paperwork that he threatened to move his art from the gallery if you were ever fired."

"Oh, that." She waved a hand. "I doubt he really meant it. It's just that I was at the gallery when he first visited and I'm the one he works with the most."

"I see." Emily considered this. "Do you think he's sweet on you?"

Mamie crossed her arms again. "Absolutely not. He has never made a pass or an inappropriate remark to me. He treats me with only friendship and respect."

"Is he as temperamental as I've heard?"

Mamie tapped her chin. "He can be short-tempered and brusque, and he is reclusive and not very social."

Emily smiled. "Well, it's a coup for the gallery to get him."

"Yes." Mamie took out a plastic pass card to gain entry into the final gallery area. "This is our exhibit room. One of us has to open this room and stay with any visitors for security reasons. We exhibit our traveling shows of famous art here. Much of the work is priceless, so we simply can't allow people to wander around in here at will—children carrying sticky taffy or tourists not understanding they can't walk up and touch and handle these works."

Emily clapped her hands in pleasure as she looked around. "Oh, you have Norman Rockwell's work here!"

"Yes, that's our current show. We rotate the shows, most staying about three months, some less. I'm sure you will be a help to us in finding shows for the exhibit room with all your contacts. We generally try to display work that most people can relate to, and when a new show comes in, we host an opening event at the gallery. Our openings are very popular with art lovers in the area."

Leona leaned into the exhibit room, interrupting them. "Mamie, could you come to the phone to talk to Mr. Craddock? He said they've made a decision about a couple of the paintings they looked at with you yesterday."

"Excellent." Mamie made a thumbs-up sign. "This will be a big sale for the gallery." She handed Emily the pass card. "Look around at the Rockwell prints while I take this call. You can lock up and come to the front after."

Emily walked around the room slowly, entranced. She'd always loved Rockwell's work—although many in the art field thought it too illustrative. As a girl, she'd visited the Norman Rockwell Museum in the Berkshires at the artist's studio home of Stockbridge, Massachusetts, with Hal and Mary. Most of their trips and vacations involved stopping at one gallery or another along the way. She knew there were traveling exhibitions of Rockwell's work, but they'd never been quite appropriate for the Newman Gallery. However, they seemed perfect here—homespun scenes anyone could relate to.

She stopped to look at one of her favorites—a young girl in a white slip looking into the mirror, a movie magazine in her lap and a doll lying on the floor. Every young girl encountered that moment between childhood and womanhood, looking into the mirror and wondering if she was pretty, or if she would be pretty one day like the glamorous movie stars. The painting's title, *Girl at the Mirror*, was written on a gold plaque below it.

As Emily leaned in to look closer, something felt odd about the painting all of a sudden—something about that doll, lying akimbo on the floor, its arm at an angle. Emily couldn't put a finger on what it was, but something seemed off.

Feeling an odd prickle, Emily walked around to study all the other paintings in the exhibit. They seemed okay, but she slowed at another favorite—of kids traveling in a car, hanging out the window in a morning and an evening scene, the parents worn and frazzled in the latter. Something didn't feel right here, either. The big, pink gum bubble the little girl was blowing in the first scene didn't look right in some way. Emily had always admired that huge gum bubble in the Rockwell scene, and she remembered wishing she could blow one that size as a girl. She'd even tried to blow one that big while studying the painting in an art book. Now the bubble looked smaller than she remembered. Was it only because she'd grown older and bigger? That her perspective had changed?

Shrugging, Emily finished viewing the full exhibit, locked the door with the pass card, and headed back towards the front of the gallery. *You must still be tired*, she told herself, *or simply imagining things because you're in a new place.*

At the front counter, Mamie greeted her with excitement, having just finalized a large sale of several paintings with the Craddocks.

"That sale will make our month at the Creekside," she said as she led Emily into the mat shop to finish their tour.

The door into the mat shop opened directly off the gallery. Customers could walk through to the shop from the gallery or it could be closed off. Here Mamie introduced Emily to Marty Russo, a handsome middle-aged man with a European demeanor. He was tall and well built, reminding Emily of an Italian movie star whose name she'd long ago forgotten.

Mr. Russo lifted his brows appreciatively as he took Emily's hand in a courtly manner. "I hoped I might meet you today, Miss Lamont. *Bellissimo.*"

"Oh, quit flirting, Monty," Mamie admonished, frowning at him. She turned to Emily. "Emily, you'll soon notice Monty's Italian heritage tends to surface whenever a pretty girl comes in the shop."

He grinned, showing even white teeth in a handsome face. "A man who doesn't notice a pretty girl must be partly dead."

Emily smiled and then walked over to examine the mat that Monty was cutting for a wildflower print.

Mamie glanced at her watch. "Emily, since we've toured the gallery and since Monty is here now, I think I'll let him show you around the mat and frame shop. I'd like to get some things done at the house this afternoon." She placed a hand on Emily's arm with fondness. "After you talk with Monty, you can head upstairs to find Cooper and get started on that porch furniture. I'll take Mercedes for a nice walk and then see you at the house around dinnertime."

Agreeing, Emily let Monty show her around the shop and talk to her about the Creekside's linked side business. Emily found the mat shop neat, orderly, and very similar in layout to the mat room at the Newman Gallery, if smaller. Monty, a charming host for the tour, also took her into the back storage area, dusty and piled with boxes and supplies.

"Does no one use this area anymore?" she asked, glancing around at the large space with its long windows in the back looking towards the patio and garden.

He shook his head. "No, not except for storage now. It used to be a framery. That's why there are so many built-in cabinets and work tables. Leon Jacobs liked to work with wood and he often cut frames for local artists—and for the gallery here—when the Creekside first opened. Now we let Ben Lee do all the custom framing."

Emily smiled, letting her eyes move around the room with its big windows spanning across the back wall. "I think I have a little plan for this space," she said, knowing she'd be back to explore this area more later.

CHAPTER 6

Cooper spent the morning hanging the wallpaper in the bedroom of the apartment. Prepasted paper made the job a lot easier. He'd started by rough-cutting the paper, then trimming each sheet for a more precise fit. It took a little measuring and extra work in the corners of each wall to get a professional finish, but Cooper had handled more difficult jobs before. Fortunately, the walls were plumb. He'd used a level often to check. Working with the stripes proved a challenge, but the room looked good now, if you liked a lot of yellow and little flower sprigs everywhere.

"Oh, it looks wonderful," Emily said from the doorway.

He turned towards her. "I didn't hear you come in." She wore another million-dollar outfit today. Cooper scowled.

"I hope I'm not interrupting," she said, obviously picking up on his frown.

"No, I just finished."

"You did a beautiful job, Cooper." She walked around the room, looking at everything, peeking into the bathroom to notice he'd papered there, also, above the chair rail. "Thank you so much for doing this."

"I only need to paint the trim work and the rails on the porch. Then I'll be finished up."

"Will I be in your way out on the porch if I paint the furniture?"

"No. Rafe already painted the inside walls there the other day." He started cleaning up the wallpaper remnants on the floor. "I'll be working on the outside porch; you can do your painting in the sun porch area inside."

He'd almost forgotten she might come up today. "I'll go down to get the paint and the drop cloths after I finish picking up here."

"I can help." She started to lean over to pick up a pile of trash.

He held up a hand. "No, you're dressed too nice. Wallpaper paste is messy. I'll do it." He stuffed some more leftover paper scraps into a sack, his eyes drifting over her. "I hope you brought some other clothes to work in."

"I did." She gave him that sweet, sunny smile of hers. "I'll change in the bathroom while you finish up if it's all right."

"Sure. I think there's an old shirt you can use in the storage room."

"Oh, Mamie gave me one." She held up a tote bag. "But thank you."

While she changed, Cooper's mind kept wandering to the idea of her undressing right behind the bathroom door. Dadgumit, he needed to get a grip on himself.

Loading his arms with wallpaper scraps and work supplies, he headed down the stairs to the outdoor trash cans and then inside to the storage area. After throwing a few drop cloths over his shoulder and picking up two cans of paint and a couple of paintbrushes, he came back upstairs.

Walking into the newly papered bedroom again, he saw her examining the wicker chairs on the sun porch. "I'm glad it's warm again today," she said, hearing him come in. "This porch is enclosed and sunny, of course, but the deck porch where you'll be painting is outside." She paused. "I think I'll open the French doors leading to the deck and let the fresh air in while I work. It feels like it's in the sixties today, absolutely unbelievable for February."

"March and spring will soon be here." He sat down a can of white paint and two brushes for her, dumped a few drop cloths on the floor, and headed out to the exterior porch with the rest. He'd always liked the way the Jacobs renovated this upstairs apartment, turning one back room into an enclosed porch that led out to an open-air porch looking over the gardens and down to the stream.

Seeing Emily examining a wicker chair, getting ready to work, he walked back indoors. "When we started cleaning out the apartment last week, Rafe and I took all this furniture outside and used a couple of wire brushes to get off the old flaking paint. Then we hosed the pieces down to get the dust and grime off. After you left yesterday, I primed everything, so the furniture only needs a coat of fresh paint now. You'll see I brought up oil-based paint because that's what the pieces had before. You can't put water-based paint over oil."

She nodded, moving a can of paint onto a drop cloth near the chair.

Cooper glanced at his watch. "Have you eaten any lunch? It's one thirty."

She looked up with surprise. "Is it? I guess Mamie fed me such a nice breakfast I hadn't even noticed the time."

Knowing it would be rude to go grab lunch without including her, he asked, "Have you met the Bolinger brothers?"

"Who?"

"The two brothers who run the coffee shop next door to the gallery, your other renters."

"Oh, I knew that name sounded familiar." She brushed a hand through her hair, pushing back a loose strand. "I haven't met them yet, but I met Leona and Monty in the gallery earlier today."

"Well, let's go down and get a sandwich before we get started here. I've been working all morning and I'm starved."

"Oh, goodness." Her mouth dropped open. "I don't look like going out to lunch."

"And you think I do?" He grinned, glancing down at his University of Tennessee T-shirt and old blue jeans, both spattered with blotches of paint.

She bit her lip, considering the idea.

"Listen, you've got on cute jeans and a nice T-shirt under my mom's old paint smock. Just take off the smock and drape it over the chair there. This is a tourist town, Emily, and not Philadelphia. You look fine." He grinned at her. "Actually, you look more than fine, as always, but I guess you already know that. You're a pretty girl."

A blush rose up her neck and spread across her cheeks.

"Not used to compliments?"

She lifted her chin. "Not in blue jeans and a paint shirt."

"I'm a construction guy; that's my favorite look." He let his eyes rove over her with appreciation.

"Now you're starting to sound like Monty." She took off his mom's smock and tossed it over the chair. "Let's go to lunch, Mr. Garrison. I hadn't wanted to meet my tenants for the first time in blue jeans, but I'll have an opportunity to make up for such a casual appearance later, I'm sure."

"I'm sure you will," he repeated, starting towards the door.

"Tell me about the Bolinger brothers," she asked, following him.

"Floyd and Arnold Bolinger came here from Indiana about thirteen years ago, the year before my dad died. They leased the former candy store next door and renovated the place into a little business they call Bolinger Brothers Coffee Shop. Both men had recently retired from the military and Arnold had lost his wife. They were at loose ends, looking for something to do. Floyd had always cooked a lot in the service in one role or another, and Arnold did a lot of the baking at home. Their dad had run a bakery, so they'd grown up around cooking."

He turned to lock the door to the apartment after letting her through. "They're great guys. You'll like them. Floyd is a whiz in the kitchen, makes a fresh homemade soup and a variety of sandwiches every day. Arnold bakes sweets to sell with coffee in the morning and with the lunches they serve. His sweets are legend around here."

Cooper led Emily around the side of the gallery to the front door into Bolingers. The shop wasn't big, but it had a scattering of sturdy wood tables covered in aqua-blue check tablecloths to match the front windows on the Creekside façade. In the back stood an order area and a refrigerated case holding the daily sweet choices on one side and an assortment of deli meats on the other.

"It's a cute place," Emily said as they walked in the door.

Behind the counter, the brothers looked up, sending Cooper a wave and a hello.

"Hey, Cooper, good to see you," Arnold said, wiping his hands on the apron stretched over his full figure. "Who's that pretty thing you brought with you?"

Floyd laughed. "Yeah, and how'd an old construction worker like you get a pretty girl like that?" Taller and slimmer than his brother, he had silver threads through his dark hair and a lean, fun-filled face.

"Now, now, let's don't spoil Cooper's possibilities, Floyd." Arnold shook a finger at his brother. "This may be the only date he'll have this month."

"I guess I forgot to mention these two guys are a couple of comedians." Cooper chuckled, moving to introductions. "Floyd Bolinger and Arnold Bolinger, meet your new landlord, Miz Emily Lamont."

"Well, Lord have mercy, didn't we hit the jackpot!" Arnold came around the counter to offer Emily a hand. "We figured on some sour-faced, citified matron but look how the day shined on us."

Cooper saw Emily grin as she took Arnold's hand and then Floyd's as he came around the counter.

"We're both delighted to meet you, young lady." Floyd staged a little bow. "I hope you've come for lunch, because if so it's on the house for you."

The men moved back behind the counter, chattering about the menu. "I'll spoon you out a bowl of my homemade vegetable soup. That's today's special," Floyd said. "You tell me what kind of sandwich you want to go with it."

Emily studied the menu on the wall. "How about a half sandwich, turkey with provolone, on wheat bread with lettuce, tomato, and mayonnaise, plus iced tea."

"A fine choice," Floyd said, turning to make it.

"What will you have, Cooper?" Arnold asked.

"A bowl of soup, tea, and one of your Philly cheesesteak sandwiches, in honor of Miz Lamont, who comes from Philadelphia."

The two men grinned as they worked.

"You know, that sandwich did get its origins right in downtown Philadelphia," Floyd said. "I read about it in a magazine once. Two brothers, kind of like us, Pat and Harry Olivieri, developed it in the 1930s at a hot dog stand with grilled beef and onions and later added cheese. Served it steaming hot on an Italian roll just like we do."

Emily smiled. "It's still a favorite sandwich in many restaurants in Philadelphia. Some places add green peppers, mushrooms, and hot sauce, too."

"We can do that." Arnold grinned, pushing Cooper's sandwich tray across the counter. "You want any of those extras, Coop?"

He shook his head, picking up his tray and dropping a bill on the counter.

Emily suddenly giggled. "Oh, how clever! I just noticed your bulletin board." She pointed to an old whiteboard hanging on the wall. "I love the saying you posted: *A balanced diet is a cookie in each hand.*"

Cooper glanced towards it. "Arnold and Floyd write up something nutty like that every day. Underneath it Arnold always posts his sweet special."

"Yes, and in harmony with our little quote today, I've made two original cookie recipes—one for each hand—a white chocolate macadamia nut for one hand and a peanut butter chocolate chip for the other."

Floyd came out carrying Emily's tray for her. "I put one of each on your tray, little lady. I think you'll love our peach tea, too."

"They make everything fresh here," Cooper told her as they sat down at one of the tables by the window.

He waved at Floyd as he walked back towards the counter. "I'll have two each of those cookies, too—knowing how good they are—and pack me up several to take home for later."

A big group of tourists came in then, keeping Arnold and Floyd busy while Cooper and Emily began to eat.

"Ummm, this soup is wonderful." She licked her spoon. "And the bread on my sandwich tastes homemade."

"It is," Cooper said after swallowing a big bite of his own sandwich. "I often kid these guys that I rented the space on the other side of the gallery just to be close to their restaurant for lunch every day." He looked across the room at the brothers. "My dad died not long after Arnold and Floyd moved here. They were wonderful to Lance and me then, fathered us through a rough time."

"I like them," Emily said as another sweep of customers filed in the door. "And they seem to stay busy."

"Yes. The locals love this place—as well as the deli at Old Dad's on the Parkway. You can walk over there for lunch another day. It's also an old-time grocery store. You can pick up milk, eggs, bread, and a lot of your small groceries without driving to the big food store on Highway 321."

"Do you live close by?" she asked.

He took a long drink of tea before answering. "I live about a mile away. If you follow the River Road to the Parkway and then head up the street across from the light—that's Natty Road—you'll end at the driveway to my log cabin at the top of the hill."

"Did you build your house?"

"Garrison Homes did; I helped."

"Maybe I'll get to see it someday."

He glanced up from his sandwich, wondering if anything more than curiosity about his house was implied. But she seemed intent on her eating.

After lunch, they headed back to the apartment to work. Cooper helped Emily set up and get started on her job, but then found it hard to stay focused on his own painting with her working, and humming, in the next room. Every time she leaned over, his eyes moved to where they didn't need to go, and when he passed through the room near her, he felt the proximity to her prickle along his skin. Sometimes he caught a waft of vanilla scent on the air around her. Dang woman.

At his next trip down to the storage room to get more paint,

Cooper brought his CD player back with him. He stuck a CD in it and flipped it on, hoping the music would distract him. Looking up from his work a short time later, he saw Emily leaning in the open doorway.

"What are you listening to?" she asked.

"Just some country music." He brushed a line of paint down the top of the porch rail as he answered her.

"I've never heard any of these songs before." She tapped her fingers on the doorframe. "I really like this song."

"Honey, that's Hank Locklin's 'Please Help Me I'm Falling.' Everybody knows that old classic."

She shrugged a little apologetically.

He shook his head. "Well, I'm sure you knew the song before that—'Walking after Midnight,' by Patsy Cline."

"Her name sounds familiar." She bit her lip as if trying to place it.

Cooper shook his head. "Patsy was a big 1960s country music star. She sang 'I Fall to Pieces' and 'Leavin' on Your Mind' and a lot of other great songs."

"I guess I've never listened to country music much. Do you really enjoy it?"

"Yeah, I do." He filled in a spot he'd missed on the railing. "It's my favorite kind of music and I especially like the old greats like these."

A new song came on, and he watched her face brighten as she listened. "That sounds like an old jitterbug tune."

"That's Roy Orbison's 'Dream Baby' and what would you know about jitterbugging? That style of dancing dates back to the 1940s; you weren't even born then."

She passed him a sassy look. "I learned it in ballroom dance classes, I'll have you know."

"Is that right?" He laid his brush across the top of the paint can, stood and reached out a hand to her, moving her into some easy jitterbug steps.

Surprised at first, she stumbled over the first dance movement, but then she relaxed and joined in playfully, letting him twirl her under his arm, keeping up easily with his moves and turns.

"You're good," he said, swinging her under his arm.

"So are you." She flashed bright eyes at him. "Where did you learn?"

"Our folks taught us. Mom and Dad were great dancers, loved the old rock and roll songs and loved country music, too."

Spinning in another jitterbug move, Emily slipped on a drop cloth and fell against him, laughing. Instead of letting her step back though, Cooper held her, looking down at her, both of them panting a little from the dance. He saw pretty flushed cheeks, clear blue eyes, soft lips. And he wanted to kiss her.

His voice husky now, he put a hand to her face. "Like the song we've been listening to, you've started me dreaming sweet dreams that won't do, Miz Lamont."

They stared at each other, not moving, like moonstruck teenagers, but then Cooper pulled away, resisting the urges he struggled with. "I guess we need to get back to work if we're going to get done here," he said, his voice tight.

"Yes." She glanced at her watch, avoiding his eyes, and then started back towards the inside porch room, her steps a little shaky.

It didn't help that a slow romantic country ballad came on next, making him wish he could go pull her into his arms again, dance her around the room, and kiss her until he felt crazy with it. Dang, he hadn't felt this goofy around a girl for a long time, and it was sorrowful indeed these feelings had gotten stirred up by the new owner of his mother's gallery. It just wasn't a place Cooper wanted to go.

Later in the afternoon, they finished up their painting projects. Cooper came to help Emily finish the porch furniture once he got through with his own work, but he kept a careful distance, mostly painting the pieces on the outside porch. He kept CDs going to entertain them, and to help the time pass and fill the silence.

Any more conversation they engaged in related to their work or mundane comments about the weather. It was danged awkward, but Cooper told himself it was better this way. Emily just wasn't his type.

She insisted on helping him clean up this time, carrying drop cloths and supplies back to the storage room. He pulled a can of turpentine and a clean rag from a shelf so she could clean spatters of oil paint off her hands and arms.

"There's a spot on your face, too." He started towards her to wipe it off with his rag and then hesitated, not wanting to risk putting his hands on her again. "You can go in the bathroom there to see it." Cooper pointed her towards the hallway.

When she didn't come back within a short time, he looked down the hallway and saw her standing in the open doorway of the old frame shop. He walked down to stand beside her. "I need to come in here and clean this place out; I didn't realize it had gotten so dusty."

"Do you think it would be all right if I cleaned it out and used it?"

His eyebrows lifted. "Are you bringing a lot of extra stuff from Philadelphia you need to store here?"

"No." She shook her head. "But I'd like to use this as a work space."

He considered that. "Do you paint as well as manage a gallery?"

She lifted a glance to him and then shifted her eyes from his, obviously still a little uncomfortable about their earlier dance scene. "I build dollhouses and this would be a perfect place for working on them."

He couldn't help laughing. "Well, that's a hoot. You build homes for little bitty dolls. Is there a market for that?"

She glared at him this time. "You might be surprised to know there is. Some of my custom houses go for quite a high price."

"Is that right?" He smirked at the idea. "Maybe I'll have to drop by later and check out some of these fine homes you build."

Emily turned on him, putting her hands on her hips. "There's no need to be sarcastic, Mr. Garrison. You may build beautiful homes for real people to live in but little girls love to have a dollhouse they can cherish and enjoy, too."

He checked the quick retort on his lips. "I guess I always thought dollhouses were a little silly," he said, not ready to totally back down yet.

Her face flushed. "With that snide attitude you can be sure I won't ask your opinion on any construction questions I might have."

He bit back another laugh. "I doubt I'd be much of an expert on houses for dollies." He knew he rolled out the last word too slowly, provoking her further.

She crossed her arms, her color heightening. "If you're intentionally trying to make yourself disagreeable, Mr. Garrison, you're doing a very good job of it." With those words, she turned her back on him, pulled the framery door shut, and stalked down the hallway towards the back door.

"I'll clean out the frame shop for you when I get a little extra time," he called after her, realizing he'd really made her mad.

"Don't bother," she threw back. "I wouldn't want to take any more of your *precious* time."

Cooper blew out a whistle as the back door slammed. "Dang. Guess I hit a sensitive nerve." He pushed back his hat, staring at the door.

He started to go after her and then thought better of it. She was ticked; he'd give her time to cool off. He pushed open the door into the frame shop instead and walked inside to look around. The room had broad built-in counters on three walls, tall cabinets, a sink for washing up, and a big butcher-block worktable in the middle of the room. It was a good space for a hobby shop, with big windows in the back to let in the light. He wandered around, pulling out drawers, glancing in cupboards. Leon Jacobs had left a lot of old tools behind, too, some in better shape than others.

Opening the closet in the corner, he saw a push broom and a dustpan leaning against the back wall. "Guess I'll clean up this place before I head home. It won't take long, and it might go a ways towards defusing Miz Emily Lamont's anger the next time she looks in here." He located an empty box to dump trash in, collected cleaning supplies from the storage room behind his office, and settled in to work.

Cooper always found work helpful when his emotions got stirred up. He wasn't sure how he should handle the situation with Emily Lamont, and her anger just now was the least of his worries relating to her. A lot of thoughts had originally crossed Cooper's mind about this woman coming to take over the gallery from his mother, mostly sour and resentful ones. He heaved a sigh as he swept a pile of dust and trash across the floor with the broom. She sure had turned out to be different than he imagined. And she'd certainly turned out to be a lot more trouble than he expected—in ways he was downright uncomfortable with.

CHAPTER 7

Emily was furious when she walked out the back entrance of Cooper Garrison's office. Exasperating man! Nice one minute, nasty the next. Coming on to her and flirting with her one minute, acting interested in her, and then turning around, snubbing her abruptly and treating her like she suddenly had the plague the next. What was wrong with him anyway?

Knowing she needed to work off some of these feelings before she drove home to face Mamie—who was Cooper's mother, for heaven's sake—she walked through the parking lot and down the sidewalk of the River Road. On impulse, she turned left by Bennett's Pit Bar-B-Que restaurant onto a little side street. Moving away from the busy traffic of Gatlinburg now, Emily soon wound her way into a suburban area of charming homes on little back lanes, each with small-town appeal.

This will be a good place to walk Mercedes, she thought to herself, beginning to calm down finally.

At the end of a cul-de-sac, as Emily turned around to start back up the street, a small white bichon frise raced out from a shaded yard, yipping and barking.

"Buster, come back here!" a voice called.

The dog paused, lifting its ears, looking back and forth between Emily and a young woman now crossing the yard with a leash in her hand.

"Sorry he barked at you." The girl shook a finger at the dog, causing him to whine and look chastised.

"I don't think he'd have hurt me," Emily said, squatting to the dog's level and holding out her hand in greeting.

He raced over, wagging his tail in a friendly doggy fashion.

"Are you visiting in the area?" the girl asked.

"No, I just moved here from Philadelphia."

The girl's eyes brightened. "No kidding? Do you live on this street? I remember seeing the blue house on the corner for sale."

Emily shook her head. "No, I live on the River Road above the Creekside Gallery."

"Wow. I didn't know they'd decided to rent that apartment again. It's been empty a couple of years." She put out a hand. "I'm Sara Russell. I live here." She pointed behind her to a cute white cottage trimmed in blue shutters.

"I'm Emily Lamont." Emily took Sara's hand. "And I love your house. It looks like a dollhouse."

Sara rolled her eyes. "I know. My mom owns Dora's Dolls in the Laurel Mountain Village Mall on the Parkway. She's crazy about dolls and immediately painted the house white with bright blue shutters and doors when she bought it. With the house's paint job and its cottage-style exterior, it looks exactly like a little dollhouse. Of course, Mom loves it like that."

"I like it, too," Emily said. "It has charm."

"I suppose." Sara flashed Emily a grin, pushing a hand through her short blond hair. "Look, I don't mean to sound presumptuous or anything, but I'm really glad to meet you today. I'm eager to make some new friends. I recently moved here from Alabama, and I hardly know anyone in Gatlinburg yet. Maybe you could walk with me sometimes when I take the pest out." She grinned at the little dog, leaning down to snap the leash on him. "He's Mom's dog and he isn't as well trained as he should be. When I'm not working at the store, I take my turn getting him outdoors for some exercise."

Emily studied Sara Russell while she talked. She stood a little taller than Emily, lean and athletic in build, with mischievous green eyes and a playful smile. She wore jeans, a black long-sleeved knit shirt, and she looked like fun.

"I could use a friend," Emily told her. "I have a dog, too—Mercedes; she's a standard poodle. We could walk our dogs together."

"Great! I'm sure Buster would love that. He's good with other dogs, despite being a little feisty and high-spirited." She stepped into pace with Emily as she walked along. "Do you want to go get your dog now? We could stop by your place for her and then walk the Gatlinburg Trail. It's a short hiking trail that cuts off the River Road and wanders through the backwoods along the stream. It's pretty there and quiet. And dogs are allowed."

"I'd love that but Mercedes is at Mamie Garrison's house where I'm staying right now. I don't move in until Saturday."

"Ah, I guess that explains the paint." Sara glanced at Emily's paint smock and then tapped Emily's cheek.

"I guess I missed a spot." Emily rubbed at her face. "It's oil paint, too; I'll probably need to get it off with turpentine later. I've been painting some old wicker furniture the past owners left behind."

"It's only a tiny dab. Let me wipe it off for you."

Emily paused so Sara could try.

"See?" She grinned. "That came right off. You're fine."

"Thanks." Emily glanced at her watch. "I can walk with you for a little while today, but then I probably need to get back to Mamie's to check on Mercedes. Mamie will be expecting me, too."

"Okay. We'll only walk around the neighborhood streets today." Sara reined in the bichon from spritzing a mailbox. "What are you doing tomorrow? I'm off all day. Maybe we can do something then."

Emily frowned. "I planned to drive to Sevierville to the Walmart and a fabric shop Mamie told me about to buy fabric to re-cover the wicker porch chairs I painted. I also need stuff for the apartment, too—shower curtain liners, an entry rug, a little valance for the kitchen window, sundries . . . you know. With the movers coming on Saturday, I really need to shop tomorrow."

"Oh fun!" Sara's eyes sparkled. "I can go with you. I know where everything is around here. We can shop, visit, and have lunch. What do you say?"

"Well, if you wouldn't mind dragging along with me."

"I'd love it. We can meet at your new apartment after breakfast tomorrow and you can give me the tour. Then I can help you find what you need."

"Okay." Emily's heart lifted. "I'm sure Mercedes will be all right at Mamie's for another day. If not, I'll leave her in the apartment while we're gone. Thanks for offering, Sara."

"My pleasure." She grinned while slowing at the street corner.

"So tell me about yourself," Emily said as they turned to start up a hill.

"Well, I was born in Birmingham, Alabama, the city founded on industry and known for the giant Vulcan. It's the world's largest cast-iron statue, standing proudly atop Red Mountain, overlooking the city." She intoned this like a tour guide, making Emily laugh. "Kidding aside, it was a great place to grow up. We lived in a nice suburban area outside town near a country club, where I swam on the local swim team."

She continued. "My daddy was a banker—first a bank manager and then a bank vice president. Mom stayed home with my younger sister, Natalie, and me in our younger years. Then she started working part-time in a specialty shop that sold children's toys, books, and dolls. She wanted something to do to stay busy."

She waved her hand in a flourish. "Mom always loved dolls, collected them, sewed clothes for them—so she really liked working there. We had a pretty normal home life, I guess, until Dad died in my high school years. That was a pretty difficult time for Mom, but she came around, started working in the shop full-time. In my senior year of high school she walked in the house one evening saying she'd decided to buy a dollhouse store in Gatlinburg."

Sara laughed. "Natalie and I thought she was kidding, but she wasn't. We'd vacationed in the Smokies a lot when I was growing up. Dad like to camp and we stayed at Elkmont. We had one of those silver Airstream campers you can pull behind your station wagon. Mom knew the area here really well but still . . ."

She wrinkled her nose remembering it. "If we held any reservations about a move, she absolutely did not. I remember she got so excited. She'd driven up here to see the store and really wanted it. She put our house up for sale, and then she and Natalie moved here right after settling me into the dormitory at the University of Alabama. I went there four years on a swim scholarship, majored in finance and banking." They paused to let Buster nose around a bush.

"I had a good head for math and numbers, like Daddy," Sara continued. "After college, I got a job in the bank and moved into a little apartment with a friend. I worked as a teller, then as a loan officer."

"What brought you here?" Emily asked.

"I broke up with a boyfriend, got passed over for yet another job promotion—mostly for being a girl—and had one of those moments when I felt disillusioned with life. I drove up to Gatlinburg to spend a long weekend with Mom and Natalie and it felt good here." She shrugged. "Family means more than you think sometimes. And Mom was losing her assistant manager and needed a new employee. I saw her working really long hours at the shop while I visited, more than I thought she needed to, and I realized I could help with the store and help with Natalie, too. So I moved here and now I work as Mom's assistant manager at Dora's Dolls."

"How do you like it?"

A faint smile played on her lips. "More than I thought I would. We're all doll lovers—Mom, Natalie, and me—and it's a kick working with the public in retail and talking about dolls every day. Plus I'm good with the books, which Mom really needed help with. We make a good team and even Natalie helps, although she's only eleven."

Emily blinked. "Your sister is much younger than you."

"Yeah. Evidently I was the unexpected early child to my parents, while Natalie showed up as the unexpected late arrival when I was thirteen." She laughed. "It was a real surprise to everyone. Especially to Mom."

"I'm glad things worked out for you. You're lucky to have close family."

Sara raised an eyebrow. "Are you not close to your family?"

"I don't have a family anymore." Emily stopped to sit with Sara on a bench by a small park area. "My parents were killed when I was ten and the godparents I went to live with passed away in the last two years."

"Gee, I'm sorry." Sara took Buster off the leash for a few minutes so he could romp around. "So what brought you to Gatlinburg?"

"I inherited the Creekside Gallery."

"Wow! That's cool." She studied Emily's face. "Why do I get the feeling that wasn't a thrill to you?"

Emily looked out across the park, watching Buster chase around a tree. "Hal and Mary Newman, my godparents, raised me to one day run their gallery in Philadelphia. I was managing it when they died. They also wanted me to have their home and their art collections and to take care of their longtime servants, who'd worked for them most of their lives." She paused. "But there was a problem with their will. It hadn't been properly executed, so everything went to their nephew Leonard, except for the gallery property here in Gatlinburg. That property had been put jointly in my name when Hal bought it from Nelle Jacobs." She hesitated. "It's a sad mess. Leonard, who inherited all their estate, terminated the servants, threw the Philadelphia gallery into a turmoil, and plans to sell most everything in the house. Leonard had a strained relationship with Hal and Mary."

"And I assume with you, too." Sara cocked an eyebrow.

Emily nodded. "He was very glad to see me leave town and he didn't mind saying so. Leonard felt I undermined his authority at the gallery—even though I wasn't working there anymore."

Sara crossed her arms. "Sounds like a creep. I've known some of those."

"Yeah, I guess he is a creep." Emily felt herself smile.

Sara punched Emily with an elbow. "Well, life goes on, and at least you did get the gallery here. It could have been worse. I hear the Creekside does pretty well, so maybe you'll be happy here, Emily." She grinned at her. "Especially now that you have this charming new friend to keep company with."

Emily laughed. "There is that."

"Did you leave a boyfriend behind, too?"

"No one special, only a few people I went out with now and then." She turned to Sara. "Do you date anyone special here in Gatlinburg?"

"One guy maybe. His name is Giles Sutherland and his family owns the Smokyland Candy Store in the same mall where my mom's shop is. He really likes me." She hesitated. "Mom really likes him, too. So does Natalie. He's a great guy but . . ."

"But what?"

Sara shook her head. "I don't know. There just isn't that zing there between us. I mean, I realize a great friendship can grow into more but . . ." She paused again.

"You want more zing."

"Is that dumb?" Sara turned to Emily. "Giles is a good man, stable, easy-tempered. You'd think I'd be on cloud nine after dealing with the jerk who dumped me in Birmingham. But there's something missing I keep finding myself looking for."

She whistled for Buster, who was wandering too far away. "Have you ever been in love, Emily?"

Emily considered this. "I don't think so, not seriously."

Sara laughed. "Well, it's an emotional roller coaster sometimes. But it makes you feel so alive. You can't get the guy out of your thoughts or mind; you feel it in your bones every time he comes into a room; you notice his every move and mood. You recognize his cologne, wish you could sleep with his shirt every night just to have something of his close. It's goofy and crazy but it's great, too. It may be dumb of me—but I want that again. I don't want to settle."

Sara's cell phone rang. She pulled it out of her pocket. "Speak of the devil," she said, rolling her eyes. "It's Giles."

Emily listened while Sara talked for a minute, confirming a date for dinner later.

Sara ended her call, tucked her cell phone back in her pocket, and stood up to call Buster. "I guess I'd better head back to the house. Natalie's probably home; I don't like her to stay too long by herself even if she is in sixth grade now." She snapped Buster's leash back on. "And Giles is coming for dinner with us tonight. He's bringing pizza."

She blew out a breath. "See what I mean? He doesn't even mind a date with Natalie in tow since Mom is working. And he'll be a great sport and play board games with her. The latest favorite is Life. You drive your car around this board highway of life, get married, have kids, buy insurance. Natalie and Giles put real pressure on me to play it."

Emily laughed. "Do you mean he's interested in getting married?"

"Oh, yeah. Hints around about it all the time."

"Well, at least he's not ignoring you," Emily said, thinking of Cooper. "That could be worse."

"Yeah, I suppose that would be worse," Sara said, clipping Buster's leash back on and leading the way out of the park.

Later at Mamie's, over dinner, Emily shared about meeting Sara—leaving out any information about her disagreement with Cooper, of course. There was no point in dwelling on thoughts of that exasperating man.

"Oh, the Russells are a nice family," Mamie said, putting dishes on the table for supper while she talked. "I've known Dora Russell since she moved here, Natalie, too. Dora is absolutely thrilled Sara has come to help her in the store."

She gestured to Emily to sit down at the table to eat. "I'm so glad you found a friend so quickly."

Mamie had fixed a chicken casserole for dinner, with sides, and as they ate, she shared with Emily more about the workings of the gallery, the clientele, and the neighboring businesses along the River Road. After helping Mamie clean up from dinner, Emily excused herself early to head upstairs for a hot shower and to settle into the cozy armchair in her bedroom for some quiet time. She felt worn out from her long day at the gallery and the paint job after.

As she showered and got into her pajamas, Emily tried not to let her mind drift back over the day with Cooper. To divert her thoughts, she pulled out her laptop to check her e-mail and found a message from Daniel Stelben, asking her to call—even if late. She toyed with whether or not to even comply.

Daniel's number was still on Emily's speed dial, since he'd been the assistant manager at the Newman Gallery and Hal Newman's assistant for years before. Emily loved Daniel like another father, and she missed seeing him every day. Reuben Parrish had been right that Daniel was outraged Leonard inherited the gallery. In the weeks before Emily left Philadelphia, she'd heard a daily barrage of complaints from Daniel, as well as from the office manager, Christine Moore, and the longtime frame shop manager, Lewis Hearst, about the problems Leonard was creating in the gallery. Michael Zucchi threatened to quit in the first week when Leonard insulted him right in front of one of the gallery's best clients, and Julianne Fontes broke down and cried when Leonard made disparaging remarks to her about taking off to be with a sick child and showing no dedication to her job. Even longtime clients of the gallery had contacted Emily to lodge complaints on how they were now being treated—as if she could do anything about it. Then, of course, every time someone phoned her, word of it got back to Leonard in some way, and his irate and threatening calls to her soon followed. Emily knew any call to Daniel would probably not bring good news.

However, loyalty won out, and Emily made the call. "Hi," she said, hearing Daniel's voice. "I hope it's not too late to call."

"No." A small silence ensured. "Michael Zucchi quit today. Leonard insulted him again and went into a rage, right in front of a group of clients in the gallery, for what he termed Michael's 'insubordination.' Basically, Leonard lied blatantly to a client and Michael called him on it. Leonard totally lost it. The Carmichaels, the

Braxtons, and the Hunts will probably never return to Hal New-man Gallery after what they witnessed today."

"Oh, my." Emily sighed and settled back in her chair. "I am so sorry to hear that. All three of those families have collected with the Newman Gallery for at least fifteen years. It's a big loss to the gallery—and a bigger loss to lose Michael. He was wonderful in sales, often did our graphics, and filled in helping Lewis in the mat room whenever he got overloaded. Michael will be hard to replace."

"Yes." Daniel sighed. "And word is getting out on the street that the gallery is a mess now. It may be hard to hire good people."

"Again, I'm so sorry, Daniel." Emily looked across at the photo of Hal and Mary Newman beside her bedside table. "I know Hal and Mary would both have hated this."

Daniel snorted. "Frankly, I'd like to kick both of their butts from here to China for leaving us in this mess. I know Hal tended to be a little lax keeping up with paperwork and remembering to get needed verifications and documentation in the gallery sometimes, but this action of his with an important document like a will was purely stupid. Leonard's going to run this gallery into the ground, Emily, and there's not a blessed thing I can do about it."

"Perhaps eventually, if the gallery goes under, someone better will buy it, remembering its past reputation."

"I could say a curse word to think it will come to that, Emily, but you're right—it could happen. What a wretched shame. Hal's father started this gallery seventy-five years ago. The place holds a long and prestigious history. It tears me up to think it may end."

"Maybe things will turn around, Daniel. Perhaps Leonard will see the harm he's doing, back away, and let you run things. He likes money and I know he likes the money the gallery brings in."

"He's also as proud as a peacock. He loves strutting in here, lord-ing it over everyone, bragging and trying to sound like he knows two cents about art to the clients who come in. My mind starts counting every day to see if he can break the past day's record of stupid comments and idiotic actions."

Emily almost giggled. "Leonard has always been one of those people who dislikes admitting he doesn't know everything."

"Thou sayest," Daniel quipped.

"Do you think if I called Michael he might come back?"

"No, and he said to tell you not to even *try* when I talked to him." Daniel blew out a breath. "He told me the day Leonard Newman is out of the picture for me to give him a ring and no sooner."

"How is everyone else doing?"

She heard another long sigh. "Several are looking for other positions. They don't want me to know, of course, but I do. Word gets around in the business. Christine, Lewis, Margaret Kimbrough, and I may hang around—for the love of the gallery and the Newmans—and because we're older and have more patience with idiocy, but I worry that Julianne may be next to go."

"That would be a shame. She has a brilliant knowledge of art, excellent credentials, and a skillful way of persuading clients to purchase."

"Sounds like you, Emily. Hal always called you the 'hand in the velvet glove'—said you looked soft but could disarm a client with kindness and diplomacy and then move in for the sale like a pro."

Emily smiled at the memory, looking across at the picture on her bedside table again. A tall, noble-featured white-haired gentleman looked back at her, dressed impeccably in a casual tux, his arm crooked around a beautiful, silver-haired woman draped in smiles, fur, and jewels. Every inch a lady, Mary Newman had also been a charming hostess, an astute businesswoman, and a loving godmother. How she missed them both.

Hanging up from her call, Emily indulged in a good cry. It broke her heart to hear the sorrows going on at the gallery. She'd learned from Claus and Edda that they'd found a new position as houseparents in a children's home in Hershey, Pennsylvania. They were happy, and Emily was glad, but she still felt grieved they hadn't received the settlement Hal and Mary wanted for them. And she didn't even want to think about the auction Reuben Parrish said Leonard planned for Hal and Mary's collections and antiques.

She supposed her fresh sorrows and griefs made her especially vulnerable to the emotions Cooper Garrison stirred in her right now. She'd never felt this way about a man before, drawn like a moth only to get burned by a cruel tongue or rejection whenever she allowed herself to get close. Why did he do that? Flirt with her, come near to her, stir her up, stare at her as he did—hunger evident in his eyes—and then push her away? It hurt to be treated like that. Especially now with her emotions so raw from all she'd been through.

It would be good when she settled into her own place, got busy with the routine of work again—and got out of Cooper's mother's home. She loved Mamie Garrison already, but she was Cooper's mother. Pictures of Cooper and Lance sat all over the house and reminders dropped from her tongue in casual conversation constantly . . . *Cooper this* and *Cooper that.* It was natural, of course, and Emily knew she needed to get used to it. Even when she left Mamie's house, she'd be working with her every day. Thinking about this, she desperately hoped Mamie would never witness one of those scenes that seemed to happen all too often between her and Cooper. What would she think? What would she say?

Seeming to understand that she felt upset, Mercedes padded across the room to give Emily's hand a wet lick.

"We'll simply have to try to keep our distance from Cooper Garrison, girl. He seems to have some personal problems I totally do not understand. And I've been hurt enough in this last year. I don't want to set myself up to be hurt anymore." She crossed her arms. "I also don't want to be someone's doormat to wipe their feet on, either, as though I don't have feelings or a right to be respected."

Emily crawled under the covers, settling in for the night. Tomorrow she'd shop and enjoy time with Sara. On Saturday the van would come, and she'd be busy unpacking and settling in. Then on Monday she wanted to work some hours in the gallery, beginning to get to know the staff and the routine of the Creekside. In the coming weeks, she planned to start scheduling meetings with all the gallery artists, so she would know each of them, and she wanted to begin getting acquainted with the major clients of the gallery, the collectors who came back again and again. With all she had to do, it wouldn't be too hard to tactfully avoid Cooper Garrison altogether. It seemed the best plan.

CHAPTER 8

The last days of February slipped away, and March swept in, bringing warmer weather as each week went by. Cooper saw little of Emily Lamont. Of course, he'd hoped that would happen, but somehow it bothered him how easily his wish had come true. He found himself thinking about her far too often.

Emily's moving van had arrived on schedule, and Sara Russell spent the weekend helping her move in. His mother chattered on and on about what a bond the girls had formed and about how nice it was for Emily to have a friend. Cooper scowled. He'd planned to offer to help her settle in himself, but he'd obviously not been needed. And now he often saw the girls out walking their dogs together while he walked Brinkley on his own.

Emily carried a natural warmth with her that drew friends her way. Mamie said everyone in the gallery loved her and that she possessed a charm and casual ease that drew clients to her, causing them to look for her when they returned to shop again. Evidently, the smarmy rep with the company that handled the traveling exhibits in the gallery had seen that, too, hanging around an extra day, taking Emily out to dinner. Cooper had wandered into the gallery the day he arrived and watched him schmooze out his charm on Emily, like he did to his mother.

Cooper pulled up to the Mayfield house, where the Garrison Homes crew worked, and looked around in satisfaction. The house was nearly complete now, with work on the interior in progress and the landscaping beginning. He parked the truck and grabbed the sack of lunch orders he'd picked up from town—burgers and fries from Five Guys on the Parkway.

"Boss is here with the grub," Rafe called out, climbing down from a ladder on the porch where he'd been adjusting a gutter.

With the day nice outdoors, Cooper dumped the food on a picnic table the men carried from house to house to use for eating and work breaks, while Rafe headed to Cooper's pickup to get the cooler of ice and drinks.

Cooper's work crew soon lounged around the table, pulling out their cheeseburger orders from the sack, distributing fries and canned colas. They brought lunch with them most days they worked, but other days someone ran out to buy lunch and everyone chipped in on the expense.

Cooper looked around with fondness at the men he'd worked with for years now, all who'd worked with Lance before and many with his father, too. Delbert Hilton, his construction supervisor, started at Garrison Homes the year his father, Price Garrison, began the company. White-headed now, his thinning hair covered by a familiar battered straw hat, Delbert was like a second father to Cooper. Delbert and Dottie's boys, Fleenor and Mackie, had grown up with him and Lance, and the two families were close. Mackie, with his reddish-brown hair and easy grin worked with Garrison Homes, too, while Fleenor and his wife, Beth, managed the Hilton Hardware Store that Delbert bought out of bankruptcy ten years back.

"We need to keep a hardware store in Gatlinburg," he'd told Cooper. "I don't want to be driving all the way through tourist traffic to Lowe's or Home Depot in Sevierville every time I need a dratted nail or two."

Cooper knew he'd bought the business in part for his boys, so they'd have something for the future besides only construction work. Fleenor, in particular, loved the store and worked it full-time, but Mackie liked to work construction.

"I don't want to be cooped up in a dang store all day, catering to fussy folks," he'd said in past, sounding like his father. "Besides, I like the satisfaction of seeing a house come into shape."

Cooper's other primary crew members were Buddy Dean, excellent with cabinetry and interior details; Rafe Harlan, good with gutters, a skilled roofer, and a great painter; and Leroy Johnson, who handled all Garrison Homes' electrical work with an enviable skill. All possessed a wide array of general construction talent, but each carried an expertise, too. Between the four men and Cooper, they could do most of the work of building a log home, whether from a kit or scratch, and Cooper contracted the other work needed.

Even in early March, all the men were sun browned from time out of doors, except for Leroy, African American and already naturally dark. Cooper was lucky, too, to have Leroy's wife, Radonna, to manage the Garrison Homes office inside the model log home on Highway 321 northeast of Gatlinburg. Leroy and Radonna lived in a renovated farmhouse a quarter mile behind the model home, along with their three kids and Radonna's mother, Mae Dean. One of the old barns on the property was utilized for storing Garrison's equipment, supplies, and lumber.

Leroy and Delbert were the only married men on the crew. Buddy, Rafe, and Mackie, like Cooper, were in their late twenties and early thirties and not married yet, although Buddy had a steady girl now.

Rafe banged his cola can with a screwdriver pulled from his back pocket, interrupting Cooper's thoughts. "Big news flash for the day," he announced, grinning. "Buddy and Lisa Marie set the big date to get married."

"Is that right?" Cooper looked across at Buddy—lanky with dark hair cut army short, and probably the quietest of them all.

Buddy blushed a little, pulling his cap down to hide his eyes. "Yeah, I figured it about time."

"Well, Lisa Marie Vann's a fine young girl," Delbert put in. "Comes from a good family, too. When's the wedding date?"

"About the end of next month, I reckon."

"Well, we'll need to plan a little party to celebrate your engagement." Delbert grinned at the idea, and then looked at Cooper.

"How about if we hold it at your place? You've got a lot of room and extra parking space. It's a good place for a party."

"What about a barbecue party?" Leroy chimed in. "I can slow cook a couple of pork roasts in my smoker, and Radonna and her mama will be glad to make their homemade potato salad." He turned to Delbert. "You think your wife, Dottie, could bring some of that great slaw she makes and a pan of baked beans?" He paused. "And maybe Fleenor's wife could bring a few loaves of that homemade bread she's famous for."

"Sure," Delbert answered. "No problem. We'll all kick in and supply the food if Cooper will provide the place. Some of the others coming can bring desserts and more sides, too."

"I'm in," Cooper said, deciding hosting a party with friends sounded better all the time.

"I'll bring the drinks," Rafe offered. "You know I'm no good in the kitchen. And Buddy, Johnny Vann, and I can bring our instruments and do a little pickin' and singin' after dinner."

Buddy offered a shy grin. "That's how I met Lisa Maria," he said. "She came along to our gigs with her brother Johnny."

Rafe, Buddy, and Lisa Marie's brother Johnny played and sang bluegrass and country music in a well-known local group.

Rafe laughed at Buddy's words. "Shoot. I remember how long it took you to get up the nerve to ask her out, too."

The two sparred back and forth before Delbert asked, "Cooper, what's a good date for you for this shindig?"

Cooper pulled out his phone to check his schedule and then to Google the weather. "How about this Saturday? The weather's looking good for this weekend."

They all called their spouses and texted or phoned friends and family to confirm the date.

"Well, I think we've got about everybody lined up we need to invite." Rafe raised an eyebrow at Cooper. "Maybe you ought to ask the new gallery owner for us, boss. Although I hear from the Bolinger Brothers you muffed it with her and that she's been avoiding you ever since she moved in. Dang shame, that. She's a fine-looking girl.' "

Cooper bristled. "Emily Lamont stayed at my mother's a few days and I helped to get her apartment ready at Mom's request. That's all, Rafe. We don't have—and never have had—a relationship."

Rafe grinned. "Yeah. Isn't that what I was saying, boss, that you don't?"

Annoyed at the teasing, Cooper busied himself wolfing down the rest of his burger while the men talked about plans for the party on Saturday.

As they gathered up lunch trash, he glanced at Delbert, ready to move the talk back to business. "Did the bathroom fixtures get delivered this morning?"

"Yeah, but you'll need to drive into Knoxville to the lumber company on Middlebrook Pike today to pick up that skylight and the hardware we ordered." He followed Cooper out to the truck as they talked. "While you're at the lumber company, get another piece of board to replace that deck rail in back. It isn't as straight as it should be. I called and they said they'd throw one in free for the warped one."

"Okay, anything else?" Cooper opened the truck door, eager to leave.

Delbert looked at him. "Yeah, I think you should be the one to invite that Lamont girl to the party. Sounds like there's a fly in your relationship from what I've been hearing, and she is our landlord and your mother's boss. I figure even a less-than-charming guy like yourself ought to be able to invite a nice girl to attend a party at his house."

Cooper kicked at the tire on his truck. "It isn't like what Rafe says."

"Isn't it?" Delbert pushed back his old straw hat to look into Cooper's eyes. "You've been scowling around here for weeks since she came. I figure there's a relationship of some sort there. Ain't like you to be a coward and run from a little challenge."

Cooper scuffed his foot across the ground, knowing he couldn't lie to Delbert. "She rattled me up, I admit, but I don't think she's the kind of girl I ought to pursue a relationship with."

"Hmmm. And you know this for a fact because you've been avoiding her?" He put a hand on Cooper's shoulder. "Son, you've worked real hard to carry all the load your daddy and brother left you at a young age, but that doesn't mean you don't need to indulge in a little social life now and then. Rafe said some real sparks popped in the air between the two of you when you met—that you both just stood there riveted to each other. Seems to me like you ought to look into an attraction like that, see what there is to it."

"Rafe talks too much," Cooper groused.

"Maybe." Delbert opened the truck door for him. "And maybe not. You think on it, Son."

Cooper did, driving down the mountain. It was seldom Delbert offered him advice that wasn't helpful, many times taking the place of the father he'd lost.

He was still thinking over Delbert's words when he stopped by the Gatlinburg office before heading to Knoxville and heard someone humming in the frame shop. Cooper opened the door and looked in to see Emily at work on what looked like a large wooden dollhouse structure sitting on the butcher-block table in the middle of the room.

Hearing him, she turned. "Don't say anything," she said in warning, her eyes moving from the dollhouse to him.

He bit back a grin, remembering how mad she'd been when he'd teased her before about building houses for dolls.

"Looks like you've got the place fixed up real nice," he said, ignoring her warning and looking around. He saw cans of paint and supplies on the shelves and a surprising collection of building tools and equipment scattered around the room—a couple of small saws, a jigsaw, a few drills and chisels, two or three hammers, screwdrivers, a miter box, marking squares, a pin vise, a small lathe, sandpaper, tape. Impressive.

"Yes. The space is perfect for my work." She turned back to the two-story frame house on the table to begin sanding it again with a piece of fine sandpaper.

"That's quite a fancy house," Cooper said, walking closer to examine the structure.

She continued sanding without looking up at him. "This is a one-inch-scale Greenleaf Beacon Hill dollhouse—Victorian in design. It will be pink, trimmed in white with a gray roof when completed, and then it will be decorated and furnished to period."

"Who built the base house structure?"

"Sometimes I do, but this is one that a man in Philadelphia did for me before I moved. I just haven't had time until now to set up shop to work on it."

"Where'd you learn to do this?" he asked, curious.

"My parents owned a dollhouse shop before they died. They built custom houses and sold furnishings for dollhouses." She brushed off some sanding debris from the little porch of the house with an old paintbrush, not adding more to her conversation. Well remembering she could be talkative enough with others, Cooper knew she was still giving him the cold shoulder.

He tried to think how to smooth things over. "I remember you saying your parents had a shop in Knoxville. In Bearden, I think you mentioned."

She paused in her work. "Yes. I sometimes wonder if it's still there. I've never been back."

Cooper smiled. "Wanna go see? I'm heading to Knoxville to pick up some building supplies on Middlebrook Pike. That's right near the Bearden area. You can ride with me and we'll go by and check it out."

She turned to look at him for the first time. "Why would you offer that, Cooper?"

He crossed his arms, learning against a counter. "I wasn't real nice to you the last time we spent time together. I'm sorry for it. I'd like to make amends for being a little tactless."

"I see." She studied him, as if trying to decide if he was telling the truth.

He looked around, gesturing with one hand as he did. "I did

clean up the shop for you."

Cooper watched her try not to smile. "I wondered who did that," she said.

"It was my way of trying to make nice."

Her eyes met his. "You needed to make nice. You hurt my feelings."

"I figured that out after it was a little too late." He didn't bring up her banging out of the room and slamming the door outside in a snit.

She ran a hand along the side of the house, testing to see if she'd sanded it smooth. "Well, I am off today."

"It's pretty weather out," he put in. "A drive into Knoxville would be nice."

"How far is it? I can't remember."

"About forty miles. It will take about an hour to drive."

She glanced at her watch. "All right, Cooper. I must admit I'd love to see if the shop is still there and if the house where I grew up is still there, too. It's only a few blocks away from the shop. Maybe we could drive by there, too."

"Sure thing. After I pick up my supplies, we can drive around in Bearden and see any old sights you want."

Emily studied him again, wary. "You're being awfully nice to me. I'm not sure why."

Cooper decided to be honest. "Neither am I, Emily, but I think we ought to try to be friends. People have been noticing and making comments about the fact that we've been acting frosty with each other—avoiding each other's company."

"Is that right?"

He nodded.

"Well, we can't have that, can we? Mamie might think poorly of me for it." She pulled off the work apron she wore. "I'll run upstairs to wash my hands and get my purse and then I'll be ready." She glanced down at herself. "I'm only wearing jeans. Is that all right?"

He glanced at his own jeans. "My favorite look, Emily."

About two hours later, having driven to Knoxville and picked up the supplies on Middlebrook Pike, Cooper drove his truck up Kingston Pike into the Bearden district of West Knoxville. "Did you ever learn where the neighborhood name of Bearden came from?" Cooper asked.

"I probably did in school when I lived here, but I've forgotten."

"It was named for a Tennessee state legislator, Marcus De Lafayette Bearden. I read a write-up about Bearden's history in a local magazine article not long ago. I remember reading that in the 1800s the area was called Murderer's Hollow because so many Indian massacres occurred here."

"No kidding? That seems hard to imagine with so much commerce here now." She glanced around. "Everything looks so different than I remember but a lot the same, too." She leaned forward, peering out the truck window. "Watch for a Naples Italian Restaurant ahead on the right. If it's still there, turn right after the restaurant on Homberg Drive. A few blocks down that road is where Mom and Dad's dollhouse shop stood."

Cooper followed her directions and soon pulled his truck up beside a little cottage house she pointed out. It looked vacant and neglected, and a For Sale sign sat in the yard.

Emily got out of the car and stood looking at the small building. "It's still here, but it's all sad, empty, and boarded up now." To his surprise, she started to cry. "I really shouldn't have come here today, not when I've known so much loss recently."

Feeling awkward, Cooper walked over and put his arm around her, patting her back. "It's okay, Emily. I guess anyone would feel emotional coming back to see a place they hadn't visited since a little girl."

She leaned against him. "Thanks. That's kind of you."

An unexpected wave of tenderness passed over Cooper. "Sometimes I see something that makes me think of my dad or my brother and I get a moment, too."

She looked up at him, her face still damp with tears. "You cry, too?"

"No, but I feel bad." He brushed a tear or two away from her cheek with his thumb. "Sometimes I get angry, too. Think it isn't fair that I lost them."

"I know what you mean." She gave him a small smile and walked over to look into the windows of the house. "So many memories come back to me being here. I guess Mother and Daddy never had much money with a little business like this, but I only remember them being happy working here, happy with each other—and that I was happy with them. My father could do the most intricate carpentry work. I loved watching him, and I helped my mother pick out delicate wallpapers, tiny furniture, and decorations for the houses they made."

"Did they create small-scale houses like the one you're working on?"

"Yes," she answered. "When I went to live with Hal and Mary I had to put that part of my life behind me, except for keeping one special dollhouse Daddy and Mother made for me. It wasn't until I got out on my own after college, in my own town house, that I started playing around with making dollhouses again."

She put a hand on the window, leaning closer to look inside. "I suggested making dollhouses a time or two to Hal and Mary but they seemed to think it was a hobby or interest I shouldn't pursue. I realized later Mary thought Mother and Daddy somewhat foolish for wasting themselves and their educations with a little shop like this that provided such a poor return. And leaving me so destitute when they died." She turned to Cooper. "But my parents didn't expect to die so young."

"I understand what you're saying. My dad didn't leave much for my mother either and a lot of people criticized that, but he kept plowing all the money he made back into growing the business." He ran a hand through his hair. "I didn't understand that much as a teenager, but I do now."

She turned to smile at him. "Your mother is happy, and she loves her little home in Mynatt Park that your father built."

He nodded. "I know and she likes her work, too. But I'd love to do more for her." He propped his foot on a small wall near the house. "She grew up an orphan. I don't know if you knew that. She has no idea who her father is. Her mother, who was only a kid from what little she knows of her, turned her over to the children's orphanage in Sevierville when she was born. She didn't think she could take care of a baby, and her family wasn't supportive. Later she died, so Mom doesn't know if her mother ever hoped to come back for her or not. She has no other information about her family because all the records were sealed."

"I didn't know that." Emily picked a sprig off a shrub, looking at the small buds beginning to form on it. "Was she unhappy in the orphanage?"

"No, she holds pretty good memories, and she goes over and volunteers in a number of ways at the Smoky Mountain Children's Home, tries to help out."

Emily considered this. "I guess I was lucky to know who my parents are and to know their love for ten years. It would be sad not to have those memories." She turned the sprig over in her hand, thinking. "I know, too, that I was blessed Hal and Mary took me in after Mother and Daddy were killed. I might have been sent to an orphanage, maybe even that one, if Hal and Mary hadn't stepped up. I really had no one else."

"Do you think you could find your family's house from here?" Cooper asked. "It might still be there, too."

"Yes, it sits across the highway on a small side street. Sometimes we walked to the shop, so it isn't far."

Emily led Cooper right to the small house, a two-story cottage, not even as large as his mother's place. The house looked less neglected than the shop, and it was painted a crisp white with black shutters.

She smiled, studying it. "It hasn't changed much, except that it had green shutters when I was a girl. And the trees have all grown taller." She pointed. "My room was upstairs in the back, and my father would take me on walks in the big cemetery nearby, on its quiet roads."

Cooper let his eyes run over the house. If this was the place where Emily grew up, she wasn't really so different from him. And in an odd sense, her father had been a builder, too—except of dolls' houses instead of mountain homes for tourists.

"It's getting late," he commented, glancing at his watch. "I think we'd better head back. If you'd like we can stop for dinner some-where."

She started for the truck. "No need to do that, but thanks for bringing me with you today. I'm truly grateful, Cooper. It meant a lot to me to come here just now."

He opened the door of the truck for her and took her hand to help her up onto the high seat. Keeping her hand in his, he said, "I enjoyed being with you today, too, Emily, and I'd really like to take you out to dinner if you'll go."

She looked away. "Well, then," she said, using another of those phrases that said little of what she was feeling.

"Is that a yes?" he asked.

She nodded. "Yes. It would be nice to share dinner. Thank you."

"Good. I know a little place on our route home I think you might like." He walked around to climb in the truck. "I haven't been there in a long time myself. I'd enjoy stopping in again, too."

About thirty minutes later, he pulled into the parking lot of Ye Olde Steak House on Chapman Highway. The highway was one of the roads leading from Knoxville towards the mountains. Cooper doubted that he would need reservations on a weekday, but he'd called just in case.

"Oh, how nice. It looks like an old log cabin." Emily's eyes lit up as she got out to study the restaurant.

"Yeah, this place started in the late 1960s and is still owned by the same family. With so many chain restaurants around, I thought you might enjoy this one with local history and a little charm. Their specialty is flame-grilled steaks. I like the filet and shrimp combo, too."

Once inside, and seated at a cozy table by a big fireplace, they ordered steaks, salads, and baked potatoes with all the fixings. As

they ate their dinner, Emily shared memories of growing up—
both in Knoxville and in Philadelphia, afterwards. Entertained by
her childhood stories, Cooper opened up with memories of his
own, of growing up around Gatlinburg. He found Emily easy to
be with in this setting and easy on the eyes, too. Her pretty heart-
shaped face glowed in the soft light from the candles on the table,
her smile frequently lighting up her face, and her eyes twinkling
when it did.

She put her chin on one hand, studying him. "I've seen you smile
more tonight than I have since I met you," she said with a sigh.
"It's nice. You're very handsome when you smile."

"Does that mean you've forgiven me for the last time we were
together?" He watched her fidget.

"Of course," she said at last, but Cooper knew it a half-truth.
She still didn't understand why he'd pulled away from her after they
danced, when he'd wanted to kiss her so much it was like a sucker
punch.

"Because you're working with my mother, I thought it would be
better if we're just friends." He watched to see how she'd take this.

"Oh, I agree," she said, seeming relieved at his words. "I've
thought the same thing."

It irked Cooper somehow that she agreed with him so readily.
"Well, that's good." He offered her a half smile.

The waiter came then with their check, since they'd both decided
dessert wasn't needed after such a big meal.

On the way home from the restaurant, they chatted about the
gallery and their work, but Cooper found himself intensely aware
of Emily Lamont, sitting so near him in the darkened truck. He
could smell that vanilla scent of hers and feel a building tension as
the miles stretched out before them.

"I'll walk you in," he said as they pulled into the parking area
behind the Creekside Gallery and her apartment.

"Oh, no. You don't need to," she replied, a little too brightly,
obviously picking up on the tension in the air herself.

"It's the gentlemanly thing to do," he insisted, following behind her to her door.

She turned, biting her lip, to look back at him. "Do you want to come up and see how I've fixed up the place?"

"I'd like that, but right now it might not be a good idea." His eyes locked with hers, and he knew she understood exactly what he meant.

As they stood there, frozen, looking into each other's eyes again, she finally made a move and licked her lips nervously.

"Dagnabit. That did it," he said, pulling her into his arms and finding her lips with his. She tasted as sweet as he'd envisioned, and he drew her closer, savoring the kiss and the joyous feel of her in his arms finally.

She gave a soft little sound, and when Cooper put his hands to her face to touch her, she wrapped her arms around his back, pulling him nearer and sighing with pleasure. He felt like a drowning man who'd found a lifeline. She impacted him in a way no other girl ever had before, not just arousing him but touching him right down into his heart and soul. He felt a sweep of tenderness with her that was new to him and found himself wanting to care for her, protect her, keep anyone from ever hurting or harming her again.

He drew back at last to look down at her in the dark hallway. "I lied about only wanting to be friends, Emily."

"So did I," she whispered. "I thought it would be better for us, but I didn't know . . ." She let the words drift away.

He traced a finger down her cheek. "I don't know what we're going to do about this, Emily Lamont, but I don't think we can keep ignoring each other."

A little smiled touched her mouth. "I'm always so aware of you, Cooper, even when I try to pretend I'm not."

"Hmmm." He let his hands drift down her arms. "One of the reasons I stopped to talk with you earlier today was to invite you to a party to celebrate the engagement of one of the guys who works with me, Buddy Dean."

"Oh, when is it?"

"This Saturday night at my place. There will be a lot of people there you know from the gallery and from Garrison Homes."

She looked hesitant.

"You can bring your friend Sara if you like."

She brightened. "Oh, could I? She'd enjoy that. And then I'd know someone I can hang out with."

"I'll be there, too." He grinned at her.

"Well, I know that." Her face flushed pink.

He watched a frown cross her face. "What? Tell me what you were thinking."

"With everyone there that we work with and all, maybe we should decide how we'll act. I mean . . ." Her voice drifted off, and she look uncomfortable.

"You think we should just act like friends at the party."

She bit her lip. "Would you get mad at me if I said yes?"

"No, I think it's a good idea." He let his hand drift through her hair, feeling its softness under his fingers. "We're only starting to explore these feelings between us. I'd sort of like to keep it to ourselves for now."

She sighed. "I'm glad you're not mad."

"No, and you've started me dreaming more sweet dreams tonight, Miz Lamont."

She blushed. "You're remembering the words to that song when we painted out on the porch together."

"I am—and I'm remembering how much I wanted to kiss you then." He kissed her again, wondering now why he'd waited so long.

She traced her fingers down his shirt a little shyly after he pulled away again. "I enjoyed our dance that day, too," she said.

"Maybe we can dance at the party if some jitterbugging gets started."

Emily giggled. "Most people don't jitterbug today."

"I can guarantee Mom will get some jitterbugging going. She always asks Rafe, Buddy, and their little band to play a few lively tunes so she can spin around the floor again."

"I'd like to see that." Her eyes lit with humor.

"I'm sure you will."

She reached up a soft hand, touching his face. "Thanks for today, Cooper. I was so unhappy thinking you didn't like me all these weeks."

"I like you all too much, Emily Lamont. That's the problem." And he kissed her one more time to prove it before he left.

CHAPTER 9

Emily enjoyed sweet dreams after her evening with Cooper, and her heart felt glad the next day as she worked in the gallery. She'd kept the ongoing work schedule as Mamie set it up, since it suited all the employees. And she'd set her own schedule with alternating hours to learn the gallery at different times, to get to know each of the employees, and to lighten their workloads. This afternoon, she worked in the gallery alone while Monty matted a new shipment of prints next door in the mat shop. She could hear him singing along to songs on the radio occasionally when she walked by the shop door.

Mercedes and Sugar Lips had gradually developed a grudging tolerance for each other. Mercedes, playful by nature, tried to induce the cat into occasional games by tossing one of her cat toys or rising on her hind legs at the checkout counter to study the cat in her bed by the sunny window. Sugar Lips, for the most part, met these friendly advances with hisses and growls, but Emily noticed her responses more routine now. She often saw the cat watching the dog with lazy interest and one day watched her stalk Mercedes in fun.

Today, however, Sugar Lips slept in a pool of sun, and Mercedes followed Emily as she made rounds through the gallery. While there were no customers in the store, she checked the art collections and cleaned, straightening picture frames and using a soft rag and cleaner to wipe smudges off the glass cases. Letting herself into the Rockwell exhibit room, she paused again in front of the two paintings that still didn't feel right to her. Emily wasn't sure why these works kept drawing her attention. The others seemed all right. She'd certainly examined the entire collection often enough, but her eye kept returning to these two.

A soft growl from Mercedes alerted her to the fact she was no longer alone. Emily turned to see Randy Lawson standing in the doorway she'd propped open. "Hi," she said. "I didn't see you come in."

Randy was the rep from Delamar, the company Creekside obtained its traveling art exhibits from, like this one of Rockwell's work from Rankin Exhibition Services. Randy dropped by the gallery every few weeks to check on the exhibit, his company always cautious about security with valuable properties out in the public. At his visits, he let Emily and Mamie know about new availabilities and confirmed scheduling on future exhibits.

Like many sales reps, he was young, handsome, charming, and very extroverted. When here last, he'd targeted Emily with his charm, taking her out to dinner and feigning an intense interest in her life. It was a sales ploy Emily had grown accustomed to in the business end of running a gallery, but Randy was cute and harmless—and fun company.

"How's the gorgeous new gallery owner?" he asked, leaning nonchalantly against the doorframe. "Are you settling in comfortably to the Creekside now?"

"Yes, thank you," she answered, noticing the casual, expensive suit he wore with shiny designer shoes. "What brings you by today?"

He grinned. "Besides hoping to see you, I brought some information on a possible new exhibit you might want to carry next year when it's available, and I wanted to confirm delivery of the Grandma Moses exhibit next on your calendar and verify the pickup date for the Rockwell collection."

Emily walked closer to the Rockwell painting titled *Going and Coming* as Randy talked, leaning in to study the area that still concerned her.

"I hope you haven't spotted damage to one of the pieces," he said, walking into the room to stand beside her. "Usually with exhibits in a locked room, there is never a problem."

"No." Emily waved a hand. "It's just something about this painting that bothers me."

"What do you mean?" he asked, sounding edgy.

"Oh, it's nothing, really, and I'm probably being silly."

He walked closer. "Silly about what?"

Mercedes growled as Randy drew closer, and he backed away a step.

She spoke to the dog and then shrugged. "As a little girl, I always admired the size of the bubble the child in this painting could produce." She pointed at the bright pink gum bubble and laughed. "It seems smaller now than I remember but it's probably only because I'm older. I don't know why it keeps troubling me."

He smiled. "I remember a fish I caught as much bigger, too." He spread his hands. "It seems to me it was *at least* this long."

Watching his hands, she laughed. "Yes. Memories get distorted."

"Come and let me show you the exhibit folder I brought," Randy said, turning towards the door. "And if you're free, I'd like to take you to dinner later."

Emily followed him out of the exhibit room, ushering Mercedes ahead of her and locking the door. "I'm not free for dinner, but thank you for asking."

Cooper had called earlier and invited her to his place tonight. He wanted her ideas for the party on Saturday night, and she looked forward to the evening—and to seeing his home.

Randy rattled on cheerfully about the Grandma Moses exhibit next on their exhibit schedule and told stories about his clients that made Emily laugh. She almost wished, for a minute, that she could have dinner with him instead of Cooper. Randy was so easy and comfortable to be with, never displaying any of the moodiness she encountered with Cooper, and never making her edgy and uncomfortable in his presence either.

As she studied the exhibit folder with Randy at the front counter, the bell on the door rang and Cawood Gentry strolled in.

"Where's Mamie?" He snapped the words out in his usual sharp tone, looking around with a frown. "This is one of her days to work."

"She went home early," Emily answered, overlooking his brusque manner.

"Is she sick?" Cawood's brow furrowed.

"No, she planned to meet a friend for lunch so I suggested she take the day off afterwards to shop and enjoy herself." Emily smiled, noting the relieved look on his face. "Mamie works too hard."

"She does." He leaned against the counter, his eyes moving to the exhibit materials fanned out across the surface. "Nice examples of Grandma Moses's works. Always liked that *Shenandoah Valley* painting."

Randy looked up in annoyance. "Listen, sir, we're busy here, so since you didn't find who you wanted to see today, maybe you could let us continue."

Cawood's eyebrows shot up at Randy's dismissive remark. He was an imposing man, very tall and mustached, with an angular, distinguished face and a shock of white hair. He intimidated most people but obviously not Randy Lawson.

"Listen, you little whippersnapper, I could buy and sell you— from your fancy city suit down to your spiffy overpriced shoes. Who the heck are you?"

Randy, a little short in stature, tried to pull himself up to his full height, one hand pulling into a fist, his face reddening. He obviously didn't recognize Cawood Gentry.

Emily laid a hand on his arm. "This is one of my best artists, Randy." She gave his arm a little warning squeeze. "And we had a previous appointment set for this time. I think you and I have finished all the business we needed to accomplish for today." She closed up the portfolio. "I'll see you when you come to pick up the Rockwell exhibit, and I'll look forward to seeing the Grandma Moses paintings." Drawing him with her, she walked towards the door, opening it with a small smile.

Taking the hint, Randy nodded, sending Cawood a warning scowl before pushing his way through the doorway.

Cawood studied her. "You're a diplomatic little minx. We didn't have an appointment at all, you know."

"No," she replied, shutting the door and stilling the bell on it with one hand.

He waited, obviously expecting her to say more.

"Hmmph," he said at last, a small smile touching the corners of his mouth. "I think that kid might have tried to punch me if you hadn't stepped in."

"I doubt that would have happened." Emily straightened a flyaway strand of hair, pushing it behind her ear. She'd certainly done her best to see that didn't happen.

Cawood reached a hand over to stroke the cat, curled in her basket on the counter. Glancing down at the dog, lying below the counter with one ear alert and watching him pet the cat, he said, "Looks like Sugar Lips has accepted the dog in her own way and the dog's even acting protective."

Emily nodded, letting Cawood set the tone of their visit, wanting him to feel comfortable. She'd met Cawood Gentry another day with Mamie in the shop. He'd focused his attention on Mamie that visit, making it very clear he wanted Mamie to handle his business, new owner or not.

Today, with Mamie gone, Emily decided it might be time to establish more of a relationship on her own with this major artist of the Creekside Gallery.

"What can I do for you today, Mr. Gentry?" she asked, deciding to see if he would let her help him.

He looked around, frowning, as if making a decision about discussing any business matters with her. "I have a contract offer on a painting hanging in the display room," he said at last.

The gallery agreement with Cawood allowed him to also personally advertise and sell any paintings he displayed in the gallery on his own; they held no exclusive on his work.

"Come and show me which one," Emily offered graciously. "And perhaps you have another in mind for the space."

They walked towards the back of the gallery. He pointed to a vivid painting, on the back wall of the Cawood Gentry display area, with a long slash of dusty road winding down into the depths of a rocky western canyon.

He cocked his head to look at his own work. "The couple who inquired about this painting live near the painting's setting. I've met them." He reached out a hand to run a finger down the gold frame. "I own a small place in New Mexico. I've always liked the contrast of the starkness and open majesty of the western mountains to the green, thick landscape and rolling hills and valleys of the eastern mountains."

"It's a fine piece. I especially like the play of light, the way you've captured the afternoon shadows."

"You have a good eye."

Emily studied the wall space that held the painting. "If you have a finished work of a similar size, we can hang it without rearrangement of the other pieces. If not, I can reassemble the wall whenever you can bring your new piece in."

"I finished a painting of the same dimensions last month, a scene of a twisting cascade dropping over a rock cliff I spotted on a hike in the mountains here. It will sell better here in the Creekside than the western piece and make a good replacement."

"Sounds perfect. Bring it over one day when Monty is working and he'll help you swap out the paintings and pack the canyon piece for shipping."

A little grin touched the corner of his mouth. "Maybe Monty will bring me a bottle of the Russo family wine, too."

"I'm sure you can count on it, Mr. Gentry." She laughed. "I'll pass the hint along to him."

He studied her more closely. "I think Cawood will be all right between us now instead of Mr. Gentry—that is if Emily is okay for you, Miss Lamont."

"I'd like that." She offered him a smile.

He glanced back towards the front of the gallery. "You know, I've seen that smart-ass kid in this gallery before. Who is he?"

"He's the rep for Delamar. His company handles delivery and pickup for most of the major exhibits we bring in from Rankin Exhibition Services."

"Does he know his stuff?"

"He seems to." She hesitated, another thought popping into her mind. "Do you know Norman Rockwell's work very well?"

"As well as most, not as well as some. Why?"

"I'd like to see if you notice anything irregular in any of the Rockwell pieces on display."

His eyes popped. "You suspect fraud?"

She rubbed her arm. "I shouldn't think so. I know Rockwell's work primarily from catalogs and girlhood visits to the Norman Rockwell Museum with Hal and Mary Newman. My memory is probably not all it should be."

"I met Hal and Mary Newman a few times," he said as he started towards the exhibit room with her. "Fine people. They spoke of you with both fondness and respect when they talked of the gallery."

"Thank you," she said, sliding her key card into the door. "I really miss them."

"Mamie Garrison speaks well of you, too." He followed her into the room. "That means a lot to me."

"She's been kind to me."

He nodded, looking around at the paintings in the room as she switched on additional lights. "Show me which pieces trouble you in the exhibit."

She did, letting him study both at length and then look around at the others.

"I'm not enough of an expert to judge any irregularity. But take some photos of all the paintings and send them to this man." He pulled one of his business cards out of his pocket and scribbled a name, e-mail, and phone number on the back of it. "He's a friend of mine and possesses a keen eye. Send the photos to anyone else you know, too—anyone who knows what to look for."

"Daniel Stelben in the Newman Gallery has a keen eye. I should have thought of that already. I'll send photos to him, also."

He looked at her. "Have you talked to Mamie about this?"

She blushed and shook her head. "No, I didn't want to worry her."

"Nor to seem overly critical as a newcomer," he added.

"Yes, that too."

"Well, you'll need to speak with her. See if there have been any past instances or concerns about other works. She might have been reluctant to mention anything to you just as you have to her. As you say, it could be nothing, or it could be something." He paused. "Have you ever faced this at the Newman Gallery?"

She shook her head. "Few would try with Hal Newman and Daniel Stelben there. As you say, both were known for a keen and discriminating eye."

"Perhaps you've been trained to have one, too." He walked closer to Rockwell's *Girl at the Mirror* depicting the young adolescent, the second painting Emily worried over. "You do know the market value of this work and the other. It would be worth a risk for a good crook."

"I know. You never like to consider it happening, but it does."

"When you've been raised around art, trust your instincts. Check into this before the exhibit is picked up."

"I will, and thank you for your advice."

The gallery grew busy after Cawood left. When things quieted at last at five, Emily left Monty with the gallery until close and hurried upstairs to put on more casual clothes before heading to Cooper's.

She pulled on red paprika chinos, a white T-shirt, and a cashmere cardigan in red, white, and black stripes. Knowing Mercedes needed the exercise, she decided to walk to Cooper's, confident he'd run her home after dinner. Mercedes would enjoy the company of Brinkley, too, always more eager for a chase and tumble on the floor than the cautious Sugar Lips.

Cutting over from the River Road to the Parkway, Emily savored the sights and sounds of Gatlinburg, a very different city from Philadelphia with its high skyscrapers, tall church spires, darting cabs, and busy professionals hustling down the sidewalks in business attire. Here the pace was more relaxed as tourists strolled along the sidewalks enjoying time away from work, traffic often slowing amiably so drivers could gawk out the windows at the colorful shops and scenery.

Knowing she was early, Emily took a detour through the Mountain Laurel Village Mall to say hello to Sara Russell at Dora's Dolls. The mall, like many in Gatlinburg, was built with wandering walkways among colorful shops. Walled garden areas full of shade trees, plants, and soothing fountains decorated the whole, with benches and tables scattered about in shady corners. Emily had already explored the shops often, the mall being the closest to the Creekside Gallery.

Mercedes, in familiar territory now, pranced towards Sara's shop, probably hoping her walking partner, Buster, would be in the store.

"Hi," Sara called out, seeing Emily and Mercedes come in the front door. "I see that you two are out taking a walk."

She came around the counter to squat down to pet Mercedes. "Sorry, Mercedes. Buster, the pest, is home with Mother today and not in the store."

Emily looked around with pleasure at the busy shelves filled with dolls, doll clothing, and doll accessories. "I do love to come in here," she said, smiling.

Sara leaned against the counter. "Spoken like a dollhouse maker. When are you going to build and furnish us a house to put in the store? I know we can sell it and we can take orders for you, too."

"I'm flattered at your interest, Sara, and I'm thinking about it." Emily walked over to pick up a Madame Alexander doll, dressed like Meg in *Little Women*, with other characters from the classic storybook clustered nearby. "These are new," she commented.

"Yeah, the *Little Women* dollhouse in your apartment inspired me to order these. The classic book and the characters are all still popular, and the movie remakes have helped to push the sales of the dolls."

Emily sat the dark-haired doll back on the shelf with the others. "My father made that dollhouse you saw the year before he and Mother were killed. Mother and I decorated it together. It's very special to me. I'm so glad I got to keep it when I moved to live with Hal and Mary."

"Well, it's a fantastic dollhouse, and Natalie made me promise she could come over to see it one day."

"Any time." Emily smiled, picking up a book from the shelf beside the dolls. "You ordered some of the *Little Women* books, too."

"Only a few copies to go with the display—I thought they might inspire purchase." She grinned. "I stock American Girl books, Barbie books, and other titles that coordinate with our dolls when I can order them economically. The *Madeline* books sell well with the dolls to match and I turn over a lot of Disney books with the Disney Barbie Princess dolls we carry."

Sara snagged a water bottle from under the counter to take a swig and then changed the subject. "I wish I could go walking with you, but I'm working until close tonight." Her eyes slid up and down Emily thoughtfully. "You look really nice for a walk with the dog. Pretty outfit under your jacket."

Emily felt a hint of a blush rush into her face. "I'm going up to have dinner with Cooper."

"Is that right?" Sara smirked.

"He wants me to help him with ideas for the party he's giving on Saturday for one his workers who's getting married—Buddy Dean. Cooper is hosting a potluck dinner and engagement party." She twisted the bracelet on her wrist. "I stopped by to see if you'd like to go with me on Saturday night. Cooper wants me to come but I don't know many of the people who work with Garrison Homes. I told him if you came I'd have someone to talk with."

"Sure, I'm off Saturday night, and I'd love to go. It will give us both a chance to meet more people around Gatlinburg. I like parties." She grinned. "Maybe we'll meet some eligible guys, too—unless you've already zeroed in on one."

Emily offered Sara a practiced smile. "I think a lot of the men who work for Garrison Homes and their friends are single, and I'm sure we'll meet a lot of new people."

Sara tut-tutted and shook her head. "If you're trying to sidestep the issue that you're interested in Cooper Garrison, it's not working."

Emily crossed her arms. "All right. I admit there is some interest, but don't say anything to anyone about it. We're only beginning to get acquainted to see how things will go. . . ."

"My lips are sealed, Emmy dear," Sara interrupted. "Friends keep each other's secrets, you know. I don't want you telling anyone I'm looking around when Giles is so nice to me either. I'm still not sure what to do about that situation."

"Is Giles still hinting about getting married?"

She rolled her eyes. "All too often! Sheesh. And I'm getting pressure from Mom and Natalie because they simply love Giles."

"You're still waiting for that zing, aren't you?"

Sara sighed. "Silly, I guess. Do you get a zing around Cooper?"

Emily dropped her gaze.

"You do! I can tell by that blush on your face." Sara punched at her. "I am so jealous."

"We've barely met, Sara. Don't read too much into this."

"All right, all right." She looked heavenward dramatically. "But it's so sweet when that zing happens. Sweaty palms, beating heart, a rush every time that special someone comes into the room, your eyes going to their lips—wishing."

Emily laughed. "Sara Russell, you're an incurable romantic under that pixie exterior!"

Sara wrinkled her nose. "I know, isn't it awful? And you'd think a person with a mathematical bent would be very staid and practical."

"Well, those genes certainly missed you." Emily glanced at her watch. "And I'd better head up the road to Cooper's now; he'll be expecting me. Come over to the apartment at about six on Saturday, and we'll go up to the party together."

"What should I bring if it's a potluck dinner?"

"Maybe we can go in together and make an hors d'oeuvres plate. I'll ask Cooper about it tonight."

"Okay. Have fun." Sara wiggled her eyebrows.

"I'm sure I will," Emily said primly, heading out the door and avoiding a response to Sara's giggle that followed her.

Emily cut through the side entrance of the mall to start up Natty Road, leading to Cooper's. The road passed the Garden Restaurant, a couple of shops, and the Highland Cumberland Presbyterian Church, which Emily had visited with Mamie one Sunday, before curling away from commerce to wind uphill. Here only a few tidy mountain homes and rustic log cabins lay scattered along the roadside in peaceful wooded settings.

She slowed to look at flowers popping up along the way, nearly ready to bloom. It charmed her how small side roads out of Gatlinburg turned quickly rural like this, an unexpected surprise after the hustle and bustle of Gatlinburg's downtown streets. Emily marveled, too, that she needed only a jacket on this March evening in east Tennessee. In Philadelphia, the weather would still be bitterly cold and blustery. Daniel e-mailed only yesterday complaining about another snowstorm moving in. Emily often experienced homesick moments for friends and familiar places in Philadelphia, but she certainly didn't miss the colder weather of the North, and that was a fact.

As Natty Road came to a dead-end turnaround, Emily spotted the rustic mailbox Cooper had described, saw his name on it, and turned down the quiet driveway beside it. Around the first bend, she saw his log home nestled in a perfect mountain setting, with ample parking on the street and in a grassy lot by an outdoor pavilion. It was beautiful. Open, rustic porches jutted off the front of the house and picturesque gables peeked out of the gray metal roof. Trees shaded the house all around, and Emily caught a glimpse of the mountains in the background, misty blue with overlapping layers.

Brinkley's barking assured Emily she'd come to the right place, and Cooper soon opened the door to her and Mercedes. He helped Emily out of her coat after he closed the door and hung it on a hand-carved hall tree.

"Come on back," he said, leading her through an open living area with a vast stone fireplace at its center, a grouping of soft brown leather sofas and chairs scattered around it. "I'm working on dinner in the kitchen."

Mercedes and Brinkley bumped and greeted in doggy fashion as Emily followed Cooper into a broad open kitchen and dining area, with rustic beams overhead. The big space looked out long windows to a picture-perfect scene of forest and mountain ranges.

"Lovely view." She paused to gaze outside.

"The log homes that we build higher on the mountains have even more stupendous views than this, but I didn't want the ongoing hassle of driving up and down those winding, steep roads to and from Gatlinburg every day. In winter, mountain roads can be a real pill, too."

Emily sniffed the air. "Ummm. What are you cooking?"

"Spaghetti, a single guy's staple. Mom taught me her sauce recipe; that's the real key. The rest is easy—cook a little pasta, toss a salad, pop a loaf of French bread in the oven to warm. My kind of meal."

"What can I do to help?" She watched him stir a pot of sauce on the stove and then taste a sample.

"You can get the salad out of the fridge and hunt up a couple of wine glasses." He pointed to a cabinet. "I've about got it."

Emily's eyes slipped over him while his back was turned. He wore faded jeans and a sun-washed sandstone-green shirt that matched his hazel eyes. His dark hair looked a little damp, as if from a recent shower, and he smelled of a spicy cologne when she moved by him towards the refrigerator. She noticed he didn't wear his usual ball cap tonight and that he wore nice leather camp mocs rather than his usual battered work boots. For Cooper, Emily would guess this was dressing up for a girl. Her lips curled with pleasure at the thought.

CHAPTER 10

Cooper experienced a moment of possessive pleasure when he'd opened the door to Emily Lamont. Now, as she busied herself in his kitchen, he let his eyes drift over her nicely shaped backside as she reached into the cabinet for wine glasses. She wore red again, like when he first met her—bright crimson slacks and a long, striped sweater, another of those soft cashmere ones she favored. Under the sweater, her white T-shirt cupped her breasts in a tantalizing way that rattled Cooper's composure.

This is your mother's boss, he told himself. *You can't go after her like you might some other girl.* This thought reminded him again that he had no business furthering this relationship with Emily Lamont at all or even yielding an inch to the attraction she jacked up in him. Dang Delbert Hilton for challenging him to pursue this relationship or further examine it. He should have left things as they were.

Cooper dumped the pasta into the colander and then prepared two plates of spaghetti. He carried them over to the table, setting her plate across from his. She brought the wine, glasses, and salad to the table. The rest he'd set up before she arrived.

He gestured for her to sit down, realizing the silence had stretched out too long now, waiting for him to fill it as the host.

Cooper cleared his throat. "Did you notice the redbud and dogwood blooms starting to form on the trees as you walked up? They'll be a show next month."

"No, I didn't." She sent him one of those sweet smiles that crinkled the corners of her eyes and caused a set of dimples to wink in her cheeks. "It still seems so incredible to me, coming from Philadelphia, that the trees are beginning to leaf here at all. I even noticed green buds forming on daffodils along the roadside."

"Yeah, hints of spring are starting to show around the mountains, but it's in April when everything will really start to pop out. It's the best time of year for wildflowers in the Smokies. You'll find trillium, fire pinks, violets, and white bloodroot right here on my property later—and more flowers if you go deeper into the woods."

He filled a salad bowl with greens while he talked. "A trail behind my place leads up into the Smoky Mountains, then funnels into a horse and walking pathway called Grassy Branch Trail. You can follow it through the woods, over a ridge, and then down a winding trail to the backside of my mother's property at Mynatt Park." For a man of not many words most of the time, he felt like he was babbling.

She didn't seem to notice. "I am so excited about being in the Smokies for spring this year." She lowered her eyes shyly. "Maybe you'll take me on a hike, like the one to your mother's place or on another one you like, since you know so much about the area. I'd love to learn more about the mountains and the flowers and trees."

"Yeah, well, maybe we can do that." He focused on his spaghetti, seeing himself already sinking deeper into this relationship than he wanted to go.

Cooper tried to think what else to talk about. "How are things at the gallery?"

"Well, I got to know Cawood Gentry a little more today," Emily told him between bites. "He's not quite as gruff as he seems." She hesitated. "I also asked him to look at the paintings in the Rockwell exhibit. One or two didn't look like I remember."

Her frown caught his attention. "What do you mean?"

She twisted at the diamond earring on her ear, obviously a little uncomfortable. "In a gallery, you always need to be very vigilant about highly expensive art work moving in and out of your exhibit rooms—in fact about any art work of value moving in and out—

for authenticity."

Cooper felt a thread of alarm. "You think there might be some phony work?"

"I don't know. I hope not." She shook her head. "Cawood couldn't see anything irregular but he said I should check it out. He gave me a contact, a specialist, to send some photos to for an opinion. It's probably nothing, but Cawood said I should trust my instincts enough to check. I can have someone come in if an out-side specialist thinks I should."

"Have you talked to my mother about this?"

"No." She sighed and rubbed her arm in an abstract way. "I so hated to worry her or to seem critical when I've only just come."

He waited.

"Cawood said I should talk to her, though, to see if she'd ever encountered any problems in past. He also suggested she might be equally reluctant to discuss this type of problem with me." Her eyes met his now, blue and clear. "Has she ever said anything to you about any past problems of this nature with the gallery?"

"No." He reached for another piece of bread. "But Cawood is right that you should talk to Mom about this. He's right, too, that you should always check out suspicions of fraud—or anything else that seems smarmy."

He shook his head. "There are a lot of good and decent people in the world, but a lot who aren't, too. That famous psychologist Viktor Frankl, the one who lived through imprisonment in the Ho-locaust, said that even in that heinous prison camp environment he found people either decent or unprincipled."

"Yes, but I'd hate to live my life suspicious and untrusting."

"I agree." He poured a little more wine into her glass. "But you can't live stupid either. With the building business, I face a lot of the same kinds of things—dealers attempting to pass off inferior materials, contractors hoping to get away with shoddy work, com-panies trying to tack charges onto their bills and overcharge me." Cooper glanced across at her. "You should be used to this kind of thing, having worked in an even bigger gallery for so long."

She picked at her spaghetti with her fork. "Yes, but that's the gallery I grew up in. I knew everyone."

Cooper smiled then, realizing why she'd brought this issue to him. "Mom won't fault you or feel bad about you talking to her about this, Emily, and neither do I. Bottom line is, you're responsible for the Creekside now, and you should use all your expertise to check into anything that raises your hackles. You won't have a problem with Mom or with me in following through on this issue or with any other problem that troubles you."

She sighed with relief. "Thanks."

He grinned. "I'm not that much of an old ogre, am I?"

A flush touched her cheeks. "Well, we've had our moments," she said with candor.

Cooper rubbed his neck. "Yeah, well, it's awkward dealing with feelings about your landlord and your mother's boss." He rubbed his finger around the rim of his wine glass, considering his words. "I think we're real different people, too."

Her eyes trapped his. "So why did you invite me up here with such misgivings?"

"I'm trying to sort things out," he answered with honesty.

"Well, at least you've been candid." She ate for a few moments quietly, obviously not very happy with this turn in the conversation.

Cooper got up to get more spaghetti for himself. Coming back to put his plate on the table, he sat down and then watched Emily until she looked up again. "Despite all that talk, Emily Lamont, you attract me like no other girl I've ever met. I'm real uncomfortable with all the feelings you stir up in me, and regardless of whether I think it's wise that we get more involved, I can't deny the attraction. It keeps me antsy and I don't know if I like the feeling of it churning around in me all the time."

Her lips twitched. "Sara calls it a zing. She says it drives you crazy but it's great, too. She wishes she had it with the guy she's dating. She says theirs is a comfortable, easy relationship but that there's no zing."

"Sara dates Giles Sutherland, doesn't she? His family owns the Smokyland Candy Store in the mall near her mom's store."

Emily nodded. "Yes, and don't say anything to anyone about this. I sort of blurted it out without thinking. Sara's trying to work out that relationship and isn't sure what to do about it."

"And you told her we're seeing each other?" The thought didn't please him.

"No, she guessed. Good friends do, you know."

Thinking of Delbert and even Rafe, he agreed with her.

They ate quietly, thinking about their words.

"I guess Mom will figure it out pretty soon, too, if other people are noticing we've gotten interested in each other."

Emily bit her lip. "Do you think she'll mind?"

He shook his head. "No, I don't think she'll mind—but I think I'll mind. There isn't much I can do to stop it though, I guess. Mom is always pushing for me to date what she calls some 'nice girls.'"

Cooper saw Emily smirk. "And you've been dating girls that aren't nice?"

He scowled and stood up. "I think we've said enough on this subject. I'm going to make some coffee. While it's brewing I'll show you around the house, if you like. You said you wanted to see one of the homes Garrison builds. We all worked on this one." He headed to the coffeemaker. "While we're walking around, see if you can think of any ways I could spruce up this place for the party Saturday. I could use some ideas on that."

"You have a great place for a party here, with all the open areas," she said, standing and beginning to gather up plates to take into the kitchen.

"Just put those plates by the sink," he directed. "I'll scrape them off and put them in the dishwasher later when I clean up all the rest." He gestured to the tumble of pots and utensils already piled in the sink.

She didn't argue, and he soon led her on a tour around the house, with Emily exclaiming over and pointing out things she liked. One thing Cooper appreciated about Emily was her willingness to let go of a testy discussion when it started getting out of hand, without insisting a guy keep gnawing around on it.

It didn't take long to see the two-story house. The floor plan of Cooper's log home was a typical design in most ways—a big open living area around a massive fireplace with a beamed ceiling downstairs, large kitchen and dining area with a fine view off the back porch, spacious office, huge master suite and bath. The upstairs held three bedrooms, two more baths, and a game area with a large pool table. Porches curled around most of the front and back of the house, with one downstairs section enclosed to enjoy in both winter and summer.

"I think this is one of my favorite rooms." Emily looked around the sun porch on the backside of the house. "It's cozy, homey, and comfortable."

He smirked. "Yes, and there's a lot of yellow and red in the décor out here, too, more color than inside."

"Yes. I like a little color." She refused to let him bait her, following him back inside.

"Coffee's ready," he said, glancing towards the kitchen. "And I picked up a peanut butter chocolate cheesecake in one of those cheesecake stores in Pigeon Forge earlier for our dessert." Cooper pulled the box out from the refrigerator and opened it. "Let's take our coffee and a piece of this cake into the living room around the fire."

"Oh, that looks divine." She edged closer to the box to peek inside. "Cheesecake is one of my absolutely favorite desserts."

"Bettie mentioned it one day."

Emily smiled. "There's very little that woman doesn't know. She's a walking encyclopedia on most anything around Gatlinburg."

"And most anyone." Cooper poured their coffee, letting Emily cut the cake. "Be careful you never tell Bettie Chase anything you don't want to see in tomorrow's newspaper. She's good-hearted for sure, but she's not known for her discretion."

They carried their plates into the living room and settled on one of the big brown leather sofas dominating the room. Cooper stirred up the fire and added another log before sitting down to pick up his plate and cup from the large coffee table between the cluster of sofas and chairs.

Both dug in to their dessert for a few minutes, enjoying the crackling of the fire, before Cooper spoke again. "The weather is holding in a warming trend and it should be in the eighties this Saturday. It's one reason we decided to schedule the party then. My idea was to let everyone gather outdoors around the pavilion most of the evening."

"What about tables and seating?"

"We store tables and chairs in the shed up on Hwy 321 behind the model home. We can haul them down here in one of the trucks and set them up. Delbert said he'd bring some hay bales from the farm to put around for extra seating, too." He paused to eat another bite of cheesecake. "Maybe you didn't notice but there's a fire pit outside we can use to knock off the chill of the evening and for the pleasure of watching the fire in the darkness. The band likes to set up at the end of the outdoor pavilion and that leaves room for a little dancing, too, when everyone gets in the mood."

She glanced across at him. "Sounds like you have this already planned. What did you need my ideas on?"

"It's a wedding shower thing, along with being an engagement party. I didn't want it to seem too much like a guys-only event—the kind of get-togethers we usually have." He scratched his head. "What would Lisa Marie like to see or expect? That's the girl Buddy is marrying."

Emily sipped at her coffee, considering this. "Maybe a gift-opening time before heading back to the dining area to fill plates and go outside to eat. With weather this glorious and a fire pit, it would be a shame not to enjoy most of the evening out of doors in this setting." She heaved a small sigh. "It's wonderful you can host an outdoor event here in March. I think a foot of snow is predicted in Philly this weekend."

He grinned. "We occasionally get snow and cold weather in March, too. I can remember some big snowstorms. But this weekend is expected to continue with warm, springlike days. It sure is nice right now."

"It is and those two sets of French doors to the back deck will give plenty of access from the dining and kitchen area of your house to the outside. Guests can drift in and out easily for drink refills or seconds on food."

She looked around, thinking. "For the wedding shower, you might order a colorful basket of flowers and put it on this huge coffee table here. You can pile the gifts around it as people come in, and then Lisa Marie and Buddy can open their gifts in a small preparty before the potluck dinner. I think the food will keep for the short time it takes for that, don't you?"

"Yeah, that sounds like a good plan. I agree, too, about keeping the food indoors. I don't want to set it up outside. It draws bears."

Cooper saw Emily's eyes widen.

He laughed. "These are the mountains, Emily Lamont. Bears start to mill around after sleeping and hibernating through the winter."

Seeing her still considering this with a troubled look, he added, "Don't worry. It's rare to see bears around my place and rarer still to encounter problems with them. They're just hungry and maybe curious when they come around."

She sat up straighter. "Well, as you say, it's *certainly* an added reason to keep the food inside."

He chuckled, but she ignored him.

Still in planning mode, she added, "It would also be nice if you set up some extra tables in the kitchen with nice tablecloths over them to put all the food on. Your dining table alone won't be big enough. You can set up the drinks and ice on the bar between the kitchen and dining area."

"I can do that." He set his plate on the table, dessert finished. "I'm glad you don't think I need anything fussier."

Her smile popped out again. "I don't think you need anything fussy or formal for a gathering in a log home." She glanced across at him. "Do you need help to set everything up?"

Cooper leaned back on the sofa to put his feet on the table. "My mom, Bettie Chase from the office, Delbert's wife, Dottie, and a couple of the other women—like Buddy's mother and Lisa Marie's mom—plan to come early to set everything up and to help direct the food aspect as people arrive. They can order flowers and do up the tables and such, too."

"I'm sure the party will be very nice." Emily sat her plate down, leaning forward to look at the fire.

Cooper watched her in the quiet of the evening, enjoyed seeing the firelight flicker over her face and hair. She was such a beautiful woman—soft and rounded in all the right places, with her pretty social skills and that fine mind. Cooper liked a smart woman. So many were dippy. With dinner and business out of the way, he felt the sweet rush of attraction and desire begin to swirl around in the room.

She fidgeted with her sweater, obviously sensing it, too.

"I should probably head for home now," she said, glancing at her watch. "It's getting late. I hope you don't mind running Mercedes and me back to the gallery."

"No, I said I would." He scooted closer to her on the couch, turning her towards him now. "But first we're going to do a little kissing to see if that zing Sara talked about will kick up again." He settled his mouth on hers before she had time to offer a reply.

CHAPTER 11

A little later, Emily walked hand in hand with Cooper down the winding road from his house towards the gallery in Gatlinburg. With a full moon outside and the weather so fine, Cooper had suggested he walk her home. The dogs, delighted with the idea, now pranced along beside them, stopping to sniff in the shrubbery when allowed.

Emily glanced shyly at Cooper's profile in the darkness. That zing certainly still sizzled between them. Emily couldn't ever recall feeling such a swamp of emotions with a man.

Cooper's words interrupted her reverie. "Could you get off tomorrow to take a hike?" he asked, surprising her. "This weather is glorious. It would be a great day to go. I could get away tomorrow if you can."

"Yes, I can arrange that. Mamie and Leona are both working tomorrow during the day and Monty in the evening. I won't be missed at the gallery." She turned to smile at him. "I'd be delighted to go."

He'd dropped her hand to rein in Brinkley, not as well trained to heel as Mercedes, but then he reached for it again. "You said earlier you'd like to try out a trail. It's a shame you've hiked so little in the Smokies."

"Sara and I walk the dogs on the Gatlinburg Trail sometimes."

"I walk Brinkley on that trail a lot, too. It's one of the few that allow dogs and it's actually a great walking trail not many people even know about." He slowed to let Brinkley spritz a bush by the roadside, letting her hand go again.

Emily slipped her hand from his with some reluctance. It felt so sweet holding hands and walking with a man. She couldn't remember how long it had been since anyone simply held her hand with affection.

Focusing her thoughts on his last comment about the Gatlinburg Trail, she added, "It's amazing how that trail slips away from the hustle and bustle of the Burg so quickly to move through such a quiet, wooded area."

Cooper grinned. "A lot of early mountain settlers lived in that trail area at one time. You can tell families lived there from the old chimneys and cabin remains you pass along the trailside." He paused. "I think we'll hike another nearby trail, the Old Sugarlands Trail, tomorrow. It carries a lot of early history, too. What do you think?"

"It sounds wonderful. In fact, I'd love to explore and hike all the trails around the park now that I live here."

His smile winked in the dark. "Then I'd better pick you up a good hiking guide so you can start reading up on the trails. There's a nice day-hiker guidebook called *The Afternoon Hiker,* complete with photos illustrating every trail. You'd like that one. It's geared primarily for short pleasure hikes you can do in a morning or an afternoon."

"Sounds perfect. I'd love a copy. Those are the kind of trails I want to do."

It felt good, walking along congenially with Cooper, talking about hiking and planning time together. So different from the moody man earlier, who'd talked as if he'd only invited her to his home to sort out his thoughts and misgivings about her.

"Are you feeling better about the two of us now?" she asked, hoping his reply would help her understand him more.

He swatted her lightly on the rear. "As Sara says, when there's a zing there's a zing. I guess we'd better go with it a little and see where it leads."

Her eyes widened in surprise at the swat.

Cooper leaned over to pull her into a half hug with one arm, moving his lips down to cover hers in a slow kiss that made her knees weak. "It is a nice zing, and that's a fact," he said against her mouth, his breath warm.

He caught her hand in his again as they walked on, Emily still trying to catch her breath and slow down her heartbeat.

"You tell Sara Russell to hold out for the zing," he said with a chuckle after a few minutes. "Sure as the sun shines, it's worth it, don't you think?"

"Uh, yes," she said, not quite sure how to reply. She shifted the subject to get on safer ground. "What time do you want to leave in the morning for the hike?"

"Let's say eleven," he answered. "It will allow the day to warm up first, and I need to take care of a few things on the site before I leave. Would that be all right with you? We can carry a lunch with us and eat along the trail. I know a good spot."

She nodded.

"Do you have a sturdy fanny pack—one of those belt packs with a small zippered storage area you can clip around your waist?" he asked. "We don't really need a backpack for a short hike, just a waist pack to put water and a few lunch items in."

She thought. "I'm not sure I own one. Where can I pick one up in the morning?"

"I have an extra." He fussed at Brinkley to quit jerking on the leash before adding, "It's even red, one of your favorite colors."

"I do like red," she replied, glad to see he noticed so much about her.

"What about hiking boots or outdoor shoes?"

"I have some good Merrells. They're even waterproof."

He snorted. "It figures they'd be name brand and pricey. Emily, I don't care what kind of boots they are, just as long as they're well broken in and you can hike comfortably in them."

She shook her finger at him. "Quit being so prissy because I own some nice things."

"Me? Prissy? What about you, Miss Philadelphia?"

Emily sighed. "There you go again, making a big deal about the fact that I lived in a large metropolitan city most of my life. I'm still me, Cooper, whether I live in Philadelphia, Gatlinburg, or Knoxville, Tennessee. You saw where I grew up. I don't feel so different from that little girl raised in Bearden."

He released her hand to adjust Brinkley's leash. "I do razz you a lot about the money thing, don't I?"

"Yes, you do." She paused to look at him. "Having money doesn't always ruin people, not if they don't let it."

"I guess I'm overly judgmental in that area. If you'd met many of my wealthy clients I build houses for, you'd understand why."

"A little prissy, are they?" She giggled.

"A lot prissy and very full of themselves."

"But seriously, Cooper, not all of your clients are like that, are they? Think about it and be honest."

"No, not all of them. You have a point." She watched him consider this. "I guess the few negatives tend to stand out and color the whole perspective."

"It can happen. I've dealt with clients in the gallery who've made me think the same thoughts."

As they walked by the church now, Emily saw a man heading down the sidewalk, waving at them.

"Cooper, is that you?" The young man, dark-haired, lanky, and about their own age, walked closer to reach out a hand to Cooper, smiling in recognition. "Good to see you again."

"Nice to see you," Cooper replied.

The man glanced towards Emily pointedly, and Cooper remembered his manners. "Perry Ammons, this is Emily Lamont, who now owns the Creekside Gallery where my mother works. Emily, this is Perry Ammons, the pastor of the Highland Cumberland Presbyterian Church here on Natty Road." He gestured towards the building. "Although Perry is a minister now, I still remember him mostly as one of the Jack Gang boys around Mynatt Park, a group of guys a little older than me that my friends and I thought were cool."

Emily smiled. "It's nice to meet you, Perry—or should I say Reverend Ammons?"

"Perry will do. Please. And Cooper and I did grow up here in Gatlinburg together and went to the same schools. I was three years older than Coop and three years younger than his brother Lance—right in the middle between the two in age. My friends and I looked up to Lance and his friends."

Emily watched Cooper stiffen with the mention of Lance's name, his smile shutting down and a frown replacing it.

Perry noticed it, too, and put a hand on Cooper's shoulder. "Lance has been gone a long time, Cooper. Isn't it about time you let go of that anger you're still harboring about the past? I'd like to see you come on back to church, too, and get over being mad at God."

"I don't think we need to discuss this in front of Emily." Cooper crossed his arms, scowling. "And I come to church now and again with Mother."

"Yes, and on the few times you do, you sit stiff and angry on the pew and wish you were anywhere else. It's hard for your mother to see that."

Cooper backed up a few steps. "You've got a lot of nerve, Perry, and a lack of tact for a minister."

Perry kept his eyes steadily on Cooper's. "Sometimes honesty is needed, Cooper. God isn't responsible for your brother's death."

Cooper clenched a fist. "Well, God didn't do anything to stop it, did He? And He didn't do anything to stop my dad from dying after that heart attack either." His voice rose in volume as he spewed out the words. "What's the point of being all-powerful and omnipotent if you can't stop bad things from happening to good people?"

Perry sighed. "God doesn't send death, hurt, destruction, pain, and tragedy, Cooper. The devil does that—and all too well from what I've seen."

"Hmmph. I remember being taught God is stronger than the devil and that the devil is no match for God."

Emily watched Perry Ammons consider his next words. "A man has to use wisdom in his life, Cooper. He needs to walk close to God, be mature and strong in his faith, and keep his armor on daily to defeat a crafty enemy. Walking in the protection of the Kingdom of God isn't guaranteed to any man because he's a nice person in the world. It's an aspect of faith. You know that."

He paused. "God is a good God, Cooper. I'll stand for Him in that. He wants above all things for His people to prosper and be in health, for them to be blessed coming in and blessed going out, for life to go well for them, for each of His people to have peace and protection from harm. But God's people don't always walk in a strong place with Him. They don't always use wisdom, and sometimes the enemy gets a toehold into the lives of even the best of men. Only God knows each man's heart, Cooper, and why these things occur. But destruction is never God's doing and never from Him."

"Well, thanks for the sermon." Cooper tossed the words out with sarcasm. "But I still say God could change outcomes if He wanted to. And I don't much respect Him for not intervening to prevent two people I loved a lot from dying much too young."

Perry leaned over to pet Brinkley, who was weaving around his leg. "Maybe we could sit down and talk about this a little more someday soon."

"Thanks but no thanks, and I need to get Emily home now." Cooper took Emily's arm. "The dogs are getting restless. I'll see you around, Perry."

He nodded. "Nice to meet you, Emily Lamont. Hope to see you visiting in church again soon."

Cooper practically towed her off with him down the street. "I didn't know you'd been going to church at Highland."

"I visited once with your mother and another time with Sara." She disengaged her arm from his grip to slow their pace down. "But this is the first time I've talked with the minister."

He walked on, not saying more, acting broody again now.

"Tell me about your brother," she said at last.

"I don't want to talk about Lance." He snapped out the words in an angry tone. "And I don't want to talk about my father either."

Emily sighed and let it go, quickening her pace to keep up with him. This was obviously a touchy subject.

They crossed the street and cut across the Parkway in Gatlinburg, taking the shortcut through Old Dad's parking lot towards the River Road and the Creekside Gallery. Emily could still feel the anger seething in Cooper as they walked along.

A motorcycle roared up beside them as they neared the sidewalk that followed the River Road. A young woman in black leather brought her big Harley to a halt, dropping her booted feet to the ground on either side to support it after the motor stilled. She pulled off her helmet to reveal long black hair tied back with a leather string, her face angular but striking.

Cooper directed an angry gaze towards the motorcycle. "Get that dang thing out of here."

She looked around casually. "This is a public place, Cooper. My Harley and I are as welcome here as you."

"I am not in the mood to deal with you tonight, Venetta."

"You're never in the mood to deal with me, so what else is new." She shrugged. "How's your mother?"

"I'm not discussing my mother or anything else with you." He grasped Emily's arm as if to pull her along once more.

"Ouch, Cooper," she complained as his fingers bit too hard into her upper arm.

"Whoa! You're hurting that girl. Just a friggin' minute." The girl propped her cycle with a kickstand and followed after them.

Seeing Venetta catching up to them, Cooper let go of Emily's arm and turned to look down at her, his eyes flashing with a mix of remorse and anger. "Listen, I'm sorry. But this is an old friend of my brother's that I hold no affection for and I really can't deal with her tonight. I hope you don't mind seeing yourself home from here. The gallery is in sight now." He pointed towards it before turning on his heel and literally walking away, Brinkley all but running to keep up with him.

The girl rolled her eyes. "Well, that certainly went well." She turned to Emily, moving closer to study her arm. "Did he hurt you?"

"No." Emily rubbed her arm even as she denied the claim.

"Hmmm. You'll probably have a bruise there tomorrow. These construction men don't always realize their own strength." She held out a hand to Emily then. "I'm Venetta Renaugh."

"I'm Emily Lamont, the new owner of the Creekside."

"Ahhh. I didn't think we'd met. I was Cooper's brother's fiancée."

Shocked, Emily blurted out. "You were Lance's fiancée?"

"Yeah, Lance Garrison was the best. I still miss him."

Emily's mind worked around these statements.

"You're wondering about how Cooper acted just now," she stated, picking up on Emily's thoughts. "He blames me for Lance's death. You'll hear it from someone soon enough. Lance and I were riding our motorcycles on The Dragon the day Lance died."

Seeing Emily's confused look, she added, "The Dragon is an eleven-mile stretch of mountain highway that motorcyclists love to ride. It's over on the western side of the Smoky Mountains. The road twists and twines around the mountainside, giving a thrill of a ride."

"How did Lance die there?"

"He went off the road on one of the turns. I rode ahead of him that day and I didn't see it happen, but riders behind him said they thought he misjudged his speed as he approached Guardrail Cliff, a notorious bend about four miles down The Dragon. He slid over the edge of the road and down a steep embankment; he fell sixty feet and then tumbled down another sharp drop after the first. They said he died instantly."

Emily watched Venetta pause, closing her eyes in remembrance before saying more. "The curves are sharp leading into this turn on The Dragon and the road dips a little to one side. A lot of accidents have happened at that point. Lance knew that, of course. Maybe he lost traction, overbraked or lost control. No one knows for sure." She sighed. "Lance always lived life to the fullest and then some, took too many risks, but I loved him with all my heart."

"How could Cooper blame you when you rode ahead of Lance?" Emily tried to puzzle out Venetta's words.

"You must not know Cooper Garrison very well yet." She ran her hands through her hair, smoothing it. "He blames a lot of people for Lance's death—me, Lance's friends we rode with that day, God, even himself."

Emily considered this. "How could Cooper see himself at fault? Was he there that day?"

"No." She laughed. "Cooper never liked motorcycles much but Lance always tried to get him to ride, pushed at him to try them out and to get into biking. He harassed and cajoled Cooper that day to go with us. He even said he needed Cooper to 'keep him in line.'"

"Oh, my. I'm sure those words came back to haunt Cooper."

"You bet. It was a tragic thing, for sure, but it was nobody's fault—not even Lance's. I'm sure Lance didn't mean to pick up too much speed or lean in too far. And maybe there was oil on the road or too much wind that day. All sorts of things could have played into what happened." She rubbed her neck. "I did a real number on myself for a time, too, blaming myself, thinking I might have done something to change what occurred."

Emily felt sympathetic to that statement. "I've lost people I love, too. I know how those feelings can rise up and overwhelm your good reason."

"Yeah, but most of us get past it after a few months or maybe a year and find a way to move on." She studied Emily. "Are you dating Cooper?"

"A little," she admitted.

"Good, I'm glad to hear it. He's kept most everyone at arm's length emotionally for a long time. My shrink says he's afraid to love, afraid to love and lose again, and that he's still punishing himself by even denying himself the chance to be loved."

"Does your therapist know Cooper?"

"Very well." She nodded. "He grew up around here, too, like all of us did. Gatlinburg is a small town despite the tourism. The longtime locals know each other."

She glanced towards her motorcycle, checking on it. "Look. I didn't mean to mess up your evening or anything, but I'm always hoping Cooper and I can reconcile. We used to be close friends." She hesitated. "In all honesty, I got invited to Buddy's party this Saturday, the one at Cooper's place. When I saw him tonight, I hoped to ask if he'd mind if I came. I like Buddy and Lisa Marie." She made a face. "But I guess the obvious answer is no."

Emily wasn't sure what to say.

Venetta picked at the zipper on her leather jacket. "The guy I'm dating—he works for Cooper and he's afraid to even tell Cooper we're seeing each other." She laughed. "Isn't that a kicker? First time I've found a guy that I care about since Lance died six years ago and we're sneaking around on the sly because Cooper still holds me responsible for Lance's death. My boyfriend's afraid Cooper will fire him if he finds out we're dating."

"That's sad," Emily said.

"Yeah, it is." She put her helmet back on. "Do you want me to ride you around to your door?" Venetta gestured towards the cycle.

"No, I have Mercedes with me." Emily glanced down at the dog sitting patiently beside her. "I'll just walk on across the street. I'll be fine."

"Well, you put an ice pack or a bag of frozen peas on that arm when you get home and it might keep it from bruising."

Emily smiled. "Thanks, I'll try that."

"Nice to meet you despite the circumstances," Venetta said, starting to walk away. "I'll try to stop by the gallery some day. Say hello. I haven't seen Mamie for a while and need to drop in anyway. She doesn't have a problem with me, only Cooper does."

After Venetta fired up her motorcycle and rode off, Emily looked down at Mercedes. "Well, I guess we'd better get on home, girl. It's been a strange evening, that's for sure."

After letting herself into her apartment, Emily found a text message on her phone from Daniel Stelben, asking her to call. Somehow, she knew it wouldn't be good news and dreaded it. The situation at the gallery in Philadelphia grew worse daily. Emily received threatening calls and e-mails from Leonard occasionally, too. Unable to see himself as responsible for the increasing problems at the Newman, he now focused his bitterness and blame on Emily.

"I know you're behind this," Leonard told her one day when she answered the phone at the Creekside. "Somehow you're turning people against me, causing problems with my employees, trying to make the gallery fail in order to get even with me for inheriting instead of you."

He sounded so bitter, and Emily didn't know how to respond to his unreasonable accusations. Concerned, she'd talked to Reuben Parrish about it. He'd urged her to start a record of the calls, to physically save and authenticate them so they could be used as evidence if further trouble ensued. But it felt awful trying to do so. In some ways she felt a little sorry for Leonard. He'd never been able to see how responsible he was for his own problems. He always saw them as someone else's fault.

"I just want it all to be behind me, Mercedes," she said, curling up on the sofa to rest, the dog climbing up beside her to lay a head on her lap.

In so many ways the move here to Gatlinburg had proved to be a happy one. Emily loved her large apartment with its views out over the garden. She'd settled her furniture in a way she felt happy with; she'd made new friends. The art collectors seemed more congenial and less intense than the patrons of the Newman, the store demands and staff easier to work with. The little gallery and the cheerful array of carefree tourists breezing in and out made for pleasurable workdays.

"It's turned out to be a good move in many ways for us, except for the problems with Cooper," she told the dog, rubbing Mercedes's ears in one of her favorite spots. She'd experienced problems with Cooper from the start, which in many ways hadn't improved.

"I'll need to talk with him about what I learned tomorrow," she said. "*If* he still takes me hiking."

Until then, she'd read a good book, call a few friends, and savor her memories of the sweeter moments with Cooper Garrison before his gloomy Hyde side had emerged again. Honestly. He really seemed like a Dr. Jekyll and Mr. Hyde mix sometimes.

CHAPTER 12

Cooper slept badly and woke in a sour mood. He knew he needed to offer an apology to Emily Lamont for his behavior last night, and he dreaded it. He dreaded even reintroducing the subject that brought about the problem, and he dreaded the questions she'd probably ask about Lance, Venetta, and the way he'd acted towards Perry Ammons. Dang it. He probably owed Ammons an apology, too.

As he showered, shaved, and dressed, Cooper considered calling to cancel his hiking afternoon with Emily, but truthfully, he had no excuse not to take her. With the weather unseasonably warm, he admittedly looked forward to getting out of doors for a hike himself. And he looked forward to enjoying the day through Emily's fresh eyes.

After finding needed hiking items to pick up later, he loaded Brinkley in the truck and headed for the work site just as the sun rose in a blaze over the mountain. Delbert often arrived early, and Cooper hoped he might get a chance to go over the work schedule and any problems needing to be resolved before taking off for the afternoon.

Cooper soon pulled up to the Perkins house, Garrison Homes' current project high on the mountain behind Gatlinburg, and spotted Delbert's old green truck parked under a tree. After looking inside the house for him, Cooper wandered out back to find Delbert sitting at a battered picnic table, with his head dropped between his hands.

"Hey, you okay?" he asked as he drew closer.

Del looked up with clear gray eyes out of a weathered, workman's face.

"I'm fine. Just having a little quiet time with the Maker before the day starts. Always makes my day go better when I take time for it."

Remembering the conversation with Perry Ammons yesterday, Cooper hoped to skirt this subject. "If you're done, maybe we can talk about the work schedule for today. If not, I'll go check the subfloor in the house and then come back."

"Sit down, Cooper." Delbert nodded towards the bench across the table from him.

Cooper hesitated, recognizing that look in Delbert's eyes. Then he remembered all the times this older man had helped him after the deaths of his dad and his brother, stood by him in the business, fathered him time and again.

"Yes, sir," he said, taking a seat.

"I hear you had some trouble last night."

"How'd you know about that?" Cooper clenched a fist.

"Don't matter, but you've been raised better than to act like you did."

"In which instance?"

Cooper watched a smile pull at the corner of Delbert's mouth. "Guess you'll need to tell me about each so I can identify which one I'm referring to."

Cooper shook his head, resigned to the inevitable now, and told Delbert about his evening and about running into Perry and Venetta.

"Hurting women with your tongue or your hands ain't the way your daddy raised you, Cooper. He'd be ashamed to hear of it, as I am."

"I got angry." Cooper looked off towards the mountain ranges visible from the backyard of the house site.

The look Delbert gave him let him know the excuse he offered seemed a flimsy one. "Perry's right that you need to let your anger go about losing your dad and your brother. It is way past time."

The older man paused, running a hand through his silvering hair, thinner now than in his younger years. "Cooper, it's been hard on everyone watching you harbor so much resentment and anger, watching you take it out on others and punish others for your dad and Lance's deaths, and watching you punish yourself."

Cooper tugged at his cap and shifted his shoulders. "I do better most of the time now, Del, but it really made me mad when Perry said God wasn't accountable for what happened and that sometimes we're responsible ourselves for the bad that comes our way." He crossed his arms. "Dad and Lance were good men. I didn't like him saying that."

"Well, I wasn't listening in on the conversation, so I can't judge it, but I will say this. Your dad and your brother were both good men and that's a fact, but they weren't saints. Lance was a risk taker, often careless about his life. He saw that aspect of character as his own business, of course, but it affected others."

"He was young . . ." Cooper began.

Delbert cut him off. "So were you, Cooper, and I didn't see you taking the kind of risks Lance did."

"Lance and I were always different."

"That's exactly my point." He drummed his fingers on the tables absently. "And concerning your dad, you and I both know he smoked like a fiend and wouldn't give up the cigarettes. Your mother and I stayed after him all the time to give it up. He told me, 'I like to smoke—and if it kills me, it will.' That ain't healthy talk or a healthy attitude."

He looked out over the mountains as he spoke. "Price worked too hard, too. Didn't keep enough balance in his life. He showed up in church on Sunday, that's true. Claimed it was good business to do so, but he spent no time in prayer or study. No offense, Son, but your daddy had a low level of faith and he didn't mind his ways or his words about his life." Delbert twisted his old battered hat as he talked. "I hated that for his sake. You remember yourself he always laughed and said, 'This business is going to give me a heart attack one day—I'm just going to keel over and check out.'"

"Dad was only kidding around when he said that."

Delbert gave him a tolerant look. "You ain't a dumb boy, Cooper. Bible teaching aside, you know all sorts of research shows the things we think and believe and the words we say over our lives exert a power."

Cooper jerked out of his seat, getting angry now. "You're saying Dad's words killed him."

"No, I'm not. Sit down, boy." He reached a hand across to grasp Cooper's arm in a strong grip. "Price Garrison was my best friend in the world. I loved him like a brother. You know that. But I'm saying you can't canonize him—or Lance—and say they never did or said a wrong thing. We all fall short in our lives, and sometimes that opens a door for the enemy to slip in. Like the Garden of Eden story. You remember the devil stood behind all that trouble there, too. It wasn't God's fault what happened."

"But if God's all-powerful why did He let that happen?"

"You know the Garden of Eden story. They had a choice." He rubbed his chin, thinking. "Here's how my daddy explained it to me. He said it was like owning a big ranch and being responsible for it. You need to constantly ride the ranges checking the fences, staying diligent about rustlers and problems. It keeps your spread, your business and your family, from problems. If a fence line breaks down or gets cut by a rustler, you go get after it real quick before the problem grows worse. He taught me that when you're diligent in your faith, it's a way to keep your fences safe. You keep your life and those who depend on you safe."

He stopped to consider his next words. "So, in order to have the best life, you need to think of each day like taking care of your ranch. You do that in regard to your physical life, with your business and your work, with your relationships with others and with your spiritual life. You care for your ranch, keep it protected—and you keep yourself strong. Then if you run head-to-head with a rustler one day, you're ready. You understand?"

"Yeah, I get it." Delbert's stories were the way he always explained a lot of things to Cooper, his own boys, and even the men he worked with.

Cooper smiled at Delbert, knowing the older man only meant him good. "I guess it's like the Bible story about building your house on the rock, with a sure foundation, versus on the sand. Seems like you've told me that one, too. It assures the house will stand when the storms come."

"Yeah, that's another good analogy. And it might be easier for us to think on that one since we're builders." He chuckled. "You might not remember me telling you, but my pa preached on Sundays in a small church near our ranch out west. That's where I lived all my life before I moved here. We lived way out in the country in those years and our church couldn't get no ordained minister to come and settle that far out in the middle of nowhere for such a small congregation."

"I remember you told me that."

"Well, Dad, he preached often on the words of our mouths and their power over our lives and I've never forgotten those teachings."

He laughed then. "I recall one Sunday Bertha Albright came in saying God had put a cancer on her to strengthen her and for His glory. She asked Pa to pray for her to bear up under it. He told her, 'Well sure, sister, and we're going to pray, too, that God puts more cancer on you. If He's bringing cancer on you to strengthen you and for His glory then we ought to pray for more of it.'"

Delbert slapped his hand on the table, chuckling. "I thought that woman's eyes were going to bug out of her head. I don't think she realized how ridiculous what she'd said even sounded until she heard it come back on her like that."

Cooper grinned. He'd always loved Delbert's stories. "So what does all this have to do with my dad and Lance dying, Del?"

"That neither of their deaths were for God's best or glory—or by His design. That like Bertha's cancer, it was an attack from the devil, like Perry tried explaining to you. We do have a bad devil just like we have a good God. And like the ranch story I shared with you, we need to work hard at strengthening ourselves in the good ways and growing ourselves in our faith daily so we can keep up the best fencing and the best hedge we can around our lives."

"Okay." Cooper glanced at his watch.

"Okay, what?" Delbert leaned forward.

"Okay, I get the message." He started to stand, but Delbert put a hand on his arm, stopping him.

"Son, you ready to have a little prayer with me here this morning and forgive everybody you've been blaming unjustly? You about ready to take a step forward and put the blame more rightly where it belongs?"

"I can pray on my own." Cooper frowned.

"Nah, we need to get it done right here and now. I know a kind mother of yours that needs you to get it taken care of today, that's tired of feeling guilty because she hasn't been able to say the right things to help you move on. You need to do it for the men who work for you who are getting tired of your temper flashing out whenever that anger triggers up in you."

He gave Cooper a stern look. "You need to do it now because there's a boy who works for you who's sweet on Venetta Renaugh and he's afraid you'll fire him if you find out about it. And then there's Venetta herself, who lost the man she loved and wanted to spend her whole life with, who had to see him dragged dead up from that embankment, see his torn-up motorcycle carried out. Then in her grief she's had to put up with your unjust resentment and unkindness when you should have offered her a brother's love and comfort. And, finally, there's a young girl that's getting sweet on you, and you on her, who you're driving away with your angry moods and surly ways."

Cooper closed his eyes. Delbert's candid words were hard to take.

He felt a hand close over his. "Finally, Cooper, there's also yourself you need to quit blaming and forgive, Son. You weren't at fault in any way for the fact that your dad or your brother died. I hate it like the dickens it happened, and I've had my moments of wishing there was something I could have done to prevent it. But that kind of thinking is harmful."

Cooper fell quiet for a moment. "How come this is all coming up now? It's been six years."

"I guess God decided you weren't going to deal with this and so He finally sent some folks along to kick your butt. The question is whether you're ready to hear good advice, break out, and get free—or not?"

"How can I do that, Del?" Cooper rubbed at his arm. "Wishing I could move on will hardly make it happen."

"My pa called it breaking up the fallow ground. We're going to pray out each area you've hardened yourself in one point at a time. You'll forgive each person, ask God for forgiveness for harboring anger towards them, and ask God by faith to cleanse you from guilt and wrong relating to each one. Then you're going to turn over a new leaf and walk on."

"Will it work?"

"It will if you want it to and if you work at being changed." He put his calloused workman's hand over Cooper's. "I'll pray and you repeat, Son. Sometimes that helps the words get formed right."

An hour later, as the men began to arrive at work for the day, Cooper looked around at them with a new fondness. He did feel better.

"I hear you got a new girlfriend," Leroy punched at his arm. "Bettie told Radonna she's a real pretty little thing, and I hear we're going to get to meet her this Saturday night at the party."

Rafe walked by them, carrying a ladder in from his truck. "If Cooper don't mess it up by then, maybe we will. His track record with Miz Lamont ain't none too good."

"Maybe I'll get lucky and won't mess it up this time." Cooper punched Rafe on the arm as he passed beside him.

"We'll see." Rafe grinned at him.

"Looks like a lot of us boys are getting lucky," Buddy put in, heading over to help unload the lumber from the back of Leroy's truck.

"Well, some might not think it lucky to be getting hitched." Rafe laughed. "Just dating's better, to my way of thinking."

"Who's dating Venetta?" Cooper dropped the question into their ongoing banter, bringing the group's laughter to a quiet standstill.

The men shifted with discomfort, avoiding his eyes.

Cooper reached into the truck to pick up another stack of boards. "I thought whoever it is ought to invite her to the party this weekend," he said, shifting the boards to his shoulder. "She's right good friends with Lisa Marie; isn't that right, Buddy?"

"They've been known to run around," he answered carefully.

"Well, I suppose I could ask her myself but I'm not the one dating her," Cooper replied, stacking boards on the porch and heading back to the truck for more.

Another silence ensued.

Rafe cleared his throat. "I've been seeing some of Venetta," he said at last. "I could ask her, if you're sure."

Cooper turned to Rafe, seeing the caution in his eyes.

He clapped him on the back as he headed past him to the truck to pick up the next load of boards. "You do that, Rafe. It's time life moved on."

Cooper heard Rafe's breath heave out behind him. "I'll see if she's free," he said, trying to sound nonchalant.

Cooper grinned to himself.

The men settled to work then, feeling easy and comfortable again—laughing and joking in their usual way. Cooper worked for a time alongside them and then loaded up Brinkley and headed back to the house. He had a few more fences to mend before this day was out.

He knocked on Emily's door a few minutes before eleven. She opened the door and waved him in, her cell phone to her ear. She mouthed to him that she'd be off in a few minutes.

"Daniel, I'm so sorry Julianne has quit," he heard her say. "I guess we've been expecting it, but I'm still truly sorry. The Fontaine Gallery outside Philadelphia in New Hope is really lucky to get her. She'll love the culture in that city. It's always attracted artists and has easy access to Philadelphia and New York. It will be a change for Julianne, but I think she'll like it, as will her family. It's wonderful her husband could transfer to a bank branch there, too. I know you'll miss her, but like you said, Leonard has been bullying her and making her life a misery. No one needs that."

Cooper watched her listen with a frown on her face.

"Listen, I don't care what Leonard says, I had nothing to do with Julianne's decision. Yes, I did give her a good reference. I gave Michael Zucchi one, too. I would give a good reference to any of the staff I worked with at the Newman for so long. Why shouldn't I?"

Cooper watched her pace around the room, Mercedes watching her with concern, sensing she was upset.

"Perhaps, as you say, Margaret may leave next. I can't say. What you tell me about how Leonard is treating his employees would tempt anyone to look around for a better work environment. How can you blame them?"

She listened again. "I'm sorry, Daniel. I know this is a difficult time for you. I don't know what else to say."

She put the phone down a few minutes later and then slumped into a butterscotch plaid sofa against a stack of colorful pillows. Cooper chose an armchair across from her and sat down, too.

"Bad news?" he said at last.

"Yes." She sighed, picking up a pillow and hugging it to herself. "Another employee quit at the Newman. I guess you heard."

"You feel like it's your fault."

She glared at him. "Well, I'm sure you would be an expert on that subject," she snapped, her voice laced with sarcasm.

He pulled his cap off and grinned at her. "Yeah, I would. And believe it or not, I got free of a lot of that baggage this morning."

She raised her eyebrows.

"Never mind that now. Just don't you carry around a pile of guilt about the gallery as long as I did in thinking I could have prevented Lance's death. It might give you a permanent scowl." He grinned at her.

"You're in a good mood," she said.

He stood and walked over to sit beside her. "Let's see your arm." He pushed the T-shirt on her left arm up and uncovered the red bruises his fingers had left. "Ah, dadgumit, look at that. I'm so sorry, Emily."

"It's not too bad. It doesn't hurt."

"That doesn't excuse it." He leaned over to press his lips to the bruises. "I wish I could kiss it better like my mom used to do with my skinned elbows and knees."

He heard her quick intake of breath. "I think it might feel a little better already." Her voice softened, her eyes meeting his.

Cooper ran his fingers down her cheek. "Let's see if I can improve the situation even more." He moved in to let his lips find hers.

Heaven. She was so sweet to kiss and hold. Cooper pulled her closer, enjoying the feel and taste of her.

"Ummm, this is nice," she said at last. "But I thought we were going hiking."

He kissed her a last time on the nose before he let her go.

"We are." He let his eyes skim over her. "And your jeans and T-shirt look perfect for our hike today."

She blushed. "You said you liked girls in jeans."

"That I do," he said, letting his eyes linger on the snug fit of her jeans over her curves before drifting down her legs to her feet. "And the Merrell boots are very nice and practical."

"Thanks."

Cooper stood and looked around the room. "This is the first time I've seen your place since you moved in. Everything looks really nice, Emily. You've fixed the place up well."

She gave him a quick tour around the apartment so he could see how all the rooms had turned out. Her furniture looked great with the paint colors she'd chosen, and the porch furniture had taken on new life with the colorful striped fabric she'd re-covered the cushions in.

Cooper looked around a little more on his own while she took Mercedes out a last time.

"I guess I'm ready if you are," she said, coming back.

"Here's your waist pack." He picked it up from the table by the door, where he'd dropped it. "It has water and some lunch items in it. You can add any girly things you want, ChapStick or a small hairbrush, Band-Aids if your boots aren't well broken in, definitely a package of tissues. Keep in mind toilet facilities will be off the trail behind a shrub."

She ran around the house, tucking a few more items into her waist pack, and then they were off.

Cooper drove his Jeep today instead of his truck, more fun for treks like this around the mountain. He enjoyed the wind in his hair as they sped down the Parkway away from Gatlinburg. It felt great to be a guy out with a pretty girl today. And to be a guy with a lighter heart.

CHAPTER 13

Emily put a hand up to tighten the clip on her hair as they flew down the road in the open Jeep. She glanced across at Cooper and saw him grinning. He was obviously feeling better today and said he'd gotten some help or counseling that morning. Maybe he went to talk to Perry or to the counselor Venetta mentioned. Anyway, Emily felt glad to see him happier.

Turning right off the highway, Cooper parked his Jeep by the park headquarters building. They snapped on their waist packs, and then Cooper led the way down the roadside and across the highway to a trail sign.

"Wait. Let me take a picture." Emily pulled out her phone to snap a photo of Cooper beside the sign and then let him take one of her.

"You'll find better photo shoots along the way." He handed her phone back and turned to start down a slight hill from the road and onto the park trail, Emily close behind.

The pathway they followed spread wide and flat ahead of them, like an old roadbed, and it soon passed tall rock cliffs on their left.

"This was an old rock quarry at one time." Cooper paused to run his hand over some of the smooth rocks. "The CCC—that stands for Civilian Conservation Corps—had two work camps in this area during the 1930s and early 1940s. They took rock out of this quarry to build many of the roads, walls, and tunnels around the Smokies."

"Oh, look at this little rock, Cooper. What is it?" Emily reached down to pick up a shiny white rock from the ground.

"That's white quartz. Sometimes a vein of quartz runs through the rock formations in the mountains, as in this sandstone mix here." He pointed to a line of white zigzagging across the rock wall. "You'll probably see more quartz pieces as we walk on."

She did, picking up several more to examine.

The trail soon dropped to wind alongside the river. Emily enjoyed listening to the roar of the water as it tumbled and cascaded over the huge boulders scattered throughout the stream. She took photos as they walked, and Cooper called her attention to birds twittering high above in the trees, leafy ferns growing by the trailside, and two lively gray squirrels skittering up the trunk of a pine.

The path rose gently as they followed the water, gradually turning away from the river and narrowing, as it wound through a green woods. To Emily's delight she found early purple violets along the trailside and clusters of delicate white-petaled wildflowers Cooper called hepatica.

After passing an intersection, Cooper slowed, turning down an unmarked path off the main trail. He led the way to a tall rock structure amid the trees that rose up high over both their heads.

"Looks like an old chimney," Emily said, studying it.

"It does," he agreed, "but actually, it's an old CCC clock tower, a reminder of how many men lived and worked here building the park."

Emily dug out her phone from her waist pack to take another photo before following Cooper back along the trail.

A short time later, he paused at another intersection marked with trail signs. "Continuing on straight ahead takes us towards the heart of one of the old CCC camp areas and then up an old macadam roadbed to the end of the trail. But today, I want to angle off down this side trail instead."

She followed him down an old roadway with a grass line between the worn-out wagon tracks. "What's that?" she asked, pointing out another rock structure to the left of the trail. "It looks like the remains of an old fireplace."

"That's pretty accurate. It was a CCC trash incinerator." He waited while Emily went over to examine it. "One of the reasons I chose this trail is because there are so many interesting signs of the past camps and the places where the settlers lived all along the way." He pointed ahead. "At the end of this road lay a big mountain settlement, with a school, mills, and many farms and homes."

They walked on along a narrowing trail, enjoying the new green of early spring beginning to show on the trees and relishing being outdoors on such a fine day.

At another intersection ahead, Cooper found a fallen log for them to stop and take a short rest on. "We've walked a little over two miles at this point. If you're tired, we can turn back. If you're still okay, we'll hike on another mile to the ruins of an old stone house and eat our lunch there." He pulled his ball cap off to lay it beside him when they stopped and dug into his waist pack to find a bottle of water and a snack.

"I'm all right," Emily said, searching for her water, too. "Walking around the streets and parks of Philadelphia keeps you in pretty good shape." Turning to look at him sitting beside her, she felt another catch in her heart as she studied his tanned face and dark hair, mussed a little from the soft wind whispering through the trees on this warm March day.

Unaware of her observations of him, he opened a bag of peanuts and offered her a handful before upending the rest into his mouth. Then after gulping down part of his water, he started them on their way up the path again.

"I think you'll like the Old Stone House," he said, striding ahead of her with long steps.

Emily smiled. It was nice spending time with Cooper today. He wasn't grumpy or moody. This was the side of him she most liked.

The trail climbed a little more steeply now up a ridge, the ground a little rougher and rockier. At the top of the hill, Cooper led Emily into the woods on an unmarked trail. She could see little trace of a clear path in front of them, but Cooper seemed to know where they were going.

He helped her rock hop a stream a short time later, and then she followed him over a wooded hill and down to yet another stream. "This one is trickier to cross." He stopped until she caught up to him. "Some days if it's been raining a lot, I don't even try it, but today there are some rocks we can make our way across on. I'll go first and then give you a hand as you follow me."

Emily slipped a time or two on the slick rocks, wetting her boots, but she managed not to fall. On the other side of the bank she clambered up a steep hill behind Cooper, pushing brush aside and heading towards a thicket of rhododendron. As they wound their way through this thick undergrowth, Emily suddenly looked ahead to see the stone walls of a house.

"Is that it?" she asked.

"Yes." He led them through the last of the thicket into a clearing, revealing the walls and ruins of an old stone cabin. "This place lay hidden and undiscovered for seventy-five years before someone found it. As you can see, it's still difficult to find. The park hasn't cut a maintained trail to the place either because the foundations and walls of this old ruin aren't very stable. They probably think someone could get hurt if they popularized it. I've heard talk that they're planning to tear the place down, but so far it hasn't happened."

"What an interesting place." Emily walked around to peep into the doorways and windows still remaining of the stone structure. Inside the walls, she spotted rusting relics of an old bedstead, crude tools, a primitive stove, and the corroded remains of aged pots and pans.

"There are some large rocks in the room next door we can sit on to eat our lunch." He led the way to the spot he had in mind.

They chatted amiably over a sandwich lunch, Cooper telling her interesting stories about the history of the area and about the Pi Beta Phi settlement that once occupied the area. He explained that as an offshoot of the national Mission Movement of that era, the Pi Beta Phi women's fraternity created a settlement school in nearby Gatlinburg to help the mountain people that grew to later become the Arrowmont School of Arts and Crafts.

On the way back, Cooper led her down another side trail to a beautiful spot on the stream. He took her hand to lead her out onto a huge boulder where they could sit to watch the water cascading and rushing down from the mountain.

"This is the West Prong Little Pigeon River, the same river that later turns to run along behind the Creekside Gallery." Cooper leaned over to run his hand through the water. "This is one of my favorite places along this river."

"It's a larger and more rushing stream here than behind the gallery." Emily curled her legs underneath her and leaned her head back to look up at the blue sky. Then she watched Cooper skip stones across the water, so content and happy.

"Cooper, what happened this morning to make you feel so much better than last night?" she asked, hoping he wouldn't get mad at the question.

"Delbert Hilton had a talk with me." He smiled at her and pulled his cap off to run his fingers through his hair. "He and my dad worked together in the business and were best friends. When Dad died, Delbert sort of stepped in as a father figure to me. He helped me through the hard time after Lance got killed, too."

She waited, watching him.

"It seemed to be my time to let go of a little of the anger over losing Dad and Lance. It never seemed fair to me. I guess I always wanted to blame someone."

She understood the feelings. "After Mother and Daddy were killed in the car wreck, I went through a time of being really angry, too—angry at the man driving the truck that went out of control and hit them, angry at the doctors at the hospital who couldn't save them, angry at God for letting them die. I thought of those feelings again when Perry talked to you last night."

Cooper rubbed his neck. "I probably need to drop by to give Perry an apology for last night."

She didn't reply to that, thinking her own thoughts. "I can still remember some of the things people in our church said to me when my parents got killed."

"Things that helped you?"

"No." Emily shook her head. "Exactly the opposite. One lady said God took my parents to heaven because he wanted two more angels. An older man patted me on the head and told me God had sent me this hard test early in my life to strengthen me for some purpose of His."

Cooper turned towards her. "Do you believe any of that is true now?"

"Definitely not, and fortunately, Hal and Mary helped me over some of that nonsense thinking as did the Quaker teachers where I went to private school in Philadelphia. Miss Mary Pennington, my fifth-grade teacher, explained clearly to me that people do not become angels. That's a religious myth. When people die they go to heaven to be saints with God, to help in ruling over angels, but they never become angels. I remember she seemed quite provoked that so many people seemed to persist in believing people become angels when they die. She blamed it on books and movies that perpetuate the concept."

Cooper laughed. "She'd get along well with Hadley Bennack in the Creekside Gallery. He does all the angel paintings and can fill your ears complaining about the misconceptions people have about what angels look like as well. He claims to have seen angels and says they are not chubby little cherubs or soft, wispy ethereal women, but strong, valiant beings capable of warring in the heavens and carrying out the work of God."

She smiled. "I do love Bennack's work."

"Me too." Cooper grinned. "And I like thinking I have angels like the ones Bennack depicts on my team, as guardians and helpers."

"Do you think we have angels assigned to us specifically?"

"Why not?" Cooper picked up a rock to skim it across the stream. "If I were God with a vast army of host, I'd assign them around to help folks I care about."

"Yes, it seems like something a loving God would do. Have you ever seen an angel?"

"Nope, not that I could describe. But Delbert has. He saw a big angel divert a falling boulder at a work site so it wouldn't hit him and probably kill him."

"I like those stories." She smiled, tossing a small rock out into the stream as Cooper had.

Cooper crossed his long legs in front of him on the boulder. "You know, if people had talked to me sooner with some sense after my dad and Lance died, maybe I wouldn't have dragged my anger around so long."

"Do you think it's finished now?"

"I don't know. I'd like to think so, but something may come back to stir it up again in the future. However, I hope it won't be as bad as times in the past. Delbert's right—six years is long enough to feel bitter, angry, and resentful about something that wasn't my fault, God's fault, or anybody else's. Sometimes bad things just happen."

"Mary used to quote that scripture, 'it rains on the just and the unjust.'"

"Yes, that's true, but everything in life isn't just happenstance either. Life isn't like a big heavenly roulette wheel that a person doesn't have any influence or control over—red you win, and God's in a good mood today, or black you don't." He paused, thinking. "Actually, Delbert told me a good story related to that this morning—stressing the importance of living your life better prepared for rains and storms." He told Emily Delbert's story about tending a life with diligence like a wise rancher.

She listened. "His story reminds me of the Bible story of building your house on a rock instead of the sand."

He grinned at her. "Yeah, I thought of that parable, too."

They sat thinking quietly for a time, listening to the birds chittering in the trees, watching the stream rush by, enjoying the insects humming by the water's edge, and catching a glimpse of a lizard darting around a rock.

Emily sighed. "I don't think I'm doing as much as I should about keeping the spiritual side of my life strong."

"And?" Cooper flipped a stone out over the water.

"And I guess I should do something about that part of my ranch." She grinned at him. "I used to read my Bible and pray more, attend church a lot, and spend time reading devotionals and other books to grow in my faith, but then I got busy at the Newman, Mary got sick, the weekends grew hectic going to the hospital and the nursing home. My life became so full helping Hal and Mary, seeing Hal through the hard time after Mary died, and then dealing with the mess of Leonard inheriting." She paused. "I guess I just got out of the habit."

"Yeah, I've done that, too, but for different reasons."

Emily traced a finger across a line of quartz in the boulder they sat on. "Maybe if you go talk to Perry you could ask him to recommend a good devotional or Bible study book and then tell me the name of it."

Cooper laughed. "Or you could ask him for the name of a book yourself."

She crossed her arms. "I could, of course, but you said you'd be going to see him, so I thought since you know him better . . ."

"Don't get ticked off at me, Emily. I'll ask him for a suggestion. Maybe I'll pick up two copies—one for each of us. We can talk about what we read every now and then. Help each other along."

She smiled at him. "I like that idea."

He leaned over to take her chin in his hands. "I like the sound of any idea that lets me spend more time with you, beautiful woman."

Before she could think of an answer, his lips covered hers in one of those wonderful kisses only he could give. Her heart hammered in her chest. He tasted delicious, even better than chocolate. She giggled at the idea, even as he kissed her.

He pulled away to look at her. "Now what are you giggling about?"

She bit her lip. "I was thinking you're even better than chocolate."

He grinned at her words. "I assume that means you like chocolate. Maybe even more than cheesecake?"

"Oh, yes." She leaned forward to kiss him again softly. But he pulled her tighter then, deepening the kiss into a passionate one that spun her senses into a whirlwind. They dropped back onto the warm rock, both savoring the moment.

"This feels like making out in high school," he said a little later, lying beside her on the rock. "But trickier out on this boulder in the middle of the stream."

"Yes," she said, sitting up and smiling at him. "I've had a great day, Cooper, but I'd better get back to the house and the gallery."

He glanced at his watch. "Yeah, time has flown, hasn't it? I need to run by the Gatlinburg office and check with Bettie before she leaves for the day, and Brinkley will want a walk."

Cooper gave her a hand climbing down from the rock and then held her hand in his again as they started walking back down the trail. They talked about trivial things as they retraced their steps to Cooper's Jeep—their favorite foods, favorite things to do, and memories of happy times in the past.

"I'm looking forward to your party on Saturday night," she told him when he walked her to her door a little later.

"Me too," he said, leaning over to catch a last kiss before they parted. "And I know I'll have sweet dreams tonight, Miss Emily." He winked at her as he reminded her of the Roy Orbison tune "Dream Baby" they'd listened to while painting. Emily found herself smiling and humming the tune to herself later as she worked in the gallery.

CHAPTER 14

The crowd at the party had grown to nearly eighty guests when Cooper slipped out the front door. He desperately needed a break from the women who'd taken over his kitchen, chattering and assembling the food being brought in.

"You escaping, too?" Mackie waved at him from a rustic bench on the covered porch of Cooper's home.

Cooper settled into a chair beside him. "Yeah, the clatter of all those women in my kitchen was getting to me."

"Well, you have to admit there's a lot of good-looking food in there already and the pile of gifts for Buddy and Lisa Marie is overflowing on that coffee table in your living room." He crossed an ankle over his knee and leaned back, relaxing. "It was good of you to host this shindig, Cooper. Buddy and Lisa Marie are going to be real pleased."

"Well, I built this big place, the pavilion beside it, and even cleared off land for parking out of the woods, just to be able to host times like these."

Mackie grinned. "Sort of like the old movie line—pardon my misquote—if you build it they will come."

Cooper laughed. "Maybe . . . and I'd say more will come yet." He glanced at his watch. "It's only five after six."

Mackie cocked an eyebrow at him. "Are you out here watching for that girl you're getting sweet on? She's not here yet, is she?"

"She'll be along," Cooper replied, not wanting to admit to Mackie that part of the reason he'd come out on the porch was to watch for Emily.

Mackie changed the subject. "Dad said the Mayfields were real pleased with how their house turned out on the mountain. He stopped by the other day when they were moving in, just to be sure everything was okay."

"Yeah, I talked to them, too. They love the place, and fortunately even the delays we encountered, building most of the house in winter, didn't bother them. They're just happy to be settling in before March is out." Cooper smoothed a hand over his hair, missing the familiar Garrison Homes ball cap he usually wore.

"We're making good time on the new place going up, too, now that the weather's cleared off," Mackie added. "The roofers came today. We can get to work inside now, starting on Monday."

"If Nathan Jeffries, the man we're building that house for, shows up on-site, try to make up an excuse to get rid of him—and don't promise him anything he suggests for changes. He's a big CEO for one of those timeshare companies and likes to give orders, but he doesn't think out what his ideas might cost him. Refer him to me for anything he rambles on about if he shows up."

"Some folks are clueless that every change they make while we're building is going to cost them money."

"That's the truth."

Cooper stood to speak to Floyd and Arnold Bolinger as they came up the porch steps and then to Bettie Chase and her husband, Ted, behind them. He started to sit back down but then saw Emily and Sara walking up the driveway.

"That her?" Mackie asked.

Cooper nodded. "Yep."

"Which one?"

"The short dark-haired one." Cooper sat back down, not wanting to look too eager.

"Pretty girl." Mackie watched the girls drawing closer. "That other one is a looker, too. Who is she?"

"That's Sara Russell, Dora Russell's older daughter. Dora owns that dollhouse store in the Laurel Mountain Village Mall."

Mackie nodded. "Yeah. Seems like I've walked by her store. Little shop between Spencer Jackson's gallery and the Smokyland Candy Store, right?"

"That's the one. Emily said Sara only moved here recently from Alabama to work for her mother at the store. She's living at Dora's right now, not far from the Creekside. She and Emily met while out walking their dogs or something."

"Is she single?"

Cooper turned to grin at Mackie. "Interested?"

"Definitely. Just look at her. I'm real partial to long leggy blonds. You introduce me, okay? And say something nice about me, too."

"That interested, huh?" Cooper chuckled, standing now to wave back to Emily, who'd spotted him on the porch. "Well, come on, Mackie. I'll see what I can do."

Cooper watched Emily's eyes light with pleasure as she started up the steps towards him. Then that sweet smile of hers lit her face even more, kicking his heart up a notch. She wore a dress tonight instead of one of her usual tailored slacks sets, a flirty little red dress with a full skirt and red sequined pumps. Sara wore a similar dress in satiny blue with shiny sandals and dangling silver earrings. They made quite a stunning pair.

"Hi, Cooper." Emily put a hand in his briefly, giving him another rush just touching her hand. "A big crowd is here already." She glanced back towards the parking area and rural driveway, both lined with cars.

Mackie stepped closer, giving the girls a big smile. "A lot of folks are here, that's for sure, but not a single one is as pretty as either of you."

Cooper tried not to grin as he made his introductions. "Emily Lamont, this is Mackie Hilton. We've been best friends since school days and we work together at Garrison."

"Hello, pleased to meet you." Emily held out a hand to Mackie. She turned to Sara then. "And this is my friend, Sara Russell. She's just moved here from Birmingham, Alabama, and is working with her mother at Dora's Dolls."

"That's the cute shop next to the Jackson Gallery, isn't it?" Mackie asked, making conversation.

"Yes." Sara said, scanning her eyes over Mackie. "Have you visited our store?" She grinned when she said it.

"No, but I might get a new interest in dolls now." Mackie reached out to take the covered tray of party snacks from her hands. "Let me carry these back to the kitchen for you. Cooper can show Emily where to put the wedding gift you girls brought." He eyed the gift bag Emily carried.

"Thank you." Sara tucked a hand through Mackie's arm. "Maybe you can show me around Cooper's wonderful house here, too. I know Emily's seen it but I haven't. She said Garrison Homes built the log house. Did you help?" Their voices trailed off as Mackie led the way into the house.

Cooper's eyes followed them. "Well, they certainly seemed to hit it off."

Emily laughed. "Yes, and neither one appeared to suffer for shyness."

He turned to look at her. "You look stunning, Emily. Red is a perfect color for you. I remember you wore red when we met, too."

"Did I?" She dropped her gaze.

"Yes. A long red sweater, black slacks, and black boots. I couldn't stop looking at you. And tonight you're even more beautiful." He looked down to her feet and raised an eyebrow.

"I call these my Wizard of Oz shoes." She grinned at him. "They may be sparkly but they're really comfortable."

"Comfortable enough for dancing later?"

"Absolutely—even for jitterbugging."

He took her arm, leading her towards the door. "I've already put in a request for a couple of numbers so we can show off our moves." Cooper glanced at her gift bag. "You didn't need to bring a gift. You haven't even met Buddy or Lisa Marie yet."

"I know, but Sara and I wanted to bring something. We picked out a pretty paperweight from the gallery—just a small gift to wish them happy."

"That was nice of you." He let his eyes drift over her bare shoulders. "I hope you brought a sweater for when it grows cooler later on."

"We both have sweaters in the car if we need them. But it's still lovely and warm out now. What marvelous weather for March. I hope it stays pretty for the next several weeks, too. Sara is taking me to that theme park, Dollywood, for my birthday in April."

"You haven't been to Dollywood?"

She shook her head.

"Well, you're in for a treat. What day are you planning to go?"

"Thursday, April fifteenth—that's my birthday. Sara said that was a good weekday to go, too, and the international festival is going on at that time. She thinks I'll like the shows and exhibits that are a part of that event. Both of us arranged our work schedules so we could be off."

"Maybe Mackie and I can tag along, make it a foursome and take you girls out to dinner afterwards—help you celebrate. I think we could both plan to get away, too, that Thursday, and from how Mackie and Sara seemed to hit it off, I think they wouldn't mind a day together at Dollywood."

Emily considered this as Cooper led her into the house. "Well, you'll need to ask Sara to see if it's okay, but it sounds like fun to me."

She put her gift bag on the floor beside the large coffee table, already covered with boxes and bags for Buddy and Lisa Marie. Cooper introduced her to friends gathered around visiting in the living room and then he led her into the kitchen to meet Buddy and Lisa Marie and more guests whose acquaintance she'd hadn't made yet.

By the time the gift opening and the dinner were finished later, at least a hundred friends and work colleagues had shown up at the party. They sat or stood around in different areas of the house now, as well as outdoors around the pavilion and fire pit. Cooper had lost track of who'd come, although Lisa Marie's mother, Evelyn, had provided a guest book for everyone to sign as a keepsake for the couple.

Although Emily had wanted Sara to come, in order to have someone to talk to, Mackie had skillfully snagged Sara for himself for the evening, and she seemed to have no complaint. The two seemed a little taken with each other from what Cooper could tell, and as they all shared dinner together at an outdoor picnic table, Mackie and Sara readily agreed to make the trip to Dollywood a foursome day.

After dinner, Mackie and Sara took off down a woods trail behind the house to supposedly look at the full moon better from an open ridge top. Cooper watched the two walk away with a little envy. As the host, he really needed to stay around closer to the house.

"They sure seem to be getting along well," Cooper commented.

Emily propped her elbows on the table. "It's been a fantastic party, Cooper. And I've loved meeting everyone—the men you work with, Bettie Chase's and Leona's husbands, Leroy's wife, Radonna, who works at the other Garrison office. She is so funny! I really like her, and I like Delbert and his wife, Dottie, too. They told me a lot of stories about when you and Lance and their sons Mackie and Fleenor were kids playing together."

Cooper frowned over the mention of Lance's name.

Emily put a hand on his arm. "I didn't mean to bring up a subject you didn't want to think about."

He rubbed his neck. "No, I'm doing better about it. It's okay." His eyes moved across the yard to where Venetta sat on the edge of a hay bale talking to Rafe, Buddy, Lisa Marie, and some other young friends.

"You were nice to Venetta when she came," Emily commented.

"It was awkward, though." His eyes rested on Venetta, dressed in tight patterned slacks and a dressy top, along with her familiar black jacket and boots. He'd heard her motorcycle pull up earlier. He thought perhaps the roar of a motorcycle would always be a sound he hated.

"She almost cried when she hugged you and thanked you for letting her come tonight."

He scowled, remembering it had been hard to receive that hug. Venetta's love for bikes had kept Lance riding the road more with those dang machines after he met her. It was hard to forget that, despite trying to forgive and forget. And now she had Rafe riding with her. He hated that thought, even though he knew a lot of people loved motorcycles.

As friends stopped by to chat, Buddy, Johnny Wade, and their two friends set up their equipment and started to perform at the end of the pavilion. The sounds of their music soon filtered out across the night with a mix of country twang, bluegrass, and contemporary songs. Couples began to migrate onto the dance floor as darkness fell in the woods around them. Cooper noticed Mackie leading Sara out onto the pavilion floor as the band began a slow, sweet number by Kenny Chesney, "Me and You," which was one of Cooper's favorites.

He stood and held out a hand to Emily. "Want to dance?"

She nodded, and he soon swept her into his arms, noticing that she followed his lead waltzing as smoothly as she kept up with his jitterbug steps.

"Did you learn to waltz in dance classes, too?"

"Yes, and it was a necessity with all the events Hal and Mary hosted and that I needed to attend with them over the years." She smiled up at him. "Did you learn from your parents like you did the jitterbug?"

"I did." He pulled her closer, enjoying the feel of her and the words of the song drifting out over the night. It did seem, as the words to Chesney's song conveyed, that every day he seemed to need Emily more, thought about her more. He enjoyed having a girlfriend again, yet he still wasn't sure how far he wanted this relationship to go.

The sweet number ended, and Cooper allowed Monty Russo a dance with Emily while he headed into the kitchen to check on drinks, ice, and food. Finding all well, he made his way back outside, stopping to talk to friends along the way.

Reaching the pavilion once more, he saw Buddy give him a high sign as the band moved into one of the jitterbug numbers he'd requested. The song was an old Buddy Holly tune he and his mother both liked, "That'll Be the Day."

Cooper found Emily and soon had her jitterbug dancing around the pavilion with him, drawing a little attention to them as her red skirts swirled and her Wizard of Oz shoes frisked across the dance floor. "You are very, very good, Miz Lamont," he said, passing her behind his back in an artful twirl.

She laughed, obviously enjoying herself. "So are you! And I haven't gotten a chance to dance like this for years."

"All work and no play?" He spun her under one arm.

"That's about it." She followed him in a couple of quick two-steps and rock steps before he twirled her under his arm again.

Cooper slowed their pace a little then, while still enjoying the fun, watching Emily's light feet tap out the rhythm of the dance and her smile light up the night.

He glanced across the dance floor and noticed his mother dancing with someone he didn't know. One of Lisa Marie's relatives, maybe? He was glad she'd found someone to jitterbug with.

"Do you know the man my mother is dancing with?" he asked Emily.

Her eyes located his mother across the floor—smiling at her partner.

"No." She looked up at him. "But there are so many people here—more I don't know than that I do." She laughed. "Do you know everyone here?"

"Most everyone." His eyes followed his mother, noticing the way she laughed and talked with her partner. They didn't seem strangers.

Moving off the dance floor a short time later, Cooper passed Bettie Chase heading back to her table with a cold drink. "Who's the man with my mother?" he asked, knowing that if anyone knew the man, it would be Bettie.

She paused to glance towards his mother, sitting on a hay bale with her partner now, talking and resting after the dance number.

"Oh, honey, that's Wade Grayling. He owns that little outdoor shop on the Parkway, Grayling's Garden Gifts, I think it's called. He's sure sweet on your mother, and they've been seeing a lot of each other—lunches, movie dates, and dinners together. It's nice to see your mother opening herself up to care about someone again. I might say the same about you." She glanced pointedly towards Emily, who stood talking to Mackie and Sara.

Cooper made some appropriate comment in response. He couldn't even remember what, his eyes moving to study his mother and the man as soon as Bettie walked away. Did his mother care for this man? It upset him to think so. He didn't want anyone taking advantage of her, possibly hurting her. Hadn't she been through enough, losing both his dad and Lance? And what did he know about this Wade Grayling, anyway? Nothing except what Bettie just told him.

He leaned against a pavilion post, watching this new stranger with his mother. Short, not tall as his father had been. Balding, with glasses, a little rounded in physique, not strong-shouldered and square-chinned liked his dad. Not handsome either. He looked more smart than solid. Not a man for work clothes and calluses, he'd guess.

As if sensing his eyes on them, his mother looked up and caught his gaze. She waved him over, and Cooper had no recourse but to comply.

"Cooper, dear, this is my friend, Wade Grayling," she said, making the introduction. "And Wade, this is my son. I don't think you two have met."

She smiled from one to the other.

Cooper took the man's hand, noticing a firm grip if not a strong one.

"Wade owns that marvelous garden shop on the Parkway with the cute green shutters and all the wonderful garden statuary. You know—the one with birdbaths, birdfeeders, and garden signs in the store." She smiled at Wade. "He's an avid bird watcher, too—can name every bird by sound. It simply amazes me. And Wade builds many of the birdhouses he sells in the store. You two have something in common there."

Cooper tried to force himself to smile. Birdhouses? He'd built birdhouses as a dang kid learning to work with a hammer and nails.

"I'm pleased to meet you," Wade offered in a cultured voice with a touch of Low-Country Southern drawl. "Mamie talks about you all the time, and she's driven me by some of the homes you've built. Your business does fine work."

Cooper couldn't think what to say.

Unaffected by his lack of response, Wade continued on. "It shows a tremendous strength of character for a boy as young as you, that you took on a large construction business to run alone when your brother died. Your mother is real proud of you for the job you've done."

A new tune from the band caught Wade Grayling's attention. "Oh, that's a favorite song of ours, Mamie." He turned to Cooper. "I hope you don't mind if I take your mother for another spin across the floor. It's been a treat finding a dance partner as good as your mother is. I used to teach dance years ago with an Arthur Murray studio. I think your mother is as good as any student I ever taught."

They whirled off onto the pavilion into a swing waltz before Cooper had time to offer another comment.

Seething, he went over to join Emily, Mackie, and Sara.

"Who's the dude with your mom?" Mackie asked.

Cooper scowled as his eyes followed them dancing smoothly across the pavilion, creating a small show among the other amateurs shuffling around on the concrete. "Some garden-shop owner who's taken up with my mom." He kicked at a hay bale in annoyance. "He's moved in on her without me knowing anything about it either. She was telling me, all wide-eyed, that we had a lot in common because the guy builds birdhouses. Geeze. What is it with all these people coming into my life that build miniature houses for birds and dolls?"

Hearing a gasp, he looked over to see both Emily and Sara crossing their arms in irritation.

"I think that was a little rude, Cooper Garrison," Sara snapped out the words, quicker than Emily could vent her hurts. She grabbed Emily's arm. "And I'm taking Emily into the kitchen to find something to drink while you get a grip on yourself and think up an apology to offer to us both. If you'll think about it a minute, you'll remember that Emily makes dollhouses and I sell dollhouses and dolls."

Mackie rolled his eyes as they walked away. "Thanks a lot, Coop. What the heck were you thinking, blurting out something dumb like that? You idiot. Couldn't you figure out that would make them mad?"

Cooper glanced towards the girls heading into the back door. "I wasn't thinking. I was upset about this Wade Grayling guy."

"Why?" Mackie glanced towards Wade and Cooper's mother on the dance floor. "Dad and Mom know Wade. They say he's a nice guy. Moved up here from some little town down on the Carolina coast—Beaufort, I think. He has a successful business, does volunteer work with the parks department, and works in various community groups. I haven't heard a dang thing bad about him."

He studied Cooper's angry face. "I think what's really got you so upset is the idea of your mom seeing someone. Anyone. That doesn't make sense, Cooper. Think how long your dad's been gone."

"That's not what's upsetting me." Cooper denied Mackie's words even though he knew he hated the idea of even thinking of his mother paired with anyone but his dad. They'd been so close, so perfect for each other.

"Well, I can't think what else it is."

Cooper stiffened. "I didn't even know she was seeing this guy until they sprang it on me tonight. Bettie told me they were dating even before Mom did."

Mackie shoved at him. "Aw, Bettie Chase knows what color your pee is before you get to the toilet. You know that." He glanced towards the dance pavilion again as the couples began to leave the floor. "Maybe your mom waited to tell you because she wanted a little time to see how things went with this Wade guy first. You've done the same. You haven't talked to your mom about Emily."

"That's not the same."

"Yeah, it is. And I think you're making too much of this and getting upset about nothing." He sat on the top of one of the picnic tables. "Your mom has a right to date the same as you, and she has a right to keep how she feels about someone to herself if she wants to. She's not obligated to tell you every little thought she has."

"I don't like this conversation."

"Not surprised." Mackie shook his head.

Cooper paced a little along the grass near his friend, trying to calm his thoughts and sort out what he'd seen and heard.

Mackie watched him for a minute and then stood up. "Well, I'm going after the girls to see if I can smooth things out with them. Try to offer some apologies for why you were such a jerk just now. When you get your act straightened out and that surly mood cooled off, you need to do a little apologizing on your own."

He walked closer to Cooper. "You can mess up your own love life all you want, buddy, but watch messing up mine. I really like Sara. I mean, I really like her. I don't think I've ever felt about any woman the way I do about Sara."

"You just met her tonight." Cooper scowled.

"Yeah, I know." He looked towards the house again. "But somehow you just get a sense. I think she may be the one. Dad always said he knew the first time he saw Mom."

Cooper looked at his friend, stunned. "Are you crazy?"

Mackie punched at him. "No, but you are. At least I know what I feel and I can acknowledge it, while you run and hide from your feelings. I've watched you and Emily together tonight. I can tell you have strong feelings about her."

"Listen, just because I like Emily doesn't mean I have to start thinking about roses and wedding rings. I think you've gotten too caught up in all this wedding business of Buddy and Lisa Marie's tonight. You need to put a brake on your thoughts about Sara. Again, let me mention that you just met the girl. You need to be careful and slow about commitments." He looked towards the house as Mackie started away from him. "I like my life as it is, Mackie. I'm not eager to be changing it."

"Suit yourself, Cooper, but you start working up a decent apology for those girls." He turned to look back at him. "And if you scowled and acted like a jerk meeting your mother's friend, you might owe them an apology, too."

Mackie kicked at a pinecone on the ground before continuing. "I sure wish you'd learn to think before you put your mouth in gear. I thought lately you were starting to act like a right decent human being again."

"And what does that mean?"

"As if you need to ask." Mackie walked off.

CHAPTER 15

April moved in with a cold snap and some rainy days, but then turned warm and sunny again. Emily felt more comfortable with her new life in Gatlinburg every day. Life had moved on for the good past all the heartaches of January.

"We're beginning to see the spring tourist traffic pick up now," Leona said to her in the gallery one morning.

Emily looked up from straightening the prints in the bins across from the register where Leona had just rung up a string of sales. "Yes, the warm weather seems to have brought people out."

"You just wait." Leona sorted through a stack of mail while she talked. "Spring breaks are coming plus Easter vacation. And the wildflowers in bloom will draw visitors in, too—hikers and photographers especially."

Emily studied a wildflower print of a white trillium. "I love the trillium in bloom now and there are so many colors and varieties in the Smokies. I've hiked a couple of trails to see the flowers when I could."

Leona ran a hand through her short boyish haircut. "You've settled in well here, and Mamie, Monty, and I are all fond of you."

"That's the truth for sure," Mamie said, coming around the corner from her office as Leona stated these words. She walked over to give Emily a hug. "It was a lucky day for all of us when you inherited this gallery."

"You two still going to lunch today?" Leona asked.

"We are." Mamie picked up one of the catalogs that had come

in the mail to study it. "The two of us are overdue for a sit-down talk about a number of things. Can you cover until we get back?"

"No problem," Leona assured her.

Emily smiled. "I ordered egg-salad sandwiches from Bolingers. I know you like them, Mamie, and if it's all right, I thought we'd take them down to eat at the picnic table in the little pavilion by the creek. It seems too beautiful today not to be outside."

"Spoken like a Yankee who's recently moved south." Leona laughed.

Emily put her hand over her heart. "I admit I am still enraptured with the glorious weather here in Tennessee. Philadelphia is warming now, but they got a spitzy snow yesterday and temperatures in Philly are only in the forties today."

"Who is Leonard Newman?" Leona interrupted. "Is he the nephew who inherited the gallery in Philadelphia?"

"Yes, why?" Emily asked.

Leona looked at her over the top of her glasses perched on her nose. "Because he called here yesterday asking for you. He sounded upset and I'd be less than honest if I didn't tell you he warned me off about you."

Emily knew her mouth dropped open. "Oh, Leona, I'm sorry about that."

She waved a hand. "I paid no attention. Don't worry. But I thought you ought to know he called." She rolled her eyes. "From his angry and resentful accusations, I'd say it's a blessing you're not up there still working for him."

"He's called when I've been here, too," Mamie admitted. "He tried to plant some ugly thoughts with me, as well, but I had my own strong words to say back to him, I'll tell you. How dare he call your gallery here and try to cause trouble between you and your employees!"

Emily winced. "That's Leonard, I'm afraid."

"Has he been calling and harassing you?" Mamie asked.

"Yes, but I changed my cell phone number and my e-mail so he couldn't readily reach me anymore. I guess that's why he's started calling the gallery. I'm really sorry. I don't know what to do about it."

"Well, he sounds like a small, vicious man—and very unprofessional."

Leona tapped a nail on the counter. "I'll make it clear to him if there are any further calls that he's not to call the gallery again. And I'll put the same word in Monty's ear. Just because he's making a mess of the Newman Gallery in Philadelphia doesn't mean he can cause trouble down here, too."

"You don't think he'd come down here, do you?" Mamie asked.

"I can't imagine why," Emily replied. "Despite what Leonard thinks, I no longer have any influence with the gallery or its clients. I've kept friendships with a few staff there, of course, and I give references for employees when they ask. But that's all."

"Petty, small people like that seldom realize the problems they create in their own lives are usually their own fault. They like to blame others. I've seen that a lot in the academic field where I work, too." Leona caught Emily's eye. "You be careful about that Leonard Newman, you hear? Some of those egoistic types can become dangerous."

"I hate to think that might be true," Mamie added, "but if he should ever show up here, you call the police. We keep their number right by the phone just in case we have trouble with shoplifting or store theft."

"Have you ever had trouble with theft?" Emily asked.

"Rarely, except for a few minor incidents through the years. Gatlinburg, by and large, is a safe little town." Mamie glanced at the wall clock. "Let's run on to lunch now. I need to get back for a client appointment later."

As Emily and Mamie opened the door to Bolingers a few minutes later, Emily's eyes moved to the bulletin board to see what proverb or saying Arnold and Floyd had put up for the day.

She read it out loud. *"An apple pie without some cheese is like a kiss without a squeeze."* Emily laughed at the words. "I always love to see what Arnold and Floyd come up with for the board."

"Me too," Mamie said.

"Apple pie with cheese is the specialty of the house today," Arnold piped in, hearing them. "You'll both need to have a piece."

"Well, warm up two slices to go with those egg-salad sandwiches Emily ordered." Mamie sent Arnold a smile. "And put in some of those wonderful homemade potato chips you make, too."

"Will do." Arnold busied himself at the counter.

"How are both of you beautiful ladies today?" Floyd asked, always the flirt of the two.

"Just fine, Floyd. And it looks like business is good for you." Emily glanced around at the tables, all full at the lunch hour.

"This spring weather is bringing the tourist traffic in. Can't complain. Can't complain." Floyd packed their lunch order into a white take-out box as he talked.

"I made peach tea today," he added. "Can I fix you two orders of that to go with your lunch?"

Mamie nodded. "Yes, that sounds wonderful. And this lunch order is on me today. Don't let Emily argue about it. She paid last time." She took out her purse to count out the money needed.

Emily knew better than to argue, so she picked up the box from the counter, tucking in a few extra napkins.

Heading out the door and around the building, the two women followed a winding pathway down to the creek. Emily couldn't help stopping along the way to notice all the flowers and shrubs bursting into bloom.

"It's pretty here in spring, isn't it?" Mamie asked, following her. "With May coming up, our clients and friends around the area will be looking forward to our open house on the first of May, when we change the exhibit out. They're already excited about the Grandma Moses show coming to replace our Rockwell show."

They turned to follow a side path to a rustic covered pavilion that sat by the Little Pigeon River. Under the wood pavilion sat a scattering of outdoor chairs and an old picnic table. Emily dropped the take-out box on the table while Mamie pulled out their glasses of tea from a white bag.

"I snagged a couple of paper towels we could use like placemats to put our food on." Mamie swept off a little debris from the table before laying them out.

"I love this spot," Emily said, looking around with pleasure at the fresh spring green of the trees shading the creekside, the wildflowers rioting along the creek banks, and the foamy white of the cascades swirling over and around the big rocks in the stream.

They settled down at the table, opening their drinks and getting out their sandwiches, pickles, and Floyd's homemade potato chips. "I still remember when my husband, Price, made this table for me so I could picnic along the stream here."

She heaved a little sigh.

"Do you still miss him?" Emily asked.

"I'll always miss him. He was the love of my life."

Emily thought of Wade Grayling, whom she knew Mamie was still dating. "Do you think a person can love more than once in their life?"

"Of course. But no love is ever quite like another." She smiled at Emily. "You're thinking of Wade, aren't you?"

Emily glanced away.

"Wade is a very nice, very kind and thoughtful man. I've been a little surprised to find a touch of love, affection, and joy again at my age." She frowned. "Of course, Cooper isn't handling it well. I suppose you've seen some of his reactions, like at his party last month."

Emily wasn't sure what to say.

"I know he was annoyed to learn about Wade and he acted rude to both you and Sara while wallowing in his irritation." She shook her head. "I want you to know Cooper used to be much more carefree and happy. Losing his father so young hurt him, but losing Lance later turned him a little bitter. We've had some talks lately, the two of us. I know he's doing better and that Delbert helped him with some good counsel. I also know that you and he are attending an evening Bible study class at the church with Perry. I can't tell you how pleased I am about that. How is the class going?"

"Very well." Emily finished another bit of sandwich before adding more. "I was surprised when Cooper invited me to go to the class with him. We'd talked about getting Perry to recommend a devotional for us, but when Cooper talked with Perry later, he suggested this class he'd just started. Perry's using a study book called *Developing a Closer Walk with God* by Vincent Westbrook."

"Vincent Westbrook used to pastor a church over in Townsend. Still comes back to visit often since his mother-in-law runs a bed-and-breakfast there called the Mimosa Inn. I've read some of his Bible study guides. They are excellent."

"Yes. Cooper and I have been collecting those and sharing them, too."

Mamie's eyes met Emily's. "So I assume Cooper came and apologized to you for that rude remark about building dollhouses?"

Emily felt herself blushing. "Yes."

"You don't need to be embarrassed with me about caring for my son, Emily. I've been hoping for more years than I can recall that he could change and get past being so angry and bitter about Lance's death, that he could begin to enjoy life more fully again, date, and find happiness with someone." She reached a hand across to Emily. "My dear girl, surely you know how fond I am of you and how happy I am that you and Cooper are spending time together."

"Thank you, Mamie. I worried from the first, when Cooper and I were attracted, that you might object. I didn't want our relationship to be damaged."

"Well, worry no more." Mamie dug the pieces of pie out of the box to pass one to Emily. "And I won't probe any further about your relationship. How it comes along is your own business."

Emily felt relieved at these words.

"I have to add that I'm tickled to see how head over heels Mackie Hilton is with your friend Sara Russell. They seem to have really clicked."

"Yes, they have." Ready to change the subject now, Emily said, "I need to talk with you about the paintings in the gallery exhibit I've been worried over."

Mamie nodded. "I've thought and thought about that since you first told me about them. And I have to admit I've hunted up pictures of the Rockwell paintings, checked out books from the library showing Rockwell's work, and gone into the gallery to hold those pictures I found next to the ones hanging in our exhibit."

"I've done the same thing." Emily stirred her straw in her tea. "But the most important thing is that Cawood's friend says he can see some slight differences that might bear looking into. I sent photos to Daniel Stelben, too, the longtime manager at the Newman Gallery."

"What was his response?"

"That it was hard to say for sure if there was clear evidence to warrant a fraud investigation. He also reminded me that to suggest such a thing can create difficult feelings with the exhibition services a gallery uses, the transportation and installation services, and the insurance companies."

"I considered that, too." Mamie finished her last bite of pie and looked out over the creek thoughtfully. "If there is fraud, how in the world do you think it is occurring? I've checked our security several times. I even had Cawood come and give his opinion of that. We can't see how anyone could be getting into our gallery to make a painting exchange."

"Neither can I," Emily said. "But I don't think this is something we can ignore, and I'm still trying to decide if we should alert the exhibition service to the fact that we suspect there could be a problem. Then it would be up to them to look into it, to examine the paintings in question when they are returned."

"Hmmm, I think that sounds like the best idea." Mamie sat forward. "If we do nothing and fraud is discovered later, it might look like our gallery had a part in the problem. However, if we diplomatically suggest we have suspicions and also provide the names of those experts who examined the works and gave their input, then it will look like we were conscientious in relation to the exhibit and tried to properly alert them to a potential problem."

"You told me that another time or two in the past you, too, suspected there might be a problem."

Mamie tapped her chin thoughtfully. "Well, I'm not the expert you are, but I had an odd sense about a work or two in a few past exhibits. Never many, you know, just the occasional odd painting sometimes. I regret now I never followed up on my suspicions." She shrugged. "But of course they could have been nothing."

"Fraudulent art is very hard to detect. Those who deal in fraud with works of this stature are incredibly competent in creating replacements only experts can detect differences in. Fraud detection specialists use tests to gauge the age of materials versus relying on the eye alone."

Mamie smiled. "Well, we could come out the hero of the day if we help reveal some aspect of fraud going on."

"Or we could create ill will for our gallery by suggesting such a thing."

They sat considering this for a few moments.

"How do you plan to handle this, Emily?"

"I think I will alert Randy Lawson that I plan to report our supposition when he comes later this month to change out the exhibit. I'm sure his company will share our concerns, if there has been some tampering with the works being loaned out to galleries. After all, we attain our exhibits through Delamar and they are very cautious about security. I already mentioned briefly to Randy that I had some reservations, so he won't be too surprised that we looked into the issue further. He might have done some checking himself already since we last talked."

"Randy's such a personable young man, always so friendly and talkative."

"Yes." She giggled. "But let me tell you about a funny incident that happened when Cawood stopped by the gallery one day when Randy was here." Emily told Mamie about Randy's meeting with Cawood, making her laugh.

"Gracious, Cawood can be so intimidating," Mamie said.

Emily packed up their lunch papers into the box to take back to the trash. "What does Cawood think about you dating Wade Grayling? Or does he know?"

"Oh, he knows. We ran into him at the Peddler one night when we were having dinner. He came over and ate with us. He gave Wade the third degree, of course. He's so protective of me."

"Not jealous?"

"No." She waved a hand. "He's just fond of me, like Monty might be, wanting me to be happy, not wanting me to be hurt."

"I like Monty. And Leona. We have good staff at the Creekside."

"We do, and I hope they will stay with us for a long time." She stood and looked at her watch. "I need to head back for my appointment with Nathan and Iris Jeffries. Cooper is building a home for them on the mountain and they want to look at paintings for when the house is completed. It could be a big order, so I want to be on time."

They started back up the path to the gallery.

"You're off this afternoon, Emily. What do you plan to do?"

"I'm going to work on finishing the new dollhouse that I've nearly completed now. I need to ship it out next month."

Mamie paused, turning to look at Emily. "Child, I've just been stunned at what beautiful, intricate work you do on those houses. I'm sure Hal and Mary must have been so proud to see the detailed, creative work you put into each dollhouse you make."

Emily glanced over to a bird feeder off the path where a red cardinal perched. "Actually, Hal and Mary never saw any of the houses I made. They didn't encourage that effort and I didn't start making dollhouses until after I moved out on my own."

Seeing Mamie's surprise, she added, "My parents were the ones I learned about dollhouses from. They would have been thrilled to see me carrying on that art. They loved building miniature dollhouses and they did such incredible work. I still have old pictures of many of their finished houses in a scrapbook I kept from the days when they owned their store."

Mamie's eyes moved to the cardinal, too. "You know, I wonder sometimes what gifts I might have received from my parents, what interests I have that might have come from them, what looks I share with them, what little quirks of personality—what inheritances I carry from them, small or large."

"Have you never looked into it?" Emily asked.

"Oh, yes, a little." Mamie crossed her arms. "I volunteer over at the orphanage in Sevierville where I grew up. The records tell me some about my mother and her family. I know her name, when she died, where she came from. Her family has never come asking questions about me, so I've never felt I wanted to go seeking them out. And I know nothing at all about the man who fathered me. Someone passing through the area was all that was written down. No name. So of course I just know my mother's last name, Simons."

Emily put a hand on her arm. "I'm sorry you know so little about your family. That must be sad."

Mamie smiled. "Perhaps that is one of those questions I'll ask in heaven one day." She laughed. "I used to make a list as a girl of 'Things I'll Ask God One Day.' That was definitely on my list."

Emily linked her arm in Mamie's. "Well, you have loving family and friends in the here and now, that's for sure, Mamie Garrison. And I'm right at the top of the list."

"Well, aren't you sweet?" Mamie laughed as they made their way back to the Creekside.

CHAPTER 16

Cooper worked with Mackie today on a renovation project for one of their old clients to make a screened porch out of an open back porch on their house.

"I can see why he wanted to screen this big porch in," Mackie said. "Being up in this remote area, I imagine the mosquitoes and bugs are a pill. Anytime you wanted to be out here in the evening, the lights would draw insects."

Rolls of four-foot screen lay scattered around on the porch. Cooper and Mackie had already attached screen to the bottom section of the porch railing all around, pulling it taut and stapling it, and then covering it with three-quarter-inch strips of wood to hide the staples.

Cooper studied the upper area of the porch still remaining. "Screening the bottom of the porch behind the rails went easily, but we need to think how to screen this large open area above the rails all around."

"Hmmm." Mackie straightened the tool belt around his waist. "These areas are too wide and open just to put up screen alone. How about if we build some frames to tuck in? We can add a post or two for support, measure and build the frames, and then screen each frame first before putting it into place."

"That's the best idea, for sure." Cooper took out a builder's tape measure from his tool belt and stretched the metal blade along the deck rail to start getting the measurements needed. "Once we build the frames and attach the screens, we can tuck each into place and screw them in to secure them."

The two men took their measurements, put up the needed center posts, and then went down into the yard where their saw was set up to cut the two-by-fours for the frames. They worked in companionable silence, talking a little about the job as they built the frames, stapled the screen on them, trimmed out their work, and then put the completed frames into place.

"Dang, this looks good," Mackie said with pleasure as the two surveyed the finished job later. He glanced towards the cooler pushed into the corner of the porch. "I could use one of those colas in your cooler about now."

"Me too." Cooper glanced at his watch. "And we're overdue for lunch, too."

"You're right there. I heard my stomach complaining about an hour ago." Mackie pulled over a metal porch table and a couple of chairs they'd pushed back against the wall to make more work space on the porch. "Did you pick up something at Bolinger's?"

"Yeah, I picked up a couple of hoagies earlier and told Arnold to pile on several kinds of meats and cheeses."

Mackie dug into the bag Cooper dropped on the table. "Everything looks great. Nothing like a good morning's work to whip up your appetite." He divvied up the sandwiches, bags of chips, pickles, and cookies from the sack.

They wolfed down some of their food and guzzled half their colas before either spoke again.

"I like the property this house sits on," Mackie commented after they'd started in on the Bolingers' cookie special of the day. "There's a nice high plot similar to this on Dad's farmland that I'm thinking of starting a house on for myself." He looked around. "I'd like a nice screen porch on my house like this one, too."

"I thought you were pretty comfortable with that apartment you created over your mom and dad's big double garage."

Mackie finished off a cookie before answering. "It's a good place but not the sort of place a guy would want to settle into if he married and started a family."

Cooper raised an eyebrow. "Is that so?"

"No need to give me that look, Coop." Mackie ran a hand through his hair. "You've got a big place, and you always said Garrison would help me build one, too, when I was ready for it."

"So now you're suddenly ready when two months ago you said you didn't want the upkeep of a house on your plate."

Mackie got up to get another cold drink from the cooler.

"Does this sudden interest in building a house have anything to do with Sara Russell?"

Mackie dropped back into his chair, popping the top on the cola. "Get off my case, Cooper. Even Dad was sharp enough to figure that out. I'm sure you can add two and two as well."

"Are you getting that serious about this girl already?"

He nodded. "I am. But don't say anything about it tomorrow when we're all at Dollywood together. We're not engaged or committed or anything yet."

"I hear you." Cooper dug into the lunch sack for another cookie. "What about that guy Sara's been seeing? Is she still dating him, too?"

"No, and it caused a little stink in her family when she called off that relationship." Mackie grinned at Cooper. "But her mom and sister are coming around since they've gotten to know me, and since Sara, Natalie, and her mom spent some time with my folks and my family."

"When was this big social event?"

"I invited all her family over for Fleenor's birthday a week or so ago. Seemed like a good time to get the families together—when Dad and I were grilling out and Mom was making cake and everything."

"I'm glad everyone's getting on so well, but I still think all this is going pretty fast."

Mackie propped a boot on a pile of screen rolls left over from the job. "When you know you know, Cooper."

They went back to work then, putting the finishing touches on their job, cleaning up the site. Cooper kept thinking about Mackie's words as they loaded up the truck. He thought about Emily. He liked her, for sure, but he didn't have the kind of knowing Mackie did about Sara. Did that mean he needed to back off from the relationship? Did it mean that if a sure knowing wasn't there now, it would never come? That Emily was simply someone to date, to enjoy being with?

These thoughts still rumbled around in Cooper's mind the next day as the two couples spent the day enjoying Dollywood. The one hundred fifty-acre theme park kept growing every year, it seemed. Cooper had first visited the place as a kid when it was called Silver Dollar City and then watched it change hands and grow as he did. He'd read somewhere that over two million people visited every year now, with the park adding new rides and attractions every season.

It was obvious from watching Mackie and Sara together that they were smitten, as his dad might have said. It almost made Cooper uncomfortable being with them, watching the looks they exchanged, the times they found to touch and make contact with each together, the ease and natural warmth in their relationship. Emily felt the difference in them, too. Cooper could tell.

As they rode the big Ferris wheel in the Country Fair section of the park, Cooper could hear Mackie and Sara giggling in the seat behind his and Emily's.

"I guess Sara's decided Giles Sutherland isn't the one for her," Cooper said.

"Yes." Emily glanced behind her, smiling. "Sara apparently has found the zing she's been looking for with Mackie. She said she was really grateful I invited her to your party that Saturday night."

"They'd have probably run into each other eventually, I guess."

"So you think it's destined?" Emily asked. "That we'll meet the one we're meant to meet?"

"I don't know." He scowled. "That sounds like the sort of thing you see in movies. Most relationships build along gradually, I think. It takes time for people to know their feelings." He wanted that to be true.

"Perhaps." She leaned forward to look around at the park below.

"Have you been enjoying your birthday at Dollywood?" he asked.

"Oh, yes." She turned her sunny smile towards him. "It's an incredible place and I especially love the flowers and landscaping throughout the park. It makes it so beautiful. And everyone is so friendly." She giggled. "I love how people call out 'howdy' to the passengers on the train when they go by. That's so cute."

The Ferris wheel slowed as it began to dislodge passengers. Emily pulled out her park map to study it. "I think we've been on almost every ride now." She pointed to different ones marked on the colorful map, commenting on them. "And we've gotten to see three of the big shows in the international festival." She turned bright eyes towards his again. "Didn't you love the Russian show with all the colorful costumes and the men doing that energetic dance squatting down? What is that called? I can't remember."

"Cossack dancing." Cooper grinned. "I liked that, too. That was a great show."

"Cossack dancing. That's the name I was trying to remember." She laughed, stepping out of the Ferris wheel seat as they reached the loading and unloading platform. Mackie and Sara greeted them as they walked down the ramp.

"Wasn't that fun?" Sara exclaimed. "I haven't ridden a Ferris wheel in years." She looked down at her show schedule. "Come on. If we hurry we can jet up the hill to see Dolly Parton's *Heartsong* show. It starts in ten minutes. You'll love that, Emily. It's got sweeping views of the mountains, homespun scenes, and Dolly singing. It's a treat to see."

Mackie tucked Sara's hand into his as they started up the hill to the theater. Cooper started to take Emily's hand, but then hesitated. If Mackie and Sara became engaged soon, would Emily expect the same with him? Was he leading her to expect more with neither of them dating anyone else?

Cooper watched the spontaneous warmth between the couple in front of them. Did he yearn for Emily to be more spontaneous and more affectionate with him? No. Not really. He almost shook his head thinking about it. He'd purposely kept a little distance between them. He knew he'd been careful in public to appear friendly but not overly so. To be sure no one got the wrong idea or assumed more than friendship between them.

He wasn't ready to commit to more than friendship with Emily, and he didn't want people to assume their relationship had moved past dating and friendship either. Did Emily feel more? He turned to look at her, wondering.

"What?" she asked, seeming to sense his thoughts.

"Are you okay to go to this show?" he asked, avoiding any personal discussion. "Sara didn't exactly ask if you wanted to go."

"Of course I want to go. I want to do everything we have time for." She tucked her arm in his, hugging it to her. "This has been such a great day. Thanks so much for suggesting that you and Mackie come with us. I know I'll always remember sharing my first trip to Dollywood with all of you."

Reaching the top of the hill, they walked by the train depot and a row of shops and then past the carousel to the theater. Deciding to put his concerns aside for a while, Cooper settled in to enjoy the rest of the day. It wasn't every day he and Mackie could get away from work on a Friday to play like this.

"I want to ride the wooden roller coaster next," Cooper said as he and Emily fell into step beside Mackie and Sara. "We missed it coming in."

"Tops on my list, too," Mackie said, turning to grin at him.

The foursome felt happily worn out by the time they rode the tram back to Mackie's SUV in the parking lot at about seven that evening. Although they'd snacked around the park and shared a funnel cake in the afternoon, they were all hungry after an eight-hour day at the park.

"Emily, Mackie and I decided we'd take you to the Gondolier Italian Restaurant in Sevierville for dinner before we head back to Gatlinburg. It has great Italian and Greek menu offerings and good service. I think you and Sara will like it." Cooper opened the back door of Mackie' SUV to help Emily inside.

"They make fantastic multilayered homemade cakes, too," Mackie put in. "We'll get a big piece and put a birthday candle on it for you."

"I don't need anything special after such a fantastic day," Emily replied. "And I'm so excited you talked me into turning in my ticket for a season pass today, Sara. That means we can come back again."

"It means we'll both come often." She laughed. "I got one, too, and we'll have to come a lot to justify the expense."

"Don't worry. There are shows and special events all year round at Dollywood. We'll all come a lot." Mackie eased the car into the line of vehicles heading out of the park. "You'll love the lights at Christmas, too. Dollywood strings lights over all the buildings and the trees. It's great to see once dark falls."

The conversation continued, light and fun, throughout their dinner out together. Mackie, Sara, and Copper had bought fun gifts for Emily at Dollywood—homemade taffy, a garden flag to hang from her outside porch, a Dolly Parton CD, and a Dollywood T-shirt. Because she'd admired it so much, Cooper also bought her an umbrella covered in butterflies.

Mackie dropped Cooper off later with Emily at the Creekside Gallery. Cooper had driven down from his home earlier, so Mackie could pick them both up at Emily's place. After good-byes and more end-of-evening chatter, Cooper walked Emily upstairs to her apartment.

She hesitated at the door. "Do you want to come in for coffee? I can make some in just a few minutes."

"Yeah. That would be nice."

While Emily made coffee, Cooper greeted Mercedes and took her for a quick walk outside. Coming back in the apartment, he noticed an unwrapped gift or two on Emily's coffee table. While Mercedes headed into the kitchen, hoping for a snack, Cooper picked up a book about building dollhouses amid some colorful giftwrap and sat down to look through it.

"That's a gift from my friend Kylie in Philadelphia," Emily said, coming back in the room with their coffee, Mercedes padding along behind her. She sat beside him on the sofa.

"The other gift is from my friend Azea." Emily pointed to a cardboard box amid the birthday paper. "Kylie, Azea, and I have been friends since school years and still stay in touch." She opened the box so Cooper could see inside it. "Look what she sent me."

Cooper lifted a brow in question. It appeared to be a set of small dolls.

Emily flashed that sweet smile of hers. "This is an Edwardian doll family. Azea said I should build a house for them." She lifted them out of the box. "She even named the couple Lord and Lady Hamilton, and you can see they have two girls, a boy, and a baby, plus this lovely English governess." She took the dollhouse book from him and opened it to a page she'd marked. "I think I might create an Edwardian dollhouse like this for them. Sara has been wanting me to build one they can put in the store. Perhaps this will be it."

"Do you build from a kit or from scratch?"

"I can do either." She sipped her coffee. "Sort of like with your log homes, it's more economical, and certainly saves time and labor, to build from a prepackaged house. And there are still wonderful ways to add individuality with a kit. Especially if you get a good one with first-class quality and craftsmanship."

Cooper studied the intricate, two-story house in the book. "Mother mentioned that you didn't start building dollhouses until after you moved out of Hal and Mary's."

She nodded. "That's true. As I told you the day we visited the old shop in Knoxville, Hal and Mary didn't encourage my interest in dollhouse building. I think they worried I might want to get involved with it as a career, like my mother and father did, and they were concerned it wouldn't be profitable."

He drank some of his coffee and then set the cup down. "I thought you told me you make good money selling your houses."

"I do, but Hal and Mary were right that building dollhouses alone would probably not be a wise way to make a living full-time. It is a nice hobby though." She smiled, picking up the Edwardian couple again. "And I'm already excited about building a new home for Lord and Lady Hamilton. Perhaps you understand that excitement of getting ready to start a new building project."

Cooper knew he hadn't always been kind or charitable about this talent of Emily's. "Show me the house your father built for you."

"If you'd like." Her eyes lit, a smile slipping across her face again. She was so beautiful, he thought as he followed her down the hallway.

"I've put it in my guestroom," she said, opening the door. "This dollhouse is a custom one. Daddy built it as a sort of replica of the house that he knew I loved in the book *Little Women*. It's larger than the small houses I usually build and made for eight-inch character dolls." She opened the two panels of the house to reveal the interior of the large home that almost filled one side of the room. "Daddy made it to house my March family of dolls—Marmee, or Mrs. March, Jo, Meg, Beth, Amy, and Laurie Laurence. I had some wonderful play times with these dolls growing up."

"And your two friends in Philadelphia knew you made dollhouses." He remembered the presents from them.

"Yes." She closed up the house again. "When we were school friends together, they played with this house with me when they came to visit, and both encouraged me when I began to make houses of my own. I made one dollhouse for my friend Kylie's little girl. She's married already." Emily pointed to three pictures in a collage frame on the dresser. "That photo on the left is of Kylie, Azea, and me when we were girls, the photo next to it is when we graduated from high school, and the third was taken just before I moved here."

Cooper studied the girls flanking either side of Emily, one fair-skinned, short, and blond, the other African American, tall with dark hair.

"I'm glad you've had a happy birthday, Emily." Cooper followed her back into the living room. He picked up the dollhouse book again to look at it. "I could help you build the main frame of the house for this if you could draw up some plans for me."

She steepled her hands with pleasure. "Oh, Cooper, that would be wonderful. Would you?"

He studied the drawing again. "I've built some house replicas in the past to show what our log homes would look like. This shouldn't be any more a challenge than that." He smiled at her. "Besides, we'll get to work together."

"I hate to take your time. You're so busy."

"We can work on it in the evenings." He squatted to pet Mercedes, who was looking up at him expectantly, before sitting down beside Emily on the sofa.

"Okay." Emily's eyes flew to the drawing in the book. "I could work on measurements and a rough blueprint over the weekend and probably sketch out some rough plans next week."

"There's no hurry. My upcoming schedule is pretty packed working on the Jeffries home we're building and with appointments that Bettie and Radonna have set for me, plus I'm driving down for this Home Builders Association meeting in Knoxville one night." He leaned back, relaxing. "The next two weeks will be busy for you, too. You've got the exhibit change and the open house to plan for."

She tapped her chin. "It is going to be a hectic time getting ready for the open house." She twisted the bracelet on her wrist. "Will you come?"

"Sure. I wouldn't miss it." He grinned. "The hors d'oeuvres that the caterer does are fantastic."

"So I've heard from everyone."

Cooper glanced at his watch. "I need to head home, but I have another little birthday gift for you in the truck. Come walk out with me and I'll give it to you."

"Oh, you didn't need to buy me anything." Her eyes widened. "Besides, you already bought me that gorgeous umbrella. I really love it."

He started towards the door. "Humor me," he said. "I thought for a long time about something special to get you."

"Okay." She followed him. "But you really didn't have to do this.

I'll just get spoiled with all this attention. I already celebrated with you, Mackie, and Sara today, and yesterday afternoon enjoyed a pre-birthday party at the gallery with Mamie, Leona, Monty, the Bolingers, and Bettie from your office."

Coming to his truck in the parking lot, Cooper dug out a small gift bag from his glove compartment. "I hope you like this," he said, handing it to her.

Emily reached into the bag, taking out the small box inside. She gasped as she opened it. "Oh, Cooper, what a beautiful ring!" She turned it around in her hand to study it.

"I knew diamonds were your birthstone, so it has little diamonds all around the heart on the ring."

Emily slipped the ring on her finger. "Oh, look, it fits perfectly," she said, admiring it.

"Mother helped me with the size," he admitted.

Emily smiled. "I remember her commenting about one of my rings a few weeks ago and asking if she could try it on. She asked what size I wore, too."

"We conspired." He grinned. "I wanted it to fit."

"It's beautiful. I don't know what to say." She leaned up to kiss him. "Thank you so much."

A little kiss led to a deeper one, and Cooper soon spooned Emily against him, enjoying the taste and feel of her. He forgot that he'd decided to keep their relationship on a more formal footing, to back away from deeper intimacy. She was so soft and sweet and fit so perfectly in his arms.

He kissed her again and forgot the time ticking by, forgot all his good intentions, falling under her spell and enjoying being close to her.

Cooper pulled away at last to look down at her soft face, touched by the full moon overhead.

She reached up to touch his cheek. "I love you, Cooper Garrison. I'm so glad you came into my life."

Her words caught him off guard, and he felt himself stiffen to hear them.

She studied his face quietly for a few minutes. "You can't say the same to me, can you?" she whispered.

He saw tears pool in the corners of her eyes.

"I hoped you'd come to care for me strongly, too." She put a hand over her mouth, obviously upset, and stepped away from him.

"Look, Emily, I do care. You know that. But I'm not ready for more."

"Yes, I see that now. I thought for a minute with the ring . . . that maybe you had begun to feel as I do."

He frowned. "I'm sorry if my gift gave you that idea."

Cooper realized that with Mackie and Sara becoming engaged, choosing a ring for a birthday gift hadn't been the smartest idea. Why hadn't his mother thought of that and cautioned him? Women were supposed to be good at sensing things like that.

She looked down at the ring again, sighing.

Cooper felt like a heel.

"It was a lovely gift," she said at last, breaking the silence. "I had a lovely day, too. Thank you." She offered him a tight, polite smile. "And I am glad we're friends."

She turned then, the cool professionalism he often saw firmly back in place now. "Good-night. I'll go in now. It's late." She turned to walk down the sidewalk.

He watched her, feeling torn apart. He wanted to care more to make her happy, but the feelings and the words she wanted just weren't there.

CHAPTER 17

The next days moved by quickly for Emily. The weekday and weekend traffic at the gallery increased as April drew to a close. And Emily put in extra time helping Mamie prepare for the open house.

"You shouldn't worry about the open house," Mamie assured her. "We host them several times a year at the Creekside and they always run along as smooth as silk. We've used the same caterers for five years. They're wonderful, and the invitations are all out. That lovely quartet from Knoxville is coming to play again, too. Their touch of quiet, classical music makes everything very posh."

"The weather report is good for the weekend, too," Emily put in.

"Yes. Even the weather is cooperating. The forecast is for a pleasant day with no rain expected." Mamie waved a hand. "And if it rains, we'll just bring everything inside, set up the food in the mat shop, and let everyone mingle around in the shop and through to the gallery. It works beautifully."

Monty and Leona also assured Emily that the open houses at the gallery always went well. Even so, Emily sat in her office now, looking over details relating to the upcoming event, wanting everything to be perfect for Saturday night.

A tap at the window arrested her thoughts.

"What are you doing with your window wide open?" Sara asked. "And without a screen?"

"I love to listen to the stream rushing along behind the garden." She grinned at her friend through the open window. "I've been meaning to get Cooper or Mackie to put a screen on this window for me."

Sara giggled. "Well, it saved me from coming inside to get you. Can you still get away for a walk? Buster is eager to see Mercedes."

"Let me check with Monty to see if he can cover. It's just the two of us working the gallery tonight, so I can't stay long."

A few minutes later, after dashing upstairs to get Mercedes and to slip into walking shoes, Emily met Sara outside.

"Let's walk down the River Road and then cut down the Gatlinburg Trail," Sara said while Buster and Mercedes greeted each other.

"That sounds good, but I can't do the whole trail. I don't want to take advantage of Monty. The gallery can get busy around the dinner hour."

"We'll just walk to the bridge and then turn around."

The young women chatted and caught up on their news as they walked their dogs down the River Road.

"How was the Sunday lunch over at Mamie's and the Bible study night with Cooper?" Sara asked.

"Strained. I wish I hadn't blurted out to Cooper that I thought I was in love with him. It's caused him to back off."

"Well, honestly, when a man gives a girl an expensive ring with a pretty heart in the middle and little, sparkling diamonds all around it, what's she to think? That they're buds?"

She reached over to squeeze Sara's hand. "Thanks for making me laugh."

"Listen, you be patient with Cooper. Mackie says he's just having a hard time allowing himself to care deeply about anyone again. It scares him that he might lose another person he loves."

"I hope you're right." They came to the beginning of the Gatlinburg Trail, and Mercedes pulled on the leash, looking ahead up the street.

"What's with Mercedes?" Sara asked.

Emily shook her head. "She thinks we might be going to Cooper's. We've walked across the highway here and up Natty Road so many evenings she knows the way now. All I have to do now is say, 'Let's go to Cooper's house' and she gets all excited. She's crazy about Cooper and Brinkley."

Sara petted the big poodle. "Well, I don't blame her for yearning after those two good-looking male specimens in lieu of time with me and little Buster. It's hardly a comparison."

Emily laughed again. "You always make me feel better, Sara."

She followed her friend into the shaded woods trail. "How are things with you and Mackie?"

"Wonderful. I could hug myself ten times a day I'm so happy." She gave herself a little hug as she said the words, causing Emily to laugh again.

"And guess what?" she added. "Mackie showed me plans for a house he's building on his dad's property on a nice piece of land with a great mountain view above the farm."

Emily's eyes widened. "Has he popped the question?"

"No, but he will." She wiggled her eyebrows as she said it. "It is so good between us. Every time we're together, it feels like we've always known each other, that we were always meant to find each other."

"That's nice," Emily said the words and meant them. She wasn't jealous of Sara's happiness. "It's obvious every time I'm around the two of you how much you love each other. Mackie has told you he loves you, I hope."

"Yes, and he found a wonderfully romantic time to do it." She looked at Emily and frowned. "I wasn't going to tell you, what with Cooper having so many issues in your relationship."

"It has been a little awkward lately." They stopped at a wooden bench for a minute to look at the stream in the sunshine before walking on. "Like you said, I can only hope that perhaps in time Cooper will be able to feel more."

As Emily let herself back in the gallery later, she wondered how long that might be. She knew Cooper would be home tonight fixing a toilet that had been giving him a problem. Maybe she and Mercedes would walk up later. She'd made brownies last night; she could take him some as an excuse to stop by.

"I never thought I'd be a girl who would chase after a boy," she told Mercedes, letting her come into the gallery to keep her company. Monty would be leaving soon, and Mamie had taken Sugar Lips home with her tonight as she often did.

Earlier when Sugar Lips zoomed into the carrier with no hesitation, Mamie had laughed and said, "With Mercedes so often in the gallery, Sugar Lips has decided she likes my little home very much. She gets to be the singular queen at my place except for the few times when Brinkley visits, and that cat loves to sit and look out the window at all the birds there."

Emily had snapped the door of the carrier shut and waved them out. "Anyone would love your little house, Mamie, even Sugar Lips."

Actually, the cat and the dog got along amicably now in the gallery, and everyone enjoyed coming in to be greeted by both.

Emily helped several customers, rang up a few sales, and then sorted through mail at the counter while she watched the store. Weekday evenings were often slow. She'd clean and close soon, and go upstairs to fix a little supper for herself. Hopefully, there wouldn't be another e-mail from Daniel waiting for her. Unfortunately, things had not improved at the gallery in Philadelphia. Business had fallen off, and Daniel said Leonard was frantic about the bottom line.

Mercedes's tags jingled in the quiet as she followed Emily around the gallery at nearly six. Daylight savings time had kicked in, and dark fell later now in the mountains, but a gallery like the Creekside didn't need to stay open beyond six on weeknights.

Emily heard the store doorbell as she walked back up to the front with the dust mop she'd just zipped over the hardwood floors in the gallery.

"Well, hello, Randy, I didn't expect you until tomorrow when the exhibit changes out." She leaned the mop against the counter. "Let me lock the door behind you and put the closed sign up."

"You look beautiful," Randy said, leaning over to buss her cheek.

Mercedes moved nearer to Randy, growling low in her throat.

Randy backed away, holding up his arms. "I can't figure out why that dang dog doesn't like me." He frowned. "I like dogs."

"Oh, she's probably feeling overly protective of me since I'm in the gallery by myself tonight."

He crossed his arms. "Well, I don't like wondering if she might sneak up behind me and chomp on my leg. Can't you put her up or something while we talk?"

Emily looked at Mercedes, still tense in posture, watching Randy. "Sure," she said. "I'll put her in my office where her bed is." She walked into the hallway leading to the gallery offices, put Mercedes inside her office at the back of the hallway, closed the door, and then put the dust mop in the hall closet on her way back.

Randy stood in the doorway, watching her. "You're a lovely woman, Emily Lamont. Why don't you let me take you out to dinner somewhere special tonight?"

She hesitated, remembering that she'd planned to walk up to Cooper's later. "It's thoughtful of you to ask, but I have a lot to do getting ready for the open house coming up Saturday. I think I'll pass on your invitation, Randy." She smiled at him. "But I am pleased you came by. I wanted to talk with you before you picked up the Rockwell exhibit."

He followed her over to the counter while she put away the door keys and started closing out the register. "Mamie said last week when I called that you wanted to talk with me when I came, that you had some concerns about some of the paintings."

"Oh, I didn't know she mentioned that to you." She leaned an elbow on the counter to look across at him. "You probably remember when you were here before that I told you something didn't seem right about two of the paintings."

He grinned lazily. "I think I do remember that, and I recall we laughed because your evaluation was based on something random from your childhood."

She laced her fingers together. "That's true, but later I had Cawood Gentry also look at the paintings."

"I've always wanted to meet him."

Emily giggled. "Actually, you did." She told him it was Cawood he'd threatened at the gallery on his last visit.

He shook his head. "I always heard the man was a difficult old guy. I guess I muffed any chance of currying favor with him in future." Randy leaned an arm on the counter across from her. "So what did Cawood say?"

"He advised me to have an expert examine photos of the paintings and cautioned you could never be too careful about potential fraud."

Randy scowled. "Those are serious accusations."

She gave him a patient look. "I'm aware of that, Randy, and don't get testy. But if there are problems going on with the paintings at a higher level, your company might get implicated. I felt you should know that the expert Cawood suggested and another I know and consulted with both said there was cause to look into the issue. I hesitated a long time over this, but I've decided to call the exhibition service and let them know of our concerns before the Rockwell exhibit ships back to them. But I wanted you to know first."

Randy tapped his fingers on the counter. "Maybe you should give this some more thought, Emily. It could damage your relationship with Rankin Exhibition Services. My superiors at Delamar won't be too happy either with the implication that they might be delivering and installing fraudulent art works."

He ran a hand through his hair. "Who have you talked to about this besides Mamie, Gentry, and these supposed art experts?"

"No one else yet. Like I said, I wanted to talk with you first." She held up a finger, thinking of an idea suddenly. "Now that you're here, we might be able to reach Rankin's tonight."

"They're closed."

"Well, I know that, but I have Miklos Knopf's home cell phone for after-hours emergencies. He was a great friend of Hal and Mary Newman's. We often had dinner with him and his wife, Edith, when in New York. I'm sure he wouldn't mind if I called him tonight. He might want to make some related calls before we load the Rockwell exhibit tomorrow and before the Grandma Moses exhibit is installed." She paused. "Has Delamar picked up the Moses exhibit already?"

"Yes. It was picked up yesterday and is en route—with a stopover tonight. It's a long trip. But it should arrive by noon tomorrow. That's why I came tonight, actually, to be here early." He hesitated. "And to hopefully spend time with you."

Emily decided not to respond to that comment. "Well, since you are here, I think we should try to reach Miklos. Then if he has questions for you as well, you can answer them. I really think we should do this."

"You've made up your mind about this, haven't you?" He frowned.

"Yes, I have and I'm sorry if you think my decision isn't the best one."

"You know, you could end up ticking this man off and making yourself look like a dang fool. And you could make me look bad, too."

She shook her head. "Again, I'm sorry, but this is what I've decided to do, Randy. I can call myself now that we've talked together. I don't have to mention that you're in the know about this situation if you don't want me to—or that I've talked to you."

Emily watched him drum his fingers on the counter again, thinking. He really was a handsome man. And pleasant company. Perhaps she should have at least gone to dinner with him. It might have made this easier.

He sighed. "Show me again the paintings you have concerns about."

She led the way back to the exhibit room, taking the entry card to the room with her. "Rockwell has such wonderful work," she said as she opened the door. "I've really enjoyed having this exhibit here. I hope whatever investigation might occur will find I'm wrong. I really do. Art fraud always reflects so badly on the business through which the fraud occurs. But perhaps, if there is any criminal activity going on, it will be through an outside source that won't hurt Miklos's business."

Emily walked over to the *Girl at the Mirror* displayed prominently on the side wall. "This is the first one I noticed a problem with." She pointed out the concern she saw in it.

He moved up behind her. "I see your concern." He put an arm around her unexpectedly. "Be very still, Emily. That is a gun you can feel against your back. You won't be making a call tonight, I'm afraid."

Emily froze in place, icy fear slicing up her spine. What could she do? She was alone in the gallery, and she'd locked the doors. Glancing over her shoulder, she could see the gun Randy held and see his face, now suddenly sinister and hard. Her breathing escalated, and her heartbeat began to hammer in her chest.

"Are you going to kill me?" she whispered at last, hearing her voice tremble as she spoke.

"Not if you behave yourself and do as I tell you." She heard him move slightly behind her. "I want you to walk in front of me back towards the front of the gallery as though there is absolutely nothing wrong—just in case anyone is walking by on the gallery sidewalks and happens to peek through the shades you've pulled down."

Emily began to walk on wobbly legs, trying to think as she did. "Guns make noise. If you shoot me someone will hear and come."

She heard a small laugh behind her. "Not all guns make noise."

Emily couldn't think what to say. She had no experience in anything like this from her past to draw on. What did people do when threatened like this? She couldn't imagine herself dramatically trying to wrest the gun from Randy. If he shot her and ran, and if she survived, no one would even find her until tomorrow. She could bleed to death on the floor. She shivered at the thought.

"I regret you stuck your nose into this. I liked you." He punched the gun into her back to move her along. "We had a nice little operation going, my partners and I. We've taken out a painting or two from random exhibits traveling to small area galleries like yours for almost five years now. Too bad you had to come along and be the little art expert. I told Hollis I worried about your background and expertise when you came to take over the Creekside." He pushed her forward again as her pace slowed. "We'd already taken the Creekside off our list for any future switches. Your Grandma Moses works, and any future works, would have been fine."

"How do you exchange the art?" she asked, curious despite her fears.

"We have art experts who create the alternate works and then we do the switches at the stopover points during transfer. I'll call my man who's part of the Grandma Moses exhibit en route now and alert him that we'll need to initiate our move-out plan, thanks to you." He punched the gun into her back in annoyance. "Before I call him, though, I need to get you taken care of."

Emily shivered.

Randy pushed her forward past the front counter and into the darkened mat shop with the gun pressing against her back. "Find me some good twine and a roll of duct tape. I'm sure you keep both here."

Emily complied, trying to think if there was anything she could do to change what was happening. She glanced around.

"Don't get that active little mind of yours thinking about trying to escape. I won't hesitate to use this gun. There is a lot at stake here." He frowned at this thought. "Our group has a huge offshore corporate account; we'll be all right despite this interruption to our plans. We only need a little lead time to remove ourselves from the country. If I make sure you're out of commission for the night, that will be all the time we need. We can move very rapidly."

He took long strips of the duct tape Emily laid on the counter, pulled Emily's arms behind her back, and began to wrap her arms together with the tape. Next she felt him tie her arms in addition with the twine.

She winced. "You're hurting me, Randy."

"I'd like to hurt you worse, you little interferer. But like I said, I like you." He turned her around and slid a hand down her face, neck, and across her breast. Then he leaned over to kiss her, pulling her against him.

He grinned as her tears started. "You keep telling yourself that a little inconvenience is better than being dead—or raped, my dear. I could take you off into the mountains somewhere, have my way with you, and then shoot you." He traced his hand over the top of her breasts and let it stray down across her abdomen. "It could be worse, Emily. But I don't want that kind of criminal record. If one of my other partners were here, he wouldn't entertain a concern about that. He already has that record."

Randy laughed as she jerked back from him, terrified and nearly tripping over a box on the floor behind her, trying to get away from him. She was so scared. How could she ever have been attracted to this terrible man?

"Come on." He jerked her by the arm. "I think that little hall closet where you put the dust mop away will be just the place for you overnight."

He pushed her forward into the back hallway off the gallery. Mercedes began to bark and scratch frantically at the door to Emily's office.

"Talk to your dang dog and see if you can get her to shut up. If she doesn't quit that barking, she's dead, you hear me? I've never liked that stupid poodle, always growling at me."

Afraid for Mercedes now, Emily tried to calm her voice to call out to her dog. "Mercedes, be quiet and go lie down in your bed. I'm all right."

Emily heard the dog whine as she repeated the command, and then, blessedly, she heard Mercedes's toenails click as she walked away from the door.

"Good girl," she soothed. "I'll be in to see you in a little while. You just lie down and be quiet."

Randy chuckled. "Good thing for you that dog is trained so well. It wouldn't bother me a minute to put her down, the pest, and there aren't serious criminal charges for popping a dog."

Emily felt a sense of shock roll through her.

Randy opened the closet and gestured towards it. "Go in there and sit down with your back against the wall. Pull your knees up, too."

She did, trying not to whine or whimper, knowing that to make too many noises would alert Mercedes all wasn't well. For now, at least, the dog was quiet—and safe.

Randy set to work next duct-taping her ankles together and tying up her legs as he'd done her arms. He studied her after he finished his work. "Well, aren't you trussed up pretty?" He leaned over to kiss her another time before putting a strip of tape across her mouth. "Too bad you and I could never get together in a sweet way before all this happened. As I said, I always liked you." He traced a hand across her breasts again, grinning.

Emily recoiled.

He stood and ran a hand through his hair, smoothing it. "Someone will find you here tomorrow when the gallery opens. It may be a long night for you, but again, remember I let you live after all the trouble you've caused me. I didn't have to." He tucked the gun back into an inside pocket of his jacket. "See you around, Emily Lamont. Perhaps one day on a sunny Caribbean beach?" He laughed as he shut the door, leaving her in the dark.

Emily heard the bell jingle as Randy let himself out the front door, and then nothing but silence.

The tears slid down her face then, tears of fear, revulsion, and anger, too. How could she have been so stupid to never even harbor a suspicion about Randy Lawson? He was in the ideal situation as middleman to be a part of an art fraud exchange. But to Emily, he simply hadn't seemed the criminal type. Handsome, charming, friendly, full of fun. Could a person have two such different natures? Emily shook her head at her thoughts. She closed her eyes, trying to calm down. Her arms hurt, twisted behind her and tied so tight, but at least he hadn't hurt her worse. And with time a factor, he probably wouldn't come back.

After twenty or thirty minutes of growing discomfort, sitting taped and tied on the closet floor with her legs growing numb now, Emily began to wiggle her face and jaw and to push at the tape across her mouth with her tongue. She lost track of the time it took working to get the piece of tape loose from her mouth, but it finally came free at one corner, and then gradually she was able to ease it away from her mouth a little more.

She considered what to do next as she freed her mouth. Would anyone even hear her if she yelled and hollered? This closet was off the back hallway. Even if she yelled, her voice wouldn't carry to the outside walkways leading to the gallery. And both Bolingers' and Garrison Homes on either side of the gallery were closed. The nearest businesses lay too far away to hear anyone's screams from the middle of the gallery, much less from inside a closet.

Working to keep her panic down, Emily tried to think. And then she smiled a small smile at last. She'd left the window open in her office. The window without a screen on it. And Mercedes was in her office.

She raised her voice and called as loudly as she could. "Mercedes, go to Cooper's house. Go get Cooper. I'm in trouble." She made crying noises, knowing Mercedes would be upset to hear them. "Go out the window, Mercedes. Go to Cooper's house. Go get Cooper."

Mercedes barked in reply a number of times, scratching at the door to the office, trying to get out to come to her. But Emily kept repeating her mantra, and praying softly in between while she did, "God, please let Mercedes mind me. Help her remember how to get to Cooper's house. I can't send her to Sara's. I know they're not at home tonight, but Cooper is. And Mercedes has walked to Cooper's house time and again. She knows the way. Please help her to hear me and to go."

A short time later, Emily heard Mercedes pacing around her office, whining, realizing she couldn't get out the door to come to her and that Emily, for some reason, couldn't get to her. "Mercedes, go to Cooper's house. Go get Cooper," she repeated. "Please, Mercedes, I need help." And then she heard the crashing sound of a chair near the window, a thumping noise, and nothing more.

"Thank God," she said to herself. Mercedes had finally noticed the window was open. She'd climbed on the chair to get to it and jumped out. Emily knew the window had been open wide enough for her to get through.

She leaned back against the wall, trying not to cry again.

Now she could only wait. And hope.

CHAPTER 18

Cooper finished changing out the valve seat in the toilet in short time. He figured a leaky valve his main problem with the water still running after flushing. Before cleaning up, he checked other washers, connections, and parts, too. Then he turned the water back on and tested the new valve before gathering up the towels from the floor to throw in the washer. After putting everything back to rights in the bathroom, Cooper picked up his trash and the empty valve box from the hardware store to carry outside to the garbage.

He'd just let himself in the back door when he heard Mercedes barking. It didn't take him more than a minute to recognize the dog's bark, especially with Brinkley wagging his tail with excitement and barking back.

Cooper grinned. Evidently, Emily and Mercedes had taken a late walk and decided to stop to see him and Brinkley. Good. Things had been a little awkward between the two of them lately. Cooper walked to the door to let them in, only to find Mercedes alone—agitated, barking, and upset. He looked around and down the driveway for Emily. Where was she?

At first Cooper thought Mercedes had simply run ahead of Emily, chasing a squirrel or something, but then he noticed Mercedes didn't have a leash on. And she wouldn't quit barking.

"What is it, girl?" he asked, walking out on the porch. The poodle ran down the porch steps and part way down the drive, turning to bark at him again.

While Cooper stood, trying to figure out what the dog wanted—and what she was doing at his place alone this late—Mercedes raced back up on the porch, bumped her head against Cooper's leg, and then started down the steps again, barking. Brinkley, whipped up with all Mercedes's incessant yapping, now started barking, too.

Something was wrong.

Cooper put Brinkley back in the house, grabbed his keys, phone, and one of Brinkley's leashes, and headed out the front door again. Mercedes still circled and barked, obviously wanting him to follow. Maybe Emily had fallen and gotten hurt on the way up, sprained her ankle or something?

He tried to clip the leash on the dog, but Mercedes pulled away, dashing down the driveway but still turning to bark at him occasionally, as if urging him on. As he followed the dog down Natty Road, he watched for Emily, worrying that she might be hurt and needing help along the roadside.

His anxiety grew as they neared the church and the highway. Where was Emily? They were nearly into Gatlinburg now. And the dog wasn't acting at all like herself. She raced across the highway between traffic now, causing a motorist to honk and send an angry gesture his way.

Cooper picked up his pace, nearly running to keep up with the dog as she headed down the road towards the Creekside. At the gallery, she cut around the path and sidewalk to the back of the gallery, where he saw her leap into the window of Emily's office.

What the heck was that back window doing open? Had there been a robbery? Cooper reached the window, moving with caution now to look inside. The room was empty, but Mercedes scratched and pawed frantically at the closed door in Emily's office leading to the hallway. Cooper paused. Should he head directly into this situation or call the police? What if a thief or intruder was still inside? Would he endanger Emily? Was she even in the gallery at all?

As the last question flooded his mind, he heard a muffled call. "Mercedes, go get Cooper," he heard. "Go get Cooper. I need help."

Emily! He leaned his head in the open window. "I'm here. Where are you?"

"Oh, thank God, Cooper." He could hear her weeping. "In the hallway. I'm in the hallway closet."

Skipping the time it would take to go around and come in from his office with a key, Cooper pushed up the window a little more and climbed through. After wrangling the dog out of the way to open the scratched-up office door, he followed as Mercedes darted down the hallway. He could hear Emily's sobs now as he neared the closet.

"How the heck did you get yourself locked in here?" he asked, turning the handle of the door. But he stopped short in shock at the sight of her tied up on the floor in the corner. Devil take it, who would do such a thing?

Cooper went into action quickly, moving into the closet and pulling out his pocketknife from his back pocket to begin freeing Emily. "Who did this?" he asked, angry now as he worked to cut through the rope and duct tape. Mercedes pushed into the closet with them to lick Emily's face, whining.

She threw her arms around the dog and next around him as he freed her hands. "Oh, Cooper I was so scared! I'm so glad Mercedes found you." She wept all over him, making it difficult to get her feet untied. He had to help her stand, too, and she was so wobbly she nearly fell trying to walk.

Cooper put an arm around her to support her. "Are you all right?" He let his eyes rove over her, looking for signs of injury. Then he tensed and paused. "Is someone still in the gallery?"

"No, not now." She leaned against him. "Help me get to the bathroom before we talk," she whispered. "Please."

He walked her the short distance down the hallway to the gallery bathroom and opened the door for her. "Do you need help here?" he asked.

She offered a weak smile. "No. I'll be okay. Just give me a minute."

He and Mercedes waited while she went to the bathroom. He heard the toilet flush, and afterwards he heard her retching. "Cripes,

Emily." He opened the door to find her on her knees, throwing up. Cooper let her finish, then wet a hand towel and squatted to wipe her face, running a hand over her hair, wanting to comfort her. Mercedes whined, coming into the bathroom to nuzzle against her.

When Emily assured Cooper the retching had passed, he helped her to her feet, but this time he swept her up in his arms. "I'm going to carry you upstairs. You're going to be okay, Emily, but you need to lie down."

She wept the entire way, shaking now, too. "I thought he would kill me," she said at one point before crying even more.

Cooper bit down on his impatience to query her more until he could get her into her apartment. He carried her back to her bedroom and laid her on the bed. She clung to him as he tried to tuck a blanket around her.

"Don't leave me, Cooper. Please don't leave me." She started crying again.

He held her tight against him until she stopped shaking and weeping. "Listen. I'm going to go get you some water in the kitchen and find a cloth in the bathroom to wipe your face. Mercedes will be right here with you until I get back. Everything will be all right, Emily. Everything will be all right."

She sighed and draped an arm around the big poodle beside her. "Wait." She caught his attention before he walked through the door. "You need to call the police department, too. We will need them. One of the criminals involved with the gallery art fraud was here." She took a deep breath. "I'll try to calm down to talk with them. But we will need them. Maybe Mamie, too."

He nodded and took his phone from his back pocket to make the calls as he walked towards the kitchen. He called his father's old friend, Gatlinburg police chief Bill Magee, and then his mother.

Returning to Emily with a glass of water and a damp washcloth, he let her drink and then he wiped her face, saying soothing things. It broke his heart to see her frightened and upset like this.

She sighed and closed her eyes. "I'm so grateful he didn't hurt me." She winced. "It was Randy Lawson," she said at last, opening her eyes to look up at him. "He was part of a criminal team changing out the paintings. They carried out their art theft not only here but in other places." She shook her head. "I never imagined it could be him."

"That smarmy little weasel." Cooper clenched a fist. "I never did like him, always sucking up to the women, turning on the phony charm."

"I expected Randy to arrive tomorrow, with the scheduled exhibit exchange, but he came tonight before close. He said he wanted to take me out to dinner." Emily winced at the memory.

"And?" Cooper bit down an expletive and encouraged her to continue.

"And I decided to talk to him about what we'd learned about the authenticity of the Rockwell pieces—since he'd come early." She turned her eyes to Cooper's. "Mamie and I had agreed to talk with Randy first before we called Rankin Exhibition Services tomorrow, since Delamar was also partially involved, handling the exhibit transfers." Emily shook her head. "We thought Randy would be concerned and want to help. I'd spoken to him a couple of months ago about the paintings in question, and he mentioned that Mamie had told him we planned to report the problem."

She petted the dog absently as she paused. "Mercedes growled at him when he came in." A small smile played over her face. "She never liked Randy; I always wondered about that. I put her up because he complained. After I shared with him what I planned to do, he pulled a gun on me. I was stunned, and then really afraid. He acted so differently after that." She bit her lip. "So horrid."

Cooper tensed, listening to her words. "Did he hurt you, Emily?"

She gave him an anguished look and put a hand over her face. "After he taped and tied me up, he kissed me, said things to scare me, and touched me." Her eyes met his. "But he didn't do anything more, thank God."

Cooper felt a surge of rage flash through him. "I'm so sorry."

"It made me feel so dirty." The tears slid down her face again. "He didn't take my clothes off or anything, but he ran his hands over me and kissed me when I couldn't do anything to stop him. It was awful."

Cooper gathered her up to hold her close again.

She pulled her head away from his chest to look up at him. "I don't want to tell the police that. Do I have to?"

"I don't think it's important to the investigation. I believe you can leave it out or simply make short mention of it if questioned. Bill Magee is a good guy; he won't push you to tell what isn't needed."

"Good." She stroked the poodle again. "I'm so proud of Mercedes, and I'm so grateful you came, Cooper. Thank you."

"Where else would I be, beautiful girl?" He kissed both her cheeks.

She glanced towards the door, hearing footsteps on the stairs. "Help me walk into the living room, Cooper. I want to sit on the couch to talk."

Cooper did so, and then listened with Chief Magee and his mother as Emily told the whole story of how Randy Lawson and his partners had worked their art fraud scheme for years through small galleries using Delamar's transfer services.

Mamie shook her head. "Randy Lawson is simply the last person I would have suspected of this. I wonder how many paintings he exchanged through our gallery before the Rockwells?"

"He didn't say," Emily answered. "He only said they'd taken paintings for five years at random from small galleries they serviced. He didn't say how many galleries were involved."

Mamie leaned forward in her chair across from Emily. "Rankin Exhibitions works with literally hundreds of galleries around the United States, small and large. I'm sure Miklos Knopf will be even more devastated than we are about these losses, and unless they can catch these criminals, they may never know which paintings have been exchanged with fraudulent copies."

"The authorities will be looking for this ring of criminals," Chief Magee said. He had called in information about the painting thefts as soon as Emily provided the basic facts needed to do so. "Finding Emily as we did tonight offers a better shot at catching them before they leave the country, too."

He turned to Emily. "It was smart of you to send the dog after Cooper and to remember you left an open window in the office she might get through." He glanced at Mercedes. "Smart dog, too."

Mercedes pricked up her ears.

"Yes, she is." Emily held out a hand to the dog, who came over to nuzzle her nose in Emily's hand, wagging her stub of a tail.

Cooper began to feel sorry for Emily as Bill asked question after question, getting the full report down of all that occurred. He knew she felt exhausted and yearned to be alone, and yet she held herself together with her usual poise.

He slipped out of the room at one point to walk Mercedes and called Sara while outside, telling her briefly what had happened. "I'd appreciate it if you could come spend the night with Emily tonight. She shouldn't be alone and it's not appropriate for me to stay." He paused. "She didn't get any dinner either, so maybe you could bring something for her, too."

Sara showed up twenty minutes later, carrying food containers and an overnight bag draped over her shoulder. "Oh my gosh, Emily," she said as soon as she walked in the door. "What an awful night you've had." She dropped the food on a table and her bag by the door and ran across the room to wrap Emily in a hug.

Cooper saw surprise flicker over Emily's face at Sara's sudden appearance. "I called Sara to come," he explained to her. "I thought you needed someone to keep you company tonight after all that's happened. Sara's going to spend the night with you."

His mother sent him a smile. "That was thoughtful of you, Cooper." She glanced towards the containers on the table and then at Emily. "And I'll bet you never even got supper, did you, Emily?"

Emily shook her head.

Mamie made a clucking sound and looked at Bill. "If you're finished with all your questioning, I think we should go so that this poor child can get some food and rest. She's been through a traumatic evening."

Bill flipped his notebook shut. "I think I have all I need for now. Emily, I may need to call or come by for more questions as the investigation proceeds." He stood, getting ready to leave. "I doubt anyone will return to the gallery tonight, but I plan to post a man outside just in case. You girls can be assured someone will be watching the property."

Mamie gave Emily a last hug. "You try to get some rest, dear. You've had such a hard time but were incredibly brave through it all—and you kept your head." She patted Emily's cheek. "You acted so wisely to pursue your suspicions about those paintings. There's no telling how long those criminals would have kept stealing and substituting paintings if you hadn't followed your instincts about those Rockwell works. I'm very proud of you."

She paused. "Is there anything else I can do before I leave?"

"No, thank you." Emily smiled at her.

"Well, Leona is working in the morning and then I'm working later tomorrow. I don't want you to even think about coming down to the gallery until you've had a good rest." She hesitated. "I think it might be wise, also, to cancel the open house on Saturday after all you've been through. We can reschedule."

Emily's eyes widened. "Oh, no, Mamie. I don't want to do that. We need to move on as always, and we need to hold the open house and be positive and diplomatic to all for the gallery's sake. I'll have all day tomorrow and Saturday to rest before the event. I'll be fine. Truly."

"Hmmm. Well, it might be best for public relations—if you're sure." She looked to Cooper for his counsel.

"Emily will be fine to hostess the event by then, Mom. You, Leona, and Monty will be there to help." He nodded at Emily. "She'll be fine."

Emily gave him a grateful smile as he ushered his mother and Bill Magee out the door. Then he walked over to pick up the food containers.

"Is this ready to eat, Sara?"

She stood up and took it from him. "I'm going to go heat it in the microwave in the kitchen and plate it first." She smiled at Emily. "It's some of Mom's homemade chicken and rice casserole, just the thing for you tonight. I put in some leftover green beans to go with it and one of Mom's rolls." She started towards the kitchen. "I also brought a carton of chocolate ice cream from the freezer for later. Chocolate soothes everything, you know."

This even made Emily giggle, which Cooper was glad to see.

He sat down beside Emily on the sofa after Sara went into the kitchen. "Will you be okay with Sara here?" He put a hand to her face. "I wanted to stay, but I didn't think it would be the right thing to do."

"It was thoughtful of you to call Sara. I probably would have tried to talk you out of bothering her, but I'm happy she's here." She looked towards the window. "It might have been a hard night to get through alone."

"Listen, Emily. Whatever ugly things Randy Lawson said or did, you erase them from your mind, you hear? Only a sick person would kiss or push intimacy on someone tied up as you were." He gritted his teeth just thinking about it. "I hope they find him and lock him up."

"So do I." She leaned her head against his. "Thanks again for coming to my rescue."

He put his hands on her face. "I can't tell you how angry I felt that someone tried to hurt you. And how scared I was thinking something might have happened to you." He traced his fingers across her lips, leaning in to kiss her good-night.

She pulled back and turned her head. "Don't kiss me, Cooper. I've been sick and I haven't even had a chance to brush my teeth."

"I don't care," he grinned, swooping in to give her a quick peck before she could argue more.

She sighed in resignation and let him give her a sweeter kiss.

"Besides." He smoothed a hand through her hair before he stood to leave. "I didn't want you to wake tonight and think of that other kiss you were forced to endure. So I erased it for you. Okay?"

"Well, this is a better memory." She put a hand to her mouth, sending him one of her sweet smiles at last.

"I'll stop by tomorrow to check on you," he said as Sara came back from the kitchen with a dinner plate for Emily.

A few good-byes ensued and then Cooper left to walk back home. It was pitch-dark as he left the lights of Gatlinburg behind and began following Natty Road to his house. He could hear night sounds in the woods and see the moon in the sky above. His heart weighed heavy with feelings as he walked along—remnants of fear that he might have lost Emily tonight, anger at the man who'd frightened, threatened, and hurt her. He also felt a painful hurting around his chest that he knew Emily had reached out to him, needed him, but that he still couldn't say to her the words she so wanted to hear. Was he just a man who couldn't love anymore after losing those he'd loved? Had the old anger and bitterness, carried for so long, damaged his heart and made him unable to love as he wanted to? Cooper didn't know, but the weight of guilt that he couldn't offer Emily those three small words followed him home tonight. Those words might have brightened a harsh night for her just a little.

CHAPTER 19

Emily slipped into the simple, but elegant, black dress she planned to wear to the open house at the Creekside Gallery. It had short sleeves, a round scoop neck, and a slightly flared skirt that fell to just below her knees. It complimented Emily's figure, and she'd worn it for many similar events in the past. If there was one thing Emily owned enough of, it was little black dresses—three short ones and two long ones, to be precise. They were staple items in the gallery business and for the professional events Emily often attended.

She'd originally toyed with the idea of wearing one of the more flirty selections but decided instead on this subtle and tailored choice. She needed poise and confidence tonight. Her attack at the gallery, and the news of the fraud ring behind it, had made the papers. She'd draw extra attention because of the media pieces splashed across the front pages of two local newspapers.

Her phone rang, and Emily picked it up from the dresser.

"I hear you almost got yourself shot." Leonard Newman's laugh rang out after his voice. "Too bad that didn't happen."

"You don't really mean that." She blew out a patient breath. "And how did you get this number?"

"Found it on Daniel's phone when he was busy in the gallery. I know you and he are in cahoots to cause the gallery here to fail. Probably that Michael Zucchi is in on it, too, to get even with me. He quit before I could fire him." He laughed again. "But don't get too excited thinking your plans will work. I can sell this gallery, you know. I've had offers."

Emily tried to think what to say. "Leonard, I am not trying to get the Hal Newman Gallery to fail. Why would I? I want it to succeed to perpetuate Hal and Mary's memory and all the loving work they put into it. I am not in cahoots, as you put it, with anyone there."

"You gave recommendations for those losers I fired or who quit."

"I helped to hire those people at the Newman. I had no problems with them when I worked with them and no reason not to give them recommendations when asked."

"Don't try to sound so innocent. You talk to the people here. I know you do."

She paused to choose her words. "The people who worked at the Newman are also my friends. And, yes, we do keep in touch as friends do."

"I bought Casteel's Restaurant and that charming little floral and gift business attached to it over near Washington Square with some of the money from the sale of Hal and Mary's monstrosity of a house," Leonard said, changing the subject. "Mother always loved it; it's divine. And I'm respected there."

"It's a pretty place and historic." Emily tried to be amenable, hoping to placate Leonard.

He hesitated. "Maybe you'd like to think about coming back to run the Newman so I'd have more time at Casteel's."

This surprised her.

"People miss you." His voice took on a whiney tone now. "You should have stayed here to work if you wanted the gallery to succeed so much. Think what Hal and Mary would say to see the gallery floundering like it is. You should come back to help out. You owe it to them to try to keep the gallery from going under. Your town house hasn't sold. I've been watching that."

Emily sat down on the edge of the bed, shocked at Leonard's offer.

"I'll give you the same salary you were making before," he put in, hearing her silence.

"Leonard, I'm really surprised you would want me back." She considered what to say. "And I'm sorry, of course, that the gallery is struggling, but I have a job here now. I've resettled and I'm happy."

"Even after nearly getting killed," he shot back.

She started to reply that he'd started their conversation saying it was a shame she hadn't gotten killed. Instead, wisely biting her tongue, she replied, "I don't think I want to come back. But thank you for asking."

"If you don't come back, I'll sell the thing. It's been nothing but trouble. And then where will your friends be—with no jobs? And whoever buys it will change the name. Hal and Mary's name will be wiped out forever and it will be your fault."

She closed her eyes. Unreasonable man. However did he manage to see things the way he did? And make the outrageous statements he did? It would only be a misery trying to work for him—even to save the Newman.

"You think about it," he threw out. "I won't put up with all those veiled looks and all that talking and conniving behind my back over there for much longer. I've just about had it, you hear?"

And then he hung up.

Emily shook her head. Good heavens, Leonard Newman proved a difficult man to deal with. No wonder Daniel and the others still at the gallery were tearing their hair out and stressed all the time trying to work with and get along with him.

The phone rang again, and Emily looked at the number with reluctance, expecting it to be Leonard once more. But it was Cooper.

"Hey," he said as she answered. "Are you doing okay? Will you be all right to get through this evening? You can still bail out, you know."

"I know." She smiled at the phone, pleased he was worried about her and glad to move her thoughts in another direction. "But I'm okay. Really. And I can't believe how wonderful everything looks since Revelta Kizer and her catering team came in and set up for the event. They've simply transformed the whole back patio into what looks like an elegant little French bistro or something. I love it."

"I told you they were good." He chuckled. "And wait until you taste the hors d'oeuvres and the wine from the Russo Cellars."

Emily glanced at her watch. "I need to finish getting dressed and stop in to check on the exhibit and talk to the two boys Revelta has working inside the gallery before people begin to arrive."

"I hear you. I'll see you there," he said, clicking off.

Looking at the phone for a minute, she thought back on how sweet Cooper had been through the last two days. Surely he harbored strong feelings for her to be so kind and thoughtful? So tender and sweet?

Mercedes padded into the room, giving her an expectant look.

She reached over to pet the dog's head. "I see that look, girl. I need to take you out before I leave, don't I? We can't stay long, though. That's why we took a long walk earlier today."

Getting up from the bed, Emily walked to the dresser to clip her diamond necklace around her neck and to put matching earrings into her ears. She slipped on a dressy bracelet watch and smoothed her hands through her hair, which she'd pinned up neatly and elegantly tonight.

Mercedes lifted one ear, watching her.

"I look good, don't I?" Emily said to her, sliding her feet into dressy black sling-back pumps. "Come on. Let me take you outside for a minute. And then I have a big evening ahead of me."

Later, with the open house in full swing, Emily looked around with satisfaction at the crowd gathered around the patio and strolling down the pathways lit with lights.

"The evening has gone beautifully, hasn't it?" Mamie said, coming to stand beside her. She wore a dark gray sheath with a glittery jacket over it and looked fantastic.

"It has." Emily smiled at her. "And you're a pro at this, I can see."

"So are you, my dear." She patted Emily's arm. "I'm thrilled, too, that we learned just as the event started that the members of the fraud ring, including Randy Lawson, were caught."

Emily turned to her. "Bill Magee said they were apprehended later the same night Randy came here, at a warehouse near Lawson's home, packing to leave the country in a private plane. No wonder Randy said they only needed a little extra time for their escape plan. He knew they owned their own airplane."

"If you'd remained in that closet until morning, they'd have been gone," Mamie said.

"I know." Emily had thought about this often herself. "Perhaps they can get those involved in the art thefts to provide information about paintings they exchanged over the years now. That could help Miklos's company and the owners of the paintings."

"You can be sure the insurance companies will be working to see that happens." Mamie waved at a client across the patio. "Anyway, I'm so glad the situation is resolved, and that Rankin was able to bring our Grandma Moses exhibit to the gallery and hang it yesterday. Thank goodness no paintings in that show were exchanged."

"And the exhibit looks wonderful, doesn't it?" Emily nodded to two of their gallery artists walking by, saying a few words to them before they moved on.

"Yes, it does, and everyone loves Grandma Moses's work." Mamie gave Emily a smile. "I'm going to go mingle, dear. The Craddocks just came in and they've brought some friends with them I want to meet. I'll see you later."

Emily stepped into the shadows of the gallery's covered walkway for a minute to lean against a post, needing a break from the crowd.

"It's a fine event," Cawood Gentry said to her, walking over to join her. "And the new exhibit looks good. The simplicity and joyfulness of Anna Mary Moses's, or Grandma Moses's, work is always a pleasure to see. I got to meet Anna Mary once at an exhibition a long time ago."

"What a treat for you." Emily smiled at him. "Hal and Mary met her once, too, although I never did. Hal told me it was because she developed arthritis and couldn't embroider well that she started painting. Isn't it a blessing she did, leaving the art world such a wonderful legacy?"

"Yes." He snagged a stem of wine from a waiter passing by. "And how are you doing, Emily?"

"All right." She looked out over the milling crowd. "Do you know what flashed through my mind the most while locked in that dark closet?"

"What?"

"The happy memories of all the people who have loved me over my life." She paused. "Randy could have killed me, you know. Coming that close to death makes you think about what's important in life. I realized that what is most important is having people to love."

She paused before continuing. "Pictures and memories of the people who have loved me filtered through my mind while I sat in that dark space, like my parents, Hal and Mary Newman, friends in Philadelphia, friends here." She turned to Cawood. "Did you know Mamie has no memories of her parents? I realized that night how blessed I am to have known mine even for ten years. I can see their faces, hear their voices, remember good times with them. After getting over my panic and sending Mercedes for help, I spent my time counting all my blessings. Remembering the names of all the people who have loved me."

"Mamie told me about her past. Do you think it hurts Mamie a lot, as you say, not knowing about her parents?" Cawood asked.

"Perhaps sometimes it hurts. I'm sure Mamie wishes she knew more." She turned to see him frowning. "It's nice that you're so fond of Mamie. I like that about you, Cawood Gentry, because I've come to love Mamie." She leaned up to kiss his cheek. "And despite your gruff reputation, I've come to like you very much, too."

He cleared his throat and shifted uneasily. "I'm an old recluse, you know, and a rambling stone."

"Perhaps, but I'm still fond of you." Emily saw Mackie, Sara, and Cooper coming across the patio, waving to her.

"I guess I'd better get back to my mingling," she said, patting his arm. "And I see some people heading your way as well." She pointed to a group walking towards them, Mamie among them. Emily moved out from the shadows of the porch to meet Sara and Mackie. Both Mackie and Cooper looked stunning in crisp suits instead of their usual work clothes, and Sara wore the satiny blue dress she'd worn to Cooper's party.

As they drew closer, Sara waved her left hand in the air. "Look, look, Emily. Mackie and I are engaged." She turned a wide smile to Mackie. "Isn't it wonderful?"

"Yes, it is," Emily said, examining the starry diamond ring now on Sara's ring finger. "And that's a gorgeous ring. Congratulations, you two." She hugged both of them. "I couldn't be happier for you."

She linked an arm in Cooper's, sensing his awkwardness over this moment. "Let's go over and get some glasses of Monty's best family wine to make a toast for this occasion."

Emily offered a toast to them before all the guests, and the quartet, performing in the corner of the outdoor patio, obliged the occasion by playing a sweet classical rendition of "I Will Always Love You" to help the couple celebrate. All those who knew Mackie and Sara came to wish them well, and Emily felt glad she could make the night more memorable for them.

The open house hours slipped by quickly. Emily's evening was full greeting and speaking with all the Creekside's guests. Besides mingling and networking among the crowd on the back patio, Emily drifted frequently into the gallery and into the exhibit room to speak to the guests enjoying the artwork there. Many of her artists stayed with their personal exhibits for much of the evening to meet and greet visitors and to talk about their work. Periodically, Leona also gave a brief, informative lecture about Grandma Moses in the exhibit room. Emily listened in once and realized why Leona's students enjoyed her classes so much.

The party wound down at last, and as the stragglers began to say their good-byes, Cawood Gentry came up to Emily, Cooper, and Mamie where they stood shaking hands and thanking friends and clients for coming.

"It was a nice event," he said.

"Yes, and thanks for coming," Mamie said to him, taking his hand and giving it a friendly pat.

Cawood looked down at her hand where it held his, shifting awkwardly. "I would like you, Cooper, and Emily to come up to my home for dinner next month when I return from my trip out west. I have an exhibit and a family funeral to attend, plus I need to check on my house there."

He offered them one of his rare smiles. "I cook a very nice New York strip roast when I've a mind to get into the kitchen and I've been told I make excellent stuffed baked potatoes. I've already talked Monty Russo out of a couple of bottles of good red wine to go with our meal. I hope you will say yes."

Emily and Mamie were stunned. No one they knew had ever been to Cawood's mountaintop home, which perched at the top of a long drive beyond locked gates.

Cooper recovered his manners first. "It would be a great honor, Cawood," he said. "You've always been kind to my mother. I'm pleased you invited us to your home."

"Yes, we would be delighted," Mamie added. "What could I bring?"

"Not a thing." He waved a hand. "I make a chocolate-hazelnut trifle that is very good, too. You might be surprised to know cooking is one of my little side hobbies." He glanced out over the lingering guests. "When you live alone and travel a lot, you have to learn to be resilient and resourceful."

"Well, I am simply charmed that we will get to share a meal in your home and especially one you've prepared just for us," Emily said. "We will eagerly look forward to our visit." She hesitated. "And I, for one, hope we will also get to see your art collection. I've heard rumors it is fabulous."

"Yes." He smiled at her. "I think that could be arranged." He turned to Cooper. "I will call you tomorrow and give you directions to my place. I think the first Saturday in June might work well for me to put on your calendars, if it works for all of you. I should be back by the end of May." And with that, he gave them a military-like nod and walked away.

"Well, blow me away," Mamie said, looking after him. "I wonder what brought that on?"

Cooper's gaze followed Cawood, too. "I don't know anyone who has ever been to Cawood Gentry's home on the mountain, do you, Mom?"

"No." She shook her head. "And who would have thought the man is also a gourmet cook? My, my. I'd say we're all in for a memorable evening. We should mark our calendars right away to keep that date open." She turned to Emily. "Gracious, Emily, what does one wear to dinner at Cawood Gentry's home?"

Emily smiled. "Something casual and elegant. After all, it isn't as though you haven't know Cawood for a long time already, Mamie."

"That's true, I suppose," she said before more guests walked up to offer their good-byes and thanks for a fine evening.

Emily finally said good-bye to the last guests and then sent all her staff and artists home with small boxes of the remaining food that Revelta had packed for them while cleaning up. Cleanup on the patio and in the gallery didn't take long with the efficient work of the caterers, and Revelta handed Emily a few extra boxes of hors d'oeuvres and party sweets, too.

"If I eat all this, I may not be able to get into this little black dress again," Emily said as Cooper walked her up the stairs to her apartment.

"You look fabulous in that little black dress," he said, leaning over behind her to kiss her bare neck. "Although I like you in red even more."

"Be careful or I'll drop these boxes." She giggled. "Wasn't it a simply wonderful evening?" she added. "I don't think anything could have been more perfect."

Emily put the boxes into Cooper's hands while she unlocked her door. "Do you want to come in for coffee?" she asked.

He ran a hand down her cheek. "No, I think you could use some rest after this long evening. I still see dark circles under your eyes like you haven't been sleeping well."

She smiled up at him. "I'll sleep better tonight after the news we received from Bill Magee earlier. It's good to know those thieves are caught and that possibly the investigators might learn from them which other art works might have been swapped out." She frowned. "However, I know it's unlikely they will ever be retrieved. Private collectors who can pay for works like that, and who will buy them through those sources, cover their tracks well and hide their art carefully."

She sighed. "So that means those wonderful pieces that were stolen may never be recovered. That makes me sad."

He leaned over to kiss her nose. "Be optimistic, Emily. Maybe they will be found."

"I hope so." She reached to take the white catering boxes from him and was arrested by his eyes as she did. Emily froze in place, feeling the flames of tension and longing suddenly sweep between them. It had been like this with Cooper from the first, this dynamic attraction riveting them in place, focusing their attention on each other.

Cooper leaned towards her, and Emily knew from the darkening of his eyes that he meant to kiss her, but suddenly she didn't want that. She stepped back and put a hand on his chest, lowering her gaze.

Sensing his puzzlement, she raised her eyes then. "Why can't you love me, Cooper?" she whispered, trying not to cry as she said the words. "Is it so very hard to love? How do you need to feel to know there is love between us?"

She watched the anguish and indecision form in his eyes.

"Love should be easy, Cooper. And it is easy if you wouldn't block off your heart and your feelings." She stepped into the doorway. "In that awful closet I realized that loving and being loved is the most important thing in life. I hope someday you will see that, too." And she closed the door between them.

CHAPTER 20

May proved a busy month for Cooper after the gallery opening. Tourist traffic had picked up in the Smokies, bringing new inquiries from visitors considering a vacation or retirement home in the mountains. Cooper sat today meeting with Ollie and Annette Buchanan of Ann Arbor, Michigan.

"We've been coming here every year for our vacations," Annette enthused. "Now that we're retired we want to build on that property we bought here five years ago. Our neighbors, the Mayfields, who live on the mountain property next door, love the house Garrison Homes built for them. We're hoping you might be willing to work with us, too."

Her husband shifted in his seat with discomfort. "The only concern the Mayfields voiced was that their house ended up costing more than projected."

Cooper smiled. "That was because they kept asking for changes and upgrades during building. I explained to them at each point what those changes would add to their overall price." He pulled out a worksheet. "The best way to keep building costs as projected is to decide everything up front and then let Garrison build the house as agreed on."

Ollie relaxed. "I've experienced similar problems in my past in road construction."

Cooper asked questions then to clarify the budget the Buchanans had to work with and the size and type of house they might be interested in. "Since I already know the lot you want to build on, I can recommend a number of plans you might want to consider."

He got up to get several booklets out of a file drawer. "All seven of these plans will suit your lot and fall within your housing budget. Why don't you study them, see if you like one of the houses, and then contact me if you want to talk further?" Cooper gave them a card. "You might also want to drive up Highway 321 to see our model home. Radonna will walk you through that house and talk to you about flooring, appliances, and other options you would have without impacting projected building estimates. If you find a house design you like, but want changes made, I can tell you at our next meeting if those changes can be made and how much they will cost." He offered a smile. "How does that sound?"

"Very good." Ollie seemed relieved to find Cooper not pushing for a decision today. Cooper never did at first meeting. He wanted his clients to be sure of their decision and to have time to think well about building a home.

After ushering the Buchanans out, Cooper started back to his office but paused at the hallway door to the Creekside's workshop. He could hear Emily humming inside as she worked. Opening the door, he saw her leaning into the now-framed Edwardian dollhouse, her back to him.

Building the framed dollhouse for Emily had helped to bridge the growing awkwardness between them this last month. He knew Emily wanted more in their relationship than he could give, but he didn't know what to do about it. Their weekly double dates with Mackie and Sara didn't help. They had to listen to the two babble about wedding plans now and endure watching them constantly gazing at each other with googly eyes. He hated Emily's forced smiles and polite conversations on these occasions and the painful glances she sent his way when she thought he wasn't watching. Once he actually thought of suggesting they date other people, but there was no one else he wanted to ask out, and the idea of Emily seeing anyone else didn't appeal much to him.

Perry Ammons had even stopped by Cooper's office one day to talk with him about the situation. "I've noticed at our Bible study classes that yours and Emily's relationship seems a little strained lately. Several have commented on it to me. Is there any way I can help?"

Cooper had snapped his head off, denying the words, and then made an excuse to leave, claiming he had an appointment.

Both feigning a busy schedule, he and Emily had spent less time together this month. Except for their double dates with Mackie and Sara, they'd only gone out once on a hike one Saturday, besides walking the dogs together a time or two. Mostly the latter was because Brinkley whined and pulled on his leash to head in their direction anytime they walked in the vicinity of the Creekside or stopped at the Garrison Homes office before heading home.

Cooper cleared his throat, and Emily looked up from wallpapering a bedroom in the doll's house to see him at the door.

"Hi," she said. "I finished painting the exterior that soft ivory yellow, whitewashed the trim, and decided on shiny black for the shutters and front door. What do you think?"

Cooper walked into the room. He hadn't seen the house since she started her paintwork. "It looks great." He ran a finger over the gingerbread trim under the roof that had taken him hours to cut out. He could certainly understand why she usually built from a kit.

"Let me get this bubble in the wallpaper out." Emily used a putty knife to smooth the paper against the dollhouse wall, frowning in concentration as she did.

He wanted to touch her then, to kiss that frown away, but he held back. He'd been doing that a lot lately—holding back—working to keep a polite distance. It seemed best.

Emily glanced up at him. "Don't forget we have that dinner at Cawood Gentry's house tonight. Mamie said he was back home. I know you talked to him earlier, but he e-mailed a reminder and directions to his house to Mamie this morning and copied you. He wants us there about six. I'll ride up with you and Mamie if it's okay. I don't like traveling those winding mountain roads by myself at night." She reached for another piece of tiny sprigged wallpaper, getting ready to start another wall.

Cooper scowled. "I'd almost forgotten about that invitation." He glanced at his watch, noting it was already four. "I'd better drive over to the site to check on things so I can get back, walk Brinkley, and get dressed. I'll come by to pick you up about five thirty."

She glanced up at him, sending him a soft smile that sucker-punched him right in the midriff. "Call your mother, too. I know she's excited about going to Cawood's after all these years. Actually, so am I." She sighed. "I can't wait to see his art collection. I've only read about it. Hardly anyone has ever seen it."

Cooper knocked on her door later, at a little before five thirty, to find Emily already dressed and ready. He walked her outside and helped her into the seat behind his mother in the Jeep. They soon left the highway and wound into the mountains bordering the park, following one back road after another, as his mother read him the directions to Cawood's. A GPS was pretty useless here.

When they finally arrived at the big wrought iron gate between two stone pillars leading into Cawood's drive, Cooper could see that the man had left the gate slightly ajar for them. He got out to push it open, drive through, and then stopped to close it again.

At the end of the driveway, they found Cawood's rustic castle of a house, perched on a promontory overlooking a stunning view of Gatlinburg and the Smoky Mountains beyond. The house rose three stories high, complete with turrets, winding outdoor porches, and a sweeping display of high glass windows.

"It's a striking place all right," Cooper commented, parking the car. "I heard he brought in a renowned architect and contractors from out west to design and build the house. It looks even more incredible than the few photos I've seen."

Mamie made a tut-tutting sound. "Now what would one man alone need with a house this size? It's practically ostentatious."

He heard Emily giggle. "Cawood works here, too, Mamie, and he houses an extensive collection of art here as well."

"And who sees all that art hidden way up here on this mountain?" Mamie waved a hand. "Oh, well, you're probably more used to all this glitz than I am."

Cawood showed them around the house a short time later, and Cooper, as a builder, couldn't help but appreciate the fine workmanship within the home. The house had beautiful arched ceilings, curling stairways, tall ornate windows opening to expansive views, and spacious rooms filled with lavish but tasteful furnishings. They enjoyed conversation and drinks afterwards—a light sangria, heavy on the fruit juice and light on the wine—while sitting in an open-ceilinged living area with a rock fireplace rising two stories high.

They moved next to a lovely dining room with a table that would seat twelve, at least. Cawood seemed totally comfortable gathering them in a cozy grouping around one end of this giant table, and he played the consummate host throughout their meal, encouraging conversation, chatting about his exhibit out west, and entertaining them with humorous stories. It was a side of Cawood Gentry that Cooper had never seen before.

Cooper wasn't crazy about asparagus in any form, but the meat, potatoes, salad, rolls, and other sides tasted as good as those in any fine restaurant, probably better. They sat now working their way through a decadent dessert Cawood called a trifle, which seemed to be a layered mixture of cake, chilled cream, vanilla ice cream, nuts, and a warm chocolate-hazelnut syrup. Nice. And especially good with the fine coffee Cawood brought out to accompany it.

"Did you really cook all this lovely dinner yourself?" Mamie asked at one point.

He smiled. "I did, although my housekeeper, Mrs. Graham, put a hand in helping me, especially with setting the table and decorating. I admit I only enjoy the creative aspects of cooking and not the other related domestic chores."

They'd learned on arrival that Mrs. Graham, who flitted in and out of the dining room as they ate to fill their glasses or check on the table, lived full-time in a cozy apartment on the lower level of the house. Most of the rooms Cawood used were on the second story of the home, while the upper floor housed Cawood's studio, office, and the art gallery.

After dinner, Cawood took them up the winding stairwell,

wrapped around a tree trunk, to the third level of his home and on a tour of his studio and gallery.

"Oh, my," Cooper heard Emily say over and over, stopping to gaze at first one and then another of the valuable works of art Cawood had collected over his lifetime.

Cawood gestured towards a massive landscape painting covering almost half a wall. "As you see, I'm fond of collecting landscapes, just as I like to paint them." He paused to let his eye follow the expanse of western mountain ranges before them. "I like the way artists capture the beauty of different places around the United States and the way they interpret what they see."

The collection of paintings, mixed with a few fine sculptures, filled two large rooms. The rooms shared beautiful windows and excellent lighting, but Cooper noted that the windows could be shaded to protect the art by the manipulation of a few dials on the wall.

I'll bet that installation cost a bundle, he thought to himself, always conscious of construction costs. The man probably had millions invested in art, too. Cooper didn't know as much about art as his mother or Emily, and he didn't like all of Cawood's collection, but he did enjoy seeing several pieces by artists he recognized and liked—a Winslow Homer painting of the sea, a Turner of ships, a Georgia O'Keeffe of a desert landscape, and a Russell classic of Indians in the Wild West days. The man had amassed quite a collection, and that was a fact.

Cawood hesitated now. "I have one more painting to show you. It's in the sitting room off my bedroom. We'll go there now, if you don't mind, and we can sit and visit a bit before you leave. It's a cozy space, and a tall window offers an excellent view across the night sky." He led the way down the stairs as he talked. "The moon is full tonight and the clear sky will give us a nice vista of the lights in Gatlinburg, too."

At the bottom of the stairs, they all followed Cawood through the open living area again and then down a hallway past his large bedroom, dominated by a massive carved bed, and into the sitting room he'd spoken of. Several of Cawood's own landscapes hung on the walls here, and on the wall to the left of the fireplace hung the portrait of a young girl.

Mamie walked closer to look at it. "This is one of yours, too." She smiled, turning to him. "It must be an early work from when you often painted portraits before you began to focus on land-scape art."

"Yes." He settled into one of the leather chairs in the room, ges-turing towards the couch and chairs for them to follow. Gas logs offered a warm glow from the rock fireplace.

"When did you do the painting of the girl?" Emily asked, settling down on the sofa. Cooper took the chair beside her, letting his mother sit beside Emily.

"I was nearing my thirtieth birthday when this was painted." He sat back in his chair, crossing his ankle over his knee. "She was pretty, wasn't she? Her youth and freshness drew my interest from the first day I saw her. A young high school girl, she cleaned the rooms in the lodge where I stayed while exploring the mountains. I asked to paint her, and she was flattered."

"You were already beginning to gain a reputation about that time," Emily put in. "You'd had a small art show or two out west and one in New York."

"You did your homework." Cawood smiled.

"Hal drilled me about artists from an early age. He said what you learn when you're young you remember for a lifetime."

"He's right, you know. I still remember so many things I learned as a girl." Mamie agreed, crossing her legs and relaxing against the sofa. "Where did you grow up, Cawood? I think I read Oklahoma."

"In the Oklahoma oil fields." He laughed. "That's where our family fortune initiated, started by my great-grandfather, passed through my grandfather, then my father and to my brothers." He paused, seeming to look back. "Paul and Stefan liked the oil busi-ness. Being the younger son, and spoiled a little by our mother, I leaned to the arts instead. I studied two years in the States and then two in Paris. After that, as a trust fund baby with no pressure to work immediately, I painted around Europe, growing in my art, developing. You learn art more by doing than by study, you know." He waved a hand absently with the words. "Even then, I was growing in my love for landscape art, but I also enjoyed painting the people in the areas I traveled to, and sometimes the girls. After all I was young."

He shrugged. "Back in the States again, I began to travel out West, where I was from, and then in the East. The mountains in both regions drew me. They still do, and as you know, landscapes became the focus of my art in time."

"Your paintings of the western and eastern mountains are what you're best known for," Mamie put in. "Our clients especially love your Smokies art."

"Yes." He smiled at her. "And while in the Smoky Mountains on my first visit, I painted this young girl."

"She was from this area?" Emily leaned forward, interested. "Does she still live around here?"

"No, she passed away not long after this painting was created." He studied his hands in his lap before looking up. "Her name was Trinity Lee." His eyes met Mamie's. "Trinity Lee Simons. She was your mother, Mamie."

Cooper watched his mother's mouth drop open, her eyes moving to the portrait on the wall.

"Oh, my," Emily said, her eyes shifting to the portrait, too. "I can see the resemblance now that I study the painting, the same blond hair, that bit of a gamine smile. But her eyes are brown and not hazel like yours."

"Mamie has my eyes," said Cawood. "I am her father."

A dead silence dropped in the room before Cooper felt his shock turn to anger. "Listen, Cawood, if this is some kind of joke . . ."

"It's no joke. It's why I invited you here tonight." His eyes moved to Cooper's. "If you can hold back that hotheaded temper of yours, probably inherited from me, I will tell you all I know."

Cooper crossed his arms, biting back the words he yearned to say to him.

He felt Emily put a hand on his knee. "Let him talk, Cooper."

"As I said," Cawood continued, "I wasn't even thirty that first summer I came to the Smokies." He closed his eyes as if remembering back. "I knew immediately I wanted to paint here. I rented rooms in a lodge in the area and then tramped out into the mountains with my sketchbook or paints every day. Fell in love with the area." He paused. "And I began to notice the young girl who came to clean my rooms every day and flirted with me."

He smiled. "I knew I was too old for her, but her freshness and simple mountain beauty fascinated me. I talked her into sitting for me."

Cooper snorted.

Cawood's eyes flashed. "She wore this blue dress for the sittings, Cooper." He pointed to the painting. "I wasn't so debauched that I'd ask an underage girl to model nude. Besides, I never painted nudes anyway. If you studied my work, you'd know that."

Emily posed a question, pulling Cawood back to the story. "How did you become involved with Trinity?"

"We became friends. Trinity was lonely and somewhat a misfit in her family. Her parents had died, and an aunt and uncle were raising her, somewhat begrudgingly. They lived down the road from the lodge, so Trinity could walk in each day to work. Despite her circumstances, she possessed a happy disposition they hadn't managed to despoil." He frowned. "I met the aunt and uncle once, both boring, colorless individuals, seeming to resent anyone who saw joy in life. You know the types."

"Yes, and you became her friend." Emily encouraged him.

"I did." Cawood rubbed his neck. "Trinity's main pleasures were in nature, and she introduced me to the Smokies in a way that, as an outsider, I might never have known otherwise. She walked and hiked with me. She was like a younger sister to me at first and then one day it slipped into more. Knowing she was too young for an affair, I panicked and left the mountains then."

Cooper scowled. "You never thought of marrying her?"

"She was sixteen years old, Cooper. I was thirty."

"Did you stay in touch?" Emily asked.

Cawood shook his head. "I was young, cowardly, and self-centered. I thought it would be better for her if I just went away. I called her the day after I left. She cried and begged me to come back. It was all too emotional for me. I ran. I took off for Europe again."

Mamie found her voice at last. "When did you learn she was carrying your child?"

He shook his head, running his hands through his hair. "I never knew she'd birthed a child until about twenty years ago."

Cooper saw his mother's eyes widen. "Is that why you came to the gallery that day, asking me all those questions?"

"Yes." He sighed deeply. "I found as I traveled around Europe that Trinity's memory stayed with me, followed me. Eventually, after a few years, knowing she would be older, I returned to look for her, and I learned she'd died giving birth." Cooper watched his nostrils flare in anger. "The owners at the lodge said she developed toxemia with her pregnancy. Her aunt and uncle, ignorant and probably uncaring as well, didn't see that she got the care she needed. She had a stroke during childbirth. The owners at the lodge also told me both Trinity and the baby died. The family had even put a little marker beside Trinity's gravestone to represent the lost child. I can show it to you." He banged a fist on the table. "They didn't want people to know they'd given the baby away to the orphanage in Sevierville."

"Ahhh." Cooper heard Mamie's sigh of understanding.

"When did you find out the baby had survived?" Emily asked.

"Not until that time twenty years later." He looked at Mamie. "I often came to the mountains to paint in the years after, and when I did I always visited the gravesites. Sometimes I hiked the old trails and visited the places Trinity had introduced me to. I carried a heavy burden of guilt around that my leaving caused her death and my child's death."

"You were probably right in thinking that," Cooper put in, ignoring Emily's warning eyes as he spoke the words.

"How did you learn Mamie hadn't died?" Emily pulled the focus back to the story again.

"I was talking to an old local one day, Elton Ogle, while painting a barn scene against a mountain backdrop. Somehow I mentioned that a girl named Trinity Simons had first brought me to that very spot." His eyes moved to Mamie's. "Elton had known Trinity's parents, remembered how the flu took them both one winter, and how Trinity had gotten parceled off to her uncle's home. He said they had five kids already and didn't want another mouth to feed. He said he'd always felt sorry for Trinity. " He leaned towards Mamie. "Elton also told me he'd heard Trinity's baby had been given up to an orphanage and not buried in that little grave at all."

Mamie smiled at him finally. "And it didn't take long for you to learn there was only one orphanage in the area and to learn I'd been raised there." She shook her head. "No wonder none of my family ever came looking for me at the children's home. I always wondered about that."

"What a story." Emily almost whispered the words.

Mamie reached a hand across to Cawood. "Are you sure about this? Are you sure you're really my father?"

His eyes locked on hers. "I'm sure, but we can do blood tests and DNA tests if you want."

Cooper watched his mother's face cloud over. "Why did you decide to tell us this now?"

"Two reasons." He kept Mamie's hand in his. "My older brother Paul recently died, and I realized life is short. It was his funeral I attended when out west." His eyes shifted to Emily. "The other reason was prompted by what Emily told me at the open house in early May."

"What?" Emily asked, obviously trying to remember.

"You told me when you got tied up and locked in the closet by Randy Lawson, and realized how close you'd come to being killed, that what your mind focused on most was all the people who had loved you."

"I remember that." She smiled. "And I told you I felt glad I'd known my own parents as a girl and felt sad for Mamie because she'd never known hers." Emily sent an apologetic glance to Mamie. "You did say to me once yourself that you wished you knew more about your parents."

"I did." Mamie sat back against the sofa.

Cawood drummed his fingers on the table beside him again. "Thinking about Paul dying, I realized I didn't want you to find out about me only after I died, which had been my plan before. I wanted you to know now that I was your natural father, even though I risked that you might hate me for leaving your mother as I did and for all the heartache I probably caused her and you."

"I'd say there's no probably to that equation." Cooper clenched a fist. "And what if you had died first? Then what? Were you planning to just have someone show up at Mom's door after your death and say, 'oh, by the way, ma'am, that old artist gent was actually your father and left a note behind for you'?"

Cawood's eyes flashed as they met his. "I think the more time I spend around you, Cooper Garrison, the more I think you inherited the disagreeable nature I'm so famous for. I also admit I don't care for it hitting me in the face so often." He pushed forward in his chair, getting angry now. "I never married, Cooper. Your mother is my primary heir. I want you to know that. I planned to do right by her at the end even if I couldn't at the first of her life."

"Well, isn't that nice?" Cooper put his hands on his hips. "Here you are loaded to the gills with money, and you watched my mother struggle after my dad's death and you did nothing to help. Then you watched us struggle again after my brother's death and didn't put out a helping hand then either. I don't even remember you being at Lance's funeral, and if all you're telling me is true, he was your dang grandson. What kind of man are you?"

A shouting match ensued between them then, with Mamie and Emily having little luck in stopping it.

"Do you realize with your help, Cawood Gentry, that Mom could have bought that dang gallery she's worked her butt off in all these years and practically run single-handedly? Did you ever think about

that? Did you?" Cooper paced the room now, his anger rising.
"Look at all this opulence." He swung his hand around. "While
you sat up here in your gilded mansion on the hill, we worked, lost,
went through heartaches, and struggled down in the valley below.
Do you know how many times I sneaked down from my room
at night to find my mother crying by herself, worrying over how
to pay the bills? And where were you? Out visiting at your other
sprawling lodge out west. I saw the photos of it earlier on the walls
in your living room. How could you let your own daughter experience such need and not do anything to help?"

"Cooper, you're out of line." Mamie's voice sliced across the
room to reach him. "We're guests in Cawood's home."

"Not any longer." Cooper's eyes met his mother's before shifting
to Cawood. "Thanks for the nice dinner and all, Mr. Gentry, but
I think we'll head on back down to where the real world is again."

"You're being exceptionally rude to me," Cawood put in. "You
may regret that later."

"Why? Because you might cut me or Mom out of your will?"
He pulled his car keys out of his pocket, preparing to leave. "Gee.
Then maybe we'll get screwed, too, like poor Emily did and lose
our big inheritance. Well, get this, Mr. Gentry, I don't care. I've
taken care of Mom as best I could since we lost Dad and Lance,
and I can keep taking care of her. Thank you very much. And if
you think about it, she's done a bang-up good job taking care of
herself all these years, too, and of me and Lance until we grew up."

Cooper paused. "It looks like it didn't do me or Lance any good
to have a rich grandad we didn't know anything about or for Mom
to have a rich daddy who wouldn't own up to being her father.
What's the matter, Cawood, do you think it might spoil your artist
image to have the press suddenly talking about a little knocked-
up mountain girl and her bastard child you walked out on in the
Smoky Mountains?"

Cawood jerked out of his seat to head towards Cooper, anger
flooding his face. But Mamie jumped up to move between them.

"Oh, no," she said, placing herself firmly in his path. "I won't have you two starting a punch-out fight here, do you hear me?" She burst into tears. "This has been a very emotional night for me, and you two are now turning it into a total nightmare."

Emily stood and walked over to put an arm around Mamie. "She's right, and I think we need to take Mamie home, Cawood. This has been a big night of revelation for her and she needs time to think on all you've told her." She patted Cawood's arm with her free hand. "I'm sure Mamie will want to talk with you more once she's had a chance to digest all this information you've shared with her. Won't you, Mamie?"

Mamie nodded between her tears.

Emily sent Cooper an angry look. "And I'm sure Cooper will want to talk with you in time also when he can get his temper in check."

"I doubt that," he mumbled, turning to stalk towards the door.

He paused at the doorway, turning back to see Mamie throw her arms around Cawood. "I'm so glad you've told me this, no matter how hard it has been for you and for us. It's good to know about my mother, and about you, and about how you both met. I will want to talk with you more later, to let you share your memories with me, to tell me more about my mother and about you both in those years."

Cooper watched Emily retrieve her purse from the sofa and tuck her arm around his mother like a good daughter.

She turned to Cawood. "Thank you for a beautiful meal and for allowing us to share this evening in your home," she said, remembering her manners. She gave him a hug. "You were very brave to share all you did with us tonight. I know it wasn't easy."

Cooper rolled his eyes. Easy for whom? First he'd had the injustice of dealing with Emily's lost inheritance and its effects, and now this fiasco. Didn't rich people ever think at all about the ways they screwed up people's lives with the things they did?

Cawood's eyes met Cooper's in a steady gaze. "I'll think on what you've said, even in anger, Cooper. And you think on what I've said." He walked to the door to see them out as he spoke. "Despite the past and all my mistakes, I want to try to build a relationship with you and with your mother."

Cooper bit his tongue not to reply. With Emily and his mother both glaring at him, he decided it better to simply nod.

CHAPTER 21

Emily had thought her life at the gallery in Philadelphia busy, full, and often a little stressful, but those days looked placid now in comparison to the events of her months in Tennessee. She flipped the calendar from June to July as she worked the front counter of the Creekside this first day of July. Where had the last weeks gone?

The phone rang, interrupting her thoughts, and she picked it up.

"Hi," Mamie said. "Is all well there? I thought I'd call before your day got too busy. Stock in several areas is getting low with the tourist season in full swing. I left some notes on your desk of calls to make. We need to ask several of our artists to bring in more work and there are a few other orders that need to be placed and clients you need to call."

"Thanks." Emily perched on the stool behind the register. "How was the dinner with Cawood and Cooper last night?"

Mamie laughed. "Well, they didn't start a fight and neither one of them hollered at the other the whole evening."

"Probably because you threatened both of them ahead of time."

"A lesson for you about the power of being a woman." Mamie paused. "I wish you would have joined us. I cooked a nice dinner."

"I'm sure you did." Emily twisted the phone cord while she talked. "But I felt the three of you should have this time together without me." She started to add I'm not family, after all, but thought better of it. Best to avoid getting Mamie started on that subject.

"Cooper is still a little bitter towards Cawood for not owning up sooner about the past, but he's realized that at least Cawood did finally acknowledge his parentage to me." She hesitated. "He didn't have to, you know. No one would ever have known if he didn't."

"Except himself."

"Yes, and I'm glad his brother's death and Cawood's little talk with you pushed him to come forward. It's opened other doors for me so that I can learn more about my extended family. Admittedly, I don't care much for the Simons branch who took me to an orphanage after my mother died, but I've found other Simons family members I like very much, many who thought I'd died with Trinity." She laughed. "It was funny seeing my own grave in a cemetery. In those small family cemeteries in the past they weren't very careful about overseeing burials."

"I'm glad you had the cemetery remove that marker."

"Yes, well it did seem time. This has certainly been an eventful month."

The front door opened to let in a group of tourists.

"I'd better go, Mamie. Some customers just came in and I see more coming up the walk behind them."

"Have a good day, dear. Leona will be in later."

Emily hung up and walked out from behind the counter to talk with her customers. Introducing people to the world of art, talking about the process of creating different works, and telling visitors about the artists behind the creations were some of Emily's favorite parts of her job.

A little later in the day, after Leona arrived to work in the gallery, Emily took care of the calls Mamie had suggested in her office, answered her e-mails, ordered needed supplies, and generally caught up on all her paperwork. Her cell phone rang after an hour's work, interrupting the quiet. She glanced at it to see Daniel Stelben's name.

"Hi, Daniel," she said, answering her phone.

"Hello, Emily, do you have a few minutes to talk or are you too busy in the gallery?"

"I'm in my office finishing a pile of paperwork and orders. It will be nice to take a short break." She hesitated. "How are you?"

"Actually, feeling very good, thank you."

"That's a change." Emily smiled to hear Daniel's old jovial voice back again. "Did you get a new job or something?"

"Sort of."

"Well, tell me about it." Emily knew the gallery struggled more financially every day to stay afloat. She couldn't blame any of the remaining employees for looking elsewhere for work.

Daniel's next words confirmed her worst fears. "I think Leonard is going to sell the gallery."

Emily bit her lip. "I admit he threatened something like that to me some time ago."

Daniel laughed. "And he also let it slip to me later that he offered you your old job back."

"Daniel, I hope you don't fault me for not accepting."

"Not for a minute." She heard the squeak of Daniel's old office chair as he settled back into it. "But what if the new owner offered you a job?"

"Hmmm. I don't know." She giggled. "A new owner might be as difficult to work with as Leonard, although that seems hardly probable."

"What if I were one of the new owners, Emily, and if you came back to partner with me?"

"Is this daydreaming?"

"No. I've been a prudent man and can arrange half the capital needed. I actually have a partner now, one of our clients—Benton Shield, who has agreed to put up the rest. But he's also agreed to sell out to you when you can sell the gallery in Gatlinburg to buy in. It will be enough with the two of us partnering." He grew quiet for a moment. "I know it wouldn't be quite the same as having the gallery all your own as Hal and Mary wanted, but it would be close. And I think you and I could work well together."

"Oh, I'm flattered." Her mind went into a spin. "But I'm surprised that Leonard would sell to you."

Daniel chuckled. "He doesn't know I'm a part of the buyout. Benton is doing the sale through one of his corporations. The

Shields own many properties in downtown Philly. They know it is a good investment to buy in on the gallery and Benton Shield is particularly pleased to think you might come back. He and his wife, Jermaine, have known you since you first came to live with Hal and Mary."

"Benton and Jermaine were great friends of Hal and Mary's, and they are good people."

"Yes, and they love the gallery. They've bought art here for years, and they want to see the Newman saved for Hal and Mary's sake before Leonard completely bankrupts and destroys it."

She considered all Daniel was telling her. "This is really wonderful news."

"I hoped you'd think so." She heard his fingers tapping the desktop. "You know Leonard has bought Casteel's."

"He told me that."

"The woman helping him manage the restaurant and the little gift shop attached to it seems to know how to flatter and suck up to Leonard to make him happy. I hear she plants ideas in his head and then congratulates him for thinking of them." He chuckled. "She also seems to find him attractive."

"Really?" Emily considered this. "You mean they have a relationship?"

"Yes, and in an odd way they seem to suit. It's the first time since Leonard's mother fawned over him for so many years that he's found someone to stroke his ego and make him feel important."

"Is that changing how he acts at the gallery?"

"Oh, no, he's as nasty as ever with us, but he now says we are simply ungrateful and unappreciative of him and all he's tried to do for the Newman. He blames us, and you, that the gallery is failing, and he is positively gloating around us now, warning us that he has a buyer interested in the place who will probably throw us all out on our ears."

"Hmmm . . . he'll be angry when he learns you're one of the buyers. And he will be even angrier to learn Benton wants to sell to me to be your partner."

"He'll get over it." He drummed his fingers again. "The main thing is that the gallery will be out of his hands and saved, that it will continue as the Newman, that Hal and Mary's legacy and all they built will live on. Also that Lewis, Christine, Margaret, and I can keep our jobs. I've talked to Michael quietly, too. He plans to come back if the sale goes through, although the others who left seem happy where they've reestablished themselves. We're the only ones who know about this possible sale, Emily, so be careful who you talk to. If this should get back to Leonard, the sale might not close later this month."

Emily turned her chair to look across the garden of the Creekside and to the Little Pigeon River behind it. She had the window cracked today, even with the air conditioner running, in order to hear the sounds of the mountain creek rushing over the boulders. It was a peaceful setting. She'd been happy here in many ways.

"Will you think about it, Emily?"

"Yes, and I'm so happy you're doing this—you and Benton. Bless him and bless you for wanting to save the Newman and to keep it as it's always been."

"If everything goes through, we're going to host a change of ownership celebration in early August, invite all our old clients, let everyone know the Hal Newman Gallery is turning around, and that Leonard has sold out. That little chamber ensemble is going to come to play while everyone mingles and celebrates over one of Drummonds Caterers' fine spreads. Can't you just picture it?"

"Yes, I can." This was the caterer and small orchestral group they used for all their openings, and everybody loved them. It was tradition at the Newman.

"I'm sure I can get several of our artists to supply a stunning new work for the event, providing sort of a potpourri of new art rather than an opening event to support only one artist. Don't you think people will love that?"

"I do." She could hear the excitement in Daniel's voice.

"We could work well together, Emily. We always have."

"Yes, we have. You helped to train me—and to raise me." She

smiled in remembrance. Daniel had come to work at the gallery as a young man about the time Hal and Mary brought her to Philadelphia to live with them.

"Well, keep your toes and fingers crossed that all goes through. Leonard has agreed to the sale, and a closing date is set for later in July. But with that unpredictable man I won't fully relax until the signatures are on the line and everything is legally complete and finalized."

"I'll be believing with you that all will go well—and I'll be praying," she added, realizing that her efforts to grow in her faith these months had begun to impact her daily thinking.

Mercedes got up from her bed in the corner to bark now, running across the room to put her paws on the windowsill. Emily wasn't surprised to hear Brinkley bark back at her a few minutes later.

"Someone is here, Daniel. I need to go. You news has made my day today. Please keep me in touch with how everything goes."

"I will," he said, clicking off.

In a few moments, as Emily expected, Cooper and Brinkley came into view.

"Hey," Emily called, waving at Cooper through the window.

"Hey yourself," he said, reining Brinkley in from jumping up on the windowsill to scratch the new screen Cooper had installed. "Do you and Mercedes want to take a walk on the Gatlinburg Trail with me and Brink? It's not so hot this afternoon." He looked in the window at her. "But you'll probably want to go change into shorts. I have some for myself in the truck I think I'll put on, too. What do you say? Can you get away from the office?"

"Yes," she said, her heart lifting at the idea of time with Cooper. He was the main roadblock in considering Daniel's offer.

Emily went to speak with Leona before leaving the gallery. With the afternoon waning, Monty would soon arrive. And Monty's nephew, Brice, was helping part-time this summer now that the tourist traffic had picked up. An art major in college, he'd been working summer hours with them for two years. He worked part-time for the Creekside and part-time at the Russo Cellars to make money for school—a personable kid and very responsible.

It didn't take long for Emily to change into casual clothes and to lace on her walking shoes. She and Mercedes found Cooper and Brinkley on a bench outside the back door, and the four soon headed down the River Road towards the Gatlinburg Trail.

"I sometimes wish more Smokies trails were open to dogs," Emily said, stretching out her stride to keep up with Cooper. "Mercedes is always disappointed when I head out in hiking clothes without her. She seems to sense I'm going on a trail she might enjoy."

"Yeah, only the Gatlinburg Trail and the Oconaluftee River Trail, near Cherokee on the North Carolina side of the mountains, are open to dogs." He paused. "A lot of people take their dogs on other trails, but it's dangerous."

"Why?"

"For several reasons. For the dogs' sake, because they can become prey to predators like bears or coyotes or can lead a predator to you. Dogs being dogs, too, they can behave unpredictably, barking at wildlife, digging into nesting sites like those of yellow jackets, which could whip up the jackets, and then get themselves and others stung. They can get into burrs, stickers, or thorns, and they can carry diseases into the park's wildlife population."

"I never thought about the ways they could be a problem in the park."

"I've seen a dog jerk its leash out of an owner's hand to charge after a bear with her cubs. As you'd expect, the dog got the worst of that encounter." They turned off the road onto the trail as Cooper talked. "I've watched dogs root around rocks by the stream and stir up a snake, too. People don't realize that domestic dogs don't understand dangers in the great out-of-doors and how to avoid them."

Emily adjusted Mercedes's leash in her hand. "I'm sure Mercedes wouldn't know what to do if she encountered unexpected wildlife. We had one curiosity experience with a skunk once and I certainly haven't forgotten it."

Cooper laughed. "Been there, done that one, too."

They walked along in companionable silence for a little while. The trees shaded the trail, making the walk cooler than one in Gatlinburg on a warm July day.

Since that flare-up of Cooper's temper at Cawood Gentry's home, Emily had noticed he seemed more at ease with himself. Mamie said she thought learning about Cawood had lightened some of Cooper's load in regards to her.

"He grew so serious in his resolve to take care of me after I lost both Price and Lance." Mamie had shaken her head as she told Emily this. "Of course, he seemed to forget I'd done a rather fine job of taking care of myself. It must be a man thing, that need to protect."

Emily turned to Cooper as they walked along. "How did the dinner with Cawood go?" she asked to make conversation.

"It was an evening full of polite tension." His eyes narrowed. "Mom seems determined to create a semblance of family with Cawood Gentry, but it isn't working very well for me. I don't think he can ever expect me to call him Grandpa."

Emily giggled despite herself. "I can't imagine Cawood Gentry wanting anyone to call him Grandpa."

Cooper grinned at her. "I guess you're right."

They crossed the bridge over the stream, stopping to look down at the water rushing below.

"Since people found out Cawood Gentry is my grandfather, a lot of people have joked around saying they see now where I got my temper and my sharp tongue."

With Brinkley pulling on the leash, he walked on. "Hearing that has made me realize I want to work at being more like my father or Delbert. I don't find the comparisons very flattering." He paused to look at her. "Do you think I've been doing any better later? I've been trying."

His question surprised Emily. "I'm not with you much, Cooper," she hedged. "When I am, I've noticed you seem a little easier in your skin."

He smiled. "That's an honest answer and a nice way to put it."

They walked up a hill and into a woodsy area of the trail where the remnants of old chimneys and cabin walls still remained.

Cooper leaned over to pick up a piece of trash on the trail to tuck into his pocket. "When Lance died I decided I had to be the man of the family for Mom, to be responsible and to keep Dad's business going. All those people who worked for Garrison Homes depended on me suddenly. It was a lot for a kid. Looking back, I guess it was the same for Lance when Dad died. A weight with big expectations. It's real easy to forget how to laugh, to be carefree, and to have fun when you carry a weight like that around. I used to be different before."

"Your mother has said that."

He glanced at her. "I don't want to be thought of negatively like Cawood."

"Cawood is very respected for his work."

"Yes, but he's also known for being difficult to deal with and to approach, for being brusque and unsociable, short-tempered, imposing, and intimidating."

She felt a smile curl her lips. "Well, if it's any comfort, I don't think you've collected a reputation for all those personal characteristics yet."

"Ha, ha. But the point is I am known for a few of those less-than-stellar traits." He slowed to study a cluster of mushrooms under a tree.

Emily paused, too. "The nice thing about life is that it always gives us the opportunity to change."

"I hope that's true." His eyes met hers. "How have you changed being here?"

The question caught her off guard. "Well, I've found I can adapt to change better than I imagined, that I can handle sorrows and move on, find new joys and meaning in a new place." She smiled at him. "I've found a new respect for my work creating dollhouses here, too."

"Not from me at first."

"No, but you've come around." She patted his arm. "Thank you for all the time you spent helping me create the Edwardian. I haven't built a lavish house like that from scratch before without a kit or actually designed the house plans."

"You did good," he said. "And I admit it's been an education for me to watch all the effort and expertise you've put into every aspect of that little house. It's a piece of art of its own."

She stopped walking in surprise. "Oh, Cooper, thank you. That's a very nice compliment coming from you."

He shook his head. "Well, I should give you more. You've done a fantastic job coming in to run the Creekside. Mother constantly brags about you. You're well-loved and you've grown the business with the skills you brought with you."

Hearing the words "well-loved," Emily couldn't help but wish they applied to Cooper's feelings for her. Would she ever be more than a fond friend to him? It hurt not to have her stronger feelings returned. She still wanted more from him than he seemed to want of their relationship.

Passing the cascades in the stream, they soon neared the end of the trail, where they turned around to start back. It was only a two-mile walking trail, four miles round-trip, when they walked all of it like today.

"Do you and Mercedes want to come up to the house for dinner?" Cooper asked as they started back. "I've got some chicken for the grill and Delbert brought me fresh corn, tomatoes, and okra from the garden today."

"Ummm," she said, pleased at the offer. "I like fried okra."

"Good. Well, I'll let you make it and slice the tomatoes and stuff while I grill the chicken and the corn."

A happy, easy evening followed, the kind that made Emily's heart yearn for permanency with Cooper. It made her dream of living with him, sharing every day with him, having a family with him.

At the end of the evening, the kisses at her door were sweet, but no words of love followed. In fact, earlier in the evening, Cooper had said—probably without thinking—that he figured he might be a lot like Cawood, happy to live alone on his mountain, his life not cluttered up with anyone else's. Emily had winced at the words and turned to busy herself in the kitchen so she wouldn't meet his eyes.

"He just wants to go on as we are, Mercedes," she said to the dog as she headed back to her bedroom to get ready for bed.

She checked her e-mail a last time on her laptop before turning off the lights and saw a message from Daniel: "Enjoyed our talk. Looking forward to the change in the gallery and to partnering with you at the Newman. Say yes. We'll make a good team."

Emily knew the words were true. She and Daniel would make a good team, and together they could make the Hal Newman Gallery shine again and move to new heights. Settling into the pillows later and turning out the light, she made a decision. "I'm giving it until August, Lord," she said out loud. "If partnering as a friend is all it's going to amount to with Cooper Garrison, it's going to break my heart to keep staying here, to keep wishing and yearning for more than he can give. As long as I'm here near him, I won't be able to move on, either, or open my heart to someone else, and I don't want to end up lonely and alone on a mountain like Cawood Gentry."

She patted the bed for Mercedes to jump up beside her, feeling her prayer was a right one for her. If Cooper wasn't ready to give his heart and his love by the end of July, she'd talk to Cawood to see if he would buy the gallery for Mamie. She knew he would, and she'd go back to Philadelphia to partner with Daniel at the Newman. Her condo hadn't sold; she wouldn't even have to find a new place to live. Kylie and Azea would be thrilled to have her back, as would other friends she had in the Philadelphia area. She'd readjust quickly, and in time she'd get past loving Cooper Garrison and be able to love someone else life brought along her path. The one thing Emily had learned from her losses in life was that the heart could always love again. In the meantime, perhaps Cooper would realize his feelings went deeper than he thought. She'd just have to wait and see.

CHAPTER 22

July drifted into August. Cooper and his crew had completed much of the Jeffries' home and planned to begin work on the Buchanans' retirement home next. Outside contractors had already excavated their site and laid the house foundations. Cooper could already see that the Buchanans would be easier to work with than Nathan Jeffries had been. Frankly, Cooper would be glad to see the last of that man, calling him nearly every day about nitpicking details.

Around the Garrison crew's regular workload, all of them had been pitching in, as they could, to help Mackie get his house completed. He and Sara had set a wedding date for late fall before the Thanksgiving holidays. The couple bubbled over with talk of their wedding plans now, mixed with giggles, sneaked kisses, and occasional heated discussions on how to finish out and decorate their home.

Emily seemed to have grown quieter over the last month, as if she had something on her mind. Mamie told Cooper that Leonard had run the Hal Newman Gallery in Philadelphia into the ground with mismanagement and that the business would probably be sold. Perhaps learning this had made her worried and sad. He'd hate to think of his business failing and of how the sale of it might impact the lives of all the friends and employees he cared about.

"Maybe it will work out okay," he told Brinkley, who'd come to weave around his legs in the kitchen, where he was cleaning up after dinner. "After all, that mess earlier with the Newman Gallery brought Emily and Mercedes to us."

Brinkley's ears pricked up at Mercedes's name, making Cooper laugh. "Maybe they'll walk up after a while, Brink, and if not we might take a walk down to Emily's place, try to cheer her up a little."

A short time later Brinkley pricked up his ears at the sound of a car in the driveway. "Maybe that's her now," he said, heading to the door.

The car that pulled up to the house wasn't Emily's, though. Cooper scowled to see Cawood Gentry get out of the sleek vehicle and head up to the porch.

"How did you find out where I lived?" He crossed his arms in irritation.

"That doesn't sound like a nice welcome." Cawood paused at the steps until Cooper spoke to Brinkley that it was all right to let him come farther.

"What do you want, Cawood?"

The older man grumbled another complaint about his hospitality and then said, "I have a few things I need to talk with you about that I felt couldn't wait."

"Like what?"

"You going to invite me in and be sociable or are we going to have to stand out here on the porch and talk?"

Cooper considered his options. "We could sit down here on the porch and talk. The weather's nice. Or we could talk inside."

"Outside is fine." Cawood walked past him to settle into the wooden swing at the end of the porch. "Nice swing," he said. "You build it?"

Cooper nodded, and with some reluctance followed across the porch to settle into a chair nearby.

"Nice house, too. Mamie said you built it."

"Cut the chitchat and get to the point of what brought you here tonight."

The man grinned. "Mamie's been trying to teach me to be more sociable and less gruff. I was making an effort."

Cooper rolled his eyes.

Cawood leaned over to make friends with Brinkley before sitting back in the swing and giving it a little push back and forth.

The silence lengthened before he spoke again. "I had a visitor at my place on the mountain yesterday. Emily Lamont. She came to ask me if I would buy the Creekside Gallery for Mamie."

Cooper snapped forward in his seat.

A slow grin spread across Cawood's face. "I thought that might get your attention."

"Why would she ask that?"

Cawood rubbed his arm. "I thought you might know that."

Shifting in his chair with irritation, Cooper let his eyes meet the older man's. "And why do you think I might know that?"

The older man ran a hand through his hair now. "She said she hadn't told you or Mamie, but I wasn't sure she might not have let something slip. Or that you might have figured out what she was up to since the two of you have been seeing each other for quite a while."

Cooper gritted his teeth. "She didn't say anything to me." He wasn't sure what else he wanted to say, his mind already reeling with this unexpected information.

The silence settled in again.

"Why does she want to do this?" Cooper asked at last.

Cawood studied him. "I thought maybe you might tell me. It was my sense she'd been happy with the change here to the mountains and with her work at the Creekside. The gallery has prospered under her hand; Mamie loves her." He paused. "I don't think Mamie will be happy about Emily selling or leaving."

Cooper fought for self-control at this new information. "Leaving? When? What are you talking about?"

Cawood shook his head. "Well, it's obvious she's kept you totally in the dark about her plans. That makes me wonder if I ought to be putting my oar in this business at all."

Cooper felt his anger rising. "I think you'd better tell me what you know, Cawood."

"Why?" he asked. "Will you try to talk her into staying?"

Cooper sat back, crossing his arms, not answering.

"You're not sure. That's right sad to my way of thinking." He pushed the swing again, making the chains rattle in the darkness.

"Where is Emily going and when is she leaving?" Cooper tried to keep his voice calm and his temper down.

Cawood shifted his gaze to meet Cooper's eyes, hesitating before answering, making him more nervous with the hesitation and the look on Cawood's face. "She's already gone, boy."

Cooper's heart hammered against his ribs at the words. He felt like he'd been kicked in the stomach. He tried for words but couldn't find any. Then he jerked in air, trying to get his breath.

"I'm glad to see you're upset." Cawood said slowly, still studying him. "She's worth getting upset over."

Dang man, sitting there calm and collected while he felt like his heart had just been torn out. Cooper wanted to hit him. He felt his fists clench in his lap.

"No sense in getting mad at the messenger," Cawood said. "You'd have found out soon enough from someone."

"Where did she go?"

"Back to Philadelphia. Daniel Stelben and another partner bought the Newman Gallery from Leonard, the relative who in-herited it—and obviously mismanaged it, from what Emily told me." He chuckled. "The man doesn't know one of his own em-ployees, the gallery manager, is a part of the company that made the buyout offer, although I'd say he'll learn of it soon enough."

"Emily likes Daniel Stelben. That's good news. She's been wor-ried about the gallery there."

Cawood fixed his gaze on him again. "Daniel Stelben has offered Emily a partnership with him in running the Newman."

Cooper felt another wrench to his heart.

"What do you think about that, boy?"

Cooper glowered at him. "What does it matter what I think? She lost that gallery wrongfully. It's right she should have a chance to get it back, even if only in part."

"Is that how you see it?"

"You're getting on my nerves, Cawood."

"I can see that. And I can also see that you're a dang fool." He leaned towards Cooper. "Here's the deal. Emily left for Philadelphia yesterday after talking with me. She's going to the big reopening of the gallery now that the ownership change is finalized. I understand she planned to tell Mamie she was traveling to Philadelphia this weekend to wish them well, but she plans to stay and accept Daniel's offer to partner the Newman if I will buy the Creekside."

He gave his head a sad shake. "Emily wanted to be sure the gallery came to Mamie. Said you'd always wanted it for her. She didn't want to put it on the open buyer's market."

"And what did you say?"

Cawood leaned back in the swing and crossed his ankle over his knee. "I told her I'd buy it if she was determined to sell." His eyes met Cooper's. "Are you as pleased as she thought you might be? I know your mother won't be."

"There seem to be a few insinuations here that I don't think I like."

"Good, because I don't like you much right now. That's a fact with no insinuation about it. It seemed obvious even to an old unmarried fossil like me that someone has hurt that girl's heart and that she felt the best choice, under the circumstances, was to get away from that hurt."

"You have a lot of nerve . . ."

"That fact is established," Cawood interrupted. "But the point is, what are you going to do about it? Looks like you'll need to search your heart, what there is of it, and see if you care enough about this girl to go after her or if you want to let her go. Either way, I'll see that your mother is taken care of. The sale of the gallery from Nelle Jacobs to Hal Newman happened without my knowledge, under the table, you might say. I'd have bought the gallery then if I'd known Nelle wouldn't keep it."

"You wanted to buy it before?"

"I contacted Hal Newman after the sale and told him I'd buy the gallery if he ever wanted to sell. But he'd made a promise to Nelle he'd take care of it."

"Emily never told me this."

"I don't think she ever knew."

Cooper whistled to Brinkley, who'd wandered too far from the porch. "Maybe I shouldn't interfere in Emily getting a chance at the inheritance she should have received before."

"Is that how you see it?"

His temper flared. "How should I see it?"

"I was hoping you'd see it like a man in love, wanting to go after the woman he cares about."

"Like you did with Trinity?"

Cawood frowned at him. "That was a different story in a different time. And if I made a mistake then, as you're insinuating, are you going to make a bigger one, knowing how my decision worked out?"

The words pricked at him. "You're saying I ought to marry Emily to keep her here at the gallery."

"No, that would be monumentally stupid. And if you don't love the girl then you ought to let her go. I'll buy the gallery for your mother. Probably have to keep it in my name; you know how proud she is. But I'll let her run it and leave it to her."

Cooper stared into the darkness enveloping the mountain now, watching the fireflies wink in the edge of the woods.

Cawood stood up. "Seems to me like I ought to head on back home and let you think this thing through." He paused and put a hand on Cooper's shoulder. "Think on this situation and find the right way, boy. Don't hide your heart from yourself and regret it one day. I learned too late how much I cared for Trinity Simons, and sometimes you can't go back. As a businessman, you know that timing is everything in how things work out."

Cooper didn't want Cawood to know his own indecisiveness. He stood, too. "Thank you for coming by to tell me this. You didn't have to."

"No, I didn't. I haven't liked you much, but you're growing on me. I see too much of myself in you at times but I think in some ways you're a better and kinder man than I am. We'll see."

Cooper bit his tongue not to reply, letting the older man walk down the steps of his house and to his car. Cawood lifted a hand to him as he backed out of the driveway, but he didn't say more.

After Cawood left, Cooper went into the house to get a bottle of cola from the refrigerator. His mouth was dry from the shock of all he'd learned. Not liking the light inside, he took the drink back out on the porch to nurse it in the darkness.

How could Emily leave and not even talk to him about it? When was she planning to tell him she wasn't coming back? Never? Or with some good-bye note in the mail later on? It wasn't what he expected of Emily—taking off and planning all these major life changes without even talking to him. It hurt.

Cooper took several breaths, trying to calm himself from all he'd learned. Maybe it was all for the best, he thought. Hadn't he wished many times she'd never come to Gatlinburg? He remembered the one time she said she loved him, but he'd never been able to say it back. Did he love her? How did you know for sure? How could you tell feelings for a fact? Cooper closed his eyes, feeling wretched, sweeps of pictures and memories flooding his mind, his heart and head in a turmoil.

The sound of a motorcycle cut into the quiet of the night, and he saw Venetta rounding the corner of his drive on her Harley. He heaved a sigh. Could this night get any worse?

She parked the Harley, swinging a long leg over the side of the machine and pulling off her helmet. Even in the dark, he could see she wore her usual trademark black jacket and boots with dark boot-cut jeans.

"I am not in the mood to deal with you tonight, Venetta," he said as she started up the porch steps.

"I thought we'd gotten past that." She paused. "What are you doing sitting out here in the dark?"

"It's a nice night."

"Maybe." She walked over to sit on the swing Cawood had vacated. "Or maybe you're out here brooding."

"What makes you say that?" Cooper studied her, wondering if she, too, knew about Emily.

She leaned back in the swing. "Oh, you just sounded testy. Lance used to get that same tone of voice when he was upset about something."

Cooper bit back a retort. He definitely didn't want to get into a discussion about Lance tonight.

"What can I do for you, Venetta?"

"I wouldn't mind a drink like that one you have or a beer."

He shot her a dark look. "I don't drink beer but you can go get a cola out of the refrigerator if you want. Walk straight through to the back after you let yourself in; you can't miss the kitchen."

She returned a few minutes later with a drink and the bag of Cheetos he'd left on the counter from supper.

He raised an eyebrow.

She ignored it, holding the bag out to him. "Want some?"

"No." He watched her take the bag and dig into it. He and Lance had always marveled that Venetta could eat as much as she did and stay as thin as a rail.

"You know what tomorrow is," she said after a few minutes.

Remembrance hit him with her words that it was the anniversary of Lance's death. "And you felt a need to come remind me of that," he replied in annoyance.

"No." She looked out into the night. "I want you to go with me to put a marker on the place where Lance went off at The Dragon."

He sat up. "You what?"

"You heard me."

"Why after all this time?"

"I want to move on and I think that might help me do it."

He knew he sneered at her. "You think putting a stick cross by the road and a bunch of little flowers will make a difference?"

"Maybe." She stuck her chin up. "But I want to try to at least finalize things."

They sat in the quiet for a few minutes, Venetta eating Cheetos and drinking her cola. "I heard about Cawood Gentry being your and Lance's grandfather," she said at last. "It made me mad when I heard. Here Lance had a grandfather and he never even got to know him."

She fisted a hand. "Lance was only a kid when your daddy died. It was hard for him to suddenly have to try to step into his father's shoes and take over the business." She looked across at Cooper. "Did you know he'd been thinking of taking a year to travel around the United States before your dad died?"

Cooper knew his jaw dropped at her words.

She laughed, seeing his expression. "We planned to ride and see all sorts of places around the USA, to camp and hike and to experience a little of life while still young and fancy-free, before we settled down to start a family and all. Then everything changed." She paused. "Sometimes I think Lance grew more reckless and risk oriented after your father died, felt trapped, knowing he didn't have any choices or freedom anymore."

Venetta put a hand on Cooper's knee, surprising him with the touch. "You've been the same way, Cooper. You used to laugh and be so much fun before Lance died—even when things were tough sometimes. But then you changed, too."

She hesitated. "I see glimpses of the way you were before Lance died when you're with Emily Lamont now. She seems good for you. Don't run her off as you did me for so long. Life is short. I wish Lance and I had married. He kept putting it off after your dad died. Always putting responsibility and the business first, never giving himself time to love and be happy."

"Did Lance tell you he loved you?"

"Yes, finally, and we got engaged then. But I always sensed a part of himself that he held back. And he worried about his mother, worried about you."

Cooper raised his eyebrows.

"Oh, I know he teased you a lot, but that was his way of trying to get you to lighten up and have more fun. He worried you were too serious. Said you'd taken your dad's death even harder than he had, wanting to blame someone for it. Not wanting to see that sometimes bad things just happen, that we can't always control life. That there's evil and bad in the world and that sometimes evil gets in a sneak shot at us."

Her eyes shifted to the lightning bugs twinkling in the trees. "I've been learning that it's not so much what happens to us in the past that matters, it's how we move on. We can't live in yesterday; it's gone. And we have limited control for tomorrow. But we do have today."

She hesitated, giving him a rueful grin. "I want to let myself really love Rafe now. I know I've been holding back for Lance's sake. And I want you to say it's okay. I've spent a lot of years feeling guilty, knowing your anger towards me."

"I think motorcycles are dangerous, Venetta."

She gave him an irritated look. "Living is dangerous, Cooper. Personally, I think climbing around on roofs of half-finished houses is dangerous. I think walking across boards over open floors is dangerous and that working with saws and heavy machinery is dangerous. So what? I still wouldn't have been bitter at you if Lance had lost his life on the site. I'd have remembered he was doing what he loved. That's how I like to remember the day Lance died. He loved getting out in the mountains on his bike, loved shooting The Dragon. He was living his life the way he loved to live it when he died."

"Maybe."

"That's why I want to go put a marker where he went off."

"Why not climb down to where the motorcycle hit, put it there?"

Her eyes lit. "We can do that."

"Do you really think this will help you move on, to be ready to love Rafe? He's a great guy, too."

She twined her fingers in her lap. "I think love is a decision that you decide to let yourself know and have, like a gift you give yourself," she said at last. "I don't think it whacks you over the head, drags you off and makes you give in to it. I think it's there like a pretty flower or a hot fudge sundae, letting you know you want to pick it or taste it . . . but it doesn't come after you. You have to go after it."

Cooper thought about this for a while.

"Will you come with me?" she said. "Tomorrow is the day he died, and I want to do it then."

He looked at the sincerity in her face and gave in. "I'll come and I'll make the marker."

"Thanks." She got up and leaned over to kiss him on the cheek, and for the first time Cooper didn't cringe at her touch.

After she left, Cooper thought about Emily in Philadelphia again. Maybe he needed to let her go, too. Maybe she was meant to go back to the city, to run the Newman, to get her second chance there—like Venetta and her second chance with Rafe. Maybe going to The Dragon with Venetta would help him let Emily go just as Venetta hoped it would help her let Lance go.

Emily had said she loved him only that one time over the ring. Probably caught up in the gift, letting her feelings run away with her. What was there in him to love, after all? Especially in comparison to a glamorous life in Philadelphia? And what did Cawood Gentry know about anything anyway. It's not as if he were any expert in how to run your life. Or knew what Emily might feel or why she was doing what she was.

Cooper had kept a clamp on himself, and on his emotions, for a long time. He'd come to know this about himself in the last months. Like Venetta, he knew he'd held himself back from loving. Not wanted to take the risk to love again or to risk being hurt again. Love was risky. It gave the power to hurt.

Maybe Emily had hurt him by leaving as she did, deciding she wanted to return to the Newman, but he didn't need to run after her or try to stop her from doing what she wanted. Hadn't Emily been hurt enough, lost her inheritance before and now had the chance to get it back? He certainly didn't need to stand in the way of her regaining what she'd lost so unfairly. If she felt strongly enough about him, she'd come back and not buy the gallery after all. And if not, then they weren't meant to be, he guessed.

Brinkley came over to nuzzle his hand. Cooper looked at his watch. It was time to turn in. He'd lived through loss twice in his life; he could again.

CHAPTER 23

In her hotel room, Emily laid out the dress she'd picked to wear to the reopening of the Hal Newman Gallery. She'd chosen to pamper herself and to stay at the Rittenhouse Hotel in a luscious room overlooking the park at Rittenhouse Square. She loved the Rittenhouse Hotel and had enjoyed revisiting old memories in the Mary Cassatt Tea Room earlier. Her godmother, Mary, used to take her for afternoon tea at the Rittenhouse, and Emily had always felt so grown-up and special enjoying fine leaf teas, canapés and petit sandwiches, baked scones, sweets and savories—all in an elegant setting looking onto a charming courtyard.

Mercedes was staying at the gallery, where she felt perfectly at home, enjoying the lavish attention of old friends. She'd raced immediately to sniff out her old bed, which Daniel had put back into the office Emily always used before.

He'd hung Emily's favorite painting back on the wall, too, recreating her space as it had been before Leonard took it over. It felt bittersweet to be back, almost as if the interlude in Gatlinburg had been a vacation.

Slipping into her dress, Emily moved to study herself in the mirror, adding her signature diamond stud earrings, necklace, and dressy watch. Arly, at her old hair salon two blocks away, had worked her hair into a beautiful, smooth chignon and insisted they do her nails for the opening in a deep red to match her dress. She pulled the knee-length red sheath dress on now and thought of Cooper. He liked her in red.

She sighed, adjusting the halter neck of the dress and fluffing out the full skirt. Moving to a nearby chair, she sat down to pull on her red sequined shoes, a nice match to the sequined bodice of her dress. Emily had chosen red for a confidence boost tonight.

Two hours later she stood smiling among guests, clients, and old friends in the Newman Gallery, the rooms twinkling with special lights tonight for the opening. Several of their most famous artists had come, some with new works hung for display, delighting the guests. Drummonds had set up their usual posh and lavish buffet for all to enjoy, and the chamber ensemble in one of the gallery alcoves kept a stream of soft classical music lilting in the background of the conversation around the rooms.

"Everything is going beautifully, don't you think?" Daniel asked, coming up to stand beside her. He looked dapper and handsome in the casual tuxedo he wore with a crisp white shirt, maroon vest, and black-and-white-striped tie. His hair was turning a silvery white, reminding her of Hal.

She sighed. "Yes, everything is lovely."

"How are you doing?"

"Okay." Emily had told him all about Cooper over a long dinner they'd shared yesterday. She'd wanted him to understand her initial reluctance to accept his partnership offer, and she wanted him to understand that she might be a little moody for a season, getting past her heartbreak over Cooper.

"The man is a fool," he said softly, before Lewis and Christine came up to join them. Lewis with his gray goatee and wire-rimmed glasses was also dressed in a casual tux with a sporty yellow bow tie, typical of Lewis. Christine, who had endured as the office manager during the months with Leonard and somehow managed to budget the continual messes he created, wore a black dress with a glitzy overjacket and a million-dollar smile.

She came to put an arm around Emily, her red hair catching the lights in the room. "What a happy occasion this is, darling, and how wonderful it is to have you back—you and Mercedes."

Emily hugged her back. She felt like crying, to have all these people who loved her surrounding her with their welcomes right now when her heart hurt so.

Emily could see Michael Zucchi, mingling and laughing, obviously happy to be back at the Newman. Julianne Fontes and Margaret Kimbrough had stopped by, too, although both were happy with their new positions and weren't returning to the gallery. In time, with growth, Emily and Daniel might need a new employee, but right now as the gallery recovered, the five of them would manage.

"I can't believe Leonard came by earlier," Christine said.

"Trying to cause trouble." Lewis grumbled out the words.

"I expected him at one point or another," Daniel said. "He was bound to learn I'd become a partner in the gallery in the buyout."

"And he obviously wasn't happy about it." Christine took a stem of champagne from a passing waiter and sipped it. "I worried when he came in just as the opening began that he would try to start trouble."

"I'd thought of that possibility," Daniel said. "That's why I had my policeman friend come in uniform. He knew to watch for Leonard and to move in if he arrived."

"That did take some steam out of him." Lewis laughed.

"I knew he would be angry when he learned he hadn't simply sold out to some generic company," Emily put in. "He always believed we were plotting against him and this only seemed to confirm it."

Daniel laughed. "We were plotting against him, plotting any way we could figure to save this wonderful gallery. Emily, you may not feel a part of the plotting, but I have absolutely no guilt in my part in it."

"And I for one will be eternally grateful," said Christine. She put an arm in Lewis's. "Come on, Lewis. I see the DeFoes coming in. Let's go do a little greeting and meeting."

The two moved away, and then Daniel chuckled. "Leonard was mad but he didn't make the stink I'd suspected he might. I can't believe he actually asked us to talk up his restaurant, to put a good word in for Casteel's to our clients and friends." He shook his head. "He said we owed it to him after all he tried to do for us and for how little we appreciated it."

Emily smiled. "That's Leonard. He always views the world through his own unique perspective."

"You were nice to him."

"He is Hal and Mary's nephew. And I saw no point in being ugly. There's been enough of that."

"Caused totally by him."

"Yes, but it's time to move on."

Daniel stayed at her side as clients and guests came to greet them, seeming to realize she needed extra support tonight. Mario Benzi, with the chamber orchestra and also a member of the local opera company, sang a short congratulatory song earlier—an amusing number filled with congratulations and jubilation that had everyone laughing.

He stepped forward again now to take the microphone, smiling. "I have another little request to sing tonight," he said. "A favorite of mine and I'm sure of everyone's."

The instruments began to play the classic "Lady in Red" song, with Mario soon adding the familiar words.

Daniel smiled at her.

"Did you do this?" she asked, noticing several around the room were sending toasts or glances her way, she being the only one dressed so strikingly in red tonight.

"No, but I wish I'd thought of it. You do look beautiful tonight." He paused, leaning slightly to look over her shoulder. "Ahhh. I think we may have our answer. Is this someone you know?"

Emily turned around to see Cooper walking across the room towards her, dressed in a stunning black tux, a white pleated front shirt, and a black bow tie. He carried a red rose. Something about the look in his eyes as he drew closer prickled the hair on her arms.

"What are you doing here?" she asked as he came up before her.

He handed her the rose and then bowed slightly. "May I have this dance, beautiful woman in red?"

She fingered the rose. "This isn't an event for dancing, Cooper," she replied softly.

"Oh, I don't think anyone will mind." He glanced at Daniel. "Are you Daniel Stelben?"

Daniel nodded. "I'm Cooper Garrison. Pleased to meet you. Emily has always had only the nicest things to say about you."

Emily saw Daniel's eyebrows rise.

Cooper took the rose from Emily and handed it to Daniel. "If you wouldn't mind holding this, I'd like to dance with this beautiful lady in red."

Before Emily could argue, Cooper took her into his arms and began to dance with her away from Daniel. The crowd in the gallery parted, delighted, to watch.

Emily felt the color rise in her face. "Cooper, again, what are you doing here?"

He looked into her eyes with a look unfamiliar to her. "I came to get you, Emily. I have been stupid and blind, just like the song says, to your beauty and to my love for you."

Emily sucked in a breath and felt tears begin in her eyes. She blinked them back, trying not to overreact. "What is this all about?"

He swept her around in a smooth move before answering and then pulled her closer. "The first time we met you were wearing red. I love you in red. Did you know that? At the party at my house, you were wearing those Wizard of Oz shoes, too." He glanced towards the chamber group in the alcove. "Do you think this chamber band can play a jitterbug song?"

Alarmed, she pulled back from him. "No. Please. Dancing at all is out of character enough for the Newman and I'm already embarrassed."

"Are you?" He leaned over to kiss her. "Then prepare for this evening to get worse. I may embarrass you more, Miz Emily Lamont. I am head over heels in love with you, you know. I think I have been for months, maybe from the first time I saw you—dressed in that long red sweater. And even more amazingly so, seeing you tonight. In red again, so bright and so beautiful."

"Cooper." She glanced around the room, knowing everyone had seen the kiss. "This isn't doing my professional image much good."

"I don't care about that. All I care about is letting you know you've taken my heart, swept into my soul, changed me for the better." He kissed her nose. "You have, you know. I was only partly living until you came along. And even when you began to invade my life, I resisted like a dang fool. Not realizing you were meant for me."

He turned her around in another spin. "I'm going to fight Daniel Stelben to see which of us gets to partner with you."

Emily glanced across at Daniel, who lifted a champagne glass to her with a smile. What a situation!

Seeing her glance towards Daniel, Cooper twirled her in his direction as the song wound to a finish. He stepped away from her as Mario finished the last words, took the rose back from Daniel, got down on one knee, and then handed the rose to her, drawing every eye in the room their way and bringing conversation to a standstill.

"I love you, beautiful woman," he said, oblivious of the rapt audience. "I hope you will make me the happiest of men and marry me."

Stunned, Emily couldn't even think what to say. She put a hand to her heart while the people in the room oohed and aahed at the touching sight, some even applauding.

"Cooper, this is hardly like you," she whispered.

"Yeah, and it's a good change I plan to continue pursuing." He stood, leaned in to kiss her again, and took her hand. Glancing at Daniel, he said, "Is there any place where we can be alone for a minute?"

"Out on the back courtyard behind the gallery," Daniel answered. "Follow that hallway there." He pointed.

Cooper headed in that direction with Emily's hand in his. A little applause followed them, and Emily knew her face flamed with color once more.

She felt glad of the cool evening air as they stepped outside into the small courtyard tucked behind the Newman. Hal and Mary had put planters and a metal table and chairs out here years ago for the employees to enjoy on breaks.

Cooper lifted Emily and sat her on the table before leaning over to kiss her again. "I've missed you, Emily. How could you go off and leave me without even telling me? Plan a new life without me and not even tell me?"

She twisted her hands. "I thought it was best, and I didn't think you'd care."

"And what do you think now?"

"I don't know what to think." Her eyes moved over him, and she smiled. "I do think you look very handsome. I don't think I've ever seen you dressed up like this."

He grinned. "I do clean up nice, don't I?" He cupped her face and kissed her again. "And like the song earlier, you do look so beautiful. I know I'll never forget the way you looked tonight."

Emily sighed. "I simply cannot adjust to this new you, Cooper Garrison. I don't even know what to say to you. Whatever has happened to bring about all this change?"

He put a foot on one of the wrought iron chairs. "It's a good change, isn't it?"

"Well, yes, I suppose, although I'm still too stunned by all this to give you a proper answer to that question." She crossed her arms and studied his face. "I want to know what has happened. Something must have happened to bring this transformation in you."

Emily looked back towards the gallery. "Those guests may perceive this is your normal, gregarious, impulsive self, but we both know better."

He traced a hand down her face. "What do you want to know, Emily?"

"Everything," she said, resisting the impulse to press her lips into his hand. "When did you learn I'd come to Philadelphia, how did you realize your feelings had changed, how did you get here?" She stopped to look him over. "And how did you know what to wear?"

"That's a lot of questions." Cooper ran a hand through his hair, ruffling the smooth perfection of it. "Cawood Gentry came up to my house earlier this week to tell me you'd asked him to buy the Creekside and to add that you'd gone back to Philadelphia and planned to stay and partner with Daniel at the Newman." He paced across the small patio. "My thinking and emotions were a mess."

"I asked Cawood not to tell you or Mamie and to let me tell you in my own way later."

"When?" He turned anguished eyes to her now. "After you'd sold the Creekside, bought into the Newman, when there wouldn't be anything to say?"

She looked away. "You'd always wanted the Creekside for your mother and when Daniel called to tell me he and Benton Shield were buying the Newman from Daniel, and that Benton Shield wanted to sell out his share to me, it seemed like a good answer for everyone."

"And why would you think that was a good answer for me?"

Emily looked up at Cooper. "You'd made it clear you didn't share the same feelings that I did in our relationship, that you weren't interested in more or in the idea of marriage. You said you wanted to be like Cawood in your later years, living up in your house on the mountain on your own."

She heard him mutter an expletive. "Cawood was right in calling me a fool. Venetta, too."

Emily stared at him. "What does Venetta have to do with all this?"

He told her then about Venetta coming to his place after Cawood left, wanting him to go with her to put a marker on the spot where Lance got killed on The Dragon.

"And you went?"

"Yes. It wasn't as hard as I thought it might be, and Venetta said it did help to finalize things for her, helped her to let Lance go so she could move on." He looked out into the night. "I told Venetta I thought it helped me, too, to let you go, so you could move on."

He laughed, surprising her. "She lit into me then like a wild woman, told me I was crazy to say that. She said she needed to let Lance go because he was dead, and that I was a crazy fool to see any comparison in our situations. Venetta actually grabbed me and shook me—called me a stupid idiot and said if I had any sense at all I'd grab love with both hands if it came my way. She said I ought to go after you, put on my best suit, take flowers and words of love, sweep you off your feet and get down on my knees where I belonged, apologize, and beg you to marry me and come back."

To Emily's surprise, he threw up his hands as in surrender. "Dang if she wasn't right. I knew it the truth as I heard it, looking down at that spot where Lance died, knowing he couldn't love or dance or kiss or marry or know those kinds of earthly joys any more like I could." He walked over and put his hands on Emily's face. "So here I am, Emily. Here I am."

This time she did press her lips into his palm. "Do you really love me, Cooper Garrison? Do you?"

"Yes, without a doubt." His eyes met hers, strong and true and direct. "I feel like I buried an old dead part of me up there on the mountain at The Dragon that day. I want to live and love and laugh and enjoy this life that I have from now on." He paused. "And hopefully, God willing, to share it with you until I am old and gray-haired like Cawood."

"I've always thought Cawood Gentry distinguished and hand-some." She smiled at him.

"There's that sweet smile of yours that always sucker-punches me right in the midriff." He swept her off her feet and twirled her around the room. "You wanna get married right here in Philadel-phia before we head back home? I know Mom would fly up, prob-ably Cawood, too. And you have your friends here."

Seeing her stunned face, he grinned again. "We could beat Sara and Mackie's date, and we already have a house. I'd say you'd bring a little more color in, but that would be all right. I want you to bring color into every corner of my life, Emily Lamont."

She crossed her arms. "I haven't said yes to your proposal yet. You're taking a lot for granted here about everything."

He sat down in the chair and looked up at her. "Do you want me to get down on my knees and ask again? I will."

She studied his face. "I've told Daniel I would partner with him."

Cooper glanced back towards the gallery. "I don't think he'll be too surprised at your change of heart after what he saw tonight."

She sighed. "That's a point. But I want the gallery to continue and for Daniel to have a good partner."

Cooper considered that. "Maybe we can get Cawood to buy in; he was ready to pick up the Creekside for Mamie. We know he has the money."

"Why would he want to do that? I'm not related to him."

Cooper grinned. "But I am. Maybe we'll suggest to him that he might buy it as an inheritance for our children. One of them might turn out to be the arty type and like the idea of living up here in Philadelphia."

She felt her mouth twitch and tried not to giggle. "Well, I suppose it would be an idea." She looked towards the gallery. "Or maybe Daniel would be fine working with Benton Shield. I'm sure he'd give Daniel liberty to run the Newman as he liked."

"You see, everything will work out."

"Perhaps."

"So is that a yes, because if so I have a fantastic ring in my pocket for you."

Her eyes widened. "Oh, Cooper."

He pulled it out, opening the small box for her. "It had to be a diamond for you but I picked one with two little rubies on each side for 'my lady in red.' Do you like it?"

"I love it," she said, feeling the tears start again.

"Don't cry, sweet girl." He wiped away the tears. "We're going to have a happy life together, live on our mountain, walk our dogs and hike together, make wonderful houses—big and little—and perhaps some babies."

She knew she blushed then.

"If we have a little girl, we'll make her a fantastic custom doll-house."

"I think I could get used to this new you, Cooper."

"Good, it's time for life to move on, for a new dispensation of happiness to begin for the Garrisons. I know Dad and Lance will look down and approve. They've probably worried why I took so long to move on."

Emily looked down at her new ring, which fit perfectly, hoping everything in her life would continue as sweet as this moment.

Cooper looked back towards the gallery. "If you want we can go back in, mix and mingle, and share our good news. I'm sure all of those people are wondering how things turned out."

Emily put her hand in his. "Well, let's go show them everything turned out beautifully."

He lifted her off the table and pulled her tight to kiss her once again.

"You know I do think I'd like to be married here, in the church I went to with Hal and Mary for so many years. I think they would like that. There's a little chapel in the big church that would be perfect." She thought about it. "If we stayed the week, I think that most of the people we love and wanted to be here to share with us could come for a small ceremony. We could have another reception for our friends in Gatlinburg after we get back. What do you think?"

Cooper twirled her in a circle. "I love the idea. And I think Daniel and all your friends at the gallery will love it, too."

She put her hand in his. "I can take you to some of my favorite places here this week, show you where I lived with Hal and Mary, where I went to school."

"I want to know those things about you, Emily. And I want us to travel and do some things, too. Have some adventures."

"That sounds good."

Cooper laughed as he led her back into the gallery. "You know, it's driven me crazy watching Mackie and Sara make googly eyes and sneak kisses around us these months, talking about their wedding plans all the time. I sort of like returning with a fait accompli to them, married and one step ahead of them. After all, we met first. We should get married first."

"You're funny. I thought their behavior embarrassed you."

"No, it made me jealous out of my mind but I couldn't even admit it." He turned towards her in the darkened hallway, his voice dropping. "I don't think I've ever told you all the thoughts that have floated into my mind about the two of us, many of them a little explicit."

"Oh, well, perhaps it's good we're getting married so soon." She leaned against him, lifting her lips for another kiss and wrapping her arms around Cooper to pull him tight. "Because I've had a lot of those thoughts, too."

"How do you think Mercedes will feel, losing her spot against you in the bed every night?"

"Oh, Mercedes and Brinkley will work something out, I'm sure." She laughed. "I hope you have a big bed, though, for the two of us and those two dogs!"

They swept back into the gallery, Emily feeling suddenly happy and carefree, and from the look on Cooper's face, he felt the same. Wasn't life good?

A Reading Group Guide

LOST INHERITANCE

Lin Stepp

About This Guide

The questions on the following pages are included
to enhance your group's reading of
Lin Stepp's *Lost Inheritance*

DISCUSSION QUESTIONS

1. Early in the book, Emily Lamont is called to attorney Reuben Parrish's office to hear the will of Hal and Mary Newman. Also called to the reading is Hal and Mary's nephew, Leonard Newman, who's obviously hostile toward Emily. What outcome is expected at that meeting? What unexpected event happens instead? What are the reactions of Emily, Leonard, and Reuben Parrish at the meeting? Have you ever heard of a situation when a will was not correctly finalized, or can you remember an instance where an estate didn't go to the heirs the deceased hoped it would?

2. Emily's situation isn't desperate, although sad. She has her own condo, a trust set up for later in her life, a good education, and skills to find another job. In fact, Leonard tells her she can continue working at the Newman Gallery. Why doesn't she want to do that? What small, unexpected inheritance offers Emily an alternative? If you had been in Emily's situation, what would you have done? Fought the will legally? Stayed in Philadelphia near familiar places and friends? Gotten another job like other employees at the Newman Gallery? Or would you have picked up and moved to an unknown situation as Emily did? What did you think about Emily's attitude in all this?

3. In Chapter 2, you meet Cooper Garrison, owner of Garrison Log Homes and the son of the Creekside Gallery's longtime manager, Mamie Garrison. How do Cooper and Emily meet? What is Cooper doing when they meet and why is he so resentful of Emily? Does his mother hold the same attitude about Emily inheriting the gallery? Despite these initial problems, Cooper and Emily soon realize they are attracted to each other, even though neither wants to be. What scenes show you this?

4. Several animal characters appear in the early chapters of the book—Mercedes, Emily's big poodle; Sugar Lips, the Creekside Gallery's resident cat; Brinkley, Cooper's golden retriever; and later Sara's mother's little white bichon, Buster. How did Mercedes and Sugar Lips get their names? How did the pets in this book enhance the story? How did they help some of the characters relate and connect? Do you like stories with animals? What animals in your life enhance it or make it better?

5. The Creekside Gallery is an interesting small art gallery on the River Road in downtown Gatlinburg, Tennessee. How is the Creekside different from the Newman Gallery in Philadelphia? Did the descriptions of the artists' work in the Creekside Gallery make you wish you could visit it? Did you like Mamie? How does she reach out to Emily? How does she seem more discerning than Cooper about problems that might be going on in Emily's life?

6. Side characters in books, as well as in our lives, enrich them—bring us laughs, keep us entertained, show us the diversity of people in our world. Think back and remember several minor characters—Monty Russo and Leona Berry in the gallery; Bettie Chase in Cooper's office; Rafe Harlan, who works for Cooper building homes; and the Bolinger Brothers—Floyd and Arnold. What did you like about these characters? Did any remind you of people you know?

7. Losses, not only of inheritances, but losses of people loved, play a big role in this book. What losses has Emily known besides that of Hal and Mary Newman and the Newman Gallery? Cooper has known loss, too. When did he lose his father, Price Garrison, and his brother, Lance? How has that affected him? As the story progresses, you learn Mamie has known earlier losses, too, in her life before losing her husband and son. Where did Mamie grow up? What does she know about her parents?

8. Life is always sweeter with friends. How does Emily meet Sara Russell, who becomes her new friend in Gatlinburg? What brought Sara home to Gatlinburg after being away? Where is she working and living? Sara has a suitor, Giles Sutherland, but Sara's feelings for Giles don't match his. As she says, there's no zing. Who does Sara later fall in love with?

9. One connection between Emily and Sara is dollhouses. Sara's mother owns Dora's Dolls, a dollhouse shop in downtown Gatlinburg where Sara also works, and you learn that Emily builds dollhouses. When did Emily first get interested in building dollhouses? Why has she not done much with this skill she learned as a child? How does she envision using an unused space at the gallery for her hobby? Does Cooper encourage her in this hobby when she first tells him about it? How does Cooper's attitude on this subject create difficulty between them? Does he revise his opinion later in the book?

10. Emily and Cooper both have their reasons for not wanting to get involved emotionally. Although they acknowledge their attraction early in the book, they also make it clear they do not want the relationship to grow. Why? How does that prove to be difficult? What do you think keeps drawing them back together? As Emily and Cooper begin to develop deeper feelings for each other, Cooper seems to hold back the most in their relationship. What is behind Cooper's reluctance to get more deeply involved?

11. You first meet Venetta Renaugh riding her motorcycle near the gallery. Why does Cooper hold such hostility toward her? What relationship did Venetta have with Cooper's brother, Lance? As the book evolves, you learn Venetta is dating Cooper's friend, Rafe. Why do they keep it a secret from Cooper? How does Delbert Hilton, Cooper's construction supervisor and a longtime friend of his father's, give Cooper good counsel on this situation and other issues throughout the book? Delbert is one

of the first to sense Cooper's growing feelings for Emily. What advice does he give Cooper about Emily?

12. People often become angry with God over losses in their lives, and Cooper is angry with God. How is that anger hurting him in his life and relationships? How does some of his anger spew out in conversation with his pastor Perry Ammons on the night Cooper and Emily run into him, and later with Venetta? How do Perry, Delbert, and Emily try to help Cooper with these spiritual problems? Have you ever felt angry at God over a loss in your life? What did you think about Delbert's talk and prayer with Cooper in relation to this issue? What false things had people said that didn't help Cooper resolve his feelings toward God? Have you ever had well-meaning Christian people say things to you that hurt your faith more than helped it?

13. In her first day at the Creekside Gallery, Emily notices something in a Norman Rockwell painting, *Girl at the Mirror,* that doesn't seem right to her and she finds a second problem in yet another painting as she continues to look around. Emily gets an odd prickle about it but dismisses that early hint of intuition. What had she noticed? How does this turn out to be a problem for the gallery and for Emily later on? Who is Randy Lawson? How is Emily's life threatened by him over this issue? How do Mercedes and Cooper play a part in Emily's rescue?

14. Cawood Gentry, the internationally famous but reclusive artist, plays a quiet role early in this book and later a more important role. What link does he have to Mamie? How and when is that revealed in the book?

15. Cooper has a difficult time realizing his mother has become interested in Wade Grayling. Why is this a problem for him? He blurts out something about this that includes a derogatory comment about Emily at the party at his house. What does he say

that upsets Emily, Mackie, and Sara? This scene reveals—once again—that Cooper often speaks before thinking, causing problems for himself and with others. Do you ever have problems with that or do you know others who do?

16. It has been hard for Emily to create a new life, loving the Newman Gallery as much as she did, and old friends there like Daniel Stelben, who'd been her assistant manager. How does Leonard Newman handle his new role as head of the Newman Gallery? How does he blame Emily for his problems? What happens later in the book that enables Daniel to buy the gallery? What offer does he make Emily?

17. It has been hard for Emily to fall in love with Cooper but not see her love returned. It hasn't helped to see Sara and Mackie so quickly engaged, happy, and planning to be married. When Daniel calls Emily with his offer, to partner with her in the Newman Gallery, Emily decides she'll say yes if Cooper is unable to make a commitment by the end of July. She also decides she'll ask Cawood Gentry to buy the Creekside Gallery, knowing it will then go to Mamie. It is Cawood himself who brings Cooper the news that Emily has gone back to Philadelphia. Had Cooper known about this before Cawood's visit? How does he act? After Cawood leaves, Venetta rides up on her motorcycle—making Cooper wonder if the night can get any worse. What does she want Cooper to do with her the next day? She hopes visiting where Lance died will help her move on to commit to Rafe. How does going with her help Cooper?

18. As the book draws to an end, Emily is mingling with old friends, guests, and clients at the Newman Gallery in Philadelphia, back in the environment she so loved and lost. Dressed in a glittering red dress, she knows she looks good and should be happy, but her heart is hurting. At one point, Mario Benzi announces he's going to sing an old classic by request—"Lady in Red." Who

has requested this song? What happens next to surprise Emily? How does Daniel handle Cooper's unexpected appearance at the Newman Gallery's opening? What has Cooper come to tell Emily? How does the story finally end? Why was it especially appropriate to the story that Emily wore red that night? Do you have colors that are associated with memories in your own life?

19. What did you like most about this book? What memories—and characters—from it do you think will linger the longest in your mind?

About the Author:

Lin Stepp

Dr. Lin Stepp is a *New York Times*, *USA Today* and *Publishers Weekly* Best-Selling international author. A native Tennessean, she also works as both a businesswoman and an educator. Although not actively teaching now, she is still on adjunct faculty at Tusculum College where she taught research and a variety of psychology and counseling courses for eighteen years. Her business background

CKatie Riley

includes over twenty-five years in marketing, sales, production art, and regional publishing.

Stepp writes engaging, heart-warming contemporary Southern fiction with a strong sense of place and has eleven published novels, each set in different locations around the Smoky Mountains. Her last novel, before *Lost Inheritance* (2018), was *Daddy's Girl* (2017), with previous novels, including *Welcome Back* (2016), *Saving Laurel Springs* (2015), *Makin' Miracles* (2015) and *Down by the River* (2014) published by Kensington of New York. Other earlier titles include: *Second Hand Rose* (2013), *Delia's Place* (2012), *For Six Good Reasons* (2011), *Tell Me About Orchard Hollow* (2010), and *The Foster Girls* (2009). In addition, Stepp and her husband J.L. Stepp have co-authored a Smoky Mountains hiking guidebook titled *The Afternoon Hiker* (2014) and a Tennessee state parks guidebook *Discovering Tennessee State Parks* (2018). For more about Stepp's work and to keep up with her monthly blog, ongoing appearances and signing events see: *www.linstepp.com.*

CPSIA information can be obtained
at www.ICGtesting.com
Printed in the USA
LVHW040427040122
707780LV00001B/15

9 780998 506333